Pi...

CW00863900

of

Life

Nikki Dumigan

Acknowledgements

Since as long as I can remember, there is nothing I've wanted to do more than create characters and their stories. Lucky for me, I have had an extensive list of people encouraging me to bring this story to life. Here is where I show my deep love and gratitude for each one of you being in my life. You reflect my writing and I haven't forgotten any of you.

I'll begin with my parents. You've provided me a safe writing environment and endless inspiration, wherever we adventure to. Mom, you took the time to read over the story about ten times to make sure it was fully edited. By now you're probably sick of it yet believe in it reaching all corners of the world. I do apologize for "killing you off" but the point of it was to show how the loss of a great mother could devastate a kid's life. Dad, as many times as you've jokingly hinted that you wanted a shout out, I know you would have done all of this work to get all the details of the publishing perfect without one. All the lovable things about Andy are inspired by you. I honestly wouldn't have been able to do any of this without both of your support.

The rest of my family is equally as important. Paul, you get hyped up and proud about having an author as a sister, telling all your friends. There's a lot of you in Matty, shaking your head at my quirky writer's mind but still looking after me. Mom-mom, I can see my book being high up on your giant list of great novels. Maybe one day another mom-mom will be seeing my book on the shelf and suggesting it to her granddaughter, just as you always do. Poppy, Janice, Tom, Uncle Mark, Grandmom and Grandpop, Debi, Krista, Doll, Ruthie, and all of the Dumigans...thanks for believing in me and constantly checking in on my progress!

Since I almost forgot to put him in, I'll dedicate a nice little paragraph to my cat of many names. I call him Buzz the most and he's certainly part of the family. He's been there through all of my writing, lying on the papers, batting around the pencils, taking naps nearby when I type and have my music playing. I know he knows what he's doing yet he's too cute to be scolded. Many of my stories have cats in them and of course he's my inspiration.

To my kindergarten teacher, Mrs. Palmer, who told my mom that she can see me becoming a great writer someday. To Ms. Cat and Mrs. Kopple for seeing my talent and encouraging me to pursue publication. To Sergeant Hurt and Mrs. Pfieffer for waiting to read. To each and every one of my friends who were there for me every step of my writing process telling me that I'd reach the finish line. There are a lot of you so I'll attempt to name the prominent ones. Maddi, Maddie K, Maddie L, Anna, Dimps, Emily M, Emily S, Devin, Elise, Jess, Romy, Payten, Kathleen, Jillian, Lynsey, Megan, Melissa, Syddy, Cody, Jake, Cullen, Chase, Anthony, Bry, Becca, Andrew, and anyone who I may not have listed. I haven't forgotten you!

Anyone else who said they wanted to read my book, thank you so much! Dani (a.k.a Peanut), Julie, Michele, Al, Karleen, the Schofields, and the DeRafelos as well as countless beachgoers. I never expected anyone to even be interested so I love you all so much for it!

Finally, since I certainly can't forget, thank you to all of my favorite bands, who wrote music that inspired me to keep plugging away. The Fray, Jack's Mannequin, Relient K, Switchfoot, Theory of a Deadman, MAE, Three Days Grace, Counting Crows, Death Cab For Cutie, Kings of Leon, Matchbox Twenty, Matt Nathanson, OneRepublic, Lifehouse, SafetySuit, The Script, and Snow Patrol...I'll make sure to give you all a shout out somewhere in my writing.

I was able to write and publish my first book just how I imagined it when I started. It was like living a dream to see all of this come together...

"Life is pleasant. Death is peaceful. It's the transition that's troublesome."

-Isaac Asimov

Preface

Matty and Jenna

My favorite time of day, when we're at the beach, is when the sun has passed directly overhead and is starting to give up on killing me with its rays. I can sit down in the sand near the fence and it's not hot anymore, making it a nice time to get lost in my thoughts. In fact, I am in the middle of one of these times when my sister appears and ruins everything. I sigh loudly as she sits down next to me and gives me a wide smile. She thinks that since we're twins, we have to do everything together. I love her but sometimes I just need my space.

"Do you know what time it is?" she asks, trying to hold in an obnoxious laugh.

I glare at her. She knows just as well as everyone that I don't think of time the same as everyone else. When I was little, my dad told me that time is just something people made up to measure the amount of their life they spend doing certain things. Ever since then, I thought it was a crock and promptly decided to never pay attention to a clock ever again. I just live my life according to the amount of light there is outside and where the sun is positioned in the sky. I don't use time to know when I'm supposed to eat, I eat when I'm hungry, and I don't use time to know when I want to go to sleep, I sleep when I'm tired. This is how every other animal on Earth lives, so I decided it must give you a better quality of life.

Now one might think of me as obsessed with time and just trying to pretend I'm not. This is not the case. I believe that all time exists at once. That everything that will ever happen happens at once and we're only stuck in one certain moment. For instance, as I write this, I am not only living this moment but living every other one I already have along with everyone I ever will. It may seem hard to wrap your head around, but it's the only belief that keeps me going sometimes. Jenna likes to tease me about it but I know she hopes deep inside that it is true.

You see, I used to have another sister, Lauren. She was older than me, and when Jenna and I were only five, she was diagnosed with leukemia. She was only twelve, and she was so sick that she couldn't go to school or play or anything at all. She lost all her hair and had to wear a

7

bandana all the time. I was little so naturally I was a little scared of her. I feel bad now about it because she was my sister and I shouldn't have felt that way. One night when I was bed, things with Lauren took a turn for the worse. There was a violent snowstorm outside, and dad insisted he take her to the hospital. Jenna and I hid behind the door and listened as our mom tried to fight him.

"You can't go out in this storm alone! Why don't you just wait until morning?!" She screamed.

"We don't have until morning!" Dad screamed back.

"You're not going to make anything better killing both of you in a traffic accident!!!" And that's exactly what he did. Well, not exactly. Mom had to stay home with Jenna and I who were only seven and our baby brother who was just one. This meant that no one was there to keep an eye on Lauren while Dad drove. While Dad had his eyes on the challenging and slippery road, the cancer took over Lauren and she died in the seat next to him. Her head fell down and hit the dashboard which caught Dad's attention. He panicked, knowing very well what had come of his firstborn. He took his eyes off of the road and his hands off of the wheel to try to unsuccessfully shake her awake. The ice on the road made him slip into the opposite lane, and before he knew it, he was in a head on collision which put him instantly with his recently late daughter. That was it. They were both gone in a matter of minutes, and there was nothing anyone could do about it.

Later on in life, I was told that I was a bone marrow match to Lauren and that I had the power to save her. She would never have had to go to the hospital in a snowstorm and not only would I have had an older sister right now, but I would also have a dad. Imagine how that makes me feel. This is why I think if I believe that I'm living that moment along with this one, I can force myself back to that one and let my younger self know of my abilities. I know one of these painful days I will be able to do it.

I know instantly that today is the day to ask that particular question. Usually Matty says

something smart back or hits me. He even might start on scientific definitions about time, but the way his face looks means that he is deep in thought. I know exactly where his mind is going too and it brings me down also. I remember everything about that night as well, but I can't even imagine the guilt he feels everyday knowing he could have prevented it all. He could have given Lauren another chance at life, and he was so close with our dad that I can't even wrap my head around that.

I try to tell him that technically it wasn't his fault that he didn't stop it, but that doesn't help. Mom and Dad should have known that if Lauren died, Matty would feel this way but they still didn't tell him he was a match. The doctors told them he was just too young to go through the pain of a transplant and so they listened. I think that they should have told him so he could have made his own decision. But they didn't, so the one person I love most in the world has to put himself through hell thinking about it every day. That's not fair to me.

This is why, when Matty hates time because he can't find a way to go back on it, I hate doctors because they make stupid decisions. They make people do things that can later cause them to die along with the patient. Matty vowed never to look at a clock, and I vowed never to see a doctor, let alone step inside a hospital. I don't care what people say.

Now Matty is in a deep string of thoughts. I don't like to think either because it only leads to pain. I spring to my feet to shake myself out of it, and it shakes Matty awake too. His face returns to its normal color and he once again processes where he is and what he's doing. He looks around wildly and realizes that our brother is nowhere in sight and we are supposed to watch him.

"Where's Kelly?" he asks in panic.

I look behind me and see that he's perfectly fine jumping in the waves. We sigh in relief at the same time. "Kelly's okay, and don't tell Mom I almost lost him. You weren't paying attention either."

He laughs. "Stop freaking out. I'm not tattling."

Now you're probably wondering why both the boys in the family have girl sounding names. My dad believed that you're not a real man unless you can proudly say a feminine name when asked what you are called. Matty's real name is Mattix and that was a compromise. Dad wanted him to be named Madelyn but Mom swore that he would get teased. So Dad compromised on naming him Mattix while Mom compromised on calling him Matty, which sounds like Maddie (what Dad wanted). This is the story I was told a long time ago by Dad, who was always a little eccentric.

When I asked why Mom let Dad name her other son Kelly, she said, "Sometimes it's just not worth arguing with Mackenzie, who happened to be very proud of his name and would not stand for someone calling him Mack." I just laughed and let it go.

Matty and Kelly seem to have no problem with their names at all, so I stick up for them. I can be very tough when someone is messing with my brothers.

Kelly bounds up from the ocean to where we are. He is so nosy and if you don't tell him what you're doing at all times, he flips out. I've never seen a seven year old get so ferocious.

"Whatcha doing?" he asks, ramming his head into my stomach like a rhino. He's a very touchy-feely kid.

"Just waiting for Mom to get back from the Johnny-on-the-spot so we can head home."

He smiles and charges toward Matty. Matty puts his palm out and keeps Kelly's head from hitting him. Mom comes back then and Kelly runs toward her. She's caught off guard and Kelly knocks her right into the sand. We all laugh for awhile and all of us stop except for Kelly. We're all thinking the same thing-Dad would've enjoyed that moment.

"What's wrong?" Kelly asks. He doesn't understand because he's the only one who doesn't remember the things that happened. In a way, I feel bad for him because he doesn't remember Lauren or Dad, but then maybe it's for the best that he doesn't have to feel the emptiness we do.

1

Matty

That night, we all polish off a dinner and sit around the TV afterward. I trained my eyes not to look at the clock right under it on the VCR, and now I'm very good at it. A dinosaur comes on a commercial and Kelly pretends to be one himself. He jumps on Mom and tries to bite her. She flips him over and tickles his stomach. He can't stop laughing and it gets us all to smile. Deep down inside I feel horrible. I remember when Mom used to do that to me and I miss those days. It seems that when you're little everything is perfect and you have no problems. Then once you get to middle school, everything goes downhill and you can never get back to the way you were. I'm pretty sure I'm the only kid in the world who wants to get younger instead of older. I hate being a teenager personally. It's no big to do as every kid might think. Being seven is much more fun.

Something about seeing Mom playing with Kelly makes me sad and I want to be alone. "I think I'm going to go to bed. The sun makes me tired." I fake a yawn and step out of the room before anyone questions me. I hear Mom saying that it's early and that Kelly isn't even tired, but I zone it out.

I strip down to my boxers and turn my fan up to full blast. I have problems sleeping as it is-being hot doesn't help. I lay down flat on my back and realize I'm not tired at all. I hop back out of bed and grab a science fiction book out of my bookcase. I love science-I could watch the Discovery Channel everyday for hours and still learn something new each hour. It's fascinating. I know I sound like such a nerd but that's just how I am. I'm like my dad.

I hear Jenna come up the stairs and enter her room. I wonder what she does at night when she can't sleep. Maybe I could get some tips from her. I'd rather not be bored when I know I won't be able to sleep. I decide to find out. I open my door and tiptoe across the hall without making a sound. I peek down and see Mom is still watching TV with Kelly asleep on her lap. I know if I knock, I'll wake him up so I just open the door. As far as I know, she doesn't sleep naked so I figure I'm safe.

The lights are dim and she is sitting on her bed. She doesn't see or hear me come in so I stand in the doorway. She seems to be talking to herself. She keeps moving around and talking from different positions. I lean closer and try to hear what she's saying, but I fall over and bang against the wall. She jumps up from the bed and screams like someone is trying to murder her.

"What do you think you're doing?!?!?!?!" She yells, trying to push me out the door. I'm still a little unstable though and I fall into her arms. She lets out another scream and I know we're in trouble.

"Jenna, calm down! I just came in here to talk with you and now Mom's gonna yell at both of us!" I hiss.

She stabilizes and calms herself down. Mom comes charging up the steps with Kelly on her heals.

"What in the world is going on?" She takes one look at the both of us, me standing there in my boxers, and Jenna shaking in her cami and shorts, and starts laughing.

"Do I even want to know?" she adds. Kelly starts giggling too even though he has no idea what Mom is talking about.

"I'm not even sure what happened," I say truthfully. "It happened too fast to process."

"Why did you go to bed so early if you're just going to scare Jenna out of her wits?"

I sigh. How am I supposed to tell her the truth? "I couldn't sleep."

"You said you were tired, liar!" Jenna yells.

"I just wanted to be alone," I mutter. "Kelly was making me upset. Don't ask."

Mom can see the pain in my face. She tells Kelly to hop in bed and she will be there to tuck him in in a minute. He reluctantly goes to his room, feeling like he is missing all the fun. Mom leads us into Jenna's room and shuts the door. I flop down next to Jenna on her bed and wait for the speech to come.

"Matty honey, why did you really go to bed so early?" she soothes.

"I miss being seven. Things were much more fun then. I feel like I'm getting old, and with every minute, I'm getting farther from Dad."

"Matty! We're not old!" Jenna exclaims.

I can see tears starting to form in Mom's eyes, and I feel bad for telling the truth. If there's one thing I hate, it's seeing her or Jenna crying. I don't know what to do and I start freaking out. It usually cheers Jenna up because she says I 'flip my lid', but there's a deeper sadness in Mom. I wonder if that's just how it is when you're a widow and you see the love of your life in your son every day. I know it would drive me to drink, but she seems to keep things together. I respect her for that.

"You're not getting old, and just because you're thirteen, it doesn't mean you can't still have fun just like Kelly. You don't have to be an adult and you don't have to be strong all the time. Lord knows I'm not."

I think about what she's saying and I realize she's right. I can have moments of sadness, and if I want to be a little kid sometimes, that's ok. That thought warms my heart a little. I smile and see Mom's eyes dry. That makes me feel even better.

"Same goes for you Jen," Mom says, rubbing her hair.

"I know Mom," she replies. She gives Mom a hug and I join in. Kelly must have been getting impatient in his bed because he runs in and adds to the hug.

"Group hug!" he yells.

"I love all three of you more than myself, and I hope you always know that."

"We love you too Mom," we all say in unison. We all must be thinking of Dad again because we recite together, "I love you more than the sun loves to shine on your face, the wind loves to blow through your hair, the stars love to twinkle in your eyes, or the moon loves to smile at you. I want to protect you longer than gravity keeps the universe in orbit, and I will do that even if I have to give up everything for it." That was what he used to tell us all the time, something he made up himself. Just hearing us all say it together, I get the feeling that this family can make it after all.

2

Jenna

I didn't get my acting in that night, but it is okay. I was in the middle of a storyline when Matty

barged in my room. No one knows that I create my own soap opera. It consists of characters that I built off of my favorite celebrities. I play all of the parts because no one could do it as good as I would want and because it makes me feel good to play other people with problems that are far worse than my own. Then it's all not real if I don't want it to be.

I wish I could meet all these people I pretend to be, but I know it probably won't happen. So to make that reality okay, I pretend to be them. I don't know what it is, but that makes me feel better. People would think I'm crazy if they knew about this quirk of mine, and that's why I screamed so loud when Matty fell into the wall. I didn't know he was there, and I hope he didn't hear anything. We are close twins, but some things are just my own secrets.

The night ends with a warm family embrace and Matty dragging in his sleeping bag. He insists on sleeping on my floor that night because he says that my room is cooler than his. I don't feel that, but if it makes him sleep, then it's okay with me. I know Matty doesn't sleep much because I see his light on at all hours of the night and the sound of pages turning.

So now I hear him breathing heavily on the floor next to my bed, and I'm the one who can't sleep tonight. I always have a weird feeling in my stomach and heart when something big is about to happen, and I'm scared what it might be this time. The house seems quiet inside with a lot of rain pattering on the windows. I feel a flashback to the night of the accident coming and decide I better do something to keep my mind off of bad happenings.

I grab my music player/cell phone that I named Johnny for no reason than to give him a name, and turn up my alternative rock almost all the way. It's the only thing I listen to because it puts me to sleep. Something about the soft melody of guitar, piano, and drums, with steady male vocals, always lulls me to dream world. I tune out everything else that is going on in the world and focus on the words of the song. Before long I'm asleep. If only I could have known that the storm outside would become more than I ever expected.

The loud boom coming from the back yard is what wakes me up. It overpowers the music

and my sleep, so I know it has to be major. I cut the music and stick Johnny in my shorts pocket. I throw the covers off me and peer down at Matty. He is staring up at me. He must have heard it too, so at least I know I'm not insane. He doesn't say anything so I get up and look out the window. The storm is still raging. I used to be scared to death of them when I was little, and the sight of the lightning bolts and rain blowing sideways gives me the creeps.

It was probably just a loud clap of thunder, I tell myself. But deep down inside, I know this is something more. I back away from the window because they always say that being next to glass is not a good place to be during a storm. I go back to where Matty is laying. He is still staring, and he looks like he's going to explode. He looks as if he is in shock. He knows something!

"Matty, do you know where that noise came from?" I ask, starting to shake.

His eyes move over to me and I can see tears are running down his face. My whole body breaks out into a sweat. I start shaking him and scream, "Matty! What's wrong?"

He turns his head fully so I can see his whole face. He is purple and I wish he would say something. He's the science kid who would know what's happening. My heart is beating so fast that I feel like it's going to come popping out of the front of my chest and onto the floor.

I lie down next to Matty and ask again. "Where did that noise come from?"

He puts his lips up to my ear and whispers, "We've been hit!"

"What?" I ask, but he doesn't have to answer. At the same moment, I start to smell smoke, and I know exactly what he's talking about. If only I knew what to do about it.

3

Matty

I realize, lying on Jenna's floor, that I watch too much Discovery Channel. I watched a show on severe thunderstorms and have been frightened ever since. This is why, as soon as I hear it, I recognize the sound of lightning hitting a house. Judging on how loud the sound was, I am absolutely positive the house my family and I are in is the one that was hit. I feel my whole body go cold as Jenna screams at me, and I can't help but cry. I don't want to die and I know it is very well possible. I wonder if this was how Lauren felt as she got in the car that night, or if this was how Dad felt as he saw the headlights coming right for him.

I feel Jenna lay down next to me and ask me what happened. I know that the sooner I say something, the better chance we have of getting out of here and surviving.

"We've been hit!" I force myself to whisper in Jenna's ear. She begins to question me, but the smell of smoke reaches my nostrils, and I know there is no need for explanation.

She screams so loud that I have to hold my ears in fear that my ear drums will shatter. The smoke alarm joins her, and I know I have to do something. I punch myself in the arm, and the pain snaps me out of my shock.

"We're gonna die!" Jenna wails, and I grab her arms to hold her still.

"Not if I have anything to do with it," I say as calmly as possible. "Now let's get out of here."

"Ok," she squeaks in total fear. I grab her hand and lead her to the door. I remember from elementary school what do to in case of a fire. I feel the door with the back of my hand. It's only warm but not hot enough for the fire to be right on the other side. I grab the handle and swing open the door. The smoke is stronger and I fight the urge to cough.

"Get down like you're crawling!" I yell through the sound of the storm. I wonder why I can hear it so well as I get down to a crouch. I look up at where my room is positioned and get my answer. The lightning went right through my room, leaving a big gaping hole in the floor and a huge fire engulfing everything I ever owned. I didn't have anything that special, but I still get a tinge of sadness. I'll have to start over. Then it hits me. I would be dead if I hadn't been sleeping in

Jenna's room. It wasn't my time, I suppose. My lack of sleep and low tolerance to heat saved my life.

"What happened to the floor?" Jenna wonders aloud, and I realize I stopped moving. I start crawling, ignoring the meaning of her question. The fire keeps raging and I know we will have to split up. One of us has to go across to get Kelly while the other has to go downstairs and get Mom.

Mom! I stare at the hole in the floor of my bedroom and process that the floor had to fall through to the room below. Mom's room. The burning ceiling fell right on my mom!

"NO!!!!!" I scream. I have to save her. I can't be the reason another one of my parents dies. I don't want to be an orphan. I can't live with myself if she dies.

"Holy God," Jenna cries, thinking the same thing I just did.

I grab her shoulders and look her straight in the eye. "Listen to me."

"I am," she whispers.

"We're going to save them and we're all going to come out of this alive. I promise. Now you go get Kelly. I know you're strong enough to carry him. Carry him out the fire escape way that we practiced, and when you're safe, call 911. Don't worry about me. Okay?"

"I can't leave you," she replies, shaking her head.

"I'll be fine. I'm just going to go downstairs to go get Mom and we'll meet you outside. Please just do what I told you so I have less to worry about. And whatever you do, don't come back in here for me. Do you understand?"

"I can't raise Kelly on my own! What if you and Mom don't make it out? What if I can't make it out? I need you there to reassure me. Don't leave me please!"

She's crying out to me, but I have to be strong and not give in to her. She deserves to make it, even if I don't. "The longer we argue about this, the less chance Mom has of making it. Just go."

She takes one last look at me and runs toward Kelly's room. She has her arm over her face shielding herself from the thick fog of smoke. I feel bad for leaving her, but it is the only way I could get her to save herself. Now I have a mission to complete. I tell myself they will be fine as I make my way down the crumbling stairs. I start to feel lightheaded and know I don't have much time before the oxygen is gone up at my height. I jump as far as I can down the remaining stairs. I land on my knees and wince in pain as I feel something crack. I have to keep going.

Flat on my stomach, I slide my way in the direction of Mom. The door is closed and the fire is inside her room, so I can't open it without burning myself. In fast thinking, I pull a spindle from the railing and ram it through the door. I keep doing this until there is a large enough hole for me to fit through. I climb into the room and look around wildly for Mom. There is so much rubble and smoke and fire that I can barely see anything. My eyes are stinging and I'm gasping for breath.

Maybe she got out herself, I think, trying to give in to my body screaming to save myself. I ignore it and crawl deeper into the room. A piece of the ceiling digs into my hand and I can feel myself bleeding.

"Come on Mom, where are you?" I partly ask myself. I take one more look around and spot her hand sticking out from a large piece of ceiling.

I try to stay calm and tell myself she's okay, but I can feel myself crying again. I crawl as fast as I can toward her and try to move the ceiling off of her. It only moves an inch. I see her head move out of the hole.

"Matty, is that you?" she chokes through ceiling dust.

"Yeah, are you okay?"

"For now."

"Okay, I'm going to get you out of here. I will get this off of you."

"Matty, save yourself. Don't worry about me. Where are Jenna and Kelly?"

"They got out safely and Jenna's calling 911 right now." I assure her. I don't really know this, but I have faith in my twin sister.

"Good work son," she says, reaching her hand out to touch mine. I'm trying desperately to move the ceiling off of her, but I know without help, it is probably not going to budge. I can feel her slipping and I'm starting to panic.

"Mom, it won't move. What am I supposed to do?"

"Get out of the fire. You need to take care of Jenna and Kelly now. It's your job and I trust you will do it well. Promise you'll keep them safe for me."

I can't believe what is happening. My own mom is giving up on herself! "I promise, but I don't have to because you're going to be there with me. I'll make sure of it if it's the last thing I do."

I hear ambulance sirens outside and I know they'll save her. I just have to keep her alive until then. We're both running out of oxygen, and I wish they would hurry up and get us.

"Take these. These are the two things that meant the most to me besides you guys. Give mine to Jenna, and you wear your father's. That is until you have one of your own. You take care of Jenna, Kelly, and these. That's all I expect of you. Whatever else you do with your life is your choice. I will support anything you three do from above."

I take the wedding rings out of her hand and squeeze my palm together. I have a new weight on my shoulders. The tears are really flooding now despite the smoke that is drying out my eyes.

"I love you, Mom."

"I love you too, and tell Jenna and Kelly the same. Don't let them forget me."

"I won't."

I hear footsteps enter the room, and before I know it, hands are grabbing me. I try to fight them, but I am losing my strength quickly. "You have to get my mom!" I manage to yell.

"We'll do our best son." I hear someone tell me. "Now let us take you out."

I reach out for my mom and she smiles at me. "Let me be with Mackenzie and Lauren now. It is what is meant to happen."

I see her head drop and I lose it all together. I give up. I feel my own head snap back, and everything goes dark and silent.

4

Jenna

I take one last look at my brother, knowing it could be my last. I guard my face with my arm to keep the smoke from knocking me unconscious. I charge toward Kelly's bedroom like he does when he's pretending to be a rhino. I hope that Matty and Mom will be okay, but I promised Matty I would get Kelly out and call 911, so I have to focus on that task.

I feel the door with the back of my hand like I saw Matty do earlier, and it doesn't seem that hot. I push it open and hear whimpering. I also hear a thud and a crack. I hope that isn't Matty. I don't want to have to go to a doctor. I can't go back on the vow I made for Dad. I have to stay intact.

I drop to my knees and feel Johnny jostle around in my pocket. I'm glad I stuck him in my pocket instead of on my bed. I never go anywhere without him. I know it may sound strange, but I made good friends with my cell phone. He's my friend when I don't have any around, my family when they're elsewhere, my company when I'm alone, my pet when I miss our cat we had to leave with our grandma when we moved to keep Lauren near the best hospitals, and my boyfriend when I feel unloved. I give him a pat as I venture farther into the room in pursuit of where there is crying. Right now I need him as my guardian.

"Kelly, are you in here?" I cry out, and the whimpers get louder.

I look all around the room because I know when he's scared, he doesn't speak. He just cries, and there is no point calling for someone who isn't going to answer. I fling open the closet door, but he isn't there. I look behind all the furniture he has, but I find nothing. His sheets are turned down and crumpled, so he isn't hiding in there. Finally, I drop to my stomach and peer under the bed. I see my little brother huddled in a ball, clutching his little salamander that he can't sleep without.

"Come on out Kelly. Jenna's here to save you," I coax. He looks up at me and shakes his head no.

I sigh. "Please, or else you and Salamander are going to get hurt. And maybe even me. You wouldn't want to be responsible for that, now would you?"

He looks from me, to Salamander, and back again. "No," he whispers so silently that I can barely hear it.

"Then come out from under the bed and I will take care of the rest."

"I'm too afraid," he cries.

I stick my hand under and tousle his hair. I know we don't have time for this. I need to call 911 and make sure Matty and Mom are okay. But still I say patiently, "There's nothing to be afraid of. I'm gonna get you out of here safe and sound."

"You're sure?"

"Positive."

He slowly slides out from under the bed, still clutching Salamander. Then he stares at me, waiting. I slide my arms under him and lift him off of the carpet. I take my cami and make an air pocket above his space. That should last him until we get out of here, I think. If only I can last now.

I run out of the room, trying to make an air pocket for myself with my arm, but I'm unsuccessful. I start to cough as I hop down the remaining stairs. I still hear Kelly crying, so I know he's at least alive. That's a good sign. I turn the corner, trying to fight the urge to go to Mom's room to check on Matty. I make my way to the escape exit and out, thankfully dodging the actual fire. I breathe in the clean air of the warm summer night and feel the rain on my face. I release my shirt from Kelly's face, and he takes a sharp breath also. I fall down in the grass and it squishes on my face. I feel for Johnny and force him out of my pocket, still clutching Kelly.

I flip open Johnny, press the numbers 911, and wait for them to receive the call. I hope I get a signal in the middle of the storm or else I'm doomed.

"You have reached 911. What is your emergency?"

I sigh in relief. "My house has gotten struck by lightning and is burning down. My brother and Mom are still inside."

"Are you okay Miss?" he asks calmly. I know he's been trained for all kinds of situations.

"Yes, I'm out, but you need to bring an ambulance because Matty and Mom aren't." I'm starting to panic.

"Calm down, and don't go back in the house for anything. We will send an ambulance as fast as we can. Do you know your address?"

I tell him my address and assure him I'll stay put with Kelly. I hang up and start to let go. I can't hold on what I'm feeling anymore. I cry loudly and scream for Matty and Mom while I hold Kelly. I can feel him crying with me. I close my eyes and pray for life.

I don't know how long I fell asleep, but I hear the sirens and hop up instantly. I pick Kelly up with me. I see the ambulance swerve into the driveway and the doors fling open. Two men and a woman get out and run toward the house. Another woman gets out and comes over to me and Kelly. I stand up with Kelly on my hip. I'm surprised I'm able to support him this easily and long. Kelly isn't heavy for a seven year old, but I never thought of myself as particularly strong either.

"Are you okay?" she asks me when she gets close enough.

I nod. "I'm fine and so is Kelly."

Her brow furrows. "Who's Kelly?"

"My brother." I say, shifting him higher on my hip.

She seems surprised for a minute, and then gets control of her expressions. "Did you get him out yourself?"

"Yeah, I carried him."

"That's very brave of you."

I shrug. "I wouldn't have left him there."

"You said there were others inside?"

I nod again. I hear the fire engines coming in, spraying water on the house. "My mom and my brother."

"How old is your brother?"

She is asking a whole heck of a lot of questions. I wonder why she needs to know all these things. "Thirteen. He's my twin."

"So he could have gotten out on his own but didn't?" She asks in a disapproving tone.

"I don't like your tone lady," I say. "Matty was very capable of getting out on his own, but since he's selfless, he went into the fire to save our mother. I'm sure he will succeed."

She glares at me, but I glare back. I'm not afraid of this idiot.

"Do you have any other family members living with you that we can contact?"

"Yes I have an older sister, a father, an uncle, and a grandmother. But you can only contact my grandmother."

"Why?" she questions.

"That's none of your business, now is it?" I snap. I'm slowly losing patience with this woman. Probably because she's a doctor and I have no tolerance for them, as already stated.

I look over and see the two men carrying Matty out. His arm and knees are bleeding, and his head is hanging limply in the air. He looks much worse off than when I left him. I know I shouldn't have! Now it's my fault if anything happens. Why am I so stupid sometimes?

Next out is Mom, and she looks worse than Matty. Maybe I'm just freaking out and seeing things, but I could swear that she looks white and lifeless. No, she's fine, I tell myself. She has to be. Who would take care of us three kids if she weren't? We have no relatives left that are reachable except Grandma, who lives all the way in Philadelphia. And Uncle Slade, Mom's brother, who no one has heard from for years. He was so distraught after his wife died, that he just vanished and no one has been able to reach him.

"Come on Mom," I say softly, somehow believing she can hear me. "Hang in there for us."

I watch as her head bangs against the fireman's shoulders and something clicks in me. I have to do something before it's too late. I don't know what to do, but I have to do something. I put Kelly down on his feet and tell him to run with me. I pace quickly towards where Mom is being carried.

"Mom!" I scream, and someone tries to block me. I try to push them out of the way, but like I said, I'm not the strongest girl on record, so he has that over me. Kelly slides under his legs and runs over to Mom. He starts petting her hair, tears filling in his eyes. He shouldn't have to go through this.

"Let me go get him," I say to the man who is restraining me. "He doesn't know what's going on. Let me soothe him!"

"You kids need to calm down and let the professionals take care of things like you're supposed to," he mutters. "Bring him over here and you can all get in the ambulance."

He lets go of me and I'm off in two seconds. I hug Kelly. By this time, he's bawling.

"Mommy," he screams. "Wake up!!!"

Mom doesn't stir, so I have to reassure him. "Mom's going to be fine. We can both ride in the ambulance with her and Matty. Come on."

He lowers his hands, and I lead him to the open door of the back of the ambulance. Matty is already inside, strapped to a stretcher. They have him in a neck brace and his face looks burnt and discolored. I look away, trying to fend off the nauseous feeling in my stomach. They strap Mom to another stretcher and roll her next to Matty. This is not good seeing this. I should be the one lying there motionless, not them.

I stagger to the side of the ambulance and flop down on the little booth sort of thing. Kelly climbs on my lap. I stroke his hair as the doctors climb in and close the doors. They attach all kinds of tubes and clicking machines to both Mom and Matty and scream lots of big words that I don't understand at each other. I don't really remember much of it. The whole ride to the hospital, Mom and Matty being rushed to the emergency room, and being pushed into a seat of the waiting room is still a blur. It all runs together like a bunch of wet paint swirling on a canvas.

Before I know it, the whole experience has gotten the best of me, and I find myself vomiting all over the floor. My ribs are aching from so much "ralphing", as Matty would say, and I pass out right in the waiting room chair. Kelly yells if I'm okay and for me to wake up, but I can't get a hold of reality. Before long, I don't hear it anymore, and the whole world seems black and silent.

5

Matty

The next thing I remember is the sound of clicking machines and the crinkling of the hospital pillow where my head rests. I force my eyes open and see, as expected, a hospital room. I see white walls and white ceiling tiles. The floor is also white, with one red chair in the middle. My bed is white and my hands, which have tubes connected to them, also are white. That's not good. I look down at my nose and realize I'm wearing an oxygen mask. I must have passed out from too much carbon dioxide during the fire, I think to myself as I pull it off. I feel really tired and can't think straight.

I look over at the machines, which are measuring things like my heart rate and blood pressure. I hear the door click open, and a woman in powder blue scrubs enters. She smiles at me and I just stare. I think I forget how to smile.

"You're lucky you made it son," she says, checking my IV. "You were quite brave going in there to save your mother, but you could have very well killed yourself."

"Hmm," is all I can get out of my mouth. Then I think of how I got here and the blood starts rushing to my entire body. My mom! Jenna! Kelly! I gain strength and sit straight up.

"Whoa there tiger!" the doctor says, pushing me back down. "You're not quite ready to go for a jog!"

"This is no time for jokes!" I yell. My voice sounds hoarse, but I don't care. "Where is my family? I have to make sure they're all right."

She is still holding me down and I'm not enjoying it. "Calm down. Getting yourself worked up like this is only going to get you in trouble. I will answer any questions you have."

I sigh and relax. "Where's Jenna?"

She just stares at me. "I have no idea who that is."

"My sister! The last time I saw her was in the house!"

"Does she look like you?"

"We're twins," I say rudely.

"Then she's in the waiting room. She keeps passing out, throwing up on herself, and passing out again."

"And you think that's normal?!"

"I would appreciate it if you stop yelling at me," she says, slightly amused. She should not be amused at my total panic. "She's a little overwhelmed with the situation. She'll come to when she's ready. We can't do anything about it."

"Is she with a little boy?" I'm not going to get anywhere asking this question with his name. She looks stupid enough to have an argument with me about what a girl name and a boy name is.

"Little squirt with jet black hair and blue eyes?"

"Yeah, that sounds like him."

"I've never seen anything like that," she says in awe. "He looks just like you two, all the same contrast. He sure has the attitude too. And no, one of our kind nurses is amusing him in the play area. He doesn't speak, and he won't let go of that stupid salamander long enough to even touch another toy."

"We got my dad's genes. Apparently they were dominant. And don't make fun of him. You guys deserve it."

"Oh and where's your dad? I'm sure he's an interesting soul," she laughs, ignoring my nasty remark.

I swallow hard. I've been through this many times before. "He's not here right now."

She sees my facial expressions and says no more on the subject. "Any more questions, Mattix?"

"Don't call me that," I mutter. "My name is Matty."

She chuckles a minute and waits for me to answer her question.

"Yes, I do have another question. Where is my mom? I want to see her."

Her face changes from amused to a little sad. She slowly lowers herself into the red chair and puts her head in her hands. She's not answering, and I don't see that as a good sign. This can't be what I think it is.

"Well, answer me already!" I yell. I sit back up, but this time she doesn't try to stop me.

"Matty, I'm terribly sorry, but there was nothing we could do for your mother. She was already gone before we got her to the ambulance."

"NO!" I scream as loud and ferocious as I can. "I don't want to hear that! She can't be dead!"

Her eyes meet mine and they say that what she said was true, no matter if I want to hear it or not. That makes me so angry that I cry. Like a baby.

"You know, you guys did it again," I say through tears. "You doctors and nurses are worthless, just like Jenna has been telling me forever. All you do is make mistakes and make people do things that can lead to their deaths. First, you kill my poor older sister Lauren by telling her not to get a bone marrow transplant. Then, you kill my father because he got in an accident on the way to bring Lauren here, which he wouldn't have had to do if you hadn't convinced them there was no chance for Lauren. Then, you kill my mother because you gave up on her. You probably didn't even try, did you? All you do is kill people! When are you going to do your job and actually save someone? You answer me that question!"

She just stares at me again, not answering. I think I might have shocked her, upset her, or both, but I don't care. Maybe she should feel the way I do.

"You know what? I'm getting out of here!" I scream, pulling the tubes out of me and jumping out of the bed. "Before you kill me too."

She tries to stop me from leaving, but I push her out of the way. I run out of the room and find my way to the waiting room. I'm still in a robe and probably look ridiculous, but I have to get Jenna and Kelly out of here.

I try to walk nonchalantly to where Jenna is, but I feel a lot of people staring. She must be awake by now because she is staring at me too.

"Matty," she hisses. "What are you doing?"

"I'm getting us out of here," I whisper. The nurse playing with Kelly is getting suspicious of me. She slowly gets up and walks over.

"Did someone say you could come out here son?" she asks, grabbing my shoulder. I twist away. Why is everyone calling me son? They are definitely not my parents. Then it hits me. I no longer have parents. I have to take care of myself and my siblings on my own. I fight the urge to cry again. I have to be strong for them.

"Yes," I say calmly. "My doctor told me I could go see that my family is alright."

She eyes me up. "Somehow I don't believe a boy like you. Teenagers are known to lie. I'm going to go check on that. You stay here."

"Certainly, m' am." Of course that's a lie. I'm going to run as soon as she's out of sight. She keeps her eyes on me as long as possible, and then turns the corner. I stay very still until I know she's gone and will stay gone.

"Now, let's go," I say to Jenna. She rises from her chair and Kelly joins us at her side.

"Where are we going, fearless leader in the dress," Jenna jokes. Even in a situation like this she can't help but tease me. I have to give it to her though. She knows how to lighten the mood.

"We're going to Grandma's," I whisper. "But first the closest Wal-Mart, so I can get some new clothes."

"But we don't have any money."

I grind my teeth together. That is a problem that I hadn't thought of. "Maybe we'll get away without having any."

She widens her eyes at me but nods. "I'll pretend I didn't hear that."

"Now really, we have to find a way out of here before awful nurse comes back."

I feel a hand on my shoulder as soon as I finish the sentence. I turn around slowly and see the nurse staring in my face. She doesn't look too happy either. "You're just like all the other lying teenagers in the world. You really thought you were going to get away with escaping the hospital?"

I nod solemnly, trying to look ashamed of what I tried to do. "It was a stupid idea. I won't try anything else."

"I expect not," she spits at me. "Now I'm going to get each of you separate rooms so you can finish being examined without any trouble." She leads us down the hall and shoves Kelly in a small, kid-friendly room.

"Then what's going to happen to us," I can't help but ask, "when we're done being in the hospital?"

"We'll have to see about that. There are many different options for orphans. They have special homes, foster care, adoption centers, and much more. We'll see later what suits each one of you best."

"So you're saying you might split us up?" I choke. The thought of seeing Kelly pulled in one direction while Jenna is pulled in another makes me queasy. That would be failing them.

"We don't know yet, but it is possible."

"You can't do a thing like that!" Jenna screams, her face red. "That's awful!"

She desperately looks at me for help, but I can't get any words at her. All I do is stare back at her as the nurse shoves her in another room and closes the door. I get ushered to the farthest room down the hall, and when I get pushed in, I realize it smells funky. It's probably punishment for my attempted escape.

She leans down close to me and whispers in my ear, "I don't want any trouble from you, understand?"

I roll my eyes. "Fine, I'll be a good boy. Jeez."

She shuts the door in my face and I stick out my tongue at her. I'm definitely with Jenna on the doctors are awful belief. I look around the room and see that it is pretty much the same as the last one. All white, with a bed and a little red chair for visitors in the middle of the floor. I stumble over and plop down in the red chair. I feel really tired all of a sudden. I'm going to need some sleep if I'm going to think of a plan to get out of here. Before long, I doze off into a gentle slumber, slumped over the red chair in my hospital gown.

I wake up to hear whispering voices outside my door. I can't hear what they were saying, so I creep across the room and put my ear against the door. That makes it a little bit better, but I still have to strain to hear. I wonder who is talking because I can't recognize any voices. I spy a small window on the top of the door, so I stand on tiptoe and peek out the bottom of it. There is a police officer in a shiny blue uniform and slicked back, blond hair that looks like he used a whole bottle of gel to do it that way. Just looking at this guy, I know he is going to be trouble. He's the kind who thinks he's big and bad with his badge and that everyone should be afraid of him. Very cocky. He is talking to the doctor that was smart with me when I first woke up. After I'm done examining them, I slide down and press my ear against the door.

"Yes sir, when he woke up, he was very angry with me, and then he stormed out when I told him his mother passed," I hear the doctor say. "I understand it is difficult to lose anyone you love, I deal with loss every day, but there was no need for him to go crazy on me like that."

"I understand doctor," the cop replies. "The nurse told me earlier that he tried to get the other two kids and escape the hospital, but she caught them before they could go anywhere."

The doctor doesn't respond, but I can imagine she is agreeing with him in some way. "He seemed very unstable and attacked me. I see him as a threat, and that is exactly why I contacted you."

"I understand. I will interrogate the boy to see if it was just initial shock, and then make my decision. We might need to put him in a mental health home if I see signs. What about the girl and the young boy?"

"The girl seemed okay overall other than her excessive time unconscious. The young boy seemed fine also, except he was not getting along with our nurse. Not many kids do. She's a little rude at points, so I see that as normal. I suggest you separate the oldest boy from the other two before he contaminates them also."

"Very well," cocky cop says. "Can I speak to him now?"

"I believe he's sleeping," Doctor replies. "Let me check for you."

I push away from the door and jump in the chair in record time. I tilt my head down and shut my eyes, the same position I was when I was really asleep. I'm just realizing how much my neck is hurting, and it is difficult to hold position, but I breathe heavily anyway to make it believable.

The doctor enters the room quietly and tiptoes over to me. I feel her breath on my face, so she must be really watching my every move. I try to keep my face completely emotionless and fight the urge to blink. Pretending to be asleep is much harder than one would think.

After what feels like hours, she moves towards the door. I know she's going to turn around in the door and she if I move, so I hold just a little longer. Finally, I hear the door click. I hear a couple more whispers and then fading footsteps. I straighten my neck and open my eyes. That was very painful.

I rush over to the door and peek out the little window again. There is no one around and the coast seems clear. I know someone must be watching my door to make sure I don't try to escape. There aren't any other windows or any hidden doors in the room, so there is no other way out. I feel like I'm a prisoner. I don't think that's right, considering I'm in a hospital where they're supposed to help you, not hold you hostage. There are some shady things going on here. I have to get the remainder of my family out of this place.

I stare at the door a little longer. There's only one way to do that, I think. I have to do it. There's no way I'm going to get interrogated. My dad used to tell me about how cops just trick your mind into saying things they want you to do, and then they incriminate you. I tried to ask him how he knows things like that, and he said, "From being around the real world son." I believe him, so I know that cocky cop is going to try to make me sound crazy so he can throw me in the loony bin.

That makes my blood boil. I'm no threat to society. If anything, these doctors are. And my mental health is perfectly fine, thank you very much. Obviously it's not okay to be upset when you hear that you just became an orphan. This whole thing is ridiculous. I don't care who's watching over me, I'm going to run through those doors, get my brother and sister, and get the hell out of here!

I spin the handle on the door so it makes no sound (another thing I learned from my dad). I close it the same way. I look around and there doesn't seem to be any guards, so I tiptoe down the hall to Jenna's room. I peek through the little window and see that she's alone in there, crying. I push open the door carefully and she looks up. She smiles at me and beckons me in to say it's safe.

"Jenna," I whisper. "Did you see the cop?"

Her eyes get big. "No, why is there a cop?"

"He's here to interrogate me. The doctor thinks I'm a threat to society, and he needs to see if my mental health is okay. There is something very strange going on in this hospital."

"How long do we have before he comes," she asks, a hint of panic in her voice.

"I think he's coming back in the morning when I supposedly wake up. It pains me to ask this, but there is a very good reason. What time is it?" I wince.

She gasps. "I'm proud of you. It's almost 5 am."

I sigh. "That means we don't have much time. We have to get Kelly and find a way to escape here without getting arrested, if you know what I mean."

"I do," she chuckles a minute and then gets serious. "Do you have a plan?"

"Not yet. It seems there's no way out. Doesn't that sound wrong to you?"

She nods. I put my head in my hands and try to rack my brain for an answer. There has to be some way out of here. We're on the first floor so there is no fire escape, and the only other doors are straight through the waiting room or will set off the fire alarm.

"Maybe that will work."

"What," Jenna asks, seeing I'm having a sudden inspiration.

"Going through the fire door. It will set off the alarm, and people will be so distracted, they won't even realize we escaped. That will work!"

Jenna gets a wide smile on her face and I know she agrees. "Let's do it. But first we have to get Kelly."

"You have to," I tell her. "You're less likely to get noticed in regular clothes, and plus, you're not the mental case."

She rolls her eyes. "Fine, I'll meet you back at your room. If anything goes wrong, just open the door without me and I'll catch up."

I nod and rush back to my room before anyone sees me. I really hope this works or we're doomed.

6

Jenna

Tiptoeing to Kelly's room, I feel two different emotions at once. I feel scared because if this plan doesn't work, Matty is going to end up locked up in an insane asylum and Kelly will go God knows where. I also feel brave, like Matty has been this whole time. I feel like this part is my job and that I have to do it right. Even though there are a lot of odds against us, I feel confident. This has to work. How many bad things can happen to someone before something good does, right? I have to keep that in mind as I enter Kelly's room.

He is still sleeping in the bed and seems so peaceful. I almost don't want to wake him, but I know I must. I kneel down next to him and stroke his tiny face. His eyes open and his eyelashes brush my hand. He smiles at me and I smile back. I hope he doesn't feel pained and like there's a hole in him like Matty and I do. A boy so young shouldn't have to deal with that.

"Sweetie," I say softly in his ear. "You have to get up because we have to leave here."

"Okay," he says. He sits up and stretches briefly. Then he climbs out of the bed and gives me a huge hug. "Where are we going?"

"I don't know yet, but somewhere where we will be safe," I assure him.

"Good." I sigh and pick him up. He wraps his arms around my neck and rests his head on my shoulder. I feel like this is how it's going to be for awhile.

I cautiously leave the room, looking all around for any signs of intruders. The hall seems dark and silent so I run down it as fast and as quiet as I can. I push open the door to Matty's room, and he's waiting patiently in the red chair. He nods at me and I nod back. It's time to go.

He rises from the chair and walks past me. "Follow me."

I follow and he leads us to the fire door. "Are you ready?"

I try to keep my breathing even and my heart from beating out of my chest. I need to learn not to be as easily scared if we're going to live as fugitives. "What if there are people dying here and we kill them in a rush to get out of the supposed burning building? What if that's someone's dad, mom, brother, or sister just like us? I don't want to put someone else through that."

I see his face twist in the thought of what I said being true. Then it returns back to normal. "If you don't want to do it, tell me now, or else I'm going to."

"But what if it's true?"

"If we don't do this now, we're never going to see each other again. There's not really a fire, and I'm sure they'll figure that out soon enough. Sacrifices have to be made for the greater good sometimes Jen."

I close my eyes and try not to think of what's about to happen. "We're not going to kill anyone. Do it!"

On my command, he flings open the door, and the siren responds. Sprinklers go off and the floor is wet and slippery within seconds. The nurses and doctors run around in panic, hoping to get everyone out they can and to find the fire. I even spot the cop Matty was talking about running around in circles in the now empty waiting room. Some cop, I think. I just stand there and watch as the whole hospital becomes turmoil.

I feel Matty grab my arm and pull me, and I realize I was supposed to be running after him. I can't move from this spot, even though I know we're going to get caught soon.

"Jenna!" Matty screams over the noise. "We have to go before someone catches us! Come on!"

Kelly bites down on my neck and that gets me moving. I spin around on my heels and look Matty straight in the eye. "Sorry."

"It's okay. Just run!"

I do exactly that. I run through the cold, crisp night with the pavement smacking under my feet and Kelly bouncing against my hip. I feel his fingernails dig into me to keep from falling, and I can't help but whimper. We keep running until we reach the closest market. It's lit up so I know it is open 24 hours. We slow down in the parking lot to catch our breath. If we go in like this, we're going to look suspicious, and we have to stay as far under the radar as possible.

"You're going to have to walk in front of me until we get some clothes, or I'm definitely going to get some attention," Matty says once he can speak again.

"You do realize it's after 5 in the morning and we're going to look really strange shopping alone?" I add.

Matty's face falls. Obviously he didn't. "Let's hope no one confronts us."

I let out a nervous laugh and head in through the main doors. I let Kelly down. He's starting to get really heavy. "Don't leave us no matter what, okay?"

"Yeah," he sighs. He loves running off on his own and checking out the toy aisle. There's no time for normal things like that anymore. Sadly.

We make our way through the back to the boys' clothes section. Matty scans the shorts until he finds a pair of cargo shorts. He rips off the gown and I turn around to give him privacy. He tries them on, and when he's sure they fit, he rips off the tags. Lucky for him, there are no hard security tags that are irremovable unless purchased.

"Um, Matty," I ask, daring to turn back around. "Don't you need underwear or something?"

"Not right now, but we better get some for later," he answers. "We have to change our look or else they're going to find us easy. Go find some clothes for yourself. I'll help Kelly."

"Alright," I say. "Good luck with that."

I make my way toward the girls' section and get the sudden feeling that all this is really ridiculous. I sort through the girls' clothes and find a pair of jean shorts and a cute t-shirt that looks really soft. I take them off the rack and take off my other clothes. I try them on and when I know they fit, I rip off the tags just like Matty did. I grab a pair of flip-flops too and throw my old ones on a shelf under a bunch of tank tops. I grab Johnny out of my other shorts and shove him in the new ones. The rings Matty was holding on his way out of the building fall out. They make my heart ache and I feel tears well up. I put Mom's on my left hand and put Dad's away for Matty to wear. They're all we have left of them.

I wipe away the tears and rip open a couple packs of underwear. I ball them up as much as I can and stick them in my pockets. I do the same things with a couple packs of bras. I pull down my t-shirt as far as it will go so the bulges don't show. I take my hair out of the ponytail and shake it out so it falls in my face. I grab a hat and put that on too so I don't look the same. I wander around looking for a mirror and don't encounter anyone. It's like the place is deserted. Then again, it is really early.

I come across a mirror in the make-up aisle. I check myself out and I don't look much like I did before. That's a good thing. I see the eyeliner and lip gloss calling out to me, so I pick them up. I apply a little black eyeliner and a little pink lip gloss. Then I rip the tags off them and add them to the assortment in my pockets. A little bit of being a girl can't hurt right?

I realize I'm done so I make my way back to Matty. He looks a lot different. He's wearing the cargo shorts, which are stuffed to the max with his own supplies, a black t-shirt to blend in in the night, a pair of sneakers, and he has a pair of scissors in his hand.

Then I look up and see his hair. I gasp. "What did you do?"

"Calm down," he hisses. "I had to cut it so no one recognizes me. You did a good job by the way."

"Thank you, but did you have to cut it that short?" It used to be almost to his shoulders and now it barely reaches his ears. It's a big adjustment.

"Yes," he snaps. I can tell he's not too happy about it either, so I shut up. "I cut Kelly's the same way. Do you have everything you need?"

I know he's referring to feminine care products, but I don't need them yet. Maybe I should get some in case there is an emergency and I do need them sometime. That would be smart.

"I think I forgot something," I mutter. "You go get us some food and I'll be right back."

I can hear him snickering as I rush to the dreaded aisle. I don't know what I'm supposed to get. I scan all the brands and they all seem confusing. I grab a pack of ultra duty pads and some unscented panty liners. Then I realize I don't have anywhere to put them. I tuck them in my shirt and look for Matty in all the food aisles. I finally find him looking at bags of snacks with Kelly, a cart next to them. Kelly's look is also a shock. He's a little version of Matty.

"What are we getting?" I ask, coming up behind them.

"I found $50 in Kelly's shorts. He doesn't know how it got there, but it's our lucky day, so I'm not knocking it. Do you have a say on what food we get?"

He spins around to look at me and I see him staring at the lump in my shirt. I hug them tighter to me. "Not really. I'm really hungry; I just want to eat something."

"That looks really suspicious. We better buy whatever that is too."

"Fine, but they're just a precautionary measure, not something I need," I assure him, pulling them out.

He shakes his head. "As long as I don't know about it, I don't really care. Now help me fill the cart."

We grab everything appetizing we can find, from all different aisles, until the cart won't hold anymore. I hope that all of it isn't over $50. We check ourselves again to make sure we didn't leave any tags on and make our way to the check-out. It must be getting later because lots more people are coming in now.

The lady at the check-out counter smiles as she rings up all our food. "You kids must be awfully hungry!"

"Oh, our mother sent us out to get the food for our camping trip this weekend," Matty lies. "We're really excited."

"Oh, that's nice. I used to love camping as a little girl. I didn't get to go much, so you kids are quite lucky. Anything else?"

Matty stares at me. I smile at her and reluctantly put up the "supplies". She smiles back and rings them up. It's like she gets kids buying an assortment of strange items every day. Maybe she does, this world *is* strange.

"$49.50 is your total," she says, and we breathe a sigh of relief.

"We just made it," Matty laughs, handing her the money.

She takes it and sends us on our way with 50 cents. "Have fun camping children."

"We will," Matty and I say in unison while Kelly gives his cute little boy smile. We leave the cart by the side of the store and lug our bags through the parking lot and down the street, until we find a vacant lot. We set them down in the grass and lay down next to them.

"That went quite smoothly," Matty says, his head turned toward me in the grass. Kelly jumps in between us.

"Yeah," I agree. "But now we have to find a place to put all this."

"After we get some rest, we're going to head to Grandma's."

I sigh. "We don't even know where we are. How are we going to get to Pennsylvania?"

"Doesn't Johnny have GPS?"

I pull him out of my pocket and check the applications. "Yes."

"That's how," he says. "I have her address memorized. It shouldn't be that hard, right?"

I glare at him. "Don't jinx us please. We need all the good luck there is."

He laughs and flicks my nose. I try to hit him, but he rolls away. "I'm getting some rest and I suggest you do too. All that running took a lot out of me."

"Put this on first," I tell him, pulling out Dad's wedding ring.

His eyes widen. "I thought I lost those!"

"No, I wouldn't let that happen."

He puts it on his left hand and we embrace. Kelly comes up and joins us. This time Mom is missing, but we're still a strong family. Strong families make it.

7

Matty

The walk to Grandma's house is a rough one. We have to walk day after day after day on hard blacktop, and that takes a greater toll on one's strength than you would think. We have to stop and rest every couple hours to consult our map and raid our food supply. Jenna is also getting irritable because she is dirty and she thinks she looks awful. I had to tell her that no one really cares because we're in the middle of nowhere. The only people who are seeing her are Kelly and I, and we're just as bad off. She doesn't listen to me and continues to complain. Kelly is actually better than her. He lets out a complaint every once in awhile, but I tell him once we get to Grandma's, he can do whatever he wants, so he shuts up.

We are in the middle of a lunch break, all of us munching on poorly put together sandwiches and cheese puffs, when Jenna decides to start whining.

"I don't think my feet can take much more," she huffs, examining them. "Are we almost there?"

I pull out my map and try to make sense of where we are in comparison to where Grandma's house is. "Um, we might have a couple more days. Stop complaining; you're worse than Kelly!"

She hits my arm and lets out a cry. "Look at these blisters. I'm going to lose all my skin soon!"

"Maybe you shouldn't have chosen flip-flops for walking across states. You're smarter than that!"

"How was I supposed to know we were going to do this?" she retorts.

"You're with me Jen," I laugh. "You should have known not to wear flip-flops."

She laughs too. She knows that I'm very adventurous and one with nature, and if I see an opportunity of a long trek through the wilderness, I will take it big time over a boring bus ride. Maybe it is time we take the bus. I look down at her blisters and think they might have put a new color to the color wheel. The skin off the bottom of her feet is almost gone, and the tops have red splotches all over them. After a couple of days, the flip-flops pretty much broke in half, so she's had to walk barefoot wherever we went from then on, which had to be a week. Yeah, we definitely have to consider taking the bus before she literally loses her feet.

"Do you think we should take the bus or something?" I suggest. "I don't want you to really be endangered by that."

She looks down at her blisters again. "What if someone recognizes us? Remember we saw our faces in the paper as fugitives?"

I sigh. "We'll just have to take that chance for the sake of you being able to walk again. That's important."

"There's a bus stop over there," Kelly informs us, pointing up and across the street a ways.

"I think it might be a good idea. I mean, how many people are going to recognize us? We're in a different state now!" Jenna says.

"Ok, let's go then." We all rise from our lunch and grasp our remaining supplies. We make our way to the bus stop and wait on the bench. Soon the bus comes, and we try to sneak up the stairs without paying. That doesn't work too well.

"A dollar a person kids," the driver grunts.

We stare at each other. We all know that we only have fifty cents left and there is no way that is going to cut it with this guy. He seems like the type who hates his job and being miserable doesn't put him in the mood to help three very dirty kids.

"Sorry sir, we only have fifty cents. Is that okay?" It's worth a chance. Maybe I'm wrong about him.

I'm not. "Then stop wasting my time and get off my bus!" I think he is going to spit in my face soon.

I turn around shamefully. I don't like being poor. I look up and I'm face to face with a pretty young woman. She smiles at me, and I try to get around her, but she blocks my way.

"Where are you two going today?" she asks. Her voice is very smooth, the kind that could put me to sleep.

I can't respond, so Jenna hits me. This lady looks in her mid twenties, but she is beautiful. The kind of girl you just want to sit down and stare at for hours.

Jenna finally gives up on trying to make me respond and answers herself. "We're trying to make it to our Grandma's house, but we don't have any more money. We spent it all on food."

"Oh that's awful," she says, fluffing my hair. I grin stupidly. "Let me help."

She pulls out three dollar bills and hands them to Jenna. She slaps them in the driver's hand and glares at him. Any other time, I would have laughed, but I'm in the middle of staring at the angel in front of us.

"Thank you so much," Jenna says, and we go to sit down. She has to drag me to my seat, and I still don't stop looking at this woman. I watch her pay the driver with a crisp dollar bill, I watch her adjust her pocketbook from one shoulder to the other, I watch her take a seat across the aisle from me, and I watch her look at herself in a little mirror. Finally, she looks over and sees me gawking.

"You're a quiet one," she notes. "What's your name?"

"Matty," I manage to choke out. "M.A.T.T.Y."

"That's a nice name," she smiles. "Are you thirteen?"

I nod.

"I'm good at guessing ages. My boyfriend says that that's my special talent."

I grind my teeth together at the word boyfriend. I don't know why that makes me so mad, but it does. He better be good to her because she's special. "Are you twenty-five?"

"Yes," she says, laughing. "I guess we share a talent!"

I laugh too. We're in our own little world with this conversation. Jenna has her face pressed up against the window and Kelly is playing with his salamander. The other people on the bus don't seem to care either. Maybe if I keep talking, the bus ride won't end.

"It's nice to meet you," I say, sticking out my hand. The bus stops again and I fly forward. A bunch of people come down the aisle banging into my hand. I pull it in reluctantly. I must have looked like an idiot. Great.

"You too," she agrees when the commotion ends and the bus is moving again. "I'm Kristina."

That's the most beautiful name I've heard in a long time, I think to myself, but can't bring myself to say it aloud. "Where are you going?" I ask instead. *Way* less weird.

"Oh, I'm just headed home from work. I'm sure A is waiting for me. He's not on call today."

It sickens me that she must call her boyfriend A. "So you take this bus every day."

"Twice a day," she replies. "It's really my only way to the school since I live so far. I'm a teacher. I love kids."

I smile. That's good. "You probably make a fabulous teacher."

She blushes. "Thank you." She motions to Jenna and Kelly. "Who are you with?"

"My twin sister Jenna and my little brother Kelly. We're headed to visit our Grandma."

"I thought you were twins, but then again, the three of you look so much alike. I love that you all have the dark black hair and the blue eyes. What I'm saying is you're a cute bunch of kids."

I feel my face get hot and I'm sure it's really red. She called me cute! Gosh, I sound like Rudolph. Then I think of what Jenna has been saying about how dirty and awful we look, and I want to hide. "I'm sure we look terrible. We've been traveling alone awhile."

"Oh, no you don't," she assures me. "But why are you traveling alone?"

I swallow hard. How am I supposed to answer that question truthfully? I think I can trust her but I have to be smart about this. "Our parents can't come to Grandma's with us, so we had to make our way over here on our own. That's all."

"Oh." The bus stops again and she peers out of the window. "This is my stop."

She gets up and I feel my heart ache. "Bye Kristina!" I call out.

"Have fun at your Grandma's Matty," she yells back and leaves the bus. I stare at her as the bus pulls away.

At the sound of my name, Jenna's head snaps around. "How does she know your name?"

"I told her. Duh."

"How much else did you tell her in your fit of love?"

I glare at her. "I wasn't in love and I told her what she asked. And she told me about her. We had good conversation."

"Oh really," she retorts. "And you don't think all that good conversation could be the interrogation of an undercover cop?"

"Relax Jenna. She's not going to get us arrested."

"You just think that because you love her," she mutters, and I hit her. I glance at the map and see that we're at the next stop. I quickly fold it and brace myself to make my way off the bus.

"Wow," Kelly says, his eyes wide. "This place is big!"

I look out and see that we're only a couple blocks away from Grandma's house. I remember saying the same thing when I was little. When you live where we do for so long, a big city like this can look amazing. I sigh as I remember that Dad was there then, and he told me that I'll see some interesting sights in the city. He said never look in the homeless' eyes or they will chase you. That was true! I miss him so much.

"'Member the guy in the dress we saw down this street?" Jenna whispers in my ear.

I laugh. "How could I forget?"

When the bus stops, we leave and Jenna sticks her tongue out at the driver. He deserved it. We lug our bags down the street on our way to Grandma's. It's great to be in a place that's at least a little familiar. Only a little farther and we'll have a place to call home again, I think in happiness. At least that's what I hope.

8

Jenna

Grandma's house is exactly the same as I remember it. Gray siding and a gray roof, with a

bright pink door and shutters. It's still a huge mansion, set far back from the rest of the city in a huge shaded property, with trees surrounding it. A thick pile of dead leaves and twigs cover the lawn, and large green shrubs surround the perimeter of the house. I take in a nice breath of crisp air. The smell of wilderness has always been my favorite.

We make our way toward the door, hoping that she's there. Things seem awfully quiet. The only sound is the wind and a few birds. Matty knocks softly on the door and there is no answer. I peer in the windows, but they are tinted so I can't see inside. Who has tinted windows on their house? I don't remember that.

Matty rings the doorbell that is glowing next to the door, and I press my ear up against it. I hear footsteps inside, and they grow loud enough for Matty to hear them. He gives me a thumbs up sign and I stand back. The door swings open and Grandma appears in her nightgown. Her eyes widen as she takes in what she sees. We all wave.

"Oh my, children," she says. "Come in quick!"

We file in the door and she takes our bags. We look around at the foyer and it still looks the same. Older, but recognizable. She runs to the kitchen and returns empty handed. She makes her way to the living room and beckons us to follow. Her behavior is a little strange, I must confess. I wonder if Matty notices. I look over at him, but he has no expression on his face. We follow Grandma into the living room and sit down on the pink couch with her. There is at least one pink thing in each room that sticks out. She says it puts people in a good mood, even though it doesn't match the rest of the room at all. She's so much like her son.

"Now tell me," she says. "What on Earth are you doing here, and how did you get here?"

"Did you hear about the fire and our mother," I ask. That is the best way to start.

She nods painfully. "I was notified of the situation. Are you three alright?"

"Yes," Matty answers. "We checked out of the hospital and we're fine. But we're orphans now, and we were hoping we could live with you now."

Her face brightens. "Why of course you can, but there is one problem."

"What?" Matty and I both ask, panicking.

"You're fugitives for some odd reason. You do know that, right?"

I gulp. "There was a mix-up in the hospital and we had to run away. To here."

She nods. "I won't ask any questions. I'll hide you here, but I'm sure this will be one of the first places they look for you."

"We know," Matty says. "We just needed a recharge."

"Yeah, we're all a little dirty, and we need some ice-cream, right Kelly?" I ask turning around, but I realize Kelly isn't there with us. I freak out.

"Where's Kelly?" Matty asks, realizing the same thing as me.

I shake my head. This is not good. "Maybe he's outside. I'll go look for him and you can get Grandma up to speed."

"Ok. Good luck."

I spring up from the couch and run out the front door. I look all around the front yard, but there is no sign of him. I run up and down the street, but he's nowhere. I wander into the back yard, but it's just a huge forest. How am I ever going to find him? I think. If he's even here.

"Kelly!" I yell through the forest and my voice echoes. "Where are you?"

"Come here, real quick!" I hear him yell. I follow the direction of his voice straight into the middle of the forest. I spot him sitting in a pile of leaves, staring up at a huge oak tree.

"Look at this," he says, pointing at the bark.

"Yes, I see it. It's a very big tree. Now come back inside. You can't run off like that. We get just as worried as Mom." I grab his arm and try to pull him, but he's not budging.

"No," he whines, pulling his arm out of my grasp. "Look!"

I come down to his level and look at what he's looking at. Maybe if I stare at the tree awhile it will get him to come inside. I see that the bark is moving by itself and look closer. I gasp. Words are being carved into the tree bark in front of my very own eyes, and no one is there carving them. This isn't possible.

"Kelly, how did you find this?" I ask.

"There was a voice in my head that told me to come to this tree, and when I was here, the words appeared."

I look even closer and read what is being carved.

This is only temporary, my beloved. I hope you know when the right time is to leave. Remember I am with you as long as you wear your rings. Don't endanger your Grandmother. She doesn't deserve that. Love you all.

"Mom?" I ask. It sure sounds like her. This is unreal. There is no way that she is communicating with us like this. I don't want to take my eyes off of it in case it disappears when I turn away.

"Kelly," I say. "Go get Matty and come back here, okay?"

"Yeah," he replies, getting up from his sitting position. "Is that really Mom?"

"That's what I'm trying to find out." I hear him run through the forest toward the house, his feet crunching on the leaves. I touch the ring on my hand. It must be a way to communicate with Mom even though she's gone. What a blessing.

"Mom, if you can hear me, I miss you so much. I will make sure Matty and I always wear these rings so you can communicate with us. When we sense danger, we'll leave Grandma's and find our way on our own. I love you too."

I hear Matty come up behind me. "What? What's so important that you had to take me away from my conversation with Grandma?"

"This," I reply, pointing at the tree.

"It's a tree," Matty says bluntly.

I look up at him, now crying, and grab his arm. He falls down next to me and looks where I'm looking. When he's done reading, he keeps staring at it. I see tears leak out of his eyes too. He must be thinking the same thing as me.

"Is that what I think it is?" He whispers.

"I watched it being carved with no one touching it," I answer, "so I can assume so."

He touches the ring on his hand as I did. "So we have to keep these on?"

I nod. "I wonder why Kelly heard voices in his head asking him to come out here and we didn't."

"They say the littler you are, the more you can communicate with ghosts. Maybe that's why. I'm glad he did though or else we never would have found this."

Most brothers would have seen that and not believed me and Kelly. He would have to have seen it to believe that we weren't playing a trick on him. But the good thing is Matty is not like most brothers. He believes anything can happen at any time, and if someone says they saw something, they probably did, even if he can't see it himself. He also knows that I would never joke when it comes to something about Mom or Dad. They're just too special to us.

"This means we have to leave Grandma's sooner than we thought. The police must be after us, and this will be the first place they look. We can't get her in the middle of this. In fact, I wish you two weren't even in it because I'm the one they're after. I lost my temper and started all this mess. I should just let them take me in, and you two can go on living your lives with Grandma. You'd be better off anyway."

He puts his head in his hands and I know he's close to tears. I pull his hands away and look up at him. "We're all in this together, so we're not leaving you for anything. We need you anyway, and we probably wouldn't survive out here without you. At least I know I wouldn't."

He smiles. "Thanks Jen. Let's go inside now before Grandma thinks someone kidnapped us."

"Okay," I laugh. I grab Kelly's hand so we don't lose him again, and we all go inside. Grandma has already started preparing supper. She must have known we were coming or else she wouldn't have had a huge ham in, all the vegetables for a salad, or a pineapple salad. It all smells so good. How did I not notice all this good smelling stuff when I first came?

"I see you were expecting us," Matty comments. "This all looks so good!"

"I have a way of knowing when something big is about to happen," she smiles. She starts setting the table and I move in to help. That sounds a lot like me. I know when something big is about to happen. Maybe that's where I got it from! "I always cook when I sense adventure in the future!"

We all laugh. "I can't wait to eat it!" I say, taking a seat. She sets all the food down and we dig in. It's the best meal we've had in a very long time, and we can't get enough. Starving for a couple weeks really makes you appreciate a well prepared meal. I never knew that before.

9

Andy

My dad comes busting into my office and it scares me half to death. His face is beet red and I think the veins on his forehead are going to pop. I keep my mouth shut because I know it has been a bad day and he just might kill me if I say something wrong. "This never happens to me!" he roars, slamming his fist on my desk. Everything on it jumps a few inches into the air and rolls off onto the floor. I watch it until it all stops moving and all is quiet.

"Dare I ask?" I say, bending down to pick up all my stuff. My desk is always organized and I can't stand to see all the things in disarray. The tight dress pants I'm wearing for my uniform don't provide much movement. They don't hide much either. They scream 'this is what I've got, tell me what you think.' I miss my worn in jeans where I'm free.

I stop at the picture of my gorgeous girlfriend. She's the reason I love going home so much and hate this place. I gaze into it and for a minute and forget where I am and all the things I wish I were doing instead of listening to my angry father.

"I got tricked by kids!" He yells, and I'm snapped back into the horrible reality of things. I think I feel the room shake. I look up to make sure the ceiling isn't going to crumble and fall on me. I can only imagine what story I'm about to be told. I don't want to be crushed in the process.

"How did that happen?" I ask, confused. "I didn't hear you were after any kids."

"Three kids got orphaned in a house fire a couple nights ago, and because they were angry about it, they were an endangerment to their doctors. I was going to trap them in a nice 'interrogation', but they escaped through the fire door. They caused so much commotion that by the time someone went looking for them, they were long gone. If I don't find them soon, people are going to start talking about how reliable the chief of police really is. Who knows what crimes they're committing while I'm telling you this? Do you know what this all means for me?" He throws his hands in the air. I figure that question isn't meant to be answered.

Personally, I think this entire case is completely ridiculous. Aren't there more important things for the chief of police to spend his time on than torturing shocked orphans when they already have enough trouble?

"Correct me if I'm wrong," I say. "So you're punishing them because they lost their parents and they were upset? Because that's what it sounds like to me."

He glares at me, hoping that he can burn a hole through me right there. He fails at that, lucky for me. "Andrew!!!" he roars again. I back up slightly. I'm taller than him by a couple inches and almost as heavy, but it's still intimidating when he roars. "Why can't you be a good, understanding son like I was for my father?"

I grind my teeth together and stare at the tiny palm tree tattoo on my hand. That's the only one he can't make me hide, just like the rest of me. I don't need to get in this argument again right now. "Get out of my office!"

He continues to stand there, and I point at the door. He shakes his head and mutters, "Maybe one day he'll learn." He slams the door to my office and stops to talk to the DA a little ways down the hall. I don't know what it is about, but something makes me open the door just a crack so I can listen without anyone noticing.

"He's obviously not on our side, so don't inform him of anything on this case, okay?" he asks her. They're obviously talking about me so I have to be careful not to be seen. I slip out of my office and tip-toe up the linoleum floor of the hallway until only a thin wall separates me from them. I listen, perfectly still, which is one of the hardest things I've done in my life. Even with my meds, ADHD still has an effect on me.

"I have their files here and it says their only living relative left is their grandmother on their father's side. She lives in the suburbs of Philadelphia, and I would suggest that be the first place you look," the DA informs my father.

He sighs. "I must admit they are smart kids because they were able to escape *me*. I doubt they would go there, and even if they did, it would be a pit stop."

"Or that's what they hope you'll think."

"True. I'll look anyway, and if they're not there, it will be as expected. I will ask around all the stores and public places around where they live and the grandmother's house. I'll go to the subways and buses and every form of transportation they could have taken. I'll even ask anyone on the streets of Philadelphia that could have seen them! Anyone who tricks me is a first priority. I will take them down!"

"Very well sir," DA Gaston says, calmly. I have no idea how she could go along with this nonsense. This is insanity! Am I the only sane person in the police force? That's almost funny because I don't even want to be here. "Who should I assign to help you with that?"

"Get all our best detectives! Get anyone else who is going to find these little brats! Everyone, I'm desperate." There's a long silence and I'm sure it has to do with me. "Everyone but Andrew that is."

"I understand. I'm on that." I hear the sound of high heels clicking down the hallway and my dad's big heaving sigh. This is the first time he's ever banned me from a case. Usually I'm forced into ones I don't want to take.

Something about that thought lights a spark in my brain. These kids have no chance without me. They're scared and out there in the real world on their own, and now the whole police force of Delaware and possibly Pennsylvania is after them. I have to save them for some reason. I feel it in my bones, like it's my destiny, and I can't do that if I'm not on the case. I need to charm my dad enough to have him put me back on the case. It pains me deep down, but I have to do it.

I come out from my hiding spot and walk casually up to my father. "I heard my name on the way to the restroom. What's the problem?"

His face twists into all kinds of different expressions as he decides what to tell me. I wait patiently as possible, shifting from one foot to another. "DA Gaston and I were talking business."

He's pulling the private card on me, I think. This might be a little difficult, but I can handle it. I have mad skills. "You always tell me business." I pretend like the idea's just coming to me and ask, "Is this about the case with the orphans?"

He doesn't respond, so I continue, "I'm sorry I acted like that. I was having a difficult day and your point of view didn't occur to me until now. Any child who threatens the doctor who is helping them is not normal and should be stopped. Plus, you must protect your career."

He grins and I know I have him with all my lies. "Do you really mean that son?"

"Of course. I wouldn't lie to you."

He pats me on the back and pulls me into a hug. I slowly put my arms around him. It's awkward, but it builds the effect. I only hug three people-my mom, my sister, and my girlfriend. That's the rule and that definitely does NOT include my dad. I pull away as soon as possible.

"I knew you'd come to your senses Andrew," he beams. "You are *my* son for God's sake. You are coming to the grandmother's house with me. It will be the father-son take down of the century!" He puts his arm around my shoulders and looks up at the wall. He wipes his hand around the air like he can see the scene already on the blank wall.

"Great," I say, trying my best to fake a smile. I'm glad I'm a good liar or this never would have worked. I feel good inside. Not only am I doing a good thing for these kids, but I'm finally giving my father what he deserves. I can taste the victory on my teeth after all these years. I hope I can handle it.

"**H**ow was work?" I ask, wrapping my arms around the back of my love. She's chopping up vegetables so we can have a salad with dinner. She has this old-fashioned thing about her that she believes the woman should cook a nice meal for her man and they should sit down together and eat it. I never had that growing up because my dad was always working, and my mostly way-ward sister would have thought it was plain ridiculous. We had to fend for ourselves most of the time, and I pretty much ate toast and peanut butter and jelly sandwiches for dinner. I enjoy this much more, especially since it's a nice time to relax. It is also good because I can't even cook an egg. When I was little, my mom tried to teach me how to cook, but my dad thought it was too feminine, so I only learned two things-meat loaf and mashed potatoes. They're my favorites but even they get old after awhile. And when that happens, I'm doomed.

"It's not work when you get to give education to a group of adorable little children," she smiles. Unlike me, she loves her job with a passion.

"I love it when you smile," I charm. "It makes you more beautiful than you already are." I learned that sweet-talking her gets me what I want. She stops chopping, turns around, and kisses me. Score! This house always brings me good luck. Ever since I met Tina, she always said how she loved the beach and that her dream was to have a house on Rehoboth Beach in Delaware, where she always went as a little girl. So for her big 25th birthday bash, I bought her the most beautiful house I could afford. It isn't right on the beach, but it's 10 minutes away, and that's a hell of a lot better than 2 hours. She loved it and we moved in immediately. Tina didn't want to leave her job in Pennsylvania with the school she loves before the end of the year, so she commutes pretty far every day. She wakes up early to get there on time and makes it home by the time I usually get off work. She is already looking for a job down here for next year, so we're committed to staying. My mom told me that it was a big step to move in together before marriage because if we break up, one of us is going to end up stranded, but I figured that since we'd been together 5 years, it was not *that* big of a step. When the furniture first came in, we broke in the bed and that started my good fortune. It's been a great year too. I keep worrying that my good luck will run out and something awful will happen here, but if I start thinking dark thoughts, I'll never stop, and go places I never want to go again.

"What puts you in such a good mood?" she asks, pulling away a moment and ending my train of thought. "Usually you're pissed off after a long day with daddy."

I roll my eyes. She knows I hate it when she calls him that. "I finally found a way to get back at him."

She raises her eyebrows as she throws the salad into a bowl and shakes it around. The oven beeps and she pulls out pork tenderloin. It smells delicious and I realize that I never had lunch. "Do I want to know?"

I smirk evilly. "Oh yeah! But you might want to sit down for this. It's *that* good."

She laughs and finishes setting the table. I patiently help her place plates and silver ware on both sides of the table. She stares at the other places wishing there were little ones eating with us, but I pretend not to notice. I'm going to have enough trouble with these kids part time; I don't think I'll be able to handle any of my own all day long. Something tells me I'd be a worse father than my own, and I don't want a kid to endure that.

After we're all set up, she takes her usual place and looks up, waiting. "Go ahead. I'm *literally* on the edge of my seat here."

I take my seat and help myself to my portion of dinner. "My dad has a new high priority case. Three kids got orphaned after a house fire, got upset, and threatened the doctor. Dad was going to trick them into incriminating themselves and then lock them up like he always does. But they must have known somehow because they escaped through the fire door, and there was so much commotion, they were able to get away with ease."

"Oh no," she says, eyes widening. "Children outwitted him. There must have been a scene."

"Yeah, I got the brunt of it."

"Go on," she urges. "How does this go with your master plan of deception?"

I continue. "Well, I thought it was stupid at first and I let him know it. He tried to take me off the case, but it occurred to me how important this was to him. So I told him I finally came to my senses, and we could do a father-son take down. All lies because little does he know, I'm going to sabotage his plan and save those little mites. I feel like it's my job to help them, and plus, I get to get my dad back for years of suffering in the process."

"That's risky," she notes. "How do you plan to do that exactly?"

"Well, when we find the kids together, I will assure my father that I can bring them in myself, and when he leaves, I will let them free. I will take care of them in a place they will never be found, and in the meantime try to find them a home where they will feel safe and wanted. I'm hoping that I can find a loving family that wants all three of them at once before my plan is figured out. It's a long shot, but I have to try it, or else I'll feel like I will have failed in my duties. I haven't even met them yet, but I already feel obligated to make their lives alright."

She stabs at her pork and I know she's worried about me. My father can do things way out of character when he's mad, and that includes murdering his own flesh and blood. I know that, but I'm still not scared because I can do all this without ever running into him. "Just please don't get yourself killed."

I sigh. "I'm insulted that you don't believe in me. I can do this!"

She finally lifts her eyes to look at me. "I wouldn't be able to stand it if something..."

I lift my hand to stop her. "It won't. This will all go well." I give her a smile to reassure her and her spirits lift a little.

"You're so cute," she coos.

"Cute enough to…" I start to ask but she gives me a look and yells, "NO!" I hang my head in defeat and finish eating. "You need to get a shower to wash all that gross hair gel out and change into your normal clothes before there's even a chance."

I hear my cell ringing in my pocket and I fumble to retrieve it out of my tight pockets. After the fifth or sixth ring, I answer it. I was seconds away from missing the call. "Hello?"

"You always answer like you're confused Andrew," the voice of my mother laughs. "Are you okay?"

"Just a little flustered is all," I reply. "I always have issues with this uniform."

"Speaking of," she whispers. "You're father won't stop talking about how his son, after all these years, is finally what he wanted. How this is going to be the case of the century, and this is the best day of his life. I see through it because I know you, and he's just blinded by happiness. What's really going on?"

I smile. Mothers know everything and that's no joke. "Where are you?"

"I'm out on the deck. He's not in earshot, I promise you that."

"I have an agenda and that's all I can say."

There's a silence on the other end and I know her mind is racing, thinking of all the things I could be getting myself into. "Just promise your worrier of a mother that you won't do anything to endanger yourself."

"I can't do that because everything in life is dangerous in a way," I joke.

"Andrew," she scolds. She hates when I get like that, but sometimes I can't help myself. "You know what I meant!"

"Sorry. It was right there. But I do promise you I won't kill myself. I just assured Tina the same thing. You women need to calm down."

"How is Tina by the way," she asks, ignoring my 'you women' comment.

"Gorgeous," I reply, and she grins at me across the table. She knows when I reply with one word that I'm speaking of her.

"Stacy called today," she adds, and I know where this is going. "She said to propose to Tina already."

"She does every time."

"Maybe she's right. It's been almost 6 years."

"I know that mother," I sigh. I wish she would stop pushing me. She knows just like Tina does that I don't believe that marriage is necessary, and that I would much rather just make a commitment to someone without the big ceremony.

She sighs louder to show me she's not giving up easy today. "All I'm saying is, Stacy is only 4 years older than you, and she's been married for 3 years and her oldest is 4 now. Meanwhile, you're messing around, and we don't want you to lose Tina because she's a great girl."

"Mom," I yell. "Quit it! It's my decision and I don't care what Stacy is doing with her life." Tina gives me a strange look and I roll my eyes to tell her the usual. I never tell her about what they're *really* telling me because she might get upset and take it personally. I might never want to marry *anyone*, not just her personally.

"That reminds me." She's ignoring what I have to say again. "Stacy needs someone to watch Spencer and Tanner Saturday night so she can go out with Randy."

"I need to work then, but I'm sure Tina can do it," I answer. "She's going to be away from her kids soon and she loves the boys." I hold the phone away from my ear a minute to ask Tina, "Can you watch Spence and Tanner Saturday night? Stacy doesn't have a babysitter."

"Sure," she smiles. Stacy can always count on her because she loves little boys, especially these ones because they're so good. Spencer who is 4 was born with the lack of a voice box. They still have no idea how it happened, but they knew something was wrong when he entered the world and his cry was nothing but a mere whisper. To communicate with people, he whispers, which doesn't need the vibrations a voice box creates, but he prefers acting out the words he wants to say. He looks like a bad mime, but it's very entertaining at the same time. Two year old Tanner was born more privileged, but sometimes he decides not to talk in support of his brother.

Tina adores both of them, and they love spending time with her more than their own mother. Stacy is my one and only sibling, and most of my life she wanted nothing to do with me. She always was out causing trouble and picking on me. When I got old enough to be good enough for her, she started to think I was okay, but by that time she was off to get her own place with her many boyfriends. Not much has changed since then, and it was no surprise when she ended up pregnant before she was engaged. She quickly got married two months before Spencer was born and I'm pretty sure she's steadily cheating on Randy. Tina is exactly the opposite of her, and if I were those little boys, I'd take every opportunity to get away from wild Stacy and come see caring Tina.

"She says she'd love to," I relay to Mom. "How is Stacy feeling being thirty?"

Mom cackles into the phone. "She decided she needed to act young and made herself a nice drug deal."

"Nice," I say sarcastically. "Don't tell Dad that one."

"Never."

I laugh. Sometimes I can't believe Stacy is older than me. In fact, I *always* can't believe that.

"Andrew," she says, becoming serious again. "You're father is on a high and I don't know what will happen when he comes back down again, so please be careful."

"I will," I promise. "I love you."

"Love you too. Talk to you tomorrow."

"Alright. See you."

"Bye." She always waits for me to hang up before she does, so I close the phone and set it on the table. "Stacy is being Stacy again," I tell Tina.

"I can only imagine what she did now." She takes away the dishes and places them in the sink. She is just about to start the water when I ask, "Why don't you at least take that shower with me and forget about those for a little while?"

She thinks about it for a moment, hand on the faucet, and I hold my breath. "Fine."

"Great!" I say, racing her to our finely color coordinated bathroom.

10

Jenna

After dinner, we all feel sickly full and tired. We help Grandma clean up and thank her for the wonderful meal, but we all agree that we need to get some rest. We haven't gotten a good night's sleep in weeks and the big, soft beds are calling us. While on our way here, each night Matty and I would take turns watching out for intruders in the dark while the other and Kelly slept. Most of the time Matty would be up half of my turn as well as his own, and when it was Matty's turn, I would sleep hard and wake up with aching muscles. I don't think I've had a good dream since the night before the fire, and I miss that.

We file into the bedroom, deciding it would be best to all stick together in the largest guest room in case of an emergency. There is a king sized bed in the middle of the tan colored rug of the floor with pillows arranged nicely at the head. There is a window seat overlooking the front yard through the window that takes up the whole front wall. I pull back the tan curtains and stare in amazement. I've always wanted something like this in my room, but my windows were always little and boring, covered with annoying mini blinds.

Matty offers to sleep on the window seat because it's a little less comfortable than the bed, but I say we can all fit on the bed. It's meant for two adults, but we're smaller than adults, and Kelly barely counts as the size of a person at all.

"No," Kelly protests and we both look at him. He hasn't spoken all night. He doesn't usually decide to speak at all if it's not really important, so we wait for him to continue. "I want this." He points at the window seat and lays down on it. He's obviously not going to part with it without a fight, so we agree.

"Read?" he asks me. I always read to him once a week, and we've had no reading material for a long time. I know he's missing it so I search around the bookcase until I find a suitable novel. He likes those better than the kid's books, even though he doesn't understand half of it. Then again, he could know because his mind is very complex. I'll just take this with me when we leave here, I think. Grandma probably won't even notice.

I sit down on the window seat and Kelly climbs on my lap. Matty unmakes the bed and flops down on it. The soft mattress swallows him and it looks quite comfy. I open the book and begin to read. Before long, Kelly has fallen over so his head is in my lap. I stop reading and he looks up at me.

"I thought you were asleep," I laugh, placing the book back on the shelf. "Matty sure is." We hear him softly snore.

"I want to listen," Kelly orders. He reaches for my pocket and pulls out Johnny. He can't sleep without music even more than me, so I attach the ear buds to Johnny and carefully place them in Kelly's ears. His soft black hair brushes against my fingers, and I have to fight myself not to stroke it. He falls down on the pillow on the edge of the window seat and shuts his eyes. I remove his shoes and socks and climb into the bed next to Matty. I push over his legs so I can fit mine, and he groans.

It reminds me of the days when we used to go on family vacations that Dad would plan, where Matty and I would have to sleep in the same bed. We were five and we used to kick each other and scream all night that we wanted our own bed. After awhile, Mom and Dad used to get so fed up with us that they would make us both get out of the bed and sleep on the floor. We cried ourselves to sleep and I laugh remembering that that was the worst thing that ever happened to me. If only I could see all the things that are happening to me now, then maybe I would have just dealt with it. When you're young, everything seems like the end of the world, and then you realize that only some things are, like becoming orphan fugitives.

I turn off my thoughts before I start crying and scare Kelly. I shut my eyes and dream about my future. I dream I will be the famous writer/creator of the best show ever made and that my amazing husband and children will never be alone like I am right now. These happy thoughts lull me to sleep.

K elly's eyes flick open and he stares at me, half asleep. I woke up and Matty was already gone, so I went to look for him. He was fixing breakfast with Grandma and having a serious discussion about how girls are so much trouble at his age, so I decided not to disturb them. That isn't true by the way. Boys are trouble at thirteen; they're half as mature as girls and they do stupid things. I didn't want to get into that argument though, so I took a position cross-legged beside the bed and watched how peaceful Kelly was when he is asleep. Now we keep staring at each other and I'm not sure what to say.

Kelly pulls the headphones out of his ears and I hear a soft hum of rock music. He hands it to me and I cut the music. "My idol put me to sleep," he smiles.

"Always does." I wrap the headphones around Johnny and place him in my pocket. "Did you enjoy the story last night?"

He nods. I still don't know why he tries to speak as little as possible, but it's been since he could talk. We thought something was wrong with him when he said about two sentences a day at two years old. When the doctor asked him why he didn't talk, he simply responded, "There's nothing I need to say." He lives a unique, simple life, and I admire him for that.

"What's for breakfast," he finally asks, when I don't offer the information. He grabs his stomach and I hear it rumble.

"I think Matty and Grandma were making pancakes. Do you want to go see if they're done?"

He rises to his feet and checks his ears, like he always does in the morning. He thinks the matching gold hoop earrings that Dad got us all when we were born are going to fall out or get stolen in his sleep. They're his prize possession.

"Geen fissy?" he asks, with puppy dog eyes. I try to stare him down, but he's too cute with his jet black soft hair, his bright blue eyes, long eyelashes, and dimpled cheeks. He's a little version of Matty, who is an even littler version of Dad. Dad taught him that breakfast is not breakfast without a little candy, and he loves lime Swedish fish.

"It's 'green fishy'," I correct. He narrows his eyes at me. He can speak correctly if he wants, but Mom got tired of correcting him because he would reply, "I know, it sounds better the other way." Which to me is very smart because who says that we have to follow a rule book on how to say words some person made up eons ago? He also says 'bracet' instead of bracelet, and my favorite, 'babin' suit' instead of bathing suit.

"Ok, one green fishy," I reply. He smiles wide and I start to worry. Mom used to have to deal with these things and now I'm the mom in the household. I don't think I'm ready to be a full-time parent. I hope that we find a home where we can be loved and together and not be on the run anymore soon.

We make our way to the kitchen, my arm around Kelly's little shoulders, and the smells of pancake batter and chocolate fill the air. "Chocolate chip pancakes?"

Matty pumps his fist in the air. "I requested, and before I knew it, they were made." He licks the batter off the mixing spoon and throws it in the sink. "Yummy!"

"This is a dream," I say in astonishment. I love chocolate chip pancakes more than anything, and it feels like we haven't had them in years. I happily take a plate and stack three on it. I'm starving!

"No honey, just my short order kitchen," Grandma laughs. Matty sits beside me and Kelly stares at his plate. I almost forgot him!

"Say, Grandma," I ask. "Do you happen to have any multi-colored Swedish fish?" I say a small prayer because if the answer is no, there is going to be a hissy fit.

"You mean Aqua Life," she inquires. She pulls out a Candy Kitchen box, and when she opens it up, the Swedish fish are all different colors and shapes. "I was just up in Rehoboth last week and bought some. That's where I heard what happened to you."

I grab a lime one and place it on top of Kelly's pancakes. He squeals, "Geen fissy!" and shoves it in his mouth. I take a red one and Matty helps himself to an orange and a purple. "Pig," I say under my breath, and he kicks me under the table.

We enjoy our pancakes as a family of four, and I feel a tinge of happiness I haven't felt since that embrace before the fire. The whole kitchen is full of laughter, dirty dishes, and the smell of delicious food. Grandma has everything we could ever want, and we kids are living it up. I feel too good, I think. Something has to go terribly wrong, and soon.

11

Matty

We spend the next week at Grandma's and everything goes pretty much the same. We get pampered out of our minds, eat and sleep well, and are truly happy. We plan at night before we go to bed and check all the trees everyday to see if Mom has sent anymore guidance. The bark remains bare though, and Kelly assures us there were no more voices in his head. We all hope they will come back because they give us hope, but we never know what could happen.

Friday night, after a good amount of pizza enters my stomach, I retire to the living room to watch a little TV before I fall asleep. I pat my stomach, and my mind wanders as I stare at the television. Jenna walks in after a little while. "Kelly asleep?" I ask.

"Yeah, I just gave him his music and took off his shoes. Are you going to sleep soon?"

I nod. "There's not much on so I might as well."

She sits down next to me and I study her face. She seems concerned and I know she came in for more than just to check on me. "What's wrong?"

She sighs and picks at the loose string on her jean shorts. "I was just thinking about what Mom said. You know that this is only temporary and that we shouldn't put Grandma in the middle of our problems."

I pretend that I'm really into the cereal ad that has come on the TV and don't answer. She finally asks, "How long do you think temporary means?"

"That's an impossible question to answer Jenna," I reply. She always looks to me for answers and I admire that, but little does she know, I don't know anything more than she does. I may be 3 minutes older than her and the official 'man' of the household, but that doesn't mean I have what it takes to be the leader. And I wonder why I can't sleep at night?

"I just don't want Grandma to get hurt because we overstayed our welcome," she says, but by the end of the sentence she has become so quiet, I can barely hear her.

"I know. I'm hoping that we get a sign that tells us when it is time to leave."

"Like from Mom?"

"Maybe. I don't know. It's really something I don't know what to do about."

Her face falls even more and I feel awful. "Jenna, I wish I did, but I don't."

"You're supposed to know these things," she mutters, but I ignore it. That comment would only start a fight, and we need that like a hole in the head.

"I'm sure it will all work out," I assure her. "It always does somehow, right?"

She smirks. "Strangely, yes. I wonder..."

"Don't even start." We end up laughing and I'm glad I made her feel better. I even lifted my spirits in the process.

I click off the TV and we make our way back to the guest bedroom. Jenna checks on Kelly, and when she assures me he's long gone, we flop in our own sides of the bed. I wonder if she remembers vacation and having to sleep on the floor. That was an interesting time and thinking of it makes me drift.

I dream I'm five again and I'm running across the beach with a jellyfish sloshing in my water-filled bucket. My board shorts are filled with sand but I don't care. I dump the jellyfish on Jenna's head and her scream pierces the air, overpowering the squawks of the seagulls and the crashing of the waves. She chases me through everyone's towels and umbrellas with a handful of sand, but I know I'm faster and she'll never catch me. Mom and Dad laugh and cheer both of us on while the people we kick sand on glare. Even Lauren sits in the shade with a bandana wrapped around her head, and she smiles and silently watches us. Everything is happy and we don't have a care in the world. Summer makes everything perfect. The warm weather and the lack of responsibilities for kids will brighten anyone's spirits. Mom pats her pregnant stomach and tells unborn Kelly inside her that this is what he has to deal with soon. Before long, Jenna gives up, and we both collapse in the sand and laugh until our chests ache.

Then I feel someone shaking me and I'm not sure if it's part of the dream. I try to escape it, but it only gets worse. I force my eyes open and see Kelly standing over me. He is shaking me violently and his expression is panicked. I look over and see Jenna is still asleep and that it is still very dark outside. "Is it morning?"

Kelly shakes his head. "Then why are you waking me up? I was having a really good dream."

"I heard something," he says. His whole body is shaking and I have to hold him to calm him down.

"Was it outside or in you dream?"

"In my head."

My brow furrows. It's hard to understand Kelly because he uses as little words as possible. "Tell me what happened."

"The music cut off and there was a stern man's voice that said 'Leave, Now' in my head. It was really scary, and I don't know what that means."

"That was all he said?" I ask. I'm pretty sure what that means, but I'm not positive. I don't want to make any mistakes.

He nods and bites his lip. A drop of blood falls on the carpet and I shiver. "Was it like the time the voices told you to go to the oak tree?"

"Except that voice wasn't angry like this one." He breathes heavily, and I start to believe he will never stop shaking.

"Ok," I say, lifting him up until he rests on my hip. "That means we have to listen to this voice."

"What's it mean?" he asks. "Is it mad at me?"

"No, it's mad at me. We stayed here too long and we have to leave now, before something awful happens. Do you have Salamander?"

He jumps from my arms and grabs Salamander and Johnny. I shove his shoes back on and throw on a pair of clothes for myself. I shake Jenna awake and she stands right up from her sleep. I would have laughed if I weren't so stressed out.

"What's going on?" she asks in confusion.

"Kelly heard more voices and they said to leave here now. Get dressed and get all the stuff you need." She does exactly that. I throw all my and Kelly's clothes into the bags we came with, and Jenna follows. She packs up the rest of her things and we say our farewell to this wonderful room. We file down the stairs in a scared rush. I tell Jenna and Kelly to stay here, and I tip-toe into Grandma's bedroom. It is pitch black and I can't see a thing, but I make my way over to the side of her bed where she sleeps.

"Grandma?" I whisper. "Wake up a minute."

I hear her jump and she asks, "Matty, what's wrong?" She jumps out of bed like she's ready to fight off any intruder with merely her cane. That was a stupid simile, I think. She doesn't even own a cane.

"We have to go now. Someone's coming and we don't want to put you in the middle of this. If the cops come, tell them we left. Thank you for everything. It was the best. We'll see you when we have everything sorted out." I say all this in one breath, and I hope she understands it all.

"Ok," she says, still a little shocked. "Is there anything I can do to help you?"

I shake my head and remember she probably can't see that. "No, just the cop thing."

She pulls me and gives me a kiss on the top of my head. "Be careful out there."

"I will. Love you," I say rushing back to my siblings. I spin on my heels in the doorway and add, "Jenna and Kelly said the same thing."

"Love you all too," she whispers, and I run full speed out of there, grabbing my share of the bags when I pass Jenna and Kelly. I imagine poor, lonely Grandma standing in her nightgown in the dark while her grandchildren and only family left go out into the world, where they could die instantly. There's no time to dwell on it though; we have to get out of here now.

"I feel bad for Grandma," Jenna says while we run through the rooms of the house. The house seems endless when you're trying to escape it quickly. "She must worry herself sick."

"Yeah," I reply. "How big is this house?!"

Finally we make it to the back door, and I pry it open. We squeeze through the little space and I hear police sirens as I shut it behind us. Three cars pull into the driveway and their tires skid and screech. Men in uniform file out and I feel like we're just a little too late. There's no way to leave here without passing them and who knows what could be lurking in that forest at night. I spin around wildly as the men bang on the door and ring the doorbell multiple times. Have they no courtesy for an elderly woman trying to get her sleep?

My eyes land on the crawlspace. It's going to be tight and possibly wet with spiders, but it's either that or get thrown in the clink. "Get into the crawlspace, quick," I whisper the order.

We drop to our knees and squeeze into the unknown darkness of the crawlspace, dragging our bags behind us. We keep crawling until I estimate we're about halfway through. I try to sit up, but my head bangs the top, so I have to sit with my neck tilted. I hear another bang and Jenna lets out an expletive. I pull Kelly into my lap and we stay perfectly silent. We hear a lot of voices and sirens and footsteps that sound awfully close.

After what seems like an eternity and I think we might be in the clear, a lone voice appears almost next to us. I see a flashlight illuminate a little spot on the dark dirt and I spot a pair of men's dress shoes. "I'll check in the crawlspace. That's the only spot they would still be and then we know Ms. Thornton is telling the truth."

My heart stops with the sound of those words, and I start to have a panic attack. I talk myself down while wishing really hard for a trap door to open up underneath us and put us somewhere wonderful. Please give us a miracle God, I pray.

The flashlight shines to the left of us and we all hold our breath. Maybe he'll miss us, I think. Or maybe he'll forget the whole thing and go home. Or maybe a giant spider will eat him alive. I smile thinking of that one. The light slowly creeps toward us, and I feel more doomed than I've ever felt in my life. I also feel like I failed and that everything I did from the fire until now was all for nothing.

The light shines right in my eyes and I am forced to shut them. I try to make myself as small as possible, but I know he can see us. The light stays on us for a very long time and nothing happens. It clicks off and we're in the dark again. He's probably bringing in the troops to attack us. I hear him groan as he gets back on his feet, and he yells to whoever is up there, "Nothing. We must really have just missed them."

This is really weird. Only a blind man couldn't have seen us, but he claims he didn't. Maybe he's just trying to trick us into thinking we're safe and then closing in. I keep my position in hopes that that will help our cause.

"Big Andy's not going to like that," the women he was talking to jokes.

"There's nothing I can do about it," the flashlight cop yells. "Let him be mad. He always is anyway."

The woman laughs quietly and I hear many footsteps. I'm really confused at what is happening. I feel a rock come up and hit me on the shin. It's a big sharp one, and where it hit stings. I can't help but to whisper an "Ow!" I instantly cover my mouth and try to endure the pain silently. I hope I'm not bleeding. I'm not too good with blood. I hear the flashlight cop chuckle a little, and I know he did it on purpose. He did see us and he told the woman he didn't! He is trying to trick us after all! I let out a big heaving sigh. This is not going to end well.

12

Andy

I open the door to find Stacy sucking on a cigarette with Spencer and Tanner on either side of her. I glare at her and she keeps puffing, even in my face. She has some nerve. I hold my breath and grab for the cigarette. She pulls out of my reach and laughs, just like when she used to steal my toys as a kid. She rubs the end on the railing of my front steps and throws it on my lawn. Then she smirks at me. "Hello Andrew."

I continue to stare at her, blinking every five seconds. "Pick it up."

She rolls her eyes. "How about 'Hi Stacy. Long time no see.'"

"Hi Stacy. Now pick it up and get it out of my sight."

She makes a big deal out of bending down and picking it up, all the while huffing and puffing. She dangles it in front of my face, and then throws it in the garbage can a little ways down the walkway. "Can I come in now?"

"You stink like it," I reply bluntly. "You know I don't want that around my house, yet you do it anyway. And you subject your children to the secondhand smoke. Did you ever grow up?"

She shrugs. "Who wants to grow up? And I was just messing around with you. You need to cool it."

"You don't mess around with cancer Stacy. Now take your shoes off and come inside."

She smiles jokingly and ushers her sons in the door. She kicks her shoes off and they fly halfway into the foyer. She pulls off Spencer's and Tanner's shoes and does the same with them. They land in a heap on the hardwoods. I pick them up and place them in a line next to the door. This is what I had to live with when I was younger.

Tina comes in then and rushes up to the boys. "Hey Spencer, hey Tanner!"

She high-fives both of them, and they get wide smiles on their faces. "We love it here!" Tanner says excitedly, and Spencer nods in agreement. Tina bends down and they run into a hug. They all laugh; even Spencer, whose comes out more like a wheeze.

"Are you just going to forget about me?" I ask. They turn to me and grab my legs. I ruffle their hair and they laugh again.

Stacy rolls her eyes again. "You know this is a blow to my ego. My own sons like you guys much better than me and Randy."

"Hmm," I say. "Wonder why?"

Randy walks up the front steps and stands in the door in his dirty cowboy boots. He's wearing ripped jeans and a leather jacket. He's got a beard full of stubble and his usual big shaved head, and he folds his arms. It's the middle of summer you idiot, I think. Who dresses like that? He's the kind of guy who thinks he's tough and everyone wants him, when really most of population thinks he's disgusting and looks ridiculous wearing a leather jacket in June. My danger loving sister only likes him because the rest of us don't, and the boys are obviously scared to death he's going to murder them in the night. For that, I can't blame them.

"Have a nice day boys," he grunts. They cower in halfway behind my legs and give small waves. Even the two year old knows to steer clear of this tool. He nods at Tina and I and puts his arm around Stacy's waist. She's not very big and I'm surprised he hasn't crushed her by now.

"We're going to go now," Stacy tells us all. "We'll be back tomorrow morning, okay boys?"

"Ok," Spencer whispers, and I wave. Sometimes it's hard to hear and understand the low whispers he has to talk in, but after awhile, you get used to it. Randy leads Stacy back to the truck and they climb in it. I watch them drive away until they're no longer in sight, thinking about that cigarette. Stacy's going to end up in a lot of trouble one of these days and end up killing herself. I wish I could help her, we all do, but she's hopeless. The more you try to tell her not to do something, the more she does it. I shake my head. I always wanted a sister who actually cared about me and wouldn't smoke in front of my face after all I've been through. We used to be close when I was really little. What happened to *that* sister?

"Now it's time to have fun!" Tina yells, and the boys cheer. I smile at them and watch as they start to plug in the Nintendo Wii. They start playing tennis and run around the family room. Tanner swings wildly and almost takes Spencer's head off. I watch a little while until my cell rings.

"Yes?" I know it's my dad telling me we're ready to go.

"It's almost dinner time now. I think we better get going or else we might not catch them."

"Ok," I reply. "I'll get ready and see you at the office in an hour."

"This is going to be a good one son," he boasts.

"I'm stoked," I lie. He laughs and hangs up. I stroll into the danger zone and dodge the remote Tanner continues to throw around. "I'm gonna leave soon," I tell Tina.

She pauses the game and they all stop moving. She comes over to me and gives me a huge hug. "That's for good luck. Don't get caught."

"You underestimate me," I laugh. "I have this all under control. I'm going to go get ready and sneak out the door. Have fun."

"Oh we will," she smirks and shoots the boys a look. They hold up their remotes and smile back.

"Play?" Tanner asks, and she returns to her game. I hurry up the stairs and take a quick shower. I reluctantly pull on my uniform, which is a slow process since it's so tight. I slick my hair back with gobs of gel and cringe at myself in the mirror. I look so much like my father like this, and I hate it. I shove my feet in my dress shoes and they hurt instantly. "This sucks," I mutter to myself.

I trudge down the stairs; the only thing making me go is the fact that I'm deceiving the chief of police. I go out the back door and the sound of laughter is only a low rumble. I hop into my nice, shiny, red Mazda Miata MX-5, which had been my dream car since I started driving. I was finally able to afford it when I got my detective salary. It's really small, but it's my special occasion car, so I don't really need to put many people in it. Then again, I don't like carting around lots of people no matter what car I'm driving.

I watch out the window as I drive, seeing all the tourists shopping and squeezing as many things in their cars to take to the beach. It's always busy this time of year, right until Labor Day. Then weekends in the fall are crowded, but when the winter hits, it's a ghost town up here. That's the way I like it because you can get where you need to be fast, and there aren't as many ridiculous teenage fights to deal with on the boardwalk. That's a waste of my time.

Finally I make it through the crowds coming in and leaving on a Saturday, and pull in the police station. I lock my beauty and run my hands along her hood. The only thing that makes this car more beautiful is when Tina is in it, I think. I get to my office and see a couple guy detectives I see around a lot and Detective Jones standing in it.

Detective Jones glares at me as I walk inside. She used to be really nice to me and talk to me all the time. She used to do anything I asked, and I could talk to her about all I've been through and about how I wanted to be a performer. Then one night I stayed late to work on a case and she came to my office to see me. That's when everything changed. She unexpectedly pushed me on my desk and tried coming on to me. I freaked out and ran away, yelling I had a girlfriend and to stay away from me. She pleaded she secretly loved me but I was so shocked, I didn't even hear half of what she said. I drove back to my house in a panic and Tina laughed at me when I told her. The next day, when I came to work, she didn't talk to me and started spreading rumors. I guess she was sour I didn't love her back because all she does is make fun of me now. This is why I sighed deeply when I saw she was on the case with me.

"Well if it isn't the angry tool," she comments, and I refuse to look at her.

My dad walks in, an evil smile on his face. "Andrew! You're here!"

I nod. "Where else would I be?"

"You're just never on time for something like this."

"I'm truly into this one," I say, trying to fake my own evil smile. I know it's not too great, and I wonder if he buys it.

He pats me on the back. "Well let's get going then." Then he turns to the other detectives on the case and orders, "Jones, Cox, and Morgan. You're going to be riding behind us, and then watch around the house while Andrew and I ask the grandmother questions."

They nod and file out, making their way to their squad cars. Jones shoots me the bird on her way out, but I ignore it. I guess I'm used to her by now.

I follow my dad out of my office and we get into his special case car. I know the car ride is going to be really awkward, especially since it is two hours and I usually like to speak to him as little as possible. He's going to try to build up the case, and then when he can't think of anything else to say, he'll try to make useless small talk. His classical music, which bores me to tears, doesn't help. Music is my life, but this stuff is the worst.

"I haven't seen Tina in awhile," he informs me, starting to drive. "I heard she's watching Stacy's boys tonight." Oh no, I think. He's starting with the small talk. This is going to be a long drive.

W hen we finally pull into the grandmother's driveway, sirens blaring, I can't wait to get out.

I'd been tortured for two hours with my dad talking my ear off and the music almost putting me to sleep at 9 pm. I couldn't move the entire ride because of my constricting uniform, and my legs were numb. I undo my seat belt so fast it hits hard against the side of the car, and throw the door open. I stumble out into the warm night air. It's probably about midnight or later by now since we hit so much weekend traffic, and I can barely see two inches in front of my face. I can't walk because I can't feel my legs and try to stomp hard on the driveway to get the blood flowing again.

I stare up at the house while I do this and see that it's enormous. A real mansion, like this lady belongs in a fairy tale. How are we ever going to find a couple kids in there? I ask myself. That's going to take forever. Plus, behind the house is a full out forest, so they could be anywhere in there. I hope we don't have to look in there. It's late and I want to go home.

"Who are these kids so I know who to look for?" I ask my dad as we peer around the front yard.

"Two boys and a girl." He tries to look through the windows, but everything in the house is dark. I sigh in relief. At least I'm not dealing with three little girls. I don't think I would have lasted long if that had been the case. I haven't had much experience with little girls and when I did, they didn't like me. Little kids and me don't mix, especially ones who carry around dolls.

"How old?" Please don't say toddlers, I pray silently. I don't really want older teenagers either because they might not listen to me and go have wild parties. I did that sometimes.

"Twin 13 year old boy and girl, and a 7 year old boy. They all have long black hair and bright blue eyes. Little copies of each other. Hard to miss."

I smile. Things are really going my way. Thirteen year olds can't be that hard, and a 7 year old boy is even easier than Spencer and Tanner. Now I'm hoping they're not really like the doctor described them, evil and threatening, or else I may lose my life.

"Let's go in," he says. "I don't think we're getting anywhere out here." The other detectives have gone out back to scope it out, so it is just us.

I step up and bang on the door. When there is no answer, I continually ring the doorbell. That is usually annoying enough that people can't stand it any longer and are forced to open the door. Plus, maybe it will give the kids enough warning to get out of here, if they're there.

I try to knock again, and an elderly woman in a nightgown with silver hair wrapped in a bun opens the door. I almost punch her right in the face. I lower my fist and nod at her.

"Ms. Thornton?" Dad asks.

"Laura Thornton, please. Aren't you the great Commissioner Andrew Thompson of Delaware?"

He smiles. "That I am. Have you heard about me?"

"Of course. Great things, like you're the best commissioner they could ever have down there in the diamond state."

I almost laugh. She's charming him and only *I* see through it. "Well I'm flattered," he blushes. It's working.

"And this must be your handsome son, Andrew Jr. You two must make a great team."

I shake her hand firmly, and my father beams. "Nice to meet you Laura."

"So what brings you two fine gentlemen to my home at this hour?" We must have woken her up from a sleep, and I feel really rude. Why did we come out here this late again? I can't remember. Probably some stupid excuse of how this is a good time to trick a group of unsuspecting kids.

"Have you heard about the fire?" he asks, stepping inside the house. I follow. It's beautiful inside. Very modern and comfortable. Too bad she lives alone in here.

She gets a faraway, sad look on her face and nods. "Poor Marcella. My son loved her so and would never have wanted this to have come of her."

"Have you seen your grandchildren since they were orphaned," I inquire, jumping right in. I *really* want to go home. My father shoots me a look, but I still wait for an answer.

"Why yes," she answers truthfully. "They came over to stay awhile and have some nice hot meals and a good night's rest."

"Are they here now?"

She shakes her head. "They left a couple of days ago. They said they had to move on, and before I knew it, I was alone once again."

My father nods. "Did you know they were on our wanted list?"

She gasps, and I know the shock on her face is real. "They said they were in a little bit of trouble, but I had no idea how much. Whatever did they do?"

"They threatened a doctor and then resisted arrest," I answer before my dad can bash them and make them look like murderers. "I'm sure they were just still in shock. We just wanted to talk to them to see if they were okay mentally."

"They seemed fine, but they are long gone by now."

My father puts a hand on her shoulder. "It's okay. May we have a look around the house to see if they left anything behind?"

"Certainly. They are very neat, so I doubt you'll find anything."

"Thanks for your cooperation," I add. She smiles at me, and something in her eyes tells me she only speaks the truth. Maybe it's the sad and worried look that her grandchildren are out in the world on their own and she just lost her only daughter-in-law. It's sad to see, but I also feel a little good because this means that maybe I will be able to find them before Dad.

I help him look around the house, but as expected, there are no signs that the children were ever here. By the end, he looks exasperated, and I can't hide my excitement. I love to see him that way after all his boasting. He's not as good as he thinks.

"Why don't you check the backyard," he orders. "I'll look down the streets."

"I'm on it." I pass Laura on my way out the door, and she smiles warmly and gives me a small wave. I do the same and stumble my way to the backyard. "I'm not looking in the woods," I mutter to myself.

"What's the matter Andrew," Detective Jones chuckles. She's standing off to the side of the yard, arms behind her back, watching for any movement. I jump a little at the sight of her. She blends in with the dark night, and you wouldn't know she was there if she didn't talk. I guess she was hoping the kids would stumble into that trap. "Scared of a couple trees?"

"A couple? That's like the Everglades!"

"You're just a wimp," she laughs.

"Yet you still love me," I mumble. She flips me off again, and I add, "That's not very professional."

She rolls her eyes. "Just do your job and get out of my sight."

I wanted to come back with an 'I'm sure that's not what you *really* want me to do', but I keep my mouth shut. It's easier that way.

I walk around the yard, looking in all spots young kids could hide, like on the deck, behind chairs, and under tables, but they're nowhere. I take one last look and see the crawlspace. There's a small pair of socks lying right near it. I pick them up and conclude they must be the little boy's. He probably dropped them as they quickly dove into here. I shove them in my pocket so no one else sees them.

"I'll check in the crawlspace. That's the only spot they would still be and then we know Ms. Thornton is telling the truth." Detective Jones throws me a flashlight and it slams me in the chest. She laughs and mutters, "Stupid waif," barely audible. I ignore her once again and get down on my stomach. I prop myself up on my elbows and turn on the flashlight. It's one of those super duty ones that shine really far and wide. As big as the house is, I can still see the other end of the crawlspace. I start off at the very far left and slowly make my way across. There are lots of spider webs and creepy looking bugs, and I'm glad I'm not under there. I might have gotten carried off and turned into a dinner carcass. I hope I don't find the kids that way.

A little more than halfway across, I see a shoe. I move the light a little farther and see a teenage boy sitting with his neck tilted. He flinches and shuts his eyes at the light. There's a little boy who looks like his smaller clone in his lap, and he has the same reaction. Where's the girl? I move the light a couple of inches and see her. She is in the same position as the oldest boy, and she slaps her hands in front of her face to block the light. She is shaking, and they all look so scared, like they're doomed.

I sigh and turn off the flashlight. There's nothing I can do for them except say they're not there. Then I have to hope I will meet with them again, minus my father, and I can help them escape. They're in desperate need of some guidance, and I wish I could get them out of there right now and calm their nerves.

I get back to my feet and shake my head at Detective Jones. I groan loudly. My whole body hurts and I wish I were in my bed, not flat in the dirt past midnight. "Nothing. We must really have just missed them."

She folds her arms in disgust. She obviously thought I was going to save the day and this would have all been over. "Big Andy's not going to like that." Since my father's name is Andrew Brian Thompson also, she started calling him big Andy and me little Andy. The whole police force thought that one was hilarious and it caught on. She pulls a lot of stunts like that. It makes me believe she would be best friends with Stacy. Maybe I should introduce them and they would both leave me alone. Then again, they probably would gang up on me, so that's not a good idea.

"There's nothing I can do about it," I yell, throwing my hands in the air. "Let him be mad. He always is anyway."

She laughs quietly so her whole body shakes, but she doesn't make much sound. I search around for a decent sized rock in all this dirt and grass, leaving footprints all over in circles. I finally find a large blue one, the kind you pile at the end of your driveway, with many sharp edges. I position in front of the spot of the crawlspace where the kids were, and kick it with the side of my foot. I listen to see if I kicked it hard enough. It's a subtle way to let them know I know they're there, but I'm not going to rat them out. They probably think I'm going to trick them, but that's not true. I hear a soft "Ow!" and I know I got my point across. I chuckle to myself, thinking of all the things they could be thinking I'm doing.

I leave the scene casually and see my dad waiting by the car. "What are you laughing at?" Detective Jones asks rudely, following me out.

"You're ugly face," I retort. It isn't that ugly, but she deserves to think that I think so. Maybe if she wasn't so rude all the time, she'd be one of my good friends.

"You better shut your immature mouth before I shove my 7 ½ size shoe up you're..."

"You still want me," I yell at her before she can finish. She doesn't respond to that and I don't turn around to see her expression. I know it probably hurt, and I hate hurting people, but if she's going to be rude to me, I'm going to be rude back. I know she's only mean because she's hurt deep inside that I ran away from her, but I wish she would just get over it and be my friend. That's closer than my enemy isn't it? I don't get it. Tina says she wants me to be as hurt as her, but that doesn't make much sense to me. Women.

I climb into the passenger seat next to my father. He grips the wheel with both hands and stares straight ahead. He's very disappointed. I could do a lot to help that. I could tell him I saw the kids and we can lock them up right there, and he'll love me forever for it, but I won't do that. I'll let him stay defeated and keep up with my plan.

Detective Jones gets into a squad car with Detective Morgan. She wipes a tear from her cheek when she thinks no one can see. I feel awful. I'll have to talk to her later. I hope she listens to what I have to say without getting sassy.

"I can't believe they tricked me again!" my father growls. He squeezes the wheel so hard his knuckles turn white. I get the feeling this ride is going be even worse than the first. I put my head in my hands. This is going to be a long *summer*.

70

13

Jenna

When the coast is clear and the cop cars are long gone, we crawl back out of the crawlspace. It feels like we have been there forever. My neck aches from tilting it so long, and my legs are numb, like after a long plane or car ride. We all stretch for a couple moments before we leave the property. I stare back up at the house and hope Grandma isn't worrying too much. I feel awful leaving her all alone, but we can't take another close call like that one. That was almost unreal. The light illuminated us fully, but this cop didn't even see us! I think it's a miracle, even if Matty thinks it's all a trick.

My gaze goes back to the forest. I wish I could take that oak tree with me and cherish that carving forever, but it's not possible. I feel like it's the only thing I have left of her, and I pray that she will give us more carvings. It helps. I play with the ring on my finger and hope she can hear my prayers.

We walk in a line, me in the middle, Matty on the right, and Kelly on the left, in the middle of the night, and we're ready to take on the world. We walk down dark streets, through rocky dirt, up hills, and between buildings. Most of the times I want to cower behind Matty like a little girl, but I keep going. If Kelly's not scared, I have to be super brave for him.

We start to tire when the sun comes up, and we become afraid that we're going to be spotted. We've reached the heart of Philadelphia and things are starting to get interesting. When you don't live in the city, things you see would surprise you.

"Can't we take the bus or something," I complain. "I need to rest my feet." I still don't have any shoes and the streets reopen the blisters.

Matty looks at me like I'm an idiot. "That's the stupidest thing we could do."

"Maybe you're being too paranoid. They probably aren't watching all the buses and everything. They seemed too lazy to me."

"It's all a trap Jenna," Matty informs me. "They want us to think that so we make mistakes. They will watch everything public if we're part of the wanted list."

I throw my hands in the air. "Why would be on the wanted list? We didn't even do anything wrong!"

Matty shakes his head. "I don't know, but we probably are. So bus, train, taxi, anything like that is not an option."

I can't help but roll my eyes. I don't think I can take much more of this all day walking from state to state much longer. I didn't do much walking before this, so this is new to me. Matty is the one who used to wander around the beaches and the neighborhood all day long, constantly walking. And plus, he has shoes!

He ignores my complaints and keeps walking. I reluctantly follow. There's nothing else I can do. Then he stops abruptly, and I almost ram into the back of him. I swing my arms while on my toes so I don't knock him over. "What are you doing?"

"I have an idea," he says, smiling so widely I know he has something illegal in mind.

"I'm afraid to ask."

"We can use a car," he answers. "They can't check every car that comes by."

"You're missing two things there Matty," I snap. "One, we don't have a license so we can't drive, and two, even if we could, we don't have a car to drive."

"We're going to get one, and we're going to drive it. Well, at least I am."

I slap my forehead with my palm. This is the most ridiculous idea he's had yet. "There's no way that's going to work. Stealing a car is another crime to add to our list, and if we just drive down the highway, someone is going to notice we're too young and call attention to the cops!"

Matty shoots me a look and puts his finger to his lips. I am getting a little too loud and I didn't even notice. I look around and see no one is staring, so I turn back and glare at him.

He pulls my arm so I'm closer and whispers, "I can hotwire a car and I look older than I am, so I think I could pass for 16. We *are* almost 14. This will work, and it's the only choice we have except endless walking. We have to try it."

"No we don't, and I'm not going to let you."

He sighs a little too loudly, and I cross my arms to show I'm not going back on what I just said. I feel Kelly pulling on my shirt, and I turn around to tell to him to stop.

He waves his hands all around to show it's important when I look down at him. "What?" I ask a little too mean. Matty didn't put me in a good mood.

He points to the people waiting at the bus stop and I don't see anything significant. I wish he would just tell me what he has to say. "Just tell me."

"Nice lady from first bus," he says, pointing again. He makes a heart with his hands and points at Matty, who is deep in thought. I still don't understand.

"Remember?" he asks. I look through the people and see a familiar face. It's the woman who Matty told our life story to on the bus ride down here!

"Oh!" I say. "Come with me."

I rush up to her as the bus pulls up. Kelly follows close behind me, while Matty stays where he is, not even noticing we moved. I tap the woman's shoulder and she turns around. I smile, and she stares at me a minute until she realizes who I am.

"Hello," she says cheerily. "I was just on my way to work. How was your grandmother's?"

"It was great," I reply. "Can you help us?"

She looks from the bus to me in panic. People file into the bus and I'm beginning to think she needs some persuasion. "It's ok," I say, with a hint of disappointment in my voice. "You have to go to work. I shouldn't have bothered you."

I turn around and start to walk toward Matty with my head hanging. I pinch Kelly so he makes a pained noise. I even sigh a little to build the effect. I make it about halfway back before she calls out, "Wait!" I turn around and she tells the bus driver to go ahead. "Good job Kelly," I whisper to him. He grins.

She rushes over to us and asks, "How can I help you?"

"I didn't mean to keep you from work," I apologize, "but we were so desperate."

"I'll just call in sick," she says. "They won't mind."

"Well thank you. We need a ride to Rehoboth Beach. That's where we live, and we have no way to get there. Of course we can't drive, and we have no money to take so much public transportation. I guess we could walk, but that would take so long."

She frowns and I get frightened she might decide not to help us. "I was just there. I make the commute from my home there to my job here every day."

My eyes widen. That would be awful. "Really?"

"Yes. I had my job up here a long time before I moved to Rehoboth, and I couldn't find a new one until next year. My boyfriend was lucky enough to already work here." Boyfriend. Matty probably didn't like that if she told him about it.

"Well, once you get us there, you can stay at home and have a nice day off," I suggest to lighten her spirits toward the idea.

"That sounds nice," she admits. "You'll have to take a walk though because I drop off my car at my parent's house a few blocks from the bus stop."

"No problem." At this point, Matty is gaping at her. He can't believe that he sees her again. It's a miracle, he's probably thinking. I roll my eyes. "Get yourself together," I whisper. "She's giving us a ride to Rehoboth."

"She is?" he asks, his voice squeaking.

I nod. "But we have to walk with her to her car. Come on."

He struggles to close his mouth, and after a little while of patiently waiting, he is beside us in walking. She even carries some of our bags, which is a big relief. Much better than Matty trying to hotwire a car and drive it for two hours without being caught! I can't believe how stupid that idea is.

We arrive in front of a small wood colored home with a mahogany door. The windows are open, letting the breeze come in, and the curtains blow. I peer inside and see a woman sitting on an old couch, staring at the television. She looks over at me and I quickly duck under the window. I hear footsteps and she comes to the front door. She opens it and sticks her head out. I might as well come out and say hello, I think. I stand in front of her and wave.

"Who are you?" she asks, looking all around to see if I'm alone or not. I look over the other side of the house and see Matty, Kelly, and the bus stop woman coming to see what I'm up to. It occurs to me that I don't know the name of the woman who is helping me. I'll have to ask politely or ask Matty. He most likely knows since they had such a stimulating conversation last week.

"Mom!" she exclaims when she sees the woman in the door.

"Kristina, what are you doing back here? The bus has probably already left." Her name is Kristina so I don't have to ask. That's a nice name, except if someone calls you Kris.

She shuffles her feet, like she's ashamed of what she's doing. "I called in sick. I'm giving these nice children a ride back to their home in Rehoboth, and then taking the day off."

"Do you think that's good for the children? They need their education sweetie." Her mom talks to her like she's still a little girl. She's a grown woman! She can take a day off if she wants. I'm ready to tell her that when Kristina beats me to it.

"I need a day off, so I'm going to take one," she says sternly. "And I'm helping these poor kids in the process."

Her mom puts her hands on her hips. "Do you know these kids? And why aren't they in school?"

"Delaware gets out earlier than Pennsylvania," I chime in the conversation. It's a lie, but I couldn't very well tell her the truth. We can't finish seventh grade because we're on the run from the police.

"I see," she says. Then she looks at Kristina. "You're not wasting a day with that boy, are you?"

Kristina bites her lip. "I can spend the day with my boyfriend if I want. We are in love."

"Then you should be married," her mother mumbles.

Kristina shows us the way to her car. She's obviously done with bickering with her mother. Something tells me she hears the same thing over and over again. I shoot her mother a dirty look as we follow her. She glares at me. I hope we're not all over the news soon because I didn't win a friend with this one. She'll rat us out in seconds and bring her daughter down with us.

An orange mustang comes into view as we turn the corner. It's an expensive and beautiful car, and I'm privileged to ride in it. I look at Matty and his gaze seems to say, 'She's rich, I love her more.' I give him another look that says 'Or her boyfriend is rich', but I don't know if he gets it.

Kristina climbs into the driver's seat and puts the key in the ignition. The engine hums softly and the muffler starts really loud, like she was going 80 miles per hour. Matty and I gape. We're both really into cars, and this one is sexy. Matty leans up and whispers, "I *do* love her!"

I crack up and Kristina looks at us impatiently. She's probably excited to see rich boyfriend. "Come on," she waves us on to get inside. "You're not going to break him."

"I'm getting the front seat," Matty calls, running ahead of me. I let him go and climb in the back seat. I strap Kelly into the seat next to me. I run my fingers along the interior, the leather seats, the shiny doors, and I even reach up and touch the wheel. Kristina stares back at me.

"Sorry," I apologize. "I'm a car freak."

She chuckles. "Oh my boyfriend would *love* you then. He's the same way, and that's why we get along so well. We have the same interests. She turns to Matty. "Do you like cars?"

He nods vigorously and lets out a contented sigh. The muffler roars as she makes her way out of the neighborhood and onto the main roads. She turns the music up just enough that we can still talk but the subwoofer beats. Matty dreams of having a car like this, and to find a girl who is living his dream, I can only imagine the crazy thoughts that are going through his head. I've found the perfect girl, his mind races. Now I have to make a plan to murder her boyfriend. Maybe if I find out where he lives from her, then I can attack him in the night.

"So do you live with your boyfriend?" Matty asks over the beating of the bass. I'm a little scared. I know my brother too well!

"Yes, and it's a beautiful home," she replies. "I'll show you it when we get there."

"Nice," he smiles. I think there's a tinge of evil in it.

"Do you have Rob Thomas?" Kelly asks. He loves falling asleep in the car and that's the only artist that will put him to sleep. It's something in the husky voice I think. He's also Kelly's idol, so that makes him obsessed with his songs even more.

Kristina picks up her Zune and scrolls through the artists. "No, sorry." I look over and see Kelly pouting. He has crossed his arms and is staring angrily at the back of Matty's seat.

"That's okay," I assure her. "He can live with something else."

"Wait!" she says. "I have Matchbox Twenty. Does that work?"

Kelly raises his head and smiles again. "Yay!" he cheers. She turns on the CD, and he rests his head on my shoulder. He moves his head to the beat, and in minutes, he's fast asleep. It works every time.

"We lost one," I laugh. Matty looks back and teases me. "Looks like you became a pillow!"

"It actually doesn't bother me," I say, giving a thumbs up sign in his face. That makes him turn around. I start to nod off soon and the music makes me have strange dreams. I remember a bunch of colors bouncing around in a black background and colored rabbits jumping up and down. Pretty soon it becomes a rabbit exercise video. I jump and gasp a little when I wake.

Matty's head snaps around. "You've been asleep for over an hour."

My eyes widen. "No I haven't."

He nods to say he's not telling a lie. "Wow," I exclaim. "I guess Kelly and I have something in common."

"Well you gave us time to chat," Matty informs me, motioning toward Kristina. I wink at him, and he smiles with his tongue between his teeth. Kristina is oblivious to all this. She is too busy pulling into a long winding driveway that leads to a modern two-story beach house. It is all gray and is missing shutters. The front yard is filled with all kinds of flowers and landscaping, and the lawn is freshly cut.

"We're here!" Kristina yells, even though we already figured that. She cuts off the music and after that, the engine dies. It seems awfully quiet, and like clockwork, Kelly groans that there's no music.

"We've reached our destination," I say, smoothing his hair. He lifts his head and takes in the scenery. "Pretty."

I nod in agreement. We file out of the car and I pray that we get back in soon. This thing is so amazing I don't think I can part with it now. We walk up to the front door and she sifts through her purse until she finds her keys. She swings the door open. A foyer, with steps winding up to the second story and light hardwoods as the flooring, comes into view. A table with all kinds of pictures on it is against one wall, but we turn the other way so I don't get to snoop.

"If you don't mind taking off your shoes, it would be nice." We do as she says and follow her into the family room. There's a note lying on the couch, and she bends down a minute to read it. "You just missed my boyfriend." She crumples it up and throws it in the trash. The house is so clean, that I can barely believe a guy lives here. He must be very rare if he's not the least bit of a slob. Or maybe she just follows him around cleaning up after him.

"The guest bedrooms are upstairs if you three want to stay there," she offers. "I don't know if you have somewhere to be, but if you need somewhere to stay, you're welcome to make it here. I'm sure A won't mind."

I frown. A? That must be her pet name for rich boyfriend. I bet he's a tool and she deserves better than that.

Matty answers, "We wouldn't want to impose. We actually are supposed to be meeting back up with our parents tonight. They must be waiting for us to come back from Grandma's. We got back sooner than expected, thanks to your beautiful ride."

She blushes. "I love him too. Do you want me to take you to where you live?"

Matty raises his hand to stop her. "You've done too much already. We don't belong in your beautiful home."

"Parents?" Kelly asks. He doesn't understand that we have to lie to everyone so they don't suspect us. I shoot a look at Matty to say fix this. He stoops down to Kelly's level. "They're meeting us, remember?"

Kelly stares at him and I subtly pinch him on the back again. He flinches and it looks like he's just remembering after a long sleep what we're really supposed to be doing. "Oh, yeah."

"They'll give you a green fishy when we get there," I add. He knows now that we're pretending and that I'm going to reward him for playing along.

"Yummy!"

Kristina coos, "You're so adorable. How old are you?"

"Seven."

She pinches his cheek. "I teach 2nd graders and they're your age. They're my favorite."

Kelly gives his innocent little boy smile, where it's just lips and no teeth. "I'm special."

"Yes," Kristina agrees. "You all are. I haven't seen a more attractive group of kids. I hope mine end up that way."

Even I'm flattered. I never thought of myself as attractive. I guess I am, I think. That's a good feeling.

"They will be," Matty assures her. "Because you are."

"Oh thank you!" Matty nods a 'you're welcome' and I chuckle to myself. He's a real charmer and she's eating it up.

"You are a real heartbreaker I bet," she directs at Matty.

He shrugs as if it's no big deal, but I know he's dancing a jig in his mind. I have a better way of hiding things like that. Not that I fall in love with strangers like that, but even if I did, I wouldn't make it so obvious. I look at Matty and realize Kristina could be right. I never thought of other girls liking my brother but I guess they would. He's pretty cute: it's just that I always thought of him as my brother and not a love interest for others. I wonder if other sisters think about these things. Am I supposed to and I'm just abnormal? I always knew that, but am I more than I thought? I try not to have a panic attack.

"Well we better get going," I suggest before I go over the edge. "We don't want to keep them waiting."

Matty shoots me a look. He obviously does not agree to this. "We're early, remember?" he says through his teeth.

I roll my eyes. "We'll have some breakfast then please."

Kristina smiles wide and shuffles into the kitchen. "What would you like?"

"Do you have cereal and bagels?" Matty asks. She nods. "That sounds good."

"Geen fissy?" Kelly asks. I sigh. "Do you have any candy?"

Her brow furrows as she pours three bowls of Apple Jacks and puts three bagels in the toaster. "I don't think candy goes good with breakfast."

"Daddy says it does," Kelly argues. She still makes no move to give us any candy. Matty even is a little ticked. Who doesn't have a little candy with breakfast every once in awhile? I bet her second graders would agree with us.

We eat our breakfast without an argument about the candy. When we are finished, we help her do the dishes to make sure there is no evidence we were there. We can't be sloppy, even if she is nice and would probably never rat us out. That is the way undercover cops work though; they are really nice and agreeable so they can trap you. When we have completely covered our tracks, even Matty agrees it is time to exit the premises.

We make a quick exit, with a few small waves and are on our way. Matty touches the rock in his pocket that was kicked at him when we were in the crawlspace. His shin is bruised bright blue and he's keeping the rock to use when need be. I know his wheels are turning when he touches it.

I turn around to take in the house and that beautiful car one more time, but my eyes catch on a white object, lying alone in the grass. I try to get Matty's attention, but there is no getting him out of his thoughts. I shake my head. It probably doesn't mean anything, I tell myself. Still something tells me it does.

14

Andy

I take a permanent position on the front steps for the rest of the evening. The early evening air is warm, but a cool breeze blows through my hair and makes it comfortable. The trees rustle and a hummingbird flits by on its way to my flowers. A dog barks far away, but other than that, there are no loud noises. It's the quiet and peacefulness that only summer can bring.

I had spent the whole day listening to my father rant and rave that the search was ridiculous, and with every passing second, the little rats could be on their way to Canada or Mexico. Or they could still be wandering around Pennsylvania fresh out of the crawlspace, I think. Then I got to hear all about his reputation, and he made a statement that he was going to take them down. If he doesn't follow up on that, a lot of people are going to be really upset. It was all a lot of angry, useless banter, so I zoned him out most of the time.

And to top it all off, when I made it home, Tina informed me that three lonely kids, by the exact description as what I saw the night before, just left my home. "They looked a little suspicious," Tina had said. "They were really jumpy, but I thought that was just because they were in a strange environment." I had missed them by mere minutes. That irks me in a way that is unexplainable. It feels pretty nice to relax out here and not have to think about these things anymore.

My gaze lowers from the trees across the street to the grass, where a small white object floats in a sea of green. I look closer and scream, "Stacy!" The white cigarette butt she had has become a part of my lawn. She must have taken it out of the trash and placed it back on the grass just to mess with me. Unbelievable!

As I bend down to retrieve it, a flood of memories comes without me having a say. Suddenly, kneeling in the grass, a cigarette butt in between my thumb and forefinger, I'm back in my 21st year. I'm doing a little celebrating with my buddies in a local bar after a long week of studying. I try to slip out of the bar early with no one noticing because I feel extra tired. I barely did anything today, but I still feel winded just walking around the room. I feel like I need to rest awhile.

"Where you goin'?" my drunken best friend and roommate Ryan asks, grabbing my arm. So much for no one noticing.

"I think I'm gonna go crash."

He pulls me back into the stool beside him. "It's 8 on a Friday night! You can't be serious!"

I'm really starting to feel sick, like I'm going to pass out. I need to just go and not deal with this. "I am Ryan."

"At least stay for a burger," he slurs. I'm afraid he's becoming an alcoholic.

I shake my head. "Not hungry." The room is starting to spin.

"You're always tired, you're never hungry, you're little chest always hurts, and you're much skinnier. I mean, you were to begin with, but you look sick. Did you talk to a doctor?"

"I haven't heard back." The symptoms Ryan described had started a few months back. I went from heavy partier, to barely being able to walk from class to our apartment without having to take a nap, in weeks. I would cough nonstop and my chest ached. I had trouble catching my breath and fainted a couple times in the middle of lectures. Not to mention my big appetite was shot. I got scared; I was becoming someone else. When I told my doctor this he said, "These symptoms are suspicious. I suggest you get a chest radiograph."

I didn't ask what the symptoms suggested. I had a gut feeling and told myself there was no way. I got the chest radiograph and was told they needed to study the pictures and would get back to me. I've been scared to death for 6 days now. I try to drink it away, but I'm too tired. My mind keeps drifting to the worst.

I stumble my way back to the apartment I share with Ryan and Tina. Yes, I ended up falling for my roommate. I shuffle through Ryan's clothes and trash he scatters all over the floor, and fall on my bed. That is the one thing about living with your best friend. When you're a neat freak and he's a slob, you're friendship might not last long. Tina agrees with me.

I lay there feeling like somebody is choking me. I struggle to get air. I take my shirt off to see if that's what's constricting me, but it doesn't help. My lungs continue to squeeze. I stare at my chest. My ribs jut out way more than they used to, and my stomach is sunk in a very lot. My fingers look bony. I've always been a little guy, really tall but really skinny just the same, but this is something more. "I'm sick," I cry. "Please make me better. I'm young!" I hope someone is listening.

The apartment phone rings next to my ear, and I jump. A coughing attack starts and I have to wait to answer it. "Hello?" I begin to wheeze.

"Andrew Thompson?"

"Yeah," I cough.

"I tried to call your cell, but it went right to voicemail. Are you alright?"

I hold my breath to fight the cough, but it comes on twice as strong. This is the worst tickle of my life. "I'm sorry (cough). I can't stop (cough) coughing." He waits a few minutes until I calm down. I breathe deeply so I don't start hyperventilating. "Go on."

I wait patiently as he begins. "We studied you're chest radiograph, and there was an obvious mass in your left lung. I'm very sorry, but you seem to have what's called a non small cell lung carcinoma which is further classified as an adenocarcinoma. This starts in the peripheral lung tissue and spreads to other parts of the lung. Since you're a never-smoker, we conclude that this either came from second-hand smoke or radon gas. Luckily, we caught this in stage IA, which means you're chances of recovery are the best they can be. You are going to need to undergo chemotherapy and radiation therapy, and we'll see if that works because this certain type of lung cancer is pretty insensitive to chemo. Lung cancer is one that not many recover from, but there's hope for you Andrew."

"I have lung cancer?" I squeak.

"Unfortunately, yes." I drop the phone and it clatters on the floor. This is the worst possible news I could get. This is what I thought I would *never* hear.

"Andrew? Are you there?" my doctor calls, but I can't move to pick it up. My hands are trembling, and I feel a panic attack coming. I can't control my breathing. My heart is thumping. I even feel tears filling in my eyes, making my sight cloudy. My contacts almost fall out.

"Andrew! Do I need to send an ambulance?"

I pick up the phone like a robot. "No, thank you." I hang up. The shock starts to turn into anger, and I squeeze the phone. The only thing I accomplish is hurting my fingers, so I throw it against the wall. It breaks in half, leaving a significant dent in the wall. That makes me feel worse.

"NO!" I scream. "This isn't fair!!!" I press my back up against the wall and slide down slowly until I hug my knees. To me, cancer was always associated with death. Once you got that diagnosis, it was just a matter of time until it's all over. My grandmother died of breast cancer when I was ten, but she told me that she accepted it because she was 70. I'm not 70, that's for sure. I'm only 21! I'm too young to die. I have so many things I want to do with my life, like make my own band and maybe marry Tina when I'm ready. Worse yet, I have *lung* cancer. I've never smoked a day in my life! The whole thing just makes me sad and angry at the same time. I'm not the best guy in the world, but I certainly don't deserve to die so early. Why is it always the good people, who have so much going for them, end up with these kinds of things?

I consider ending it right now so I don't have to go through all that suffering with the chemo and radiation that I hear about. I'm going to lose all my hair that took so long to grow out and look perfect. I'm going to throw up all day long and feel sick and not be able to finish school. If I'm just going to die anyway, wouldn't it be better to do it quick and easy?

I shake that thought out of my head. I'm going to be sick, but I'm not going to die. I'm going to survive if it's the last thing I do. I can't let this be the end and let all my dreams slip away. I turn on my stereo as loud as it will go and sing my heart out. I need to get up, I tell myself. I busy myself cleaning up after Ryan so the dark thoughts don't overcome me.

When I'm halfway through the mess, Tina comes in, trying to hold up Ryan, whose hair looks sweaty and stuck to his face, so he doesn't fall and hurt himself. She throws him on his bed, taking his shoes off and covering him with the blanket. Poor girl, I think. Having to deal with us. She looks over to me and raises her eyebrows at how fast my hands are working. "What's up?"

I fight to smile. "Nothing. Just couldn't stand this mess."

"I thought you were so tired."

I can't face her. She'll know and she doesn't have to deal with this with me. I'll let her go. I have to, even if it hurts.

"You clean when you're upset, so what is it?"

"Nothing," I reply, choking back tears.

She holds my hands so I stop folding clothes. She moves my face until I look at her. She takes in my red, tear streaked eyes and cheeks. She sees the contacts I was wearing are out, and my bright blue eyes are dim. She gasps. "Andy! You were crying!"

I continue to stare at her with a pained look. She starts crying too and gives me a hug. "What happened?" she mumbles into my shoulder.

"The doctor called," I answer, stroking her hair. "I'm sick."

She lifts her head to look at me. "What do you mean by that?" she sniffs.

"I have…lung cancer."

I hear a sharp intake of breath, and she starts bawling in shock like I did earlier. We stand there for awhile until she calms down enough to speak. "How bad?"

I sigh. "There's a tumor in my left lung and I need chemo and radiation. It's going to be rough, but I'm gonna make it."

"Promise?" she sounds like a scared little girl. We've been inseparable for almost a year now, and this is just as painful and scary for her as it is for me. I can't stand to let her go now.

"I promise," I assure her. "Death is not an option."

She smiles through her tears and I feel a cough coming. I turn my head away from her and cough into my hand. It feels extra wet and I don't think that's good. I lower my fist and it's covered in blood. I wipe my lips with my other hand and come up with more blood. I try not to freak out so I don't upset Tina more. It's going to be hard to stay strong, I tell myself. I'm officially more scared than I've ever been in my entire life. But I have to do it. Ryan's cell vibrates, and when I look down, I see it's my mother.

I come back to the present and see that I reduced the cigarette butt to dust. I let go of it and watch it blow away in the breeze. I don't want to think of the way my mother cried to me, saying the doctor couldn't reach me again and that he had to call her. I don't want to think of how my father only cared that I wouldn't be able to finish college, and that he had to pull strings to get me into the police force now. I don't want to think of how Stacy didn't give me the time of day, and how she smokes in front of me to show me what I got was a fluke, and that smoking isn't going to kill her. I don't want to think of how sick and tired I was for months, and that I couldn't move. I don't want to think of how Tina struggled through every day with me, and it hurt me more to see what she was going through. I don't want to think of how I wasted a year and a half of my life fighting it off, not sleeping and wanting to break things, and now I'm wasting more years doing what I don't want to do. I never got to start that band; I followed my father's lead to avoid all the fighting, and now with every passing second, my dreams are slipping away anyway. I don't want to think of all these things, but I do.

I end up falling over onto my side on the soft grass. I just stare straight in front of me, trying not to start crying again. I don't cry unless it's really important and I have a long road ahead of me. I can't dwell on the past. I feel more than ever that I need to save these kids. If I fail, they will end up like me, wasting their lives away, except the only difference is they will be stuck in jail, when I can fix my life any minute. I choose not to and have no idea why. I'm excited to meet these kids.

As I think of this, my cell vibrates. I pick up and all I hear is, "Tonight at Rehoboth Beach. I have Jones and Morgan tracking them and they are right next to the beach. We're finally going to bust them. Be there."

"Where are we meeting?"

"By the Henlopen Hotel on the boardwalk. Then we'll move in on their hiding spot. I'll see you at 6pm?"

"Okay, I'll see you there."

"This is going to be big." I think I hear an evil cackle as my father hangs up. I smile. This is perfect, I think. He's leading himself right into my trap and he won't figure it out until it's too late. I hope I don't have too much confidence.

15

Matty

It is almost dinnertime when we finally find a good spot to hide out for the night. There is a

nice hide-out behind one of the beaches in Rehoboth. It is right next to the parking lot of the State Park, with a nice patch of soft sand for sleeping. We have enough food for dinner, and there are port-a-potties a short walk away, so we don't have to go in the woods behind us. I settle in the sand a little ways from the parking lot, and Jenna takes a spot next to me. It is very soothing to listen to the sounds of people playing tennis on the courts behind the potties. It is good to hear laughing and the sound of sneakers.

I'm almost dozing off after dinner, when Kelly screams. My eyes pop open, and I look around until I find him. He is in the forest in front of me, curled in a ball in the sand. He's holding his ears and screaming at the top of his lungs. I rush over to him with Jenna right on my heels. "Shush," I say. "You're gonna ruin the point of hiding."

Jenna shoots me a dirty look and cradles Kelly. She's such a woman, I think. "What's wrong honey?"

"He's not a baby," I mutter, but they ignore me.

"The voices," he cries. "They're loud. Tell them to stop!"

"More voices?" I ask. "What are they saying?"

"Lots of things at once, but the one is really loud. It keeps screaming 'the biggest tree. Go!'"

I search around me for the biggest tree and it's evident which one it is. This tree is a monster and stands many feet over the others. "Go to that tree," I say, pointing. "Then the voices will stop."

"Really?" he questions. Then he screams again. They must be really loud.

I nod. He wiggles out of Jenna's grasp and stumbles over to the tree, still holding his ears. That's not going to work if the noise is in his head, but if that makes him feel better, I'm not going to ruin it. He drops to his knees in front of the tree and looks down at about my knee level, as if on command. Then he slowly lowers his hands. "Look!"

Jenna and I rush over, almost tripping on each other in the process. We're both thinking the same thing. Another carving; another chance to communicate with Mom. That makes my day. We kneel beside Kelly and watch the words being carved into the wood at lightning speed, without anyone there to carve them. I hadn't been able to see the last carving in process, so this is a new experience for me. My mouth hangs open in complete awe. When the carving stops, we all look closer to read it.

Hello again children. You did a good thing by getting out of your Grandmother's when the cops arrived. Like I said before, she shouldn't be drug into this. You made it just in time and that's because I warned you. I'm sorry Kelly about the loud voices, but your mind is the only one I can get into, and I can't control the volume. I hope you understand. What I came to tell you is you will meet someone in the very near future you're not sure you can trust. I assure you this soul can be trusted, and please do what they say. It is in your best interest. Remember I love you all, and don't worry about me.

Kelly smiles. "I understand. It just hurts."

I pat him on the back. "We're lucky to have you Kelly. Without you, we would have been in jail by now."

He likes the sound of being needed. I turn to Jenna. "Who do you think we're about to meet?"

She shrugs. "How would I know? I just hope they're nice."

"I thought Kristina was enough help. Now we're bringing another person into this mess. How do you think Mom knows the future? And how do you think she's able to carve those things in the trees and put voices in Kelly's head?"

"She's an angel," Jenna simply replies. "Angels can do anything that's good."

"But do you think she's with Dad or Lauren? Do you think she can see us? Do you think Dad and Lauren could all this time?" I'm full of questions, and if only the conversation with Mom was a two-way, then I would have them all answered. In the meantime, Jenna glares at me. "Stop asking questions."

"Why 'cuz you don't know the answer?" I taunt. She pretends she doesn't hear that. I wonder if she thinks of these things like I do. I guess I'll never know because her mind is very complicated.

"Well, I guess we just wait here for this 'trusting person' to arrive. She *did* say the very near future, so I would say in the next couple days."

"Or the next couple hours," Jenna suggests. I hear something just after she says that, and it doesn't sound good. It sounds like footsteps approaching fast, but trying to be vigilant. I have excellent hearing though, so I know someone is trying to sneak up on us. I look off into the distance and then look back at Jenna to show her something bad is about to happen. I pull her back down from a stance.

"Bring Kelly and hide under that brush," I whisper. "I'll get the stuff and join you in a minute. Someone is coming, and we need to seem like we were never here."

"The cops?" Jenna asks in fear. Kelly's eyes widen, and I mouth the word 'maybe' so I don't make anymore sound. I try to run for our stuff, but I see bodies and run back to the brush. I can't make it.

We all make ourselves as small as possible and pray they go away. They don't. "They're going to come right here and see us," I breathe in Jenna and Kelly's ears. "We need a distraction to get away." Jenna nods, and we watch as four cops appear on the scene. I recognize one as cocky cop, and that's not a good sign. There are two other younger guy cops, one blond with a muscular build, and one with jet black hair who's tall and skinny. The fourth is a woman with her hair plastered to her head in a bun. She is more focused on staring at the dark haired guy than the mission at hand. They stop in front of our abandoned objects and inspect them.

"It seems they were here very recently," cocky cop notes. "That means they must have heard us coming and ducked for cover in the woods somewhere."

"Are we going in?" the woman asks. She glances over at the dark haired guy, but he doesn't notice. He's too deep in thought as he scans all the trees.

"We'll split up," cocky cop replies. He must be the boss. "Jones, Morgan, you go that way"-he points in the opposite direction of where we are-"while Andrew and I go the other way."

The woman nods. She and the blond haired guy disappear into the woods opposite us. I bet she's disappointed that she has to go with *him*, I think, laughing to myself silently. Cocky cop stands up and makes his way toward us, the distant fellow right behind him.

"I have a feeling they went this way," cocky cop says, tilting his head toward his partner. "That's why we're going this way."

"I hope we find them this time," his partner laughs. "I'm tired of hearing you scream about your failure." Cocky cop doesn't find it quite as amusing. He's the kind that believes he's invincible.

Something is very familiar about the other guy's voice too. I can't place exactly why. They come awfully close to us, and I know it's time for that distraction. Good thing I have one in mind.

I lean close to Kelly so I can tell him something without making a noticeable sound. "Jump out and make a distraction while Jenna and I try to get away. Then, when they get flustered, run after us, okay?"

He gives me a thumbs up sign, and for once, I'm glad he isn't speaking. He jumps out from the brush in a flash and screams, "Bear! Help, there's a bear!" He jumps around and runs in circles like a maniac, his hands swinging above his head. He clutches salamander in one hand, making a flash of red and black. He looks like he's trying to fight off a bee, and I fight not to laugh. Only Kelly would have thought of *that* as a distraction. If it works though, I can't blame him. He's unique.

Cocky cop and his partner stop in their tracks and stare as Kelly makes a fool of himself. "That's one of them!" cocky cop yells, but the other guy can't reply. He obviously believes what Kelly is yelling, and flinches with every rustle of the trees. They seem pretty distracted, so I take Jenna's hand and we run as fast as we can through the forest, the opposite direction of the cops. We keep one arm in front of us to keep the branches from whipping us in the face. I feel my legs being scratched, but I keep running. I even pass a gym bag sitting idly by, well hidden. Under different circumstances, I would have checked it out, but I had to pass it by this time.

Pretty soon, Kelly stops screaming, and his footsteps are coming after us. I peek behind to see how close he is and see that he's not the only one following us. "Great," I mutter. "The cops are following Kelly." We keep running anyway, hoping somehow we can lose them. But all we do is run ourselves into a dead end where the street starts. Cars zoom by inches from our feet and we're forced to stop. Jenna and I give each other pained looks as we turn around to Kelly joining us. The cops stop shortly after and raise the guns at us.

"Don't move another inch or we'll be forced to shoot," cocky cop warns us. We do exactly what he says for once. There's nowhere for us to run or hide this time. We're really doomed and no miracle will help us.

Cocky cop motions toward us. "Andrew, cuff them."

The guy called Andrew pulls out his handcuffs and tells us to turn around with our hands behind our back. "You're under arrest for endangerment, shoplifting, and resisting arrest. You have the right to remain silent. Anything you say now can and will be used against you in a court of law. You have the right to an attorney. If you cannot afford one, one will be appointed to you. Do you understand these rights as they have been read to you?" His voice sounds like he's said this a million times and he doesn't want to be bothered with us. I wonder if cocky cop senses that too.

"We know our Miranda rights," Kelly mumbles, rolling his eyes.

"Kelly," Jenna and I hiss. "Quiet!" We don't need to make any of this worse than it already is.

We're cuffed in seconds, and Andrew grabs our hands and leads us over to cocky cop. If you've never been arrested, it's a very scary thing. You feel trapped and abused, like you're whole life is ruined. The metal hurts my wrists and it's very awkward to have my arms contorted like they are. Jenna fidgets, and cocky cop holds her shoulders to keep her still. She doesn't like strangers touching her, so I know she's cursing him out in her head. It's funny how much we know each other.

"I think I can handle them Dad," Andrew says to cocky cop. That's his dad! Wow, I knew they looked alike in the face, but I would never have guessed father and son. I guess not the close kind.

His father lowers his eyes at him. "Are you sure? I can take the oldest boy. He's the dangerous one." I'm tempted to ask just how I'm dangerous. How can they honestly believe that?

"I'm sure. You go catch up with Jones and Morgan and I'll meet you back at the station with them."

Cocky cop nods. "I'm proud of you Andrew. This is big."

Andrew just stares at him, so he makes his way to leave. "I'll see you in a few minutes."

"Yup." Andrew stays still until cocky cop is completely out of sight. Then he lets go of our wrists. "Stay here," he orders. We watch as he struts through the forest and looks all around. What is this freak doing? He drops to his knees and puts one ear in the dirt. He stays there for a minute, and when he gets up, he smiles wide. "They're gone!"

"Huh?" Jenna asks. I nudge her because I don't know whether this is another trick.

"The cars just left, which means we're all alone finally," he explains. "It worked!" He pumps his fist in the air and I'm a little confused.

"What worked?" I inquire.

"My master plan of deception."

We all stare at him. "I know you're all lost, but I promise I'll explain everything when we find a good place to hide."

"I thought you had to take us to the station," Kelly reminds him. "You're meeting him in a few minutes."

He shrugs. "Yeah, well I'm a good liar. We're not going to the station, we're staying here. And my disgusting father will not be able to find us."

He spins us around and frees our hands from the handcuffs. He clips them back to his belt and starts his trek through the wilderness. The three of us continue to stand there in awe.

"Wait," Jenna calls out. "If we're not going to the police station, where are you taking us?" She is very untrusting, like me, so the two of us aren't about to go anywhere with this stranger.

He spins around on his heels. "I thought I told you, somewhere to hide. In about an hour, my co-workers will find out that I'm not coming back, and this will be the first place they look. If we start walking now, we'll be well hidden by then, and they won't catch us. I'm here to help you kids escape."

I raise my eyebrows. "Oh, really? Now how do I know this isn't all just another trap?"

He sighs and walks back to where we are. He digs around in his pant pockets until he finds what he's looking for. He takes out a little pair of socks and I recognize them as Kelly's. We all look at each other. "On your way under your grandmother's house, you dropped these." He pulls off one shoe and shows a scuff on the outer side. "And this is from kicking that rock at you, so you knew I saw you and wasn't about to tell anyone, because I'm helping you."

I take the rock out of my pocket and show him the gnash on my shin. "Thanks for that."

"It was the only nonchalant thing I could do," he says. "Sorry."

I nod. "So why would you possibly want to help us, since you swear that's what you're really doing."

He takes a long, deep breath. "Since you won't come with me until I tell you, I'll make it short, and then explain further when we're safely hidden. My father has been tricking and bossing me around my whole life, and I figured that it was time I deceived him. This is really important to him, so I'm going to screw it up. And when I saw you guys in that crawlspace all scared, I felt like I was doing the right thing. I feel good about giving you another chance in life, so I'm going to do it no matter what."

"Understandable," Jenna agrees.

"I'll answer all your questions when we're settled, but for now, please follow me."

He seems pretty trustable, and it's either go with him, or go to jail, so I give the signal to Jenna and Kelly to move. Jenna folds her arms in protest, but she doesn't want to be left alone, so she follows Kelly and me. We walk through the brush at a quick pace, with Andrew stopping to check under bushes every few minutes. It's a silent walk because we're afraid to say anything in front of a stranger.

About a half hour in, I hear another scream from Kelly. Jenna and I stare at each other wide-eyed. How are we going to keep a carving from this guy? He seems to have ignored the scream, so we sneak away to where Kelly is crouched down, holding his ears. I cover his mouth so his screams are muffled, and watch as the words appear on the tree in front of us.

I'll make this quick since I just talked to you and you have somewhere to be. All I have to say is you have met the person I mentioned previously. Trust him, he's your angel. With love, Mom.

"She signed her name," Jenna whispers when the carving stops. She traces the m, o, and m many times with her finger.

"He's the person we're supposed to trust," I sigh. "Oh great."

"At least we know it's not a trick," Kelly comments.

"True," I admit. "But I was hoping it was someone cool, like Kristina."

Jenna rolls her eyes and shakes her head at me. "You're pathetic. But we don't even know him yet. He could be cool."

She never defends someone when I question them. "Do you like him or something?"

"No!" she screams. "Gross!"

I cross my arms and smirk. "Shut up, Matty!" She tackles me, and I quickly put her in a full nelson. Kelly jumps on top of us and knocks the air out of me.

"What are you three idiots doing now?" I look past Kelly's neck and see Andrew standing over us, hands on hips. He looks a lot like a teenage girl. I remember the carving and quickly untangle myself from my siblings. I put my back up against the tree so he can't see it, and try to look innocent. I don't know why, but I feel like it's a private thing that no one else should be able to see.

"You look guilty," he notes. "What are you hiding?"

Crap, I can't lie well, I think. Jenna says, "Nothing," quickly so I don't make matters worse.

"Move," Andrew orders. I try to push up to the tree as much as I can. He sighs and grabs my arm. With ease, he throws me away from the tree, and I feel really weak. He keeps both arms straight out in a stiff arm as he peers at the tree.

"Wow," he whispers. "How did your mom write this?"

We don't have an answer for that. We actually are asking that question ourselves.

He runs his hands along the words and adds, "So you know now that you can trust me."

"Sort of," Jenna snaps. "And that doesn't mean we like you either."

He laughs. "Whatever. Just come with me. I think we're almost to the place where I left my stuff earlier."

We continue walking. "I hope the bear didn't get my stuff. Was there really a bear?"

"Yeah," I lie, amusing myself. "It was ferocious."

He gets a stressed look on his face. "I love nature, but sometimes it gets really scary. I guess I'll get used to it."

We're silent again and it's another ten minutes until Andrew stops short. It's with no warning, so I almost fall over on top of him. Jenna rams into my back, but she quickly gets her composure and stands next to me. She looks strange, like she's trying to act cool or tough or something. I'm convinced she likes him, but you can't argue with her about that kind of that stuff. She thinks she's a boy like Kelly and I and will never do any girl things. It's quite odd. And I don't know why she would like him. He seems a little awkward and goofy and not what I would think she would like. He's also got one of those soul patches where you shave all of a beard except the little patch under the bottom lip.

 Andrew comes up a few minutes later with a gym bag. That's the same one I saw on the run! "That's yours?"

He nods. "We're well hidden here. There's a lake a little ways off and of course the beach. I'm going to change out of this uniform because it's awfully uncomfortable, and I'll look a little less menacing." He grabs the gym bag and disappears behind a wall of trees.

"This is really weird," Jenna whispers in my ear. "How long are we going to have to deal with this tool?"

"Why are you acting like that?" I ask.

"What do you mean?"

"I mean you're acting tough girl all of sudden. You never call someone a tool with no good reason."

"Yes I do," she argues. "Just not to you."

"Still, you're acting different in front of this guy."

"That's because I still don't trust him."

"No. That's not what I mean. You're trying to act cool in front of him."

"No I'm not!" she yells. She tries to hit me again but I duck. "I don't like him, okay?"

"I didn't say you did. You're the one making it seem like that. And you're the one who said he might be cool!"

She grabs her head with both hands and shakes it around. "Just drop it Matty."

"Okay," I smirk. I was about to add something else smart, but Andrew comes back through the trees, looking like a whole new person. I have to take a double take to make sure someone hasn't killed him and pretended to be him. That sounded really corny, I think.

"Now," Andrew says, clapping his hands once. "I'll tell you my story and then I get to hear yours." We all sit down in a circle and get started.

16

Jenna

Matty is really confusing and embarrassing me. I'm not acting any different and he decides to make a big deal out of nothing. I wish he would just shut up. Just because he likes people that are ten plus years older than him, doesn't mean I have to do the same. Which I don't. At least I don't think so. That's why I'm confused. He's making me second guess myself. It's all just a trap, I tell myself. I know the truth, even if he doesn't believe it. I feel like hitting him really hard so he just forgets the whole thing, but then I'd feel bad because he's my brother and I don't want him badly hurt or anything. Older brothers, even if it's just by three minutes, can be such a pain. They tease you and you don't know how to handle it because you still love them.

Andrew comes out of the trees finally and saves me from all this embarrassment. I could feel myself getting red with each word Matty said, and that wasn't helping my case. He looks totally different, and my mouth hangs open a little. I don't know how one person can go through such a transformation. His blue uniform has become baggy, worn, blue jeans and a striped, button down, collared T-shirt. The shirt reveals the colorful tattoos all the way up both arms. Somehow they're mesmerizing, and my eyes keep drifting back to them. His dress shoes are gone and replaced with a shiny new pair of black and white, low-top Chuck Taylor Converse.

The most surprising difference of all though, is his hair. It used to be slicked back and shiny, basically stuck to his head, but now it is completely the opposite. He must have washed out all the gel and hairspray because now it is wet and sticking up in all directions. It is a beautiful mess of black on the top of his head. I have a hair thing, just like I do with cars, and this just enthralls me. I'm pretty much gawking over this guy and don't know why. I've never felt this way before. It's very strange. It's like I'm completely amazed by him all of a sudden, but I don't want to be. I feel like it is wrong, but I can't stop it. He's just beautiful. Why do I feel this way? I wish someone could answer that so I'm not so confused.

"Now," Andrew says, clapping and making his gorgeous blue eyes even brighter. "I'll tell you my story and then I get to hear yours." I take a seat between him and Matty, with Kelly across from me. My heart is pounding being just inches away from him. I wish it would stop. I feel like they can hear it.

Andrew begins, "We're going to be spending a lot of time together, so I want you guys to trust me and feel comfortable." I freak out that he's referring to my situation. "So call me Andy. I like that better."

We all nod. "My name's Mattix but everyone calls me Matty," Matty says, shaking his hand.

"Cool name," Andy compliments. He looks at me, "And you?"

I jump a little. "Jenna," I say quickly. I'm such an idiot, I think in my head.

He smiles. "Nice to meet you finally." He sticks out his hand, but I ignore it. I'm afraid if I touch him, I'll faint and look more stupid than I already do. He lowers it after a couple seconds and moves on to Kelly.

"I'm Kelly," Kelly says proudly. He even shakes his hand. I should have just done it too.

"That's interesting. I've never heard a boy named Kelly."

"Dad thought that to be a real man, you had to be proud of a feminine name," Kelly blurts out. "I'm a real man."

"I wish I could have met him."

"You won't," I say. The words slip out of my mouth before I can think. "No one else ever will."

"Jenna!" Matty yells. I can't look at him so I look at my feet. I want shoes more than ever so I could stare at them and draw on them. Then my feet wouldn't hurt either.

Andy ignores my comment. "I'm sorry about your parents. Mine aren't the best, but I would never want anything to happen to them. You three seem really close and that's a good thing. My sister hates me."

"Why?" Kelly asks. He has issues in knowing when and when not to use his minimal words.

He shrugs. "I honestly don't know. Stacy has issues. She gets it from my father and that's why I'm here. They say I was a miracle baby, especially since I was a boy. My father has always been the kind that wants all sons, and so he was always disappointed in Stacy. When I was finally born, he said if I wasn't a son, he was going to go insane. Lucky for me, I was, or else I don't know what would have happened to me, or the rest of my family. Anyway, since I was his only namesake, he decided I had to be just like him. He dressed me the same and made me look like his little double. He told me since I was a toddler that I didn't have a choice of what I wanted to be when I grew up; I had to be a cop."

"Wow," Matty says. He is obviously disgusted.

"Exactly. Some little boys would have wanted to be a big bad police officer with their dad, but I hated being controlled, so that was the last thing I wanted to be. I played piano since I was about

95

Kelly's age, and I even had my own little garage band in high school. I thought I was really going to escape and live my dream of being a performer, but Dad would have none of it. He took away my instruments and chased away my friends. He applied me for college when I didn't want to go, and I was forced to take police classes on the side. I didn't want to fail out and look like an idiot, so I just went wild otherwise."

"How?" I ask. He holds his hand up.

"Look at this," he says, taking a wallet out of his gym bag. He takes a picture out of it and shows it to us. "This was me in high school." I stare at it and almost don't believe him. He has blond hair, parted in the middle, which reaches past his shoulders and flows like a river. Huge glasses cover up half his face, and there are braces on all his teeth. He has his elbows propped up so his hands are on his chin, and it is evident there are no tattoos. He has a private school uniform on and there's a baby grand piano in the background.

"You were a poster boy," I laugh.

"No, I was just a nerd. I decided to change that. When I got to college, I ordered contacts and smashed my glasses. I cut off almost all my hair and dyed it jet black, the exact opposite of my dad. I got my braces removed and got tattoo after tattoo all the way up my arms. They all mean something and I love them, but they were what my father never wanted, so it gave me incentive to get them. They supposedly look unprofessional, so he always makes me wear long sleeves. Finally, I picked out a new wardrobe, and wore what I wanted, which is pretty much what I'm in now. I changed more than just my look though. I went crazy as much as you can in college. Partying, drinking, drugs, girls, the whole deal. When my father came up to visit me, he nearly had a heart attack, and I was eating it up."

Matty can't help but smirk. "I'm picturing how funny that must be. I'm sorry, but I really hate him."

Andy gives him a high five behind my back. "He's so cocky and controlling. It bothers me. No one should be able to dictate my life but me."

"So why are you a cop then," I so rudely ask. "If he can't control you?"

He looks me right in the eye. They look soulful and pained, like he's been through a lot. "I don't want all the fighting. He has a short temper because he's not really mentally stable, and he takes it out on anyone around. He might end up strangling me or one of my co-workers, or even my mother. I just do what he says to prevent that."

"Did you like college?" Kelly inquires.

He chuckles. "I did. It was a lot of fun. My best friend from my band was in the same one with me, so we got an apartment for sophomore, junior, and senior year. My girlfriend was our other roommate, and we've been together since then. Too bad I never got to finish senior year."

I want to ask all about his girlfriend because I feel a little jealousy setting in, but Matty is already wondering aloud why Andy never got to finish college. Andy doesn't like that question, and he gets a faraway look on his face as if he is drowning in memories. "I was diagnosed with lung cancer."

We all gasp, and I pretty much cry, "Are you alright?"

He nods. "I've been in remission almost four years now, and they said my 5 year survival expectancy is about 60%, so I think I'm going to be okay. I still was out of commission for over a year and could never graduate college. My dad pulled strings though to get what he wanted and got me a position in the police force. I had to take night classes and training. He is chief so he can do things like that. So now I feel like I'm wasting my life away, and my dreams will never be lived. Doing this for you three makes me feel better, like I'm finally doing something I'm meant to do."

"What exactly are you doing for us?" Matty has no feelings. I'm almost crying here and he's still looking out for us. Boys.

"I'm going to keep you out of jail for one thing. I'm going to take care of you until I can find you a loving home where, you can all be together and not have to live out here on your own in the wilderness. You deserve to finish school and be whatever you want to be without having to worry about everyday survival. I'm going to keep you from being orphans."

"I heard your Mom died in the lightening strike but how did your father die again?" He realizes that's probably a sore subject and adds, "You don't have to answer that if you don't want to."

"Our sister had leukemia," I offer the information. "Our dad had to take her to the hospital in a storm and got into a crash, killing them both. We were only seven, Kelly was one, Lauren was fourteen, and Dad was only 37. We were all too young."

"Lauren had already died in the seat next to Dad, and when he noticed, he freaked out and crashed the car, putting him with her." Matty clarifies. "Then we just recently lost our Mom to the fire, so our grandmother was our only living relative. Except Mom's brother, but he's been missing for years so we only had one place to go. Andrew Sr. there ruined that."

"I'm really sorry," Andy sympathizes. "And I don't use the Junior. I'm my own Andrew Thompson." I love that last name.

"It's okay," Matty and I say in unison. I even add, "I do like your name."

He gives me a small smile. "Yours is nice too."

Matty makes a little heart on my knee with his finger and I rub it off. I put a huge 'NO!' on his knee. He reaches over and puts 'sure' on mine and then slides over just far enough that I can't protest. Instead, I pick up a rock and throw it at his head. It clunks off his temple and he grinds his teeth. "You got me," he whispers in pain. I grin evilly.

"What's going on?" Andy asks. He looks a little scared he's going to have to discipline us. He actually looks completely frightened of us in general, especially me. I could use that to my advantage.

"Just brother sister bickering," I reply. "You're a little girl," I say to Matty.

"You are," he automatically comes back with.

I laugh. "I know."

"Okay," he says, realizing that was a pretty lame come back. He always uses that to come back to an insult, no matter what someone said, and most of the time it ends up sounding really weird. Such as when I said it's really hot and he said you are. That was a little awkward.

Andy is starting to freak out. He's lost control. "I'll get you three new clothes and a good food supply tomorrow. I'll leave every day before you go to sleep and come back in the morning. Did you have dinner yet? It's getting late."

We don't respond because Matty and I are otherwise engaged in another wrestling match. Andy huffs and pulls me off of Matty. He grabs my arm and pulls me back. His hand is really soft that it feels like how I might imagine a cloud to feel, except warmer. My heart starts thumping again, and I shake out of his grip. Matty and I stop fighting and he says, "Yeah we ate a little bit."

"I think I'm going to leave because Tina is expecting me home soon." Just then, I realize the sun is just above the horizon and is setting fast. Pretty soon we'll be in the dark, which means it must be about quarter to nine. Wow, I think. The night went quick!

"Tina?" Matty asks, raising his eyebrows.

Andy's cheeks get a tiny bit pink. "Yeah, she's my girl."

A few minutes later, Andy has left and we are alone in the forest. I find myself missing him a little already, and I shake that feeling. I can't attach to someone when they're only temporary because I'm going to end up crying. I try to cry as little as possible because I put up a tough front. I lay my head on a soft patch of grass and start to cry. My body shakes, but it's silent and no one can hear. Matty and Kelly are fast asleep. I suddenly am overcome with grief. I want my mom and my dad and my older sister. I want my grandmother and even my missing uncle. I want someone that I can attach to and know they won't go anywhere for a long time.

17

Andy

My plan has definitely worked; it's what comes afterward that scares me. I had tricked my father, and when I come home, he is at my house. He screams at me that I said a few minutes and then hours passed. I told him the bear actually came, and the kids escaped while I was trying to save myself. I show him scratches I had given myself with bushes and say the bear was attacking me and I had to save myself. Of course, he says I should have put the job first, but I ignore him. I love the sympathetic attention I am getting from Tina because I know it will all end when I tell her what really happened.

When my dad finally leaves, I flop on the couch and shut my eyes. Tina runs to the bathroom to get bandages and all that. She wraps up the gnashes on my legs and arms and puts little Band-Aids on my forehead after putting stinging medicine on them all. Then she curls up next to me. I decide this is as good a time as any to tell her the truth.

"There was no bear," I say bluntly. "I gave myself the cuts."

She laughs. "I figured that much. You fooled Daddy though."

"I hope so, because I had to hurt myself for him to buy it."

"So how were the kids?" she asks curiously. "Are they the same ones I met?"

"I'm pretty sure. They're cute and active and all that, but I have a feeling it's going to be difficult. They ask a lot of questions, the little one seems to be a whiner but refuses to talk, and the twins are constantly fighting. I had to break them up."

"Is that how you got the cuts?" she jokes.

I don't find that amusing. "I'm stronger than you think."

She chuckles softly and punches me in the chest. It takes the wind out of me and I gasp for air. "Yup, you're all man."

"Not funny," I say, wheezing. "My lungs aren't everything they used to be."

She's silent, and I decide that was not something I should have brought up right now. She was more scared than me and likes to put it behind her. "The girl was hard though."

"How so?"

"I don't know, I just had the feeling she didn't like me. Like she thought I couldn't be trusted and she wanted me away from her family. The oldest boy was obviously the leader, but he opened up to me way more than she did."

"Are you sure you're not just paranoid? Because you think that all young girls don't like you."

"I'm sure. She was the only one who wouldn't shake my hand, and she kept giving me dirty looks. It was a little intimidating since I went in a little nervous anyway. Don't you think that's funny? I'm more scared the kids won't like me than I am my dad might kill me when he finds out I'm stabbing him in the back."

"I think they'll like you," she assures me, "as soon as they get to know you."

I sigh. "I hope you're right. How do you get a thirteen year old girl to like you, since you were one once?"

"Give her stuff, talk to her privately so she's forced to communicate, and if you can, let her know about your piano skills. That's what got me."

"I think I'll get to know them all separately tomorrow. I'll teach them skills of survival."

"Have fun with that," she winks. "Tomorrow's my first day of summer; I'm done cleaning up my classroom from the year. I think I'll go visit my mom. She's a little mad at me. We got in a little scuffle the other day."

"Know what that's like."

We both laugh and she reminds me, "Just remember not to kill yourself."

"I've been through too much to do that."

I venture into the forest the next day with grocery and clothing bags in hand. I tried my best to guess their sizes, and I think I did pretty well. I got sandwich supplies, cereals, snacks, and all the necessities my mom always told me to have in my house. I prop them over my shoulders and make my way to where I left the kids. I find it easily and see Jenna and Kelly fast asleep. Matty is nowhere to be found, but I decide he'll come back soon enough. I plop the bags next to where I left my gym bag, and Jenna jumps up into a sitting position. She sees me and glares. Another reason she's going to be hard to win over.

Kelly stirs awake too, and when he sees the food, he practically dives into the bag. "Geen fissy?"

I stare at him. "What?"

They both ignore me. Jenna slaps Kelly's hands out of the bag. "No fish today."

The kid looks like he's going to cry. "I want fissy!" he squeals.

"Shush Kelly," Jenna orders. She looks up at me. "You don't happen to have lime Swedish Fish do you?"

I shake my head and Kelly starts bawling. Great, now I failed them, I think. "I have Sour Patch Kids though."

Kelly is now flat on his back in the grass, screaming and flailing his arms and legs. His shoes pound against the ground and his fists become projectiles. Jenna takes control of his limbs and holds him still. "We still have candy, cool it."

Kelly sits up, his cheeks streaked with tears. "Canny?"

I dig in the bag until I find the pack of Sour Patch Kids. I rip it open and hand him a green one. "Here you go."

He takes it and examines it. He stares hard at every speck of it and then smells it. He throws it on the ground and yells, "I want fissy!"

Jenna rolls her eyes. "Come on Kelly, it tastes the same."

He stares straight through her. "The shape matters too."

"Oh for God's sake," Jenna and I say at the same time. "You're getting candy."

He takes another green one and reluctantly shoves it in his mouth. His lips pucker at the sour part and he makes all kinds of faces, like this is torturing him. "He can be a pain sometimes," Jenna informs me.

"I can tell," I laugh. He sticks out his tongue at both of us. "Where's Matty?"

"He went down to the beach to be alone. He thinks and worries too much, and I guess the ocean helps him. He doesn't like to be bothered."

I shrug. "Oh well. You can help yourself to breakfast, and I tried my best with the clothes."

"I'm frightened."

I let that one go and take my walk down to the beach. I spot Matty's black hair blowing in the wind over near the jetty. His legs swing off the edge of it as he watches the waves. He doesn't see me coming. I scan the people setting up on the beach. There are only a few people here because it's only about 9 am. There are a lot of abandoned umbrellas and chairs, and the air is a bit chilly. The sea is rough today because a storm is supposed to be coming this weekend. They say it's not going to be that bad, but the waves are going to be huge. A few surfers are already out there. It is a beautiful sight. Very peaceful. I can see why the kid likes it out here at this hour.

I take a seat next to him and his head snaps around. I wonder what he was so deep in thought about. I hope the memories from the fire don't come back like my cancer does for me. He gives me a small wave and looks back at the ocean.

"I brought food and clothes like I promised," I say.

"Thanks," he mumbles. I can barely hear it over the wind.

"What are you thinking about?"

"My mom."

"My mom was my only good thing when I was growing up. She taught me the ways of life and how to stick up for myself when my dad went off. I can't imagine losing her."

"Yeah," he sighs. "Imagine you have the power to save her and you just can't do it."

"You know it's not your fault."

"I don't use time because I always want to go back on it, and if I watch it tick away, I go crazy. I keep thinking that that's one more minute that my dad, Lauren, or my mom never got to see because of me. Not only could I have saved my mom from that fire if I were a little bit stronger and faster, but I could have saved my sister and my dad in the process. I had the bone marrow match to Lauren that could have saved her, but I was just a little too young. If I had been a little older and had gone through with that transplant, Dad would never have had to drive in that storm. They would all be alive, but I couldn't save any of them. So really it *is* my fault when you get down to it."

I feel this kid's pain. I want to help him, but there's nothing I can do. I feel as helpless as I did the day I got that call. We sit there in silence, and I feel as awful as he does. He slides off of the jetty and starts walking back to camp. Jenna was right; he doesn't like to be bothered when he has his quiet time on the beach. I jump off of the jetty and quickly catch up with him.

"Matty," I say. "I wish I could help you."

"Hey, it's okay. I shouldn't have put that on you."

"It made me more proud that I'm doing for you what I am. I promise I'll make things better as best as I can. I actually put you up for adoption, and I'm going to meet up with families in a few days. Once I get your charges dropped, I'll have you meet them yourselves."

"Can't we go live with Grandma?" he wonders, pushing back tree branches to get in the forest. I follow.

"It turns out she's an accessory because she hid you." I try to fake a smile to make that fact a little bit easier.

It doesn't seem to work because he curses. "Now we drug her into this! That's the last thing we wanted to do." He rubs both eyes with his fingers.

Jenna runs up to us. "I heard you yelling. What's wrong?"

"Grandma's an accessory in our crimes."

"Oh no!"

"Wait you guys," I say. "I'm going to get her cleared too. You don't have to worry about it."

"You better," Jenna warns. She gives me another intimidating look. "We're counting on you."

"Yeah, you better not make all these grand statements and then not follow through," Matty sneers.

"I will do everything I possibly can," I promise. I feel really nervous. What if I can't win against my dad? What if no one wants all three kids, especially since Matty is all over town as dangerous? I don't let the bad thoughts get to me. I will win against my dad, I tell myself. I will find them a loving home. I must.

Jenna hands Matty a bowl of cereal and milk. "I fixed this for you. Kelly and I already ate."

"K thanks." He sits down to eat, and Jenna and Kelly sit with me. I walk away slowly, letting them have some alone time. I figure I need some of my own anyway. I'll just go back to that jetty. I really liked that.

18

Matty

That night, Andy tries to pull out a box of Mac and Cheese. We aren't having that. We are picky eaters and anything instant doesn't cut it. It's actually funny because we stand there, arms crossed, while Andy tries to stare us down. We're better than him and it irks him.

"Fine!" he yells, throwing the box on the ground. "What do you want?"

"You should cook for us," Jenna laughs.

"I can't cook," he admits. "Tina does that."

"Come on, your mom had to teach you how to cook something," I protest.

"Two things. Meat loaf and mashed potatoes because they're my favorite. I can't very well cook that out here, can I?"

We agree he probably can't and settle for ham and cheese sandwiches. Jenna can't help but ask, "Why is it that every guy likes meat loaf? It's disgusting and you all love it."

"It *is* not!" I argue. I love meat loaf, and Mom would never cook it because she hated it herself. She used to surprise Dad with it when I was little, but after he was gone, she had no one to surprise. I gave up going out to dinner pretty much every birthday for it, because that was the only time Mom and Jenna would choke it down. And I heard lots of complaining the entire time, so it wasn't as enjoyable as it could have been. Why couldn't they have just dealt? I ate all their dumb girl food. I ate Jenna's birthday breakfast.

"I must agree with Matty," Andy says. "It is the best."

"Thank you." I give him a high five, and Jenna attempts to stick her finger down her throat. She makes a choking sound and pretends to throw up. She's such a drama queen.

"I'll have to make you my special meat loaf one day. I got it from my mom. It's spectacular. I put melted cheese in the middle."

That sounds heavenly. "I'll be looking forward to that."

Jenna is still choking herself out. "It tastes like cardboard. It's worse than lima beans, and they're like eating dirt. I'm very disappointed in you Andy."

He chuckles and she smiles brightly. I guess she's starting to trust him after two days of no tricks. I know I do. Something about him seems pure, like he only wants so badly to do something right for us. I just hope he can do it.

"Do you want me to show you something really cool?" Andy asks Jenna and me. His face lights up like a little boy. "I found it when wandering around here a couple days ago."

I feel my own eyes get brighter. I love adventure and I'll do anything for it. "Yeah? What is it?"

Andy grins from ear to ear. "I'll show you." He looks past us. "Come with us Kelly!"

Kelly gets up from rolling around in the grass like a puppy. When he plays by himself, he gets very creative. "Where?"

"You'll see," Andy says. He pushes back a few trees, and it's like something out of a movie. The drab forest suddenly becomes a fairy tale scene. There is a small clearing in the forest and a large lake covers most of it. The lake is dark blue, and there are small ripples in it from the wind. I see a few fish fins surface and then quickly return to the bottom. There are boulders surrounding the lake that you can sit on while you dip your feet in it. I was thinking more of jumping off them myself. Behind the rocks is a ring of soft white sand. The trees rustle softly and a few birds chirp. It's the perfect little sanctuary, and I can't help but breathe, "Wow." Jenna does the same thing. We're both fascinated by it and are itching to use it.

"This is unreal," Jenna gawks. "I didn't think a little piece of land could be so beautiful."

"Actually it's more of a piece of water," I correct her.

"Shut up." She punches me in the arm and it stings.

"It's gorgeous isn't it?" Andy asks. We both nod. "So do you have bathing suits?"

"You mean we get to swim?"

"Yeah! What did you think we were going to do, just sit here and stare at a lake?"

I laugh. I do admit that was kind of stupid. I just feel like the surface of the water is so perfect that I don't want to ruin it. "No, we don't have bathing suits," I pout.

"That's okay. Who needs those anyway?" Andy says, waving that idea away.

"We can't wet our clothes," Kelly says. "Mom would never let us." That's true.

"And we are *not* skinny dipping!" Jenna yells. She sees us all looking at her like she's an idiot, and she says, "I was just making sure" in a small voice.

"You guys are too good," he laughs. He pulls off his shoes and socks and throws them in the sand. Then he takes off his shirt and puts it with them. He's actually decently built, and that surprises me since he seems so skinny and I thought he was awkward. Next come his jeans, so he's standing there in boxers. I wish I could say something smart to Jenna, but I don't want to get punched again. He runs through the sand, straight across the rocks, and jumps off them. "Rules are meant to be broken!" he yells before he disappears into the dark blue lake. It causes a big wave and leaves us three there staring. He comes up about 30 seconds later and shakes his head, sending water droplets flying from his hair.

"You're a free spirit!" I call. "You had no idea how deep that was or what was at the bottom!"

"When you almost die, you learn to just do what you want without worrying about the consequences! Now come on!"

I guess I better just go. It did look like fun. I strip down to my own boxers and so does Kelly. I grab his hand and we run through the sand together. It feels really good on my feet, like running across clouds. The rocks are really smooth and we plunge into the dark water. It's exceptionally warm, and it makes my whole body feel good, the same way a hot tub does. Kelly and I come up together, rubbing the water out of our eyes. "Wow, that's amazing," I say.

"Warm," Kelly notes. "I like it."

"I told you it was nice!" Andy says. I smile and pick up Kelly high above the surface. I spin him around a few times and then throw him as far as I can across the lake. He flops, making a huge splash. The water comes up and sprays me in the face. Kelly comes up laughing hysterically, and it makes Andy and me laugh too.

"Again," Kelly begs, swimming back over to me. I'm about to pick him up and spin him again, when I notice Jenna is still standing where she was, watching us have all the fun. She has her arms folded and her knees turned inward so they touch. She gives me a small smile when she sees me looking, but I know she's close to crying. I really feel bad for her because she's a girl and she can't really do what we did.

"Hold on Kelly," I say, swimming back to the rocks. I pull myself up out of the lake and run over to Jenna. I'm dripping wet and my boxers stick to my legs. It's really cold, but I can't let Jenna miss out on this.

"You didn't have to get out," she tells me. "I was having fun watching Kelly fly."

I give her a sympathetic look, and she knows I don't believe her. "I feel bad."

"Well, I can't very well strip down. I'll look ridiculous and be completely embarrassed in front of him."

"That doesn't mean you can't have fun. I'll be right back."

"Okay," she says. She has a very surprised look in her eyes. I run back to our camp as fast as I can and gather up a pair of gym shorts and my smallest shirt from the bag Andy brought us. They look like they could fit Jenna nicely without her being constricted. I hold them out far from me so they don't get wet and cold before she dives in the water.

"What's that?" she wonders when I return.

"The smallest pair of clothes I have. Put them on and you can go swimming with us."

She raises her eyebrows at me. "They're going to get ruined."

"It's more important that you have a good time," I assure her. "I can always get a new set of clothes. You'll never get this day back."

Her eyes light up. "I love when you get all philosophical on me."

"Just put on the clothes already," I order, trying not to laugh. That was pretty cheesy, even if it was true.

She ducks behind a tree and comes out with my gym shorts hanging past her knees and an overly large shirt. It looks like she played dress up with Dad's clothes. "Wow," I mutter. "You're smaller than I thought."

"You're bigger than I thought."

"I'm a growing boy," I laugh. "Now come on or you're getting a hug." I spread my arms out and close in on her. She screams and runs toward the lake. I chase after her and we both fall off the rocks and into the bath water. It feels like the beach day in my dream. I pick up Kelly and fling him, and then I do the same with Jenna. Andy comes up behind me and gives me a turn. My arms and legs sprawl out in all directions as I fly through the air. I hit the water in a belly flop and squeal like a little girl. Water goes into my mouth and I drink some. I come up gasping for air and end up laughing in the process. It's an amazing feeling.

"I feel alive!" I yell stupidly. The sun starts to set, but we don't care. We're having fun, and I'm starting to really like Andy. He's like the older brother I never had, but always wanted.

19

Andy

My whole body is screaming for me to stay in bed, but I force myself to get up. I have a nice surprise for the kids now that I'm sure they like me. That lake thing was a really good way to bond, and I'm proud of myself. Now things can be easier, and once I give them this present I'm planning to give, they will adore me even more. Then the rest of it will be like coasting down a mountain or hill. Piece of cake.

I take a nice morning drive down to the Rehoboth boardwalk, with the wind blowing through my hair and playing my music so it blasts down Route 1. My engine roars as I pull into Rehoboth Avenue and find an easy parking spot. Not many people are shopping before 9 am. Just the older people, and they park in front of the store they're going to because they don't want to walk. I want to get old; I just don't want to *be* old. There is a big difference there.

I feed the meter and walk to where I need to go-Candy Kitchen. I enter and the smell of candy and perfumes fills my nostrils. I smile warmly until I see the girl working at the cash register. She's glaring at me like 'you're not supposed to be here this early, get out.' Getting that present might be a little more difficult than I thought.

"Do you have Aqua Life?" I ask, coming up to the counter.

"Yeah," she says rudely. "It's right in front of your face."

I look down and see the assortment of colorful Swedish fish staring back at me. "Oh, well I'll have a pound please." The kids *liked* the Sour Patch Kids, but they're going to *love* this.

She huffs and puffs as she puts together a box of Aqua Life for me. It can't be that hard, I feel like saying. All you have to do is scoop out a little bit and put it in a box. I keep my mouth shut and wait patiently though because I feel like she might go in the back and spit in it. I'm already watching her like a hawk. I'm glad I found Tina because most girls really bother me.

"There," she says, slamming the box on the counter. "Anything else."

I grin. This is the good part. "Yes. I'd like another pound, but this time I want only lime."

She stares at me and blinks over and over. I start to believe that something got disconnected. Finally she says, "Are you kidding me?"

"No, I got a picky eater on my hands."

"I don't want to pick out all lime just because some kid or something wants it."

I cross my hands. "I'll pay you extra."

She rolls her eyes and makes a big fuss. "Fine! You're going to have to wait though because I'm taking my time."

I sit down cross-legged next to the door and look up at her expectantly. "Go ahead." I wait there whistling for at least 10 minutes, while she slowly picks out green fish one by one and sighs with each one she puts in the box. Finally, the box is filled, and she wraps the wax paper around it. She weighs it and it reads .99. She tries to sneak that by me, but I protest. "That's not a pound," I let her know.

"It's close enough."

I shake my head. "If I'm paying you extra, I want a full pound."

She rolls her eyes and picks out one more fish. It reaches a pound and she seals the box. "Now it is."

I stand up, stretching since I've been there quite awhile. I give her the money for the two boxes and then a nice tip. She puts half in the cash register and pockets the rest. She leans over something for a few seconds and then sticks it to the side of the lime fish box. "Get outta here," she says, handing me the boxes. I snatch them from her and strut to the door. I look down at the box and see a little slip of paper with a phone number scrawled on it. I rip it off, crumple it up into a little ball, and throw it next to the door where I was sitting. A kid walks in and kicks it. It skirts across the floor and disappears under the counter.

I turn around. "Sorry," I whisper. Then I leave. Ah, how I love messing with some people.

20

Jenna

After last night, we sleep really well. I wake up with all my muscles aching because I pretty much passed out in the sand next to the lake. Matty, Kelly, and I share a blanket, and I'm surprised to see that Matty is still asleep next to me. Andy left at about 9:30 last night and we had changed into pajamas. Yes, he actually remembered to get us pajamas! Now I lay in the sand thinking about all the fun we had last night. I thought for a few minutes I wasn't going to be able to swim, but like he always does, Matty swooped in and saved the day. I wanted to tell him how he's so great and I wouldn't be able to survive without him, but he probably would have made fun of me. Instead, I just let him throw me through the air, and it was so much fun. I hope we get to do that again tonight. It made all my worries disappear, and I loved that feeling.

And for a plus, Andy looked pretty hot. I have to admit I am attracted to him. I like his free spirit personality too, and I feel better just saying that than trying to fight it. He had an amazing body, with some abs and the nice arms and legs, topped off by those gorgeous tattoos. Plus he has that hair and the soul patch that makes him look more mature. Plain beauty. I would never tell him that of course because that would be extremely awkward. I usually tell the boys my age because it makes things less weird if they know how I feel straight away. But this is much different. I need to keep this a secret, and that would be easy if the blushing and fast heart beat would fade away. I hope I get used to it soon.

Matty interrupts my thoughts by kicking me in his sleep. I push him away, making him fall on Kelly. Kelly screams, waking them both. So much for my quiet time.

Matty sits up quick and looks around. "Andy here yet?"

I shake my head. "He must be as tired as us."

"I know. I think I was just unconscious all night. I had no dreams, I was so tired, and now my shoulders hurt."

"Yeah," I agree. "Same here. What's for breakfast?"

"So I'm fixing you breakfast now?"

I nod jokingly. "You're the oldest. Of course."

Andy appears out of the way where our camp is and nods at us. His hands are behind his back and I find that suspicious. "Hey. Thought you were never coming," I joke.

He grins. "I was a little spent. I did bring this though." He takes his hands out from behind his back to reveal two pink, rectangular boxes. I see the label on them and instantly get excited. Candy Kitchen means good things.

"What is it?" Matty asks, pretty much tackling him for the box.

Andy uses one arm to push him back by the chest. "Hold on there, tiger. This one is for Jenna and you to share." He hands one to Matty, and we open it immediately. Inside are all the colors Swedish Fish can be, and they look really good. We decide to take Dad's idea and eat them before breakfast. I take lots of red and green ones, while Matty goes for the blue, orange, and purple ones. We both pass up yellow at first, but when we get desperate, we'll eat them too.

Andy walks over to Kelly and hands him the remaining box. "This one is just for you. Since I failed you the other day."

Kelly rips it open like Christmas morning and sees a whole pound of just green Swedish fish. "Geen fissy!" he yells. "Yummy!" He takes a whole handful and shoves them in his mouth. He chews them with his mouth open, and a few fall out onto the sand.

"Ewww," I say, turning away. "Thank you so much!"

"We missed our candy," Matty agrees. We both munch and smile.

"No problem," he says. "I want to make you guys happy."

"Sure you're not just buttering us up?" I ask.

Matty glares at me, but I still want to hear the answer. "My intentions are pure."

I nod. "I believe you." He smiles and his blue eyes light up the whole clearing. I breathe heavily to keep from getting my ridiculous reaction.

"I even got a number in the process," he grins.

Matty gives him the thumbs up sign. "Nice. She hot?"

I push him and he almost chokes to death on the fish. He slaps his own back and gasps for air. I take out a water bottle and hand it to him. He chugs it. "I thought you were dedicated to Tina?" I ask. I don't want him to say he believes in open relationships. I have this perception of him being this perfect romantic guy, and I'm going to be really disappointed if he doesn't live up to my expectations.

"I am," he says, and I fight not to sigh in relief. "I threw it away, but it's still nice to know you're hot to everyone else, you know?"

"Sure," I draw out the word, looking across the lake.

"Can I talk to you privately?" he asks. It catches me so off guard, I choke, even though I'm not eating anything. Matty winks at me, but I'm too phased to do anything to him.

I catch my breath. "Why not?"

"Great." He walks over to the far side of the lake and sits on a rock. His legs dangle off the end so the tips of his shoes break the surface of the water. I make sure no one is looking and let out a little squeal.

I join him and my feet are far from reaching the water. I slide down a little so they're submerged. "I like your shoes," I compliment. It's always good to start a conversation with a compliment, Dad said to me once. It makes it friendly, and if they have to say something you don't want to hear, they'll say it less hurtfully. I miss my dad's wise words.

"Thanks. They're my newest pair. I have others, but they're too dirty. Only shoes I'll wear."

"Why would you wear new shoes out here?"

He smirks. "I like to start an adventure with new shoes. That way, by the end of the adventure, they'll have lots of scuff marks and dirty spots. Then I guess which part of the adventure each one came from. We can try it at the end of this."

"That's pretty cool," I admit. "I never thought of that."

"I love these shoes though. I've only worn this kind since I was a little boy; I tried every style and color."

"I wish I had a pair."

"They'd look good on you." I feel the blood rush to my cheeks when I hear that, and I quickly scoop up some water. I splash it on my face nonchalantly and smile. "I'm sure they would."

He nods. "I needed to talk to you because I feel like I pretty much know Matty and Kelly, but not you. I know that Matty lives without time, he loves science and going on any kind of adventure, he feels guilty for the death of your parents and your sister, and he loves you and Kelly unconditionally. He would do anything for you two. He's a born leader. Kelly uses as little words as he can, likes to wander off, always has candy with breakfast, especially Swedish Fish, and he won't let go of that salamander for anything. But I really don't know anything about you, and I want to know."

"Hmm, where to start," I say, holding back a fit of nervous giggles. "What do you want to know?"

"What do you think I should know?"

"I despise doctors. They put that weight on Matty's shoulders because they told my parents he was too young to donate bone marrow. I think they're the reason Mom died too. I keep away from them so I don't get killed myself. Matty was trying to prove my point to our doctor, and they said he was threatening her."

He nods. "I can see why you would stay away from doctors. And I didn't think Matty was capable of putting that one in physical danger. My dad's just trying to get a case."

"Yeah, I figured that much. On the subject of me though, I can't sleep without my alternative rock music, I love reading and relaxing with a book, and I want to be a writer when I grow up."

"Really," he says, grinning. "What kind of writer? Like fiction books?"

I struggle to explain without looking stupid. "I've written novels since I was 8, so five years. Dad never got to read any of them, but Mom was my editor. And Matty and Kelly give me lots of good ideas. I have problems saying the things I want to, so I write my opinions in the written word and I feel better. But there's more."

"Go on," he urges.

I get nervous. "Promise you won't think I'm weird."

"Promise. I'll even give you a snake shake."

I feel my eyebrows rise without me controlling them. "Am I supposed to know what that is?"

He slaps his forehead. "Sorry. I'll show you." He raises his arm, bent at elbow, with his wrist bent too. It really looks like a snake when it raises its head at you. "Do this."

I follow his lead. He brushes the top of his hand on my palm and then my palm on the top of his hand. "There," he says, lowering his hand. "It's my very own pinkie swear."

"That's really cool. Mind if I use it?"

"Nope, as long as you tell me what you were going to tell me."

I sigh. "Okay. I always have to act out my stories before I write them. And since I'm the only one who knows how it's going to go, I act out all the parts by myself each night before I go to bed. That way I know what I'm going to write the next day. I never told anyone that because I think I'd get teased and ridiculed. My dream actually is to write and produce my own show."

I watch as his whole face lights up, his eyes, and then his mouth widens into a grin. "That's amazing. I always wished I could see a whole new world in my head with all these characters. Instead I see a bunch of music notes and hear a melody. I guess that's almost the same."

"Yeah, we're alike in that way I suppose."

"I love art too," he says. He looks down at his arms. That is the first time I really notice the tattoos on his arms up close. I gaze at them. It's a bunch of strings in every color you could imagine twisting and turning into each other from his wrists to his elbows. There's a little bit of space where you can see his bare skin and it makes the design even cooler. One of the strips reaches down almost to his left hand, where a tiny palm tree is tattooed. I was never a fan of tattoos, but these are just beautiful.

"Is it supposed to mean something?" I ask. I take one finger and trace the red string with my forefinger. Then I move on to the blue one, and so on. I could do this all day.

He shrugs. "Not really. I started with the white one because I saw it in the shop, and then I kept adding colors until I had every one they made. As you can see, each arm is an exact mirror image of the other. It's just unique and awesome enough to fit me."

"It's mesmerizing," I whisper, starting to trace on the next arm.

"I have this one too," he says. He pulls up his shirt to reveal a tattoo on the left side of his chest, where you would estimate his heart is. It is a big black copyright sign, the little c inside a circle. Under it is the year '83. I thought I had seen a flash of black writing when he was running toward the lake, but I didn't know exactly what it was until now. I wonder what it's for.

Matty appears behind me at that moment and smiles. "Is that a copyright branding?"

Andy nods excitedly. "I got it when I was 18 and finally able to be independent. It represents my desire to be my own person, no matter what my dad thinks, and that I want no one to ever copy me. So I put a copyright sign and my year of birth, because as soon as I was born, I was unable to be replaced. I'm just *that* strange."

"I think I might get one of those," Matty says, almost jumping up and down. "I feel the same way." This is true. He always tells me he wanted to have a patent, so no one could copy his thoughts or feelings and try to beat him to his dreams, which is becoming the astrophysicist that makes the world better and is known for centuries after his death. This is like he finally found what he was always looking for.

"How old are you?" I can't help but ask. I could do the math, but I want to hear it from him.

"I am precisely 2.6 decades young," he replies. Matty and I are both caught by surprise.

"That's 26," I laugh, and he nods. "I've never heard someone say it that way before."

"Like I said, I like being different than everyone else."

Matty and I look at each other and smile wide. We both agree that this has to be the coolest guy ever, and we get to hang out with him all summer! Finally, something good has come along.

21

Matty

We spend another day swimming in the lake. I do wish we had bathing suits, but I'll appreciate what I have. Secretly, I admire Andy's copyright tattoo. I think that is the coolest thing ever. I'm *so* going to get one when I'm 18, and I won't change my mind for anyone. I want to be an astrophysicist when I grow up, a good one. One that will find the fate of our universe, discover new planets, and kids will read about in science class in the year 3000. Then again, there might not be schools that far in advance. They might have robot tutors and holographic friends and pets. They might not even care about me because someone has surpassed me already. What I'm trying to say is that I want to be remembered like Ben Franklin and Albert Einstein as being super intelligent and helping the world. And I don't want anybody to copy anything I do. That's why that copyright sign right there on my skin for everyone to see would be the best feeling. Andy is the coolest!

When I'm pretty much spent from throwing and being thrown through the air all day, and just want to go to sleep, Andy appears out of nowhere. My belly is full of spaghetti and nicely baked bread Tina had prepared for us. She sent it with Andy when he came back from changing out of his wet clothes, and I feel relaxed. I know with all Andy's energy, he's going to suggest we do something vigorous, so I quickly close my eyes and pretend I fell asleep.

"I know you're awake Matty," Andy says, kicking me in the side. I groan loudly and slide over to where he can't reach me.

"Now I am," I mutter.

"Come on!" Andy protests. "I planned something important for tonight. It'll be an adventure."

He knows that might get me and he's right. My eyes flicker open and I sit up. "Fine, what are we doing?"

He smirks. "We're going on an all man trip."

"Oh really?" I slowly get up, starting on my hands and knees and stretching one foot after the other. It's a complicated process, but I want to prolong standing. "What about Jenna?"

"She can come if she doesn't want to stay alone, but I didn't figure she'd like it. We're hunting!" He starts clapping and bouncing on his toes in excitement.

"Please don't tell me we're killing anything."

He flinches and steps back a little. I guess that was a little too loud. "Calm down, we're not really hunting. I'm not carrying a weapon am I?"

I have to agree. Unless we'll killing animals bare handed, which I highly doubt, we're not killing anything. He continues, "Every man needs to know how to survive on his own in the wild if need be, so I'm showing you and Kelly how to get food and start fires and all that. That way you can protect Jenna if it comes down to it."

"You're right, Jenna probably wouldn't like that."

"Like what?" she asks. I spin around to see her, hands on hips. "Don't talk about me behind my back."

I feel my hands shaking. She can really put up a fight if she has to do it. "Andy is taking Kelly and me on a hunting trip to show us how to survive in the wild."

"Oh," she says, rolling her eyes. "You're taking a manly hunting trip."

Andy smiles. "Yes, but you can come if you're afraid to be alone."

"I'm not!" she says too quickly. I know she probably is, but would never let anyone catch on to it. "Plus, I wouldn't come even if I was. I think that spaghetti didn't agree with me. My stomach is killing me, and I don't want to be stuck somewhere in the woods throwing up."

I step back a little ways. If she could throw up at any minute, not only do I not want to be in the line of fire, but I don't want the germs to catch me either. She notices and shoots me a dirty look.

"I hope you feel better," Andy says. Kelly appears with Salamander, and Andy puts his arm around his shoulders. "We'll be back in a couple hours."

"It's getting dark," Jenna points out. "Can't you wait until tomorrow?"

He shakes his head. "We're doing it now. Go to sleep soon because we might be back late. Scream as loud as you can if something's wrong and you need us."

"Okay."

"Let's go Matty," he says, guiding Kelly in the right direction. I follow them, giving Jenna a wave before we disappear behind a wall of trees. We keep hiking for a little while and the sun sets. Pretty soon we are in darkness, and the forest comes alive. That is when Andy crouches to the ground and orders us to do the same.

"Night is the best time to catch food," he whispers. "Lots of animals are unsuspecting, and the light of the moon lets you see just enough to set traps."

"Can you show us how to set a trap?" I ask. "I always wanted to know how."

He nods. He takes a vine off a nearby tree and ties it to the trunk of another. He makes a little noose with the other end of the vine and finally ties it to a little piece of stick on the ground. He uses his fingers to pretend he's a small animal walking along the dark forest floor. He tricks the vine, and his finger flies up and hangs from the tree. It looks just like what an animal would look like hanging, ready to cook up and eat. I try to memorize what he did for later use.

"Now that it works," he whispers, "we can leave it here and see what we can catch by morning."

"Cool," Kelly admires. That makes Andy smile and say, "I am only the best." He lowers down to a position flat on his stomach. He pulls himself along by the elbows until he finds what he's looking for there. He holds his hand back for us to stay where we are, and inches closer. He slowly rises and straightens his back. Suddenly, he pounces to the ground, wrapping his arms around a dark object.

"Bring me your shirt," he calls. He wiggles around as he struggles to hold on. Whatever he just caught is alive. I quickly peel off my shirt and toss it to him. He wraps the object and ties the end so it becomes a sack. He throws it over his shoulder and grins at us. "Now that was how you catch food!"

"What did you catch?" I ask excitedly. I can only imagine.

He bends down so his mouth is between Kelly and my ears. "A chicken."

"What?!" I exclaim. "There are chickens out here?"

He nods vigorously. "And we're gonna cook him up and eat him tomorrow night."

"Jenna isn't going to like that," Kelly notes. I nod in agreement. She hates it when I watch nature shows and it shows one animal eating another. I think it's really cool and is nature at its best, but she hides her eyes and screams. It must be a girl thing. I hope I can find one like Kristina who loves tricked out cars and isn't afraid to get dirty. I wonder if Andy's girlfriend is like that.

"Well, we'll kill it before she sees and cook it, and she'll think someone else caught it." I have to admit that is a smart idea. There's only one problem. I don't want to be the one who has to kill it, and I don't want Kelly to see that.

Andy must sense that as he hides behind a tree. I hear the sack being untied and then a lot of squawking. I cringe to here it stop and the silence of death, but something else happens. With my eyes closed, all I can feel is the scratching of claws on my feet. I look down to see a chicken scurry away into the darkness. Andy comes out behind the tree and I give him a questioning look.

"I can't kill him when I know we have other food and don't need to," he admits, hanging his head. "But you must know that in a starving situation, it's either you or him. Now let me show you how to catch something."

My eyes light up. "Seriously?"

"Of course. You don't think I would do that and then not let you guys have a try, do you?"

Kelly and I grin at each other. The three of us charge through the woods in search of something to catch and then release. Next, I know, we're going to start a fire and build shelters. It's going to be an all night affair and I'm shaking in excitement. This is quite an adventure, and it's going to be lots of fun. I knew having a big brother would be amazing!

22

Jenna

I wake up the next morning to find Andy slumped over a rock a few feet away. I find that as strange because he never spends the night out here with us. He always goes home to Tina and comes back with new supplies. We all were hoping he would arrive with bathing suits. I'm tired of wearing Matty's stupid clothes. I want to have my own bikini and look amazing. I spot Matty and Kelly asleep next to the rock. Matty is always up before me because he's an insomniac. That makes me wonder just how late they were out last night to make him pass out like that. I fell asleep before they got back from their "manly hunting trip", so I can only imagine what went on with it. I would have gone to observe Andy in survival action if I hadn't had that awful stomach ache. It was just below my belly button and I ended up keeling over in pain shortly after they left.

I realize the stomach ache has subsided, so I decide to get a start on finding breakfast. If Andy fell asleep here and Matty isn't awake, I'm going to have to fend for myself this morning. I fix my hair and throw the blanket off of me. I stare at my pants. There's brown all over the front of them. Maybe it's just dirt, I tell myself. I *am* sleeping on the forest floor and there could be dirt amidst the sand. But when I pull my shorts down and peek, I see it has soaked through from my underwear. My whole body goes ice cold. This can't be happening!

I pull my shorts back up and stagger back to where I slept. I know I have to do something, but I have no idea what to do. I can't tell Matty because he'll freak out worse than me, and something tells me Andy won't have a better reaction. As amazing as he is, he is a little immature. I can't very well hide this from them though. Why now? I ask the heavens.

I make the decision to wake up Andy. I pray he won't go insane. Maybe I've just judged him and he'll be cool with it. I start shaking him back and forth and he rolls off the rock. He flops in the sand and groans. It's an interesting sight, and I can't help but giggle. I cover my mouth to keep from being too loud and waking Matty and Kelly. I kick Andy to make sure that fall woke him up, and I'm almost positive I hear a growl.

"Leave me alone," he grunts. He's not being very cooperative. I know they were probably out all night and he's exhausted, but I need him.

"Andy, no!" I whisper as loud as possible. "This is important!"

His eyes fly open and he stares up at me. I have my pants turned around backward so he can't see it until I decide to show him. "What? Is someone here? Do we have to make a run for it?"

"No," I admit it's not that important. "I just have a...um...*situation*."

He sits up and continues to stare at me. I slowly slide my pants around, revealing everything. It takes a few seconds for his brain to register it, and then his eyes widen. Please stay calm, I plead him with my mind. I hope he has ESP or something and can understand my mind talk.

"Oh," he says, surprisingly calm. "That *is* an issue."

"Please tell me it's not what I think it is," I say. I close my eyes and pray I hear the words I want to hear.

"If you think it's your period, than I can't do that," he laughs. "Is this your first?"

"What do you think?" I snap. I'm sorry for that as soon as I say it. It's not his fault.

He nods. "I'm just trying to help you. You don't have to be mean."

"I'm sorry. I just don't want this right now! In fact, I don't want this for a really long time. Why couldn't it have happened at Grandma's where she could help me, if it had to happen? Or when Mom was still alive? Ugh!" The thought of Mom not being alive brings tears to my eyes. I wipe them away quickly so he doesn't see.

He gets up and stoops down so his face is right in mine. I didn't know it was possible, but it cheers me up. He's even more beautiful up close. I wish I could grab his face and kiss him. "Well, it didn't happen then, it happened now, and I'm all you got, so let me help you."

I nod. I hear Matty ask, "What's going on?" All this commotion must have stirred him awake. Kelly is still out though.

"Oh no," I whisper. I didn't hear him wake.

Andy stands up. "That," he replies, pointing at my shorts. Did he have to make it *that* obvious?

Matty screams, as expected. "Do you know how to deal with that?"

"Not really," Andy admits. "But I'm gonna try. Do you?"

"No," Matty answers, backing away. He's acting childish, like I have cooties or something. "You're the one with the sister."

"She's four years older than me and barely wanted anything to do with me. It's not like I took care of her!"

"Girlfriend?"

Andy sighs. "She's capable of dealing with it on her own."

"Still you're on your own," Matty says, "because I'm *not* going anywhere near that!"

"Jesus Matty," Andy exclaims, just as disgusted with his behavior as I am. "You're her brother! You're acting like she's a monster."

I roll my eyes. While they're in the middle of their screaming match, I'm getting worse off. I mean come on, Matty is my brother. He shouldn't be acting like I just killed someone and he can't get near me. He should know better than to let someone we've known for a little over two weeks take care of something this big. I love Matty to death, but sometimes he's just a complete idiot. "Oh for God's sake," I yell, throwing my hands in the air. "I'll just do it myself!" I storm off into the woods alone, but Andy runs after me. I continue to stomp even after he has caught up with me.

"Don't listen to him Jenny," he tells me. "He's immature. You're farther up in the world than him and he can't handle it."

I stop stomping. No one has ever called me Jenny before. I like it. And maybe he's right. "He'll get over it. Just tell me what I'm supposed to do." I stare at my feet, embarrassed.

I can feel him staring at me, trying to read my expression. He's always worried we won't like him and he's freaking out he upset me. I don't look at him to tell him it's okay though. I just want this all to be over with so I can think about other more cheerful things.

"I suggest you go to the lake and wash yourself off so you get as clean as possible. Then when you're done, you just put on a pad for now. Do you know how to do that?"

"I'm sure I can figure it out," I mumble. I kick a pinecone that has fallen in the sand, and it rolls until it falls in a footprint. It's completely hidden. I wish I could hide under the sand for a little while where no one could find me.

"I know you don't want me to help you because I'm this weird 26 year old guy you just met a month ago. For all you know, I could be some creep, which I'm not, I promise. But I just want you to know, I'm here if you need me."

"I'm smart enough to handle it on my own, I think." I hope I'm right about that.

"Okay," he says. "Go ahead."

I make my way down toward the lake. When I get to the wall of trees I have to pass to get to the clearing, I turn around. Andy is now lying flat on his stomach, facing the other way, spying on a couple of rabbits that are half hidden by a clump of brush and sticks. I smile. He's more amazing than I thought. He's really going to let me handle it on my own without hovering.

I push through the wall and run across the sand to the rocks. I quickly strip down and dive into the warm lake water. It feels sort of strange, but I pretend I'm just taking a bath. Matty had arranged soaps and shampoos on a group of rocks earlier for cleaning ourselves, so I grab a bar of soap. I clean myself, and then decide as long as I'm here, I might as well wash my hair too. I'm really glad this is a freshwater lake or else this wouldn't have worked out too well. It makes me wonder just how a fresh water lake could appear this close to the salt water ocean. I guess miracles just happen.

When I'm finished, I grab a towel off the nearest tree branch and run to where we keep our stuff. I sort through all the food, clothes, and camping supplies and find what I'm looking for. I peek over and see Kelly is still fast asleep and Matty is nowhere to be found. I'm alone, I think. Good. I rip open the pack and pull one out. I want to scream and throw it as far as I can, but I know I'm going to have to get used to it, so I don't. I quickly grab a new change of clothes. I take deep breaths to get myself together, and soon enough, I'm good to go. "That wasn't so bad," I say to myself.

I find Andy chasing rabbits, but failing to even get close to one. He keeps running around in circles, pouncing, and swearing when he comes up empty. Rabbits are just too much for our very own jungle boy. He stops when he sees me. "You all good?" he asks.

I nod. "Yup."

He sits down on the nearest tree stump and I join him. "I know you probably don't want me telling you this, but you don't have a mom to do it."

"Don't," I warn him. I know exactly what is coming.

"I'm going to anyway," he laughs. "It's tradition. You're a woman now. Congratulations!"

I glower at him and he gives me an amused smile. "No I'm not," I finally say. "I'm just a kid with woman problems that I don't want."

He chuckles. "That's one way to look at it. You *do* know what this means, right?"

I take a deep breath. I hope he doesn't start this now. He's the kind of guy who has no trouble saying what he wants, no matter how embarrassing it might be. "What?" I ask fearfully.

"This means you have to stay away from guys like me. I know what they think and it's not good."

"Please don't share," I plead.

His face falls. "Do you not like me or something?" I mean, it's okay if you don't, but I'd rather you tell me so it's out there in the open. You glare at me a lot like you're angry I'm around, and you never really want to talk. And when you do, you're rude to me."

I burst out laughing and can't stop myself. I don't know why, but I think it's so hilarious that he would even think that when the truth is, I like him so much it hurts. It's an awful feeling to find the perfect guy for you, and then realize he's unreachable. If only I were lucky enough to be this Tina he talks so much about. Then I start to freak out. If he thinks I don't like him, then that will only make things worse. I don't want him to think I don't want him around. I've been mean to hide my real feelings, which I'm really confused about. Does my staring really look angry? That's not good at all. But I can't tell him the truth. I become overwhelmed and don't know how to answer him.

"What?" he asks, panicking. "Why are you laughing?"

I catch my breath a minute. "It's just funny. I think you're very interesting. You have a different outlook on life than most, and every minute something very unique comes out of your mouth." I find that a suitable reply, given my situation.

"Is that good or bad? Because I really get the vibe you don't like me, and I don't get that from Matty or Kelly."

I start laughing again, but this time I hear it behind me too. I spin around to see Matty cracking up. He's thinking the same thing as me! But how? How much does he know that he hasn't told me?! This day is not turning out well.

"Why is that so funny?" Andy exclaims. By the look on his face, he's really lost. I guess that makes me a good actress.

"You wouldn't get it," Matty answers. Why didn't he tell me he knows for sure? "Jenna, I came to see if I could have a private chat with you. I've had time to think and feel awful."

This is unexpected. "Sure." I hop off the stump and follow him.

"You can't leave me hanging like this!" Andy calls, but we keep walking. Some things just can't be explained.

Matty and I find a nice soft, sand patch where there are no sticks, shells, or rocks, and sit down. I wait for him to start. "I'm sorry I reacted the way I did," he apologizes. "That was stupid."

"It's okay. I expected it."

"It's just that I never really thought of you much as being a woman someday like Mom, and it freaked me out. I mean, I know you're a girl and all, but I never thought you would like guys, get your period, and maybe someday a long time from now, having a baby. All these things are happening to you at once, like you're growing up, and I snapped. I didn't know how to handle this one. This all sounds really ridiculous, and it's no excuse for my actions, but it's the truth."

I smile. I'm so glad he's my twin. "It's really no big deal Matty. I don't want to think about what goes on with you either." We both laugh and Andy walks by pouting on his way back to camp. I feel bad for him. He's so lost.

When he's out of earshot, Matty suggests, "You should really tell that poor soul how you *really* feel."

"What are you talking about?" I try to act like he's making things up.

He lowers his eyes at me. "Come on Jenna. I know you too much to believe that you don't know what I'm saying."

"Just explain."

"You're my twin and I know when you're acting strange that something is going on inside you. You do like Andy more than Kelly and I, and don't even try to deny it, because I'll know you're lying."

I sigh. "Okay, you're right."

"And?"

"He's pretty hot and I love his personality. He is just plain awesome and I have a weird crush. But he never needs to know about that, okay?" I hold up my fist to show I mean business, but he just laughs at me.

"I knew it!" he exclaims. "But I don't get it. He's really goofy looking. That is your type?"

I gasp. "What?! He's beautiful inside and out. And yes, he's exactly my type, not that that's any of your business."

"Whatever you say," he laughs. "I will admit he's cool, but he's not a supermodel."

"Well obviously many other girls agree with me. He's had many girlfriends and that girl in the Candy Kitchen even gave him her number. So you must have troubled vision."

"Or you're just drawn to strange people."

I nod in agreement. "That's true."

We burst out laughing again until our sides hurt. It feels really good. "You know something?" I ask when I get myself together. "I'm really lucky to have you as a brother."

He smiles. "I'm pretty lucky to have you too, even if you creep me out sometimes."

"Oh thank you."

"What about me?" Kelly asks. I turn around to see him standing behind me. His hair is all messed up and he's clutching Salamander close to his chest. He must have just woken up after that long night they had. That reminds me to ask Matty about that. I pull Kelly into my arms and say, "You're the best little brother any girl could have."

He smiles wide and I tickle his belly. He screams in laughter, which is contagious for me. "Or a boy," Matty adds. He puts his arm around my shoulders. "I still say you tell Andy about your little crush."

I shrug. "Who knows? Maybe I will."

23

Andy

I fall back on my bed in complete and utter exhaustion. It had been another hard day. Not only did I not get home last night because I stayed out with Matty and Kelly until 3 am teaching them necessary survival skills, but I had to deal with Jenna's "woman problems" all day. I got woken up far before I needed to, and then I had to have a little fight with Matty because of his immaturity problems. I really like those kids, but they're much harder than I expected. Especially Jenna. I knew she was going to be difficult because girls usually are when they're teenagers, and even afterward for that matter. But she is giving me so many mixed signals. She tells me how cool I am and compliments me, and then she snaps and says mean things to me. I'm pretty sure she doesn't like me and just is too nice to tell me straight, but I can't be sure. Maybe she just has opening up issues because she's lost so many people. Tina walks down the hallway and when she sees me, stops in the doorway.

"Kids tire you out?" she asks.

I nod. "They're so hard! I can't remember being that difficult when I was that age. I know Stacy was, but I hope I wasn't like that."

She walks in and lies down next to me. "Try teaching them five days a week all year. You love them, but sometimes they're frustrating."

"You can say that again."

"Try teaching..."

"Tina!" I yell to stop her. She bursts into a fit of giggles. I've had too much of that for one day.

"Why would a girl laugh if you ask if she doesn't like you?" I ask suddenly. She stops giggling for a minute to stare at me, and then laughs even harder.

"What?!" I yell. "Jenna did the same thing and so did Matty."

"You really don't know the answer to that?"

I shake my head. "I wouldn't be asking you if I did."

"You don't know girls at all then. And that's why it's so funny."

"Can you please just answer me?" I ask. "I'm really confused and frustrated, and it would make me feel better if you would stop laughing at me."

She keeps laughing anyway. "You're so cute when you're mad!"

I slap my forehead. "You are no help at all!"

"Ask Jenna what you just asked me, and I'm sure she will give you the same answer I would have. I'm not going to tell you for her; that's her job. So ask her."

I cross my arms and turn away from her. "I can figure it out for myself if you are going to be like that."

"Don't be a little baby," she pleads. I don't turn back around so she changes the subject. "I got the kids something you can bring back."

I peek behind my shoulder to see her pulling a bag out of her overly large purse. It has a store name I don't recognize, so I become even more curious. "Drum roll please," she smiles as she pulls three different clothing pieces out. She shakes out a pair of shorts and I recognize it as boys' board shorts. "These are for Matty. By what I saw of him, I think they will fit." She then pulls out a woman's bikini. "Same with Jenna." Lastly, she reveals a smaller pair of the board shorts. "And Kelly."

I take them from her and size them up. "I think they'll fit, but I can't be sure. Thanks."

"I knew they desperately need them, so I picked them up. I don't have much to do without you around. So tell me if they fit, and if they don't, I'll exchange them for another size." Her facial expression becomes a little sad and I feel awful. I know she misses me, but I have to do my job. The only thing that makes me feel better is that this will all be over by September, and I can get back to my normal life.

I give her a hug and she starts to cry. "You're still my first priority," I assure her. Still, she doesn't seem so assured.

I can't figure out which of the three kids is more excited to see the bathing suits. Matty loves his board shorts, saying he never had ones these cool, and jumps right into the lake. Kelly is excited to be just like Matty and not to have his boxers chafe him. He follows Matty face first into the water. Jenna, I think, won the contest though because she hates wearing Matty's clothes.

She is more than happy to disappear behind a tree and try on her new bikini. I can tell she's never had a women's one by the look on her face-extremely excited. She jumps out from behind the tree when she's finished changing and spins around. I give her a thumbs up sign and her face lights up. She runs after her brothers and stops right at the edge of the rocks, teetering to keep from falling in face first.

"What's wrong?" I call.

"I forgot about my situation." She drops to a sitting position, hugging her knees. I run over and sit next her. I can see a tear slowly drop from the corner of her eye and run down her cheek. I wish I could comfort her, just like I wished I could last night with Tina. I'm afraid of her reaction if I touch her though.

"This sucks," she sniffs. "I feel like I'm wasting my life."

I stare at Matty and Kelly swimming around under the water and laughing like crazy. They don't even understand the troubles their sister is going through. "Boys are so lucky!" she continues. "They get all 52 weeks in each year when I only get 40. This means, if you want to really add it up, if I had this for 37 years-13 to 50-and you subtract twelve weeks from each of those years, I waste eight and a half years of my life to this. So really, I have a potential to only live about 91 years, if I even make that."

I don't know what to say to that. I've never heard of someone doing that math before. "You're only going to depress yourself if you think of it that way."

"It's true, isn't it?!" she yells, and I rock back a little. She grabs her hair with both hands and pulls. "It isn't fair!" I can't stand to watch this.

I grab her hands and pull them back around her knees. "Look," I say, fixing her hair so it doesn't stick up in spikes. "Don't live by the rules. Just jump in and forget about it. That way you're not wasting your life."

She just stares at me, so I continue. "Fight back and you'll feel better. Jump in the lake."

"Really?" She doesn't believe I'm telling her that.

"Yeah! Just change when you're done and you'll be fine. I live like this because I believe that with any moment you could die, that I can't waste a moment. I tell people everything I need to say, and do everything I want to do. Except for a bunch of things." I realize I'm pretty much lying about that. I haven't done a lot of things I want to, but I just want to cheer her up. "I'm not a good example. What I'm saying is live in the moment. Just do it and do it now!"

"Okay!" she screams. She stands up, turns around so her back faces the lake, and falls in backwards. She makes a line of waves as she submerges in the water. It looks like something out of a movie. She comes up spitting water and laughing just like her brothers. "You're right. That *did* make me feel better!"

I smile and dip my feet in the water. I have my first meeting with a family tomorrow and I'm worried it won't go well. I know that the first family is most likely not going to agree to taking in all three of them, but one can hope. They look like a nice couple that are foster parents and live down the street from me. They've known Tina and me since we moved here and are more than happy to meet with me about adopting the kids. Lucky for me, my dad is too stubborn and self-centered to post the kids' pictures in the newspaper or the plain old television news. He wants to do it himself and get publicity, so he refuses to have someone help him and give them a reward. I keep telling him he must, which is perfect because he'll always do the opposite of what I tell him. If he had listened to me, I would never have a chance to find the kids a home. Who wants to adopt three criminals anyway? I just will tell everyone that the kids are unavailable until further notice and hope they are agreeable. It's a long shot, but if I find the right people, they will take the children under any circumstances.

I watch the kids for hours, my mind racing, and I don't even realize Jenna has gotten out and is standing next to where I am sitting, until she's tapping me on the shoulder. I snap out of my own head and look up. The sun has set and Matty and Kelly are running for camp. Jenna has already changed into her lounge wear and is holding a bag of chips. Where have I been?

"What's on your mind?" She asks, munching.

"All I have to do. I have the first family meeting tomorrow."

"Best of luck to you for our sake. Want some?"

I take a chip from her outstretched hand. "Sorry I couldn't get you guys some dinner. You should have woken me up from my day dream."

"Oh we were fine. I actually came because I thought about what you said earlier."

I raise my eyebrows and pat the spot on the rock next to me. "That's a little uncomfortable."

"Okay." I climb down off the rock and lay down in the sand, a nice lump supporting my head. I fold my hands, place them on my stomach, and cross my ankles. Jenna joins me.

"You said that you always have to tell people what you want before it's too late and you regret it," she says. "And I have something I need to tell you."

I turn my head so I can see her face, but she's staring up at the starry night sky. I look up at the moon and smile. When I was a little kid, I used to think that someone on the moon had all the answers. "What is it?" I ask, since she is silent.

She sighs heavily. "It's about that question about me not liking you."

"Oh no."

"No, don't say that. You were wrong; I do like you. Maybe a little more than I should." She says the last part so quiet I'm not sure I really heard it. I can feel her looking at me though, so I must have.

"What do you mean by that?"

"Ummm...uhhh," she stutters. "I sort of have a...um...a little...uh..."

"What?" I ask impatiently.

"A little crush on you," she squeaks. "Okay, more than a little. You have to be the most gorgeous guy I have ever seen, and I love your quirks. It's like you get me more than anyone else ever has, and I love that. I mean Matty loves me, but he doesn't understand the way I am, the way my mind works, but with your whole music thing you do, and I think that's what attracts me to you. And I know it may be wrong because you're twice my age, but I can't help it. It's just the way I feel, and I thought you should know that so you don't think I don't like you. Because I do, it's just I act mean when I'm trying to hide I like someone, and I'm sorry for that. I won't do that anymore now that you know. And I'm really upset because it's like you're the coolest guy that has ever stepped foot on this Earth to me, and I can't have you. That hurts me. I don't think I'll ever find someone as good as you, and I'm really jealous of Tina. It's stupid, but it's true. Can I meet Tina sometime? You could bring her out here."

She is speaking so fast I can hardly catch the words. "Wow, slow down."

"Sorry, I talk fast when I'm nervous. And I ramble."

I laugh. "I understand. You really like me that much?"

"Um...yeah. More than you will ever understand."

I nod calmly to keep from showing how I really feel. "You shouldn't be jealous of Tina. I'm not all that great, I promise you. You will definitely find someone better than me. I'll ask Tina if she wants to come if you really want to meet her."

"I don't think I will find someone as good as you. You're like my dream guy. Does that weird you out?"

"I'm honored you think I'm beautiful and a perfect guy. I'm not."

"Really, what do you think about all this? I really want to know."

I smile, and it stretches from ear to ear. "I'm flattered and really relieved. I thought you hated me around or something, but I was dead wrong, and now I understand why you were laughing. I'm not confused anymore, which made me feel better. And I think that's really cool you're crushing on me. I've never had that before and I like the feeling. Do you think I'm sexy?"

The moonlight shows her cheeks get really red quite fast. She presses her lips to keep from giggling. "Yes," she whispers, the way Spencer has to all the time.

I start laughing to myself. Why am I enjoying this so much? I'm creeping myself out a little. I guess I always wanted to be that guy that all the girls had a poster of on their wall. "Well, that's good to know. You're beautiful yourself. And I'm not a pervert or anything."

She blushes more and says, "Why, thank you," through a fit of giggles. "You seriously aren't creeped out by me?"

"No! I really think it's cool."

"Once again, you amaze me. You're so different and I love that." And to think I thought he was immature. He just is in the exact right moments.

"Yeah, it's another one of my theories on life. If you're easy going with anything that hits you, you will get through it easier than if you have a reaction. That's why I didn't like the way Matty acted yesterday."

"You have a very interesting outlook on life."

"Listen," I say. I want to share my beliefs on life with her. "I believe that we're all connected to each other in some way because we're all made of the same things, just arranged differently. I have a strong love toward everything on this planet. We're all miracles, even the planet is. What I can't wrap my head around, is that billions of years ago, there was nothing. And I know that for sure because now we're something, and something always has to be nothing once to become something, right? Imagine nothing. Not even outer space."

"Wow," she breathes. "I never even thought about that."

"I know. We have trouble with nothing because we can't measure it, but there once was nothing. Then came us, and we're all different, yet we're all the same. It's really cool. I even have a theory on why we have different ideas of beauty."

"I'm listening."

"I think that we all see the world differently, and I mean literally. I think like all our minds are different and all our eyes are different. We see the main part of things the same, but the details are a little different. That's why we disagree so much on what is beautiful and what is ugly. Personally, I don't think anything is ugly because everything is a miracle, but that's beside the point. What I'm saying is everyone sees the sky in a different shade of blue. We all know it's blue, but we'll never agree on exactly what shade. Do you get the message I'm trying to convey?"

She takes a deep breath to try and let all this information sink in her mind. "So you're saying you don't look the same to Matty as you do to me, or even yourself. And that's why we have different opinions on taste?"

I nod, excited that she understands. It's a hard concept to explain to just anyone. "Exactly. And we'll never know if it's true because we'll only ever be able to see from one pair of eyes."

She holds her head. "I'm too tired for all this. It's amazing, but it hurts my brain!"

"Yeah, well I had a lot of time to contemplate these things about life while I had the chemo dripping into my veins. It's the most boring thing I've ever done. I'm extremely ADHD, so that was the only thing that kept me from going insane."

"You're ADHD? I never would have guessed," she says sarcastically. "You can't stay still for more than two seconds."

I laugh. "You should see me without my meds. I literally bounce off the walls. I'm like a Mexican jumping bean on overdrive. I can never forget to take my meds or else there will be trouble. I can't control myself. I also have to take medicine for my lungs, so don't let me forget that either."

"I won't," she assures me, her eyes glistening. "I would like to see you on overdrive though."

"Don't try it," I warn. "You *will* be sorry."

"You know what?" she asks. I shake my head no. "With all this you've said, I am positive you're the coolest guy to ever live. And I love the way you look from my unique vision."

"That's good," I smile. This makes me want to fix all their problems more than ever.

24

Matty

I flop onto the sand in a desperate attempt to catch a squirrel. My arms come up empty, and I get sand in my mouth. I spit it out, but some remains on my tongue. I rise to my feet, wipe the sand off of the front of me, and crouch farther into the woods. I spot a rabbit cleaning its fur and decide to take a shot at it. I hide behind a nearby tree and carefully plan my attack. Rabbits are very attentive, so I have to be almost silent and invisible. I take a few steps forward and the rabbit freezes. I freeze with it, and it stares at me out of the corner of its eye, unable to move. I yell as I attempt to pounce on it. My fingers graze its puffy little tail as it hops far out of my sight. I curse and lay my head in the sand. I have been at it for at least an hour, choosing prey, jumping towards it just as Andy had, and making a fool out of myself. I figured earlier that if he could do it, I could. It can't be that hard, I told myself, but I had been wrong. Obviously, I'm not as much of a man as he is. That's a real ego kicker.

"Maybe you should start with butterflies," Andy suggests, standing over me suddenly. I roll over onto my back and stare up at him. He has an amused look on his face and it makes me angry. Just because I can't do it now, doesn't mean I won't learn. I'm determined and will make it happen.

"What?" I ask rudely, rising to my feet. I brush off my clothes, face, and arms and wait for him to answer me.

"I said, maybe you should start with butterflies."

"I heard what you said," I say in disgust. "What do you mean by that?"

He shrugs. I don't know why he's making me so mad; maybe it's that I failed and he did it so flawlessly. I feel competitive with him for some odd reason. Maybe it has something to do with Jenna, but that doesn't really make much sense. "I'm saying I started with catching butterflies when I was a boy. You can't go straight for the hard level; you have to start with beginner's prey so you can get the hang of it."

I don't want to start easy. I want to be able to just do it, like I have my whole life. I put off riding my bike for years because I didn't want to fall and admit I couldn't do it first try. As a result, I was an eleven year old with training wheels and was humiliated anyway. "I wish you could just teach me how to go for the big guys," I mutter under my breath, a little embarrassed.

"I came here for just that," he admits. "I want to have man to man time to show you the ways."

I raise my eyebrows. "Really?" This should be interesting.

"Yeah, I thought that since I spent the whole day yesterday having a stimulating conversation with your sister, I could spend the day with you, and then tomorrow with only Kelly. I have to teach you some lessons."

To be honest, I am a tiny bit excited. I want to get into the mysterious mind of Andy and be much like him, and this is my chance. I wonder what he will teach me. What are the ways of being a man? I thought you just learned that when you turned 18 because that's when you technically where no longer a kid. Most guys are still kids mentally, so I guess that wouldn't work. I begin to think maybe every boy my age has a mentor that tells them how to be a cool teenager. If so, I got the best one of the bunch. At least in my eyes.

"When is your birthday?" he asks.

I find that as a very random question, but I answer anyway. "September 24th."

"Ahh, so you'll be 14 in a few short months."

I nod. I am ecstatic, along with Jenna. Each new age is a new experience to look forward to for us.

"That means you're no longer the baby teenager. You're now on your way to being the big teenager. If you act like the baby teenager when you're not anymore, that just leads to trouble. I'm here to show you how to act like the older teenagers."

I grin. "I'm more than willing to learn."

"Lesson 1," he starts. "We have to set a scenario. It's your birthday and a hot girl asks to celebrate it with you. What do you do?"

I have no idea. I haven't made much contact with girls my age, except a few words to Jenna's friends when they were over. I don't know much of what they think or want to hear. I'm suddenly afraid that I'm the only one who doesn't know. I try to fight off a panic attack. "Say sure."

He rubs his eyes with his hand. He shakes his head like I'm a little boy who knows nothing about the world. Which might be true, I come to realize. "No, that's not what they want to hear. They want you to say 'That would be great. I would love to spend my birthday with you over any other girl.' They'll go 'awww, he's so sweet' and before you know it, you have the hottest girl as your own."

I'm trying to absorb all of it. "Okay, so what do I do when we get where we're going?"

"She comes with a gift of course, and you show up with something for her. You use your charm to get inside her heart. What are you good at?"

"Um, science?"

He runs his hands through his hair in frustration. I watch it stick straight up and some slowly fall back down to his head, forming a miniature Mohawk. I wish mine did that. "Unless you have a science girl, she isn't going to want to hear science equations. It even takes a special one to appreciate my life theories. You have to do something romantic."

"Like what?"

"Well I write a song for the girl and that totally gets her."

Uh oh. "I can't do anything like that."

His face twists into many different expressions as he thinks of what I could do. His face lights up and I know something very scary could be coming. "You can write me a poem, right?"

My face becomes a little unsure. "I wrote some stupid ones for school."

"A song is like a poem with a melody. If you can't get the melody, you can still write the poem. Girls seem to like corny, so it's okay if it's really stupid, as long as it came from your mind. If they find you copying off of someone, you're in a lot of trouble."

"Ok, I guess I could try," I admit.

He pats me on the back. "Good, that's your homework. Give me one by the weekend." Today is Wednesday. I have barely three days.

"Now for lesson two. Once that is over and you have her hooked, you invite her to the beach. The beach is a very good place to assess the body situation. But remember she'll be looking at you too so you have to look cool. That is why I'm about to teach you the proper way to remove a shirt."

I almost burst out at the sound of the last part. "There's a proper way?" I ask, amused.

"There's many ways to do it, but I've learned there is only one way that you'll look good doing it." He sees me trying extra hard to hold in a laugh and adds, "Stop laughing at me. This is serious stuff."

That makes me laugh even harder, and I can't stop myself this time. "Sorry," I say, trying to catch my breath. "It's just you never cease to amaze me."

He chuckles a little. "Okay, I'll laugh at myself. I admit it's a little weird, but it's true."

"So how then?"

He holds up a finger to show me to wait a moment. "I'll show you."

He steps back a little so he's not in the path of any trees. I stand waiting. I'm really curious how one may take their shirt off to look good. Honestly, I never thought for a second about how I took off my shirt. I just did it and went about my business. Then again, Andy thinks about a lot of things that not many other people do. That's one of the things that makes him so awesome. There will never be another one of him, and he makes sure of it with his copyright. I think again about how I want to be like that. I want to be memorable to everyone I cross paths with and be proud of my uniqueness. He turns around, ready for his performance. What I see next should be something out of an episode of Baywatch. He pulls the striped button down polo shirt he's wearing up from the bottom so it turns inside out over his head. Then once it has cleared his head, it hangs in a straight line from shoulder to shoulder across his chest. He takes it off his right arm, slides it over so it is hanging from his left elbow, and flings it like a rubber band off his left hand. It flies into the sand in a perfect little ball. It was obviously something he has practiced many times before, because it was all in slow motion and in little steps. He smiles, knowing it came out well this time, and even gives a little bow with one arm behind his back. I clap and start laughing. It's a bit funny to me that someone would put all this time into such a simple task, but I have to admit he did look good, and I would consider trying it myself.

"Bravo!" I say, clapping like a very rich man who just saw a Broadway show.

He laughs with me and retrieves his shirt off of the ground. He shakes the sand off it, flips it back right side up, and puts it on again. He will probably need to show me that many times before I get the hang of it. "I'm glad you enjoyed my performance. Now it's your turn to try it."

I take a deep breath. Strangely, I'm a little bit nervous. It comes back to my 'want to do everything right the first try' attitude. I really need to shake that because almost always, it isn't happening. "I really don't remember where to start."

"Okay," he says, suddenly becoming a teacher. "Follow my lead. I'll do it really slow so you can keep up." I don't think you *could* do it any slower, I think to myself.

We stand side by side, out of the way of trees, and he lets me watch one more time. I try to memorize what he does so I can do it myself in a desperate situation. Then he lets me do it with him. We go through the steps, me stumbling through, trying to follow his flawless moves. Finally, after about ten or more tries, I get it right and jump up and down in achievement. It's harder than it looks, and I never thought removing a shirt could be difficult! I attempt to do it without him beside me to watch. Nervously, I use what I've learned to do it by myself. To both of our surprise, I make it look easy.

"Nice job kid," he compliments me. It feels good to do something like him. "Now remember to use that when you impress a female. It will catch their attention in a good way, I promise you."

"Lesson three," he moves on before I can say anything more about it. Obviously he thinks I can handle it. I hope his judgment is right. "If the girl doesn't ask you, you need to have a way to ask her out."

I feel my hands shake. These kinds of things scare me. I know I'll have to do it very soon, and that's even more frightening. "I have no idea how to interact with girls."

"Don't worry. That's why I'm here." He sits down in the sand and I join him. All those shirt lessons tired us both out. "The only thing I can tell you is to be yourself. I make a funny comment and most of the time that works out, but if that's not your thing, you don't do it. Whatever comes, you do, and if she rejects you, just brush it off and tell yourself that she's missing out on a lot. She won't find anyone as good as you and that's the truth. You're a cool kid."

I blush a little. "Thanks Andy. I know, although not nearly as much as you."

"I'm not as great as you might think." I don't try to argue with him. It's pointless.

"I do have one question," I say. He looks over, inviting me to ask him anything. That's a comfortable feeling, being able to share my worries and thoughts with him. He's taking the place where my dad was missing. "I see all these older kids who are really popular and stuff and all the girls and guys like them, and I want to be like them. I want to act and look cool like that. I'm sure you were one of those kids, so I was hoping you could guide me."

He shakes his head vigorously, and I feel a wave of disappointment wash over me. "You're wrong about that. I was the dork with no friends who got beat up in the parking lot. The guys you want to be like are usually tools, and the other kids only like them because they make themselves known more than the others. Trust me; you don't want to be like that. But you don't want to be like I was either. My dad dressed me like an idiot and sheltered me so much that I had a rude awakening when I had to go to public high school. All I can tell you is to just be how you want to be. Don't listen to what anyone tells you, and be your own leader. Followers end up failing in life. If you're happy with yourself, then you will be cool. And like I said, you are already cool. You just need a little confidence and you'll be a big hit."

I smile. That sounds good. "I am myself already, but most kids don't seem to like me."

"Most kids your age are stupid. When you get older, you'll understand that. The kids that do like you are the real friends who will stick with you and succeed in life. The tools will end up in jail, and the girls like that will end up pregnant."

I laugh and tip my head back. "You're honest. I give you that."

"I'm not that great of a guy, but I love myself, and that's what makes me memorable. I'm finally on my way to becoming my own person and not a clone of my father."

"I want to be like you," I admit. He finds that as a surprise.

"In a way you are," he says. "You're unique and not afraid to be it. You just need a few touch ups."

My brow furrows. "What do you mean?"

He stands up and pulls me up with him. He drags me by my arm a little way through the woods until we reach a wall of shrubs that stand at least four feet off the ground. He sticks his head through a little hole and looks around. Then he reaches his hand in and pulls out a little duffle bag. He unties the top and the sides fall away. It reveals a lot of clothing items and a few other hygiene products. I'm scared of what is coming next.

"How did that get there?" I inquire to avoid what I really want to ask.

"I hide stuff for later use. I know my way around this forest better than anyone. I used to hide here when we used to come down here for vacation. I was an adventurous little kid. But that's beside the point. What we have here is your own personal make-over."

Oh no. This is what I was afraid of happening. I'm not big on change and this especially. "I don't know if I want a make-over," I say, backing away slowly. I have my hands up in front of me in my defense.

He stops from moving any farther away. "Calm down. Not a total make-over. Just a few minor changes to make you hot."

Hot was never a word I associated with myself. "Ok, like what?"

He sighs. "Where to begin?" He searches through the pile of items and pulls out a pair of faded jeans. "Let's start with the clothes. These are always good." He grabs a t-shirt with a surf shop logo on it and holds both up to me. He nods and smiles. I guess that's a good sign. He grabs a baseball hat with red, yellow, and black stripes and places it on my head. He twists it around until he finds the right angle. He steps back to admire his work and strokes an imaginary beard. Then he strips me down and replaces my clothes with the new ones. A new pair of Vans tie up sneakers is placed on my feet. He messes around with my hair and gives me a necklace and a few bracelets, one for each wrist. I just stand there as he transforms me. Finally he throws me a stick of deodorant and a bottle of cologne. I grab them in both hands as an instinct and instantly wish I hadn't. I don't use this stuff. This is for older kids, not me.

"What's this for?" I ask cautiously.

He smirks. "If you want to be like me, you have to take care of yourself. I take longer to get ready than Tina sometimes, and I take pride in how well-kept I am."

I nod in an 'oh I see' teasing way. I still don't think it is for me. "Just try it," he urges. "If you don't like that kind of stuff, then you don't have to use it. But I do suggest the deodorant so you don't stink."

I reluctantly apply both to my body and throw them back to him. He puts them in the bag and hands me a razor and shaving cream. This is getting really out of my comfort zone. Maybe I shouldn't have asked. "I don't think I need this."

"I know. You will at some point, so I'm making sure you are prepared. You saw how Jenna is getting older. You will too."

That sends shivers down my back. How come everything is easy in elementary school and then once you hit middle school, it's like reality hits, slapping you in the face with all these things at once? I know Jenna probably has it worse than me, but it's still hard. I place the shaving supplies in the bag, careful not to touch the blade. My shirt does smell really good now. "I think I like this stuff," I admit, pulling the collar up to my nose.

"It's my favorite," he laughs. "And Tina loves it so I thought you might like some."

I nod. "Thanks."

He takes a final item out-a mirror. It is a little hand mirror, but I can still move it down me to see how I look. I do exactly that and am surprised at what I see. I actually look like an almost 14 year old should and I like it. I think I'll take Andy's advice and use this but still be myself. I actually start to believe I'm actually pretty good-looking. My black hair is now growing longer, so only my earlobes stick out under it and the bangs almost reach my eyebrows. I love it this length, halfway between just cut and ready to be cut. It's my natural color, thanks to my father's dominant gene, and it compliments my royal blue eyes perfectly. I'm pretty athletic compared to most kids my age too, because I'm always out doing something instead of using electronics. They usually show time and I steer clear of that. This adventure has made me pretty ripped too and has given me bronzed skin. Man do I look good. It's a very good feeling, one I've never had before. Andy seems impressed too because he gives a grin and a thumbs up sign. I can't wait to show Jenna and see her surprise at my transformation. Even Kelly might say a few extra words than usual to compliment me. I just wish Kristina were here to see me. She might say how I'm even cuter than before and how she didn't think that was possible. That would make me feel good all over. I have to remember to track down that boyfriend of hers so I can dispose of him and run off into the sunset with my Krissy.

I smile in my thought, and Andy snaps me back to reality. "I'm glad you like it."

I shake myself out of my admiration. "Thank you so much. I'm much more confident and ready to take on the world. I think I'll tackle that poem in no time flat."

"Yeah, that's the spirit. Just think of the coolest girl you know and let your ideas flow from your brain to your hand."

"I know who she is." There's no doubt in my mind who the coolest girl I know is. Even if she is basically a woman.

He grins. "So do I. I can never tell her how I feel through my mouth, and that's why I use writing. She has to know somehow, and that's the best way I can do it."

I can tell he loves Tina very much. I hope I can feel like that someday in the near future. Maybe I'll never have Krissy, but I can still hope to find someone as wonderful as her.

Andy's face goes from pure contentment to panic in seconds. "Look, the sun is going down. No, I promised Tina I'd be home for dinner."

"Uh, oh," I say. "You better get going. I can hold down the fort for the night."

He smiles for a minute, but it doesn't reach his eyes this time. I can tell he's very worried he upset his girl. He waves me a quick goodbye and runs through the forest full speed in the direction of the road. He usually parks a little ways down the street where no one but locals really know, so it's not easy to find, and walks down to where we are. I know it will at least take another half hour for him to get home. I pray that whoever this Tina girl is, that she will understand his situation and forgive him for being late. That's my little way of helping when he helped me so much today. I strut back to camp for the night with my new look. I can hardly wait to see and hear my siblings' reactions. I can't help but smile from ear to ear, and I haven't done that in a long time. It makes me feel much better, and for a minute, I forget all my issues.

25

Andy

I make it home as fast as I can, and my lungs hurt as I race through the door. I used to be quite a runner in my teens, but ever since my recovery, my lungs haven't been what they used to be. They still work fine and I can run and am symptom free, but sometimes I get more winded than when I was younger. I know the reason for that and have to accept it. This time I ignore my lungs though and run harder than I have in a long time. This is a very worthy cause. Tina is very big on me making dinner on time when I say I will, and I'm afraid that since I've let her down so many times before in the past month, that she'll get fed up with me. I can't let that happen. She's my everything. That is why I frantically throw open the front door, leaving my Chucks by the staircase, and race into the kitchen. Everything is dark, and I see the kitchen has already been used and cleaned up. There's a small plate on the stove with Reynolds wrap covering it for me. I open it up and see that she cooked pasta with Italian bread on the side. I throw them in the microwave because no matter what, I'm hungry and can't waste perfectly good food. I search for Tina as the food spins round and round in the dim light of the microwave. Something about the house seems very vacant, like it's been abandoned and left dark for hours. I peer into every room downstairs, flicking on the lights and calling her name. This is very unusual for her, and I get an uneasy feeling in the pit of my stomach. Since there is no sign of her downstairs, I make my way up the wooden staircase and into the small upstairs we have. There is very little floor space because we have a cat walk that looks down on the living room and most of the rest of the downstairs. She has to be somewhere up here, I tell myself. I search in all the bedrooms. There's no sign of her. I really start to panic as I finally look into the upstairs bathroom. The room is dark and I instantly turn on the light. I find Tina amidst the bubbles of the tub with her eyes closed and head leaned back. Her eyes flicker open when the lights come on, and she stares at me a few seconds before turning away.

I breathe a sigh of relief, but it comes too soon. This is still peculiar, and I know I'm in the dog house about now. "Why didn't you answer me when I called you? I thought something happened."

She shrugs, like this is something she does every day. "I needed some time to relax, and I spend so much of my day and night alone that I thought 'what are a couple more minutes as you search for me?'" She smiles crookedly. This stunt I pulled snapped her somehow.

I kneel beside her on the tile floor. "I'm really sorry. I was teaching Matty things and time slipped away. I saw the sun going down and ran home as quick as I could. I hope you're not upset."

She snickers. "Of course I'm upset. But it's okay. I understand that you're priority is the kids right now, and there's no use trying to convince you I mean more."

The microwave beeps and we stare at each other. I wish it would stop; it's ringing in my ears like the words Tina just said. I can't tell her how much she means to me in a lifetime. I give her a signal to wait there and she looks at me like 'where else am I going to go?' I flump down the stairs and into the kitchen. I take the plate of food out, poke around in it to see if it cooked the whole way through, and bring it along with utensils back up to the bathroom. I take a cross-legged position beside the tub, the plate balanced on my lap and the fork in my left hand. I take pride in being a south paw. I got the palm tree tattoo on my left hand to say that being left-handed is like paradise. I take a bite and compliment her as always on her good cooking. She just nods this time instead of beams.

"Are you okay?" I ask through a mouthful.

"I'll be over it soon enough," she assures me. "I'm just really lonely lately and this summer has pretty much sucked for me."

"I know baby, but this is everything for me. If I pull this off, I'll finally be able to escape from my dad and go after my music career. I promise you that I will be back as soon as September hits. And you are my first priority because I love you."

She rolls her eyes in disgust. "So far you've been all reassuring words and nothing has changed. It's late July and I've spent about an hour a day with you. This is my only time off, and I look forward to spending it with you. But I get nothing. You're devoted to a bunch of criminal kids, and I try to help you out. I feel like you're just saying you love me to keep me around so you're not alone at night. It's just words and no meaning, and I'm sick of it honestly. If you don't start showing that you mean what you're saying, I'm not going to be able to take living in this huge house with nothing to do anymore."

The words shock me. The thought of her leaving never occurred to me. It was some scary thing that happened to other more foolish guys, but I think I'll have Tina forever. It just starts to occur to me that maybe I have been one of those foolish guys lately. I haven't appreciated what a good girl I've got and maybe I could spend a little less time with the kids. I'll bond a little bit with Kelly tomorrow and surprise Tina with coming home early. The kids did take care of themselves pretty well before I showed up. What's a half a day? I need to make sure I don't lose the most important thing. I smile, thinking about how surprised she'll be. I'll show her what she really means, even if it is just a fraction of what I really feel inside.

I grab her hand and feel bubbles on it. "I mean every word I say. It's just that things have been hard lately, and I'm losing sight of what means the most-you. I give you my word that you can kick me to the curb if things don't change soon."

She sighs deeply and thinks it over a moment. I try to wait patiently, but even with the medicine, I still can't stay still to save my life. I fidget all around and finally dumping my plate on the floor. The fork clatters on the tile, making her laugh. "What would I ever do without you anyway?"

I smile, a little embarrassed that she thinks of me as a clown. But whatever works, right? I clean up my mess and set it nicely on the sink. I won't be able to stand it there for long because it's out of place and I have a weird obsession with cleaning, but for now it will do. I turn to her. "I know I couldn't live here without you. I can understand how lonely it must be."

She nods. "Yeah. Did I tell you you're dad stopped by today?"

My eyes widen to the point I think they're going to fall out of my head. My mouth falls open and my heart pounds. That is the worst possible thing that could have happened. Well, not the worst, but close. I can't believe she's just telling me now!

I choke on my own spit a bit as I try to regain my composure. "Why didn't you say anything until now?"

"I needed you to focus on me for a little while before you freak out about this again."

"That's understandable. What did he say? What happened? Wow, my hands are shaking like crazy!" And they are! They tremble and I have to hold them behind my back to stop them. So many things could go wrong in this scenario that could mess up my entire future.

"Calm down," she says. "He just dropped by to see how you were doing. You're mom is concerned about your long leave of sickness. Maybe if you would have made it home on time, you could have pulled off the 'on your deathbed' façade."

I glower at her. She doesn't need to rub it in my face. "So what did he say when I wasn't there?"

"He found it surprising, but I'm a reasonable liar so I think I fooled him. I told him that you were on your way to recovery from a very bad case of pneumonia and needed to get some tests done at the hospital. I said I was going to pick you up soon and had to get this dinner done so you could have something to eat when you were done. He offered to come with me, but I told him that seeing him and the thought of how you failed him with the case would only give you unneeded stress. He left with a get better request to you and not a second thought as to if I was deceiving him. I think he just wants you to get better and come back to the case so you two can bond, and the only reason he came over here was for your mother. He totally thinks you're really sick and that you're so upset about losing the kids!"

I grin and relief washes over my entire body. My hands stop shaking and my heart returns to its normal pace. What would I do without her? I would be screwed, I tell myself. It shows I work better with a partner. I wonder if she would like to help me with the kids. Jenna had said she wanted to meet her, and I could spend time with Tina while doing my job. "That's my girl," I compliment her, giving her a high five. Bubbles fly out of the tub, but neither of us care. "You're the best."

She blushes and says, "I know." I'm so glad she's not upset anymore. I hate seeing her like that.

"I can't believe how well you did. That's the greatest. Now I don't have to worry about him interfering for a while. You should really help me out with the kids though. I think you'd like them, and with all your experience, you'd have a blast. You might even find you met them before."

"That sounds fun," she smiles. "Maybe one day when you really need the help. I'm meeting my mom tomorrow for lunch at noon and then we're going shopping, so I can't go then. I loved those bus kids though. I would love to see them again if these are the same ones."

I plan on coming to the lunch tomorrow. "Where are you going to lunch?"

"Just TGI Friday's. It's my mom's favorite, and her birthday is coming up, so I thought I'd take her out on a nice surprise." Little does she know, she'll been in for one herself. I can hardly hide my excitement.

"Nice. Have fun. I'm bonding with the littlest one tomorrow. Any suggestions since you work with them?"

"Give him presents and do fun things that he'll like."

"He's a different kind of kid," I warn her. "He doesn't talk much and keeps to himself."

"Does he have an imagination?"

"Big one."

"Play imaginary war or hunting with him. He'll love it. And then give him a reward once you let him win. Something tells me that'll make him attach to you instantly."

"Thanks," I reply. "I'll do that. You're always helpful."

"That's what I'm here for. I just wish you would do the same thing for me."

"I do and I will," I promise. She smiles and stands straight up out of the tub. My whole mind and body goes crazy as the bubbles run down her and fall into the water. She grabs and towel and steps out. She lets it drain and I continue to stare. What a beauty I have in every way. She has an athletic but curvy figure and the face of an angel. It is perfectly shaped, with defined cheek bones and a gorgeous white smile. Her long eyelashes compliment her turquoise eyes that remind me of the ocean on a tropical island. Her light brown wavy hair, parted slightly to the left, falls on her face and completes the full package. I really cannot afford to lose this one. Between that and how wonderful she is to me, I need to get my act together before I do something that will make her slip through my long, skinny, piano fingers.

As planned, I spend the following day with Kelly. I find he is a very interesting kid as soon

as I get there. Matty and Jenna greet me when I arrive and show me where Kelly is playing. Matty must have told Jenna all about our day yesterday and then how I planned to bond with Kelly today. They both seem very agreeable to that, which makes me feel better. I am worried about spending the day with Kelly. First of all, he's much younger than the other two kids and I don't know how to communicate with a seven year old. Another thing is he's different than any other seven year old I've ever heard about from Tina. He barely talks at all, and he likes to keep to himself. He doesn't seem like he'll be very easy to hang out with, and to be honest, I'm a little nervous. I made such good progress with Matty and Jenna that I can't afford to mess up now. The happy faces of the twins as they lead me to Kelly make me a little less scared.

I push back a few tree branches and spot Kelly sitting cross-legged in the sand. He has his head bent over so his nose almost touches the sand and is poking the sand under his face with a stick. I hear him mumble to himself and my stomach turns. This is going to be rough. My feet don't move any further and I turn around to give a worried look to the twins. Jenna motions me on and I sigh. I feel like a little kid who really wants to get on the big roller coaster, but is just a little too scared.

I take a leap of faith and sit next to him. "What are you up to?"

His head snaps up instantly and he drops the stick. He stares at me scared to death, and I wonder if I did something wrong already. I turn around to see if the twins can help me, but they already disappeared. He continues to stare at me and I smile. He looks away and mumbles, "I wasn't talking to myself."

I almost laugh. So that was why he was so shocked to see me. "I didn't think you were."

He looks at me. "Good," he smiles a tiny bit, but only with his mouth. "I was playing a game where I befriend ants. I coax them to get on my stick and I can see how many I keep on the stick at once. My brother and sister think it is crazy, just like my other game."

"What's that?"

"I roll around in the grass until I can feel it all over my body and the sky seems to be spinning. Then I name all the clouds while lying on my back in the grass. I don't have anyone to play with, so I make up games I can play alone."

"It actually sounds fun." I feel like I'm making progress. I don't think I've ever heard him say this many words in one sitting in the whole month and a half I've known him. That makes me think he likes me.

He nods vigorously, and this time his smile reaches his eyes. It makes me smile. "I don't have any friends so I have to like it." His face falls after he says it.

"Why wouldn't a cool kid like you have any friends?" I really don't get it.

He shrugs. "I'm littler than all the other boys. My mind matured way faster than my body. Mommy used to say that I'm so smart people think I'm not. I started reading when I was only three, started talking at one, but I didn't start walking until I was almost two, if you understand what I'm trying to say."

"Yeah I do. You're saying you're really smart and you have the brain of a ten year old at least, but your body looks and acts only five."

"Exactly, which means I can't do sports like all the other boys. They all call me a girl because I have a girl name and girls can't do sports either. I don't think that's true though because lots of girls can do sports. Some are even better than boys. I think first and second grade boys are just stupid. So I like to spend time with myself. Then I don't have to deal with them. I know everything about myself and would never be mean to me."

"Wow," I breathe. "I never knew you thought all this stuff. When do you turn eight?"

"A little over half a year. My birthday's in March."

"Mine is too." They always say the strangest yet most amazing people are born in March. I think that must be true. "You just taught me something, you know that?"

He looks at me, interested in what he could have taught an adult. "You taught me even little kids can be mean, and it's better to play with yourself and be yourself than to be someone else just so you can fit in with a bunch of idiots. That's a good thing to know."

He grins, obviously proud of himself. He has a smile that is contagious. "I like being with Matty and Jenna too. They're nice to me." He looks down at the stick he dropped and starts picking some of the bark off. "And you," he adds.

I pat his back. "I like you too kid. And you don't have a girl name. Kelly is a name for both girls and boys; it's just not often used for a boy. That makes you unique."

"I like being unique." He looks up at me again and I see a longing in his eyes. He longs for people that love him for who he is and don't think he's weird. He longs for friends, no matter what age they are. He longs for a mom and a dad that he will never get back. I see a lot of my childhood in this kid. I used to long for people who understood me too. The kids used to make fun of me because of the way my dad dressed me, and they were jealous of how smart I was. My imagination used to race. I used to have to put that somewhere, so I used to write little songs. I used to sing them to myself all day long and people would look at me strange. I longed for friends and a mother and father who loved me for that weirdo I was. It's not exactly the same, but it's close. I feel the kid's pain, and I'm sad that he has to feel this stuff so young. Maybe it's because he's so much more mature than all the others his age. He's just another kid trying to find his place in the world.

"I understand how you feel," I tell him. "I used to be just like you when I was a little bit older than you. I have to ask you. Why don't you talk if you have so much to say and you're so intelligent? It makes people think there's something wrong with you."

"I don't tell people things unless I trust them. Usually I have nothing to say. I say things when I need to, but unlike most, I don't need to hear myself all the time. I don't like the sound as much as the sound of other people's voices. I love sound. I've never told anyone what I've told you."

"I'm honored," I say honestly. I even think this kid might know more about life than me.

"And I don't care what people think. I know the truth, and only the people who don't judge me are the ones I trust. I've never said this much to one person in such a short amount of time. You're a cool guy."

"You kids say that a lot to me. I don't think so, but thank you. You're a very interesting group. Matty is a science guy who lives without time, Jenna is a eccentric writer who lives without doctors, and you're little, but very strong, boy who just wants to fit in in the world. I couldn't have gotten a better group."

I think I see him blush a little. "You wanna play one of my games?"

"Sure," I say. "After I give you this." I take out the gift I got him that Tina suggested to do. It's a little hand held video game that makes you go in all of these little doors looking for keys, but some of the doors have monsters in them, and it looked fun. I thought at first it might be too hard for him, but after learning what I have today, I know that is totally wrong. I just hope he likes that kind of stuff.

He takes it from my hand and examines it. He turns it on and it beeps a few times. His face lights up. "I love it! It has cool sounds." My nervousness floods away. I shouldn't have had anything to worry about in the first place. These kids are the best I could ever ask for.

We sit around, trying his video game, cheering when we find a key, and slamming our fists into the ground when a monster kills off one of our lives. When we're finally fed up with it, we decide to try out a few of Kelly's games he made up. I actually come to like some of them, even though I would never do them alone. We laugh the entire day and I feel good inside. I'm making a misunderstood, sad kid's day, and I always feel good when I'm doing a good deed. I even have fun in the process. I have had more fun in the past month and half with these kids than I have in the two years I've been in the police force. It makes me feel severely immature. I never would have guessed that I would have three best friends thirteen years younger than me and more. But mostly it makes me feel awful about where my life is going. If I'm miserable in my job, than I'm miserable half my life. Life's too short to be miserable, and I hope with all my heart that when I'm done with this mission, I can get away from my father and start my own life. It's a little late to start my life, but I have to start somewhere. Better than living a whole life in misery and looking back on my deathbed saying "What the hell was I thinking wasting all that time?" At the end of the day, I've learned a lot. And I am more than ready to surprise Tina and tell her that I will not go back on my word. She is everything to me, and that is something she needs to know before it is too late.

26

Jenna

I wake up in panic. I had a dream where I got lost in the woods, and when I finally found Matty, Kelly, and Andy, they had forgotten who I was. I had had no idea how to fend for myself and was well on my way to starving to death or freezing to death. I feel myself breaking out into a cold sweat and can't control my breathing. I jump to my feet and run around frantically looking for my men. I giggle a little thinking of them as my men, like I'm some kind of polygamist, but I still feel awful. I push myself through the wall of trees to the clearing and get slapped in the face with a few branches. I spot Matty and Andy sitting on the rocks, their feet dangling in the lake, and Kelly swimming near the other end. I breathe a sigh of relief and run full speed toward them.

I struggle to keep my footing on the rocks, but I'm so excited, I barely notice. I slam into a hug in the back of Matty and nearly knock us both into the lake. Matty screams, "Jenna, what are you doing? You almost drowned me!"

I laugh and squeeze him tighter. "I had a nightmare and am so glad to see you."

He pries me off of him. I give up on him and run to the edge to the lake where Kelly is. I beckon Kelly to come to me, and when he does, I give him and even bigger hug, lifting him off the ground. "Okay," he says, thinking I'm acting strange also. "Love you too Jenna."

I let him go and run back to the rocks where Matty and Andy are. I want to give Andy a hug, but I'm afraid that would be too awkward. We've become really good friends in the six or seven weeks we've known each other, but I'm still afraid to touch him like I do my brothers. Instead I sit down between them, my feet dangling also, and smile brightly.

"You were so busy having this big nightmare that you missed breakfast," Matty mutters.

"We're catching lunch now since I ran out," Andy adds. I see for the first time that they're holding handmade fishing poles. They're made out of some sticks and a little fishing line. A few worms hang from each of the ends, and there's a little reel made out of vine and a little bit of plastic. It's pretty clever, and I know it is Andy's idea. He watches a lot of Discovery Channel and puts it to good use.

"Catch anything?"

They both shake their heads. "Not yet, but we're close."

I snicker. "I bet." Matty glares at me. I doubt there's even that many fish in this lake anyway. The lake still seems surreal to me. In fact, all our good luck lately is too. This whole summer has been more than any of us could have expected. And that nightmare made me appreciate what I still have a lot more.

They both seem to ignore me, so I decide to do a little acting. I haven't been able to do my hour of acting out the stories in my head since the night before the fire, and I've been really missing it. It cleanses my soul somehow and I'm really in need. If Matty and Andy are busy fishing, and Kelly is doing whatever he does all the time, I can have some time to do it without being interrupted. That would be disastrous if someone caught me. I probably would not hear the end of it, and even the wonderful Andy might think that's too strange for him to associate with me. Even though I'm not technically talking to myself because I'm becoming different characters, that's what it seems like, and there's no explaining my way out of that situation. No matter what I say, it will come out strange. I will just need to be very cautious because I can't give up precious time like this.

I sneak away without them even noticing and wander through the forest until I find the perfect spot. I clear away a few branches and I'm set to go. I take a deep breath and become someone else. This frame of mind is very difficult and requires full concentration. I forget everything about myself and imagine a whole other life, mind, body, and environment. The sand and trees become a busy street city with benches, tall buildings, public transportation, and people pushing each other to get where they need to be. I become a 20 year old woman named Juliana walking down the busy streets with my estranged older sister. I'm in Bermuda shorts, a nice t-shirt, and my long light brown hair hangs loosely down to my waist. My sister is scoping out the guy situation for me because she tells me I haven't enough boyfriends for my own good. I tell her that just because *she* has a new guy each week, doesn't mean I have to do the same. She doesn't listen though and drags me along the streets of California. I sigh loudly and let her drag me. I spot a guy on the bench that catches my eyes immediately. I pull back on my sister Jean's arm and she stops. I point over to the guy and she rolls her eyes. We have totally different taste in guys, she likes the guys who look strong and big and end up being abusive most of the time, and I like the keep to themselves guys who end up being sweet when you get to know them. This guy is scrawling quickly in a notebook, saying things to himself, crossing things out, drumming with the pencil, and scrawling again. He has shaggy light brown hair that hangs just above his eyes and well over his ears. He is in beat up blue jeans with chains connected to them and a black t-shirt. I could stare at him all day, he's so intriguing.

"Are you serious?" Jean says, throwing her hands in the air. A few people push past her and she bucks at them. "Of all the guys, you pick the lunatic who is talking to himself?"

I nod. "I like him and I'm going to go talk to him."

She refuses to let go of my arm and I tug. "I'm not letting you hook up with someone who is mentally ill."

"You don't know that," I say. "I talk to myself sometimes, it's no big deal. Now let go of my arm."

She reluctantly lets go of my arm and I make my way through the crowd to his bench. I can feel Jean's stare of disapproval on my back, but I pretend I don't and don't turn around. I sit down next to this guy on the bench and wait for him to notice me. After a little while, he looks up. He stares at me a moment and I smile. He looks way older than me, but I don't care. I really want to get to know him; he fascinates me for some reason. I peek over his shoulder and see a set of lyrics on a notebook with cross-outs and arrows and carrots all over. "Are you writing a song?" I ask with enthusiasm.

His head snaps back up and he glowers at me. He looks very lonely and angry, like he's going to be tough to get to know. He doesn't look like he smiles very often and that hurts me. "No," he finally responds. He has a very husky voice, like he's been through a lot in his day. "I'm talking to myself and writing in my diary."

I laugh out loud. "You think you're funny, don't you?"

He returns to his work without another word. I'm going to have to work to get him to say stuff. "Do you have a band or something?"

"What are you doing here?"

That surprises me. "Um, talking to you."

"Why are you talking to me? You're obviously an attractive young woman who can do a lot better than an angry old man like me."

"You fascinate me," I admit. "How old are you?"

"Twenty-two."

"Really? Or are you joking again?"

He glares again. "Why, do you think I look older?"

I nod, even though that may be rude. He's not exactly being friendly to me. "Well I've been beaten down and thrown around and it didn't make me age well," he offers. "But I don't lie about my age. What are you about seventeen?"

I glare back. "No, I'm twenty, believe it or not. You're not an old man."

That leads to him telling me about his horrible childhood and how his band is the only way he can escape. I tell him a little about myself too, and before I know it, he's actually being nice to me. He gets rid of his condescending tone and his husky voice becomes soothing. We become fast friends, even though we're so different, and spend the whole day on that bench, just talking. I don't even think about Jean or anything else except him and where we are now. He even lets me listen to some of his band's music he has recorded on a CD. I'm stunned at how good it is and encourage him to pursue a music career. He tells me about how he has to live with his mean older brother because his mother kicked him out of the house for doing drugs. He ended up from an auto-immune disease from doing drugs and gets judged every day. I feel really bad for him and invite him to come hang out with me for the weekend. We end up spending every minute together and really enjoying each other's company. Jean is drunk half the time and says rude things, but we ignore her. All in all, it's a good weekend. It's always great when you make a new friend, especially when it's a hot guy.

"Jenna?" I hear Andy's voice ask. My concentration turns to panic, and I jump at least two feet off the ground. The streets of California become the sand and trees of the forest again. I'm the orphan Jenna instead of the beautiful Juliana, and my no name guy disappears for good. I stare at Andy in pure shock. This is exactly what I didn't want to happen. I got so lost in my story world that I forgot who and where I really was. I was planning to write this story when I got the right resources. For now, I'm just acting it out to try and find the right main plot line. I will tweak it when I finally write it.

"Hey Andy," I say casually, pretending like he didn't walk in on my crazy mind coming out.

"We thought you got lost," he says. His voice sounds relieved, like he was searching for me and freaking out in the process. "We couldn't find you."

"Oh sorry, I just needed some alone time."

"You didn't seem alone," he notes. That was what I feared. "Who were you talking to?"

I bite my lip and look everywhere but into his piercing blue eyes. Some things are impossible to explain, and this is one of them. "I don't know what you're talking about." It's a lame answer, but it's all I got.

He raises his eyebrows. He doesn't say anything though. Instead, he takes out a little notepad and a pen and starts writing something. He says a few things to himself and taps his pen on his forehead. I watch patiently and am surprised to see a little of my no name face guy in him. It's his actions, definitely not the old looks or the angry attitude. He is doing exactly what I pictured the guy on the bench to be doing, and I begin to wonder if he's writing a song in front of me and even if I was his inspiration. He did say he loves writing and playing music, so it could be.

I inch closer to him, but before I can see anything he's writing, he snaps the notepad shut and puts both that and the pen in the back pocket of his jeans where they came from. I sigh; I really wanted to know what he was writing. "Sorry about that," he smiles weakly. "I had to write something down before I forgot."

"Was it about me?"

He draws a circle in the sand with the toe of his shoe, avoiding answering my question. He reminds me of Kelly in that way. "Andy?" I pry.

"You inspired an idea for a song," he admits. "I get this wave of ideas at random moments and I have write things down in the moment, or else it will be a waste. I don't let anyone see my work until it's complete and I don't have a melody yet." So he *was* writing a song!

"Interesting," I mutter. "I wish I could know what you're writing about me."

"Good things, I promise. I'm grateful for that because I've been stumped for awhile and just finally got past that." He smiles wide, almost in relief as much as gratitude. He says nothing further about how I appeared to be talking to myself, so I must ask him.

"You don't think I'm weird for what you walked in on?" I really need to know.

He seems surprised that I would even consider that. "Weird?" he squeaks. "Of course not. I think you're enthralling honestly."

"But you must think I'm crazy or something. You just saw me talking to no one."

He shakes his head. "You were obviously not yourself. You were a character you created talking to another character you imagined was there. I think that is amazing. I wish I had the mind that could really make me believe something that I can't see."

I blush a little. I never put much thought to it except that everyone would judge me. It is just something I can do and love doing, but have to hide until I'm alone and locked in my bedroom. Sometimes I can't keep it contained to only then, and it comes out in public. If one of my family members sees it, I get scolded and made fun of later. To have someone who admires that about me is new and exciting. I always knew there was a reason I liked him so much right from the beginning. I guess I knew subconsciously that he was one of my own.

"You really don't think I'm weird," I ask, just to be sure he's not just being nice.

"Nope."

A wave of happiness washes over me. That would be awful if he thought I was weird. "I think I love you," I laugh, running toward him for a hug. All that stuff about being afraid to touch him goes out the window. I wrap my arms around him and bury my face in his shirt. He hesitantly pats me on the back. It might be a little awkward for him, but it feels *so* good to me. I haven't had a good hug since the fire and am in deep need.

When I finally pull away, he looks down at me. "Do you really mean that?"

I think about that a minute. I was only joking, but maybe I really do. I do have the tendency to become overly attached to people, even when I know I have to lose them at some point. "I'm not sure, but I think I do mean it."

That makes him grin. He's like a new puppy always looking for approval from his three masters. "Why are you always scared we don't like you? We do like you, but you always seem to need reassurance."

"To be honest, you three scare the hell out of me. All my life I struggled for approval from my parents and when I got it, it wasn't as much as I wanted. I am scared to death of people in general and interacting with them. I hated getting up in front of the class and if I had to talk to someone. I didn't talk to people to get what I wanted; I would do without what I wanted. Adults were the worst when I was a kid, and now kids are the worst. I think all kids hate me for some reason, and I never would have thought you guys would be so welcoming to me. Maybe that's why I never went for dreams. What I want to be involves a lot of people and being uncomfortable, so I just waste my life doing something that makes me miserable so I don't have to be uncomfortable. I'm a scared little wimp who is extremely insecure. I give off this façade that I'm this cool guy who everyone loves when really I think I'm too skinny and ugly and will never achieve my dreams. That's the truth."

I'm taken aback. I would never have known this about him. He always acts so confident about things, just a little uncomfortable around kids. I never would have guessed he was insecure and needed reassurance from *me*. He has helped me a lot in these past weeks and I feel like I need to give some back. "You should not be insecure at all. You are sexy and amazing, and although that sounds really weird coming from me, it's the truth. You should not worry about people, because if you're just yourself, then they will all love you. I bet anything that you will make the best music of the decade and even more, and before long, you will forget all you ever doubted about yourself."

"That could be true, but I don't have the guts to start. I could barely speak around Tina at first, and I couldn't sleep the day before I came here the first time." How could someone so great think they aren't?

"I know the beginning is rough, but you have to get through that if you're going to get anywhere in life," I tell him. "I'm exactly the same, but my dad told me that I'm amazing, and if I'm ever going to show the world that, I have to get past the insecurity. You have to just do it, and if some things don't work out, you shrug it off and try again. I hear his voice all the time and that makes me feel better about things like that."

One side of his mouth turns up in a smirk. "I've heard a lot about Mackenzie Thornton and all of it has been fascinating. He sounds like a very wise man, and every time you're around him you learn something about life. I wish I could have known him."

I nod in agreement. "I'm lucky he's my dad. He was the most amazing guy you would ever meet and that's why my mom loved him so much. She was equally as amazing, but neither of them understood me. You're the first one who does, and I think that's why I'm so drawn to you. We have writer's minds."

"Matty said his motto was 'You never regret what you do, it's what you don't do that you regret' and I think that pretty much describes me. I gave up a lot in my life because I was scared, and I regret a lot of things I didn't do."

That's the same with me, I think, but don't tell him. It's not right to bring up my issue when I'm trying to help him with his. "That was his life motto and it's a good one to live by. But so is yours that you told me. You should decide to live by it now and stop regretting things. You can't go back, but you can change your future by living differently now. Wake up tomorrow and decide that you're not afraid of people anymore. You will feel better, I assure you."

He puts his arm around the top of my shoulders and pulls me into his side. "Thank you for your support."

"Anytime," I assure him. "But I still think it's funny that you would take advice from me."

"You give good advice. You help me more than you know."

"You help me too," I smile.

He shakes his head. "No, I'm failing you and your brothers, and that's why I'm so down. I've gone to all the houses I can think of that might take you and all of them have turned me down. They either want two of you or just one of you, but never all three. Most of them want only Kelly. Others that do want all of you don't look like very good caregivers, and I want to give you the best. We only have one more week of August left and then my deadline is fast approaching. I promised you that I would help you, and now I can't do it. There's only one couple left and then that's it. I failed."

I think I see his eyes start to get misty and I almost cry myself. That must be really rough for him. "It's great to know my brother is wanted more than me," I joke, in a desperate attempt to keep him from crying.

He laughs. "Don't worry, Matty's the least wanted. They all think he's going to be a danger. And I can't show you to them to prove that he's not because I can't just show you to anyone that I don't trust."

"Yeah," I agree. "It must be hard. It's worse for me though because I have that feeling that I don't know where I'm going to go when summer ends. And what about school?"

His eyes widen. "I forgot eighth grade and second grade start for you three in a few short weeks. We've had a good time over the summer, but now when the serious stuff hits, I can't follow up on what I say. Maybe I'll just show you to this last couple, since we're getting desperate and running out of time."

Something suddenly hits me when he says that that I hadn't thought of before. In two weeks we will be going back to school and living with some new family who knows nothing about us. These good times will be all over. No more beach, no more hidden forest and lake all to ourselves, no more living day by day with no cares, and most of all no more Andy. Andy will be gone from all of our lives in two weeks, and I know better than anyone how fast two weeks can go when you don't want them to end. Andy has become something I came to expect and love in my life, and the thought of him being gone for good sends shivers down my spine. I start to shake and tears fill up my eyes so I can barely see a thing. I can't control it. It's an awful unexplainable feeling when you realize that your happiness is running out.

He notices I'm crying and gasps. "What's wrong? I know you're scared of meeting some strange people, but it's all we've got. I promised I would help you and this is the way I can do it."

"You don't understand," I sniff. "You've already helped. You've brought us everything we need, but that doesn't even matter. You loved us when there was no one else that would. You listened when everyone else was convinced that we were monsters. You showed us a new way to look at life, and you made us laugh in the face of a great loss."

"I know. But I need to finish my job. I need to get you a nice, stable home."

He still doesn't get it, and I'm starting to get angry along with upset. "No! You made us happy. Not what you did to help us, but you yourself. You made our lives better by just being here with us every day, and then you're going to just leave in two short weeks. How do you think that makes us feel? We've already lost so many things we've loved. And not even us. I'm talking about me. You filled the empty void. What if I'm going to miss you just as much as I miss my parents and my sister? What if losing the one stable thing in my life will set me over the edge? What if I can't live without you anymore? Have you ever thought about that?" By this point I'm hysterical. I'm yelling at the top of my lungs and I'm barely understandable. But he gets the point, and by the look in his eyes, I can tell this is the first time he's thought about that. I pull away from him and run through that forest to the beach itself. I know I'll find Matty there, and I need to talk to him. I look back at Andy one more time before I leave and whisper, "I can't lose you too. I love you." Then I run as fast as I can until I spot Matty on the jetty. I sit down next to him and notice he's crying also. We don't ask each other why; we just somehow know we're thinking the same thing. It's that awful feeling again. We cry together for at least an hour until we're all cried out and our whole bodies are exhausted. We don't know it, but Andy's crying for us too.

27

Matty

We decide that rather than cry our last days, we might as well make the best of them. I give Andy that poem and he loves it, deciding to teach me a few things about life when we're alone together. One week flies by because as they say, we're having fun. We eat nice breakfasts, spend our days swimming, fishing, learning survival skills from Andy throughout our explorations of the woods, or just hanging out making good memories. We have large dinners sometimes that we catch and stay up to all hours of the night telling stories and laughing. For some reason, everything is much funnier after midnight, especially when you're with a severely immature 26 year old. We pass out and wake up in the mornings in awkward positions. Andy made a deal with Tina that he spends the entire week out here with us and then the last week getting everything together for our departure. I know she's probably missing him, but she can have him all the time after we're gone. As for us, we just have this time. And the entire week the looming feeling of fading happiness hangs over us. We all know very well that these could be our last happy times, our last laughs, even our last times together for a very long time, but we decide to put those feelings away and just enjoy what we have left.

September 1st comes way too quick, and it brings a depressing feeling to the air. It's always been that way, the feeling of fall and school and that the horribleness of winter is fast approaching. I always used to wish September was never a month because all it is is a slap in the face that says 'summer is over, no more fun for you.' I can almost feel it laughing at me when I wake up. I hate that my birthday is in this month. Only one more week, I think, trying to push that thought away. I don't want to break down again like I did that day on the beach with Jenna.

We eat a silent breakfast together, trying to fill our minds with memories of June, July, and August where the days are long and hot and there's nothing but happiness. Andy seems very stressed as the cool winds of the beginning of fall blow through his hair. He's deep in thought, and I wonder what he could be thinking about. Maybe Tina and how he misses her, that he still hasn't found a home for us, or that his dad could become the wiser at any time. I can only imagine the weight on his shoulders knowing he only has one week to do everything and then it's all over. He'll never get to see us again for our own good. That's an awful feeling.

"I think I'll introduce you to the family tomorrow," he says, finally coming back to the present.

There's a feeling of unhappiness in the air as he says it. He doesn't want us to go and we don't want to go, but it has to be done. "Okay," we all sigh.

"I know you don't want to, but it's all we have. They're a nice, young newlywed couple that wants all three of you and will provide you a nice home with everything you need."

"But they won't be anything like what we have here," Jenna mutters, and Kelly mumbles, "I'd rather live in the woods forever." I stay quiet, even though I could add a lot of things to their comments. Andy sighs with us. We're not making this easy on him and I feel bad. This is upsetting for him too. I'm the only one that knows because I woke up early one morning last week and saw he had misty eyes. He was singing a song that I recognized as "This is Your Life" by Switchfoot, and he was very upset. I had left him alone and hadn't shown him I'd heard anything, but it stuck with me. It made me want to be nicer to him, even though I'm not very willing to move in with a fake couple who pretends to love us just because we have nowhere else to go. This is all very unsettling, worse than the first day of middle school.

"Do we ever get to meet Tina before you're gone?" Kelly asks through all the sighing. There's a tension in the air as we all wait for the answer.

"I don't know if we have time for that." He pokes at his plate of food in his lap. "Once we win over the couple tomorrow, we're going to focus on moving you in before school starts next week. We won't be here much after today, and we might not even be seeing that much of each other."

I see my sister's face get pale white out of the corner of my eye. It makes me shiver also. We're losing him faster than we thought. When you count on one more week and then you realize you won't get that, it sure shows that no time is promised, and you should hold on to the moments you *do* have. I get a strange feeling in my stomach thinking this could be one of our last days, and I know Jenna is worse than me. I don't think she can literally live without Andy. She pushes her breakfast away and runs away covering her face. She disappears in the direction of the lake, and I don't know whether to stay here or run after her. I look at Andy. He looks as unsure as I am. Kelly is softly sobbing to himself like I hear every night. It hurts me that he's so sad for us and our family. I remember how it affected me at his age when Dad and Lauren died.

I decide I better go comfort Jenna. I run through the forest, wondering if this might be the last time I enter the hidden clearing complimented with the tranquil lake that seems untouched by anyone but us, and take my place beside Jenna. She is weeping hard and has her face buried in her arms. I pat her back and that makes her cry harder. I can feel tears welling up in my own eyes. Great, if I cry that will make this all worse, I think, fighting the tears. I come up with a quick solution and hope it works as well as I can imagine. "What if I told you I have a plan that can keep this from being our last day with Andy?" I ask, and wait for a response.

The response I get is a good one for her head snaps up. She sniffs a few times and stares at me with her red, puffy eyes. "Go on."

I smile almost evilly. "If when we meet this last chance family, they don't like us, then we don't have to leave here now do we?"

The left side of her mouth turns up and she joins my grin. "We have to look and act awful. Then we have it in the bag. I can see by Andy's face that they're already on the fence about us; a few horrible actions can turn them away from us in a minute."

"Precisely," I agree. "We just have to inform Kelly without Andy being the wiser."

Before long, we're concocting our plan and forget all of our previous sadness. We laugh nonstop and act out all the things we could do to make this family not like us. Kelly even joins after a little while and is more than happy to help us out if he gets a reward. Andy remains missing until dinner, to our advantage, and it's then that we can't hide our excitement. We have a wonderful dinner with him and stay awake until a late hour talking and making the most of what could be our last night all together. When we all but pass out in exhaustion, Andy shoots up from his spot in the sand and it startles me. I stare up at him and he gives me a little wave before he disappears. He has a weird look on his face as he leaves, and I wonder if that's just nervousness for the day to come or if there could be another problem with Tina. I turn my thoughts to our plan and really hope that we can pull off all we say we will. I'm pretty confident, but if I've learned anything about life, it's that anything can happen, and it usually does when you least expect it.

28

Andy

It had been one of the longest, most tiring, and stressful days of my summer, and it feels amazing to climb into bed next to Tina and just hold her. I had gotten so worked up in making the most of my last hours with the kids, that I had forgotten what had went down the previous week. I had showed up to the lunch I planned to and she had been extremely but happily surprised. I made sure I made it home every night for dinner and devoted all my attention to her when she was around. She seemed convinced by the end of the week, but she told me yesterday that tonight was the big test. She knew it was one of my last nights with the kids and that I could easily get wrapped up in the moment. She told me before I left this morning that she would be preparing a special evening for us, and if I failed to show up, it would show where she was on my priority list. I told her it had to be acceptable if I were a little late, considering the circumstances and she agreed, but I had completely forgotten. I know I am in hot water, but it is dumb of her to expect me to give up my last night with the kids when I can have many more with her after they're gone. To me, that's not a priority issue, it's just common sense, but girls have complicated minds. They twist things around until it's all your fault, and I can feel that I'm going to get scolded beyond belief.

I shut my eyes and try to force myself asleep before she can scream at me. I want to at least get a good's night sleep before I have to deal with what I've done. But she won't have it and squirms away from me. I know this is bothering her more than I thought it would. She turns to look at me and her face looks almost evil. I cringe. Why couldn't she have just waited until morning? It's really not that big of a deal. We've been together for so long that she should know by now that I love and need her.

"Where have you been?" she hisses, while I try to figure a way to explain my way out of this one. "You said you would come so I made a good dinner. But then I sat here alone as you failed to show."

I sigh deeply. Here goes nothing. "I'm sorry. They all had meltdowns about me leaving. They've become really attached to me like a big brother and I like them a lot too. By the time I got them to calm down, I had to prepare their dinner. We were laughing and talking so much that I lost track of time. I really meant to come; it's just I didn't have time to come with this being the night before I give them to their new family."

"Oh, so you don't have time for me now?" she sasses. Crap, I think. That was the wrong thing to say and now I've dug myself deeper. This is not going to get better; it's only going to get much worse. I'm not going to sleep anytime soon.

I smile longingly at her. "I *always* have time for you." I try to touch her face, but she pulls out of my reach.

She throws the covers off of her and jumps out of the bed. "I don't like being second to a group of kids you met only two months ago!"

"You're not..." I try to assure her, but she cuts me off.

"All you do is help those kids, which means you're always gone, and I sit here all alone because I'm off from work. I feel like you're choosing those kids over me, and I'm tired of it. I thought that since I had that talk with you, you would understand where I'm coming from and change your ways, but you just proved exactly what I thought to be true. I don't want to spend my summer waiting to see if you'll come around. How do you think that feels for me?"

I stand across the bed from her and try to think of a correct answer for that question. Obviously it was a rhetorical question because she continues, "I've decided I'm done feeling this way. I've had a lot of time alone to think about it, and I've decided that I don't care what you're doing anymore. Go hang out all day and night with a group of kids, I'm done. I'm number one, and if you're not going to treat me how I should be treated, I'm not wasting any more time on you! I already wasted too many years!" The longer she goes, the louder she gets, and I'm starting to get nervous. This is going scary places and I don't know how to get it back to good. I'm not sure there's any fixing it. I feel a little fury rising up about her saying all the time we've been together was a waste, but I do my best to suppress and go at this with a clear head.

"Tina, I'm almost done with the kids. You know I have a few days and it's all you on my mind. I promised everything is going to change once they're out of the picture, and I'm not going back on that promise." My voice is calm, but I'm scared out of my mind. One wrong word and she could be gone for good. I'm shaking more than I usually do this time of night when my meds start to wear off. My heart feels like it's going to thump out of my chest as I can see her getting ready to continue to chew me out.

"You keep saying that!" she screams. She kicks the pillows around as I watch helplessly. "But nothing changes. Between the kids, work, you're family, and even your stupid piano, I'm always your last thought! To be honest, it's quite vexing. You use me, and I finally have the strength to tell you to leave me alone!"

I move to the other side of the bed and try to calm her. She's having none of that and shrieks when I try to touch her. It's pitch dark, and it frightens me that with all this swinging wildly of her arms, she's going to injure herself or me. "Tina, you're being ridiculous. That's not true and you know it. You're just upset so you're saying things."

She burns holes through me with her eyes. I've always known her to have a short temper, but this side of her I have never seen. I shake my head at her and she screams, "OH!" She roars as loud as she possibly can and pulls at her hair with both hands. It looks like something out of a movie, and I know that there is not any reasoning with her tonight at least. "Tina?" I ask finally, making sure she's okay.

"Stop calling me Tina!" she orders, when she's done having her little tantrum. "My name is Kristina and I never wanted you to call me that! You may live your life how others want you to, but that's not me! *I* tell people when I'm upset and *I* follow my dreams!"

That hits me hard, like a sucker punch to the gut, and all I can say is, "That was low, *Kristina*." I spit her name out at the end. We agreed a long time ago, almost when we first met, that we wanted to call each other something that no one else did-our own little secret names. I chose Tina for her and she either calls me Andy or just A. It feels weird calling her by her full name, and it almost feels like I don't even know her. She's acting like a stranger. We've practically been living with each other since we met, and things have been great. Where is this all coming from?

"You know it's true!"

I just stare at her with a hurt look on my face. I fight with myself about my choices every day I can think. I feel like my moments are slipping away, and I'm wasting my life doing something I hate. I could get my cancer back any day, and yet I still avoid conflict by just doing what my father wants and not what I want my life to be. She knows all these things, and she feels them along with me. She's just trying to hurt me the way she's hurt. She has no compassion and I know she won't stop. A monster called Kristina has come out of my beautiful Tina and is choking the life out of both of us. "I'm tired of you!" she continues. "Just leave me alone *forever*, if you can comprehend that word. Get out of my house or I'll throw you out, got it?"

"This is my house too," I remind her. I feel like I have to defend myself, and I don't want to hurt her anymore, so I don't know *what* to do. This is like a bad nightmare. I plead to wake up.

"Fine," she says, throwing her hands in the air. "Have your stupid house. I never liked it anyway. It's not even a beach house being miles away from the beach! I can drive from Pennsylvania just like I can drive from here, so I'm going back to Pennsylvania. That's where I belong."

I'm getting really angry now. She can't actually be acting like this. This is almost funny, it's so absurd. "I'm glad you lied to me for years saying how you loved Rehoboth Beach and how this house is your dream. Thanks for that."

I can see her roll her eyes in the dim gleam coming in through the window from the street lights like I'm such a bother. "Andrew, just leave already! I don't want to see you again, so go hang out with your kid friends. They're probably more mature than you anyway. I think my students have more sense than you. You won't even marry me and it's been 6 years! You said all that time you supposedly loved me, but I'm starting to wonder if they're just words because you're not acting on those feelings. You're immaturity shows through. I mean come on, what grown man has to take ADHD medicine to survive the day?"

Those words shock me even more than the previous. First of all, she's the one who told me that she hated the way my family jeers my name constantly and vowed never to call me Andrew. Secondly, she told me she loved how I had the mind of a young child and that my health conditions did not bother her in the least. And finally, we had a long serious discussion about how I didn't really believe that marriage was something I wanted. She had told me that that was okay as long as we had the same connection as if we were married, and she hadn't shown any further signs of distress on the matter. She was really showing her bad side.

"I'm pretty sure a lot of people do," I snap. I pretty much have given up on trying to be nice to her. "And you know how I feel about marriage. I thought we were past this."

"I don't want to hear it. I'm just telling you what I've been keeping inside for years now. I'm finished, and I would really like it if you disappeared from my life." She points to the door and I start to leave. I'm so stunned this is happening, I can't even think of anything to say or do to protest her. "I hope your cancer comes back too so you can't hurt anybody else!!!"

I stop in the doorway, my back turned to her. I can't move, and I feel my heart shatter into a million pieces and fall on the floor at my feet. I can't remember how to breathe, and I struggle not to fall over. How could she say something like that just to rip me apart? After all we've been through? She watched me struggle all those years. I was dangerously close to death, and she was almost in as much pain as me. How could she wish that on anybody, let alone me, the love of her life? Does she have no soul and I didn't know it until now? Even with how upset I made her feel, it was wrong to go there. There's no saving this now. She crossed the line and hurt me so deeply, there's no turning back.

After what seems like an eternity of complete astonishment, I manage to speak. "I love you Tina, and I thought you loved me too. But obviously I was wrong because all along you've wanted me dead!"

She stares at her feet; she can't even look at me now. "I didn't mean that A. I'm sorry. Please leave before I hurt you more because I don't want to do that." A little bit of Tina comes through there, but I still can't get over her heart-wrenching words.

I trudge out of the room and slam the front door behind me. I run as fast as I can away from the house, hoping I can run away from the pain as well as the giver. But before long, I can't run any further. I'm about half way in between my house and my destination, the forest near Rehoboth Beach, when I fall to my knees on the pavement. My lungs can't take any more, and it takes everything I have to tilt my head to the night sky and yell, just like I did the day the doctor gave me the diagnosis. But this pain is worse. At least then I knew there was hope of recovering what I once had, and I had someone who would help me through it and understand what I was going through. This time she is gone, I have lost her just as I feared, and no one will be able to properly sympathize with me. Tina is the only thing I absolutely cannot lose, and I'm left homeless, cold, and in the dark to deal with it. This is when I first realize I am completely in love and wonder what was I doing waiting around and fooling with my luck. There is no one else for me. I should have acted on that, but instead I tried to keep up with all my little rules of not becoming attached to someone and ended up with the one thing I didn't want because of it. I rest my forehead on the blacktop and cry hard until I swear I don't have enough moisture left in my body to produce any more tears. My whole body aches. I fall over on my back and hope that a car comes by and runs me over. I don't want to deal with a new day; I don't have strength with such a large chunk of me suddenly ripped away.

29

Jenna

I wake with a feeling of dread for what is to occur today. I would do anything to stop from going to see the family today. As you may already know, I have attachment issues. When someone comes into my life for a long period of time, I come to expect them to be there forever. That is the worst thing I could do though because almost everyone isn't there to stay. I become attached to them all, I lose them, I tell myself I won't become attached again, and then I can't stop myself when a new person comes along. It's just something I can't control, like a sickness. The only way to break this cycle is to make sure I don't lose Andy. This brings me back to how I'll go to all measures to make sure I break the cycle. I frantically look for Andy in all the places he could be, and finally find him on the beach, the last place I expected. He is on his stomach long ways on the jetty with his head resting on his crossed arms. There is a miniature spiral notebook with words scrawled over the visible page lying in front of him. It is the same one I saw the other day, and I wonder if he spent the night writing a song. He doesn't look so good and I get frantic. Then again, this could be the way out of leaving here for the family meeting. I just don't know what to think of the situation.

I rush over and stand above him, waiting for a reaction. When none comes, I shake him in case he's asleep. He groans and twists his head so he can peer up at me. His whole face looks red and puffy and there are huge dark circles under his eyes. He looks as if he had a long, sad night, getting very dirty in the process. "You look worse than me," I comment. "And that is not a good thing by all means."

He sighs for a long while and sits up. His knees are bent and once again he rests his head on his crossed arms, which are on his legs. "Yeah, I had a rough night to say the least."

I take a seat next to him. "Matty said you had a look as if you had seen a ghost before you left last night. He said it probably had something to do with Tina. What happened?"

"I got kicked out of my house," he says calmly, almost laughing about it.

"What?! Why?!" Obviously I am very surprised.

He chuckles at my reaction, and I wonder why he's being so calm about this. "The dinner she had ready for me last night was a test. Since I didn't make it, she concluded that I mean nothing to her and ended it. And then she kicked me out into the night after making many rude comments."

"Why would she do that? First off, she knows that you're working with us and you'll give your full attention to her sooner than she knows, and secondly, you bought that house for her. How can she kick you out in the middle of the night?"

He shrugs. "I don't know. She just did. She was insane last night. She told me she's moving back to Pennsylvania and that she never liked the house after all."

I am irritated beyond belief at this point. After all the wonderful things I've heard about her from Andy, whom very blatantly loves her more than anything else, how could she completely change and do a thing like this? Nobody hurts my Andy like this and gets away with it. I have a strange feeling of vengeance and it is a bit scary.

"You know what else she said before I finally agreed to leave her be?" Andy asks when he realizes I'm too angry to reply.

"What?" I say through my teeth. I'm not sure I can handle it.

"She told me she hopes my cancer comes back so I can't hurt anyone else the way I hurt her." He starts laughing in a sort of crazy way when he tells me that. "Can you believe that?" I think something in his mind snapped last night because he looks a little bit unstable.

Something snaps in my head as well when I hear what she said to him. I am so furious, indignant, and irate that my entire face turns red. I am fuming. I think there is smoke coming out of my ears like a stupid cartoon. "I think I hate her with a passion."

That brings him into a fit of laughter. Unbelievably, I start laughing also. The both of us are so mad and upset we're laughing! I feel crazy. "The funny thing is," Andy adds. "I still am totally in love with her and I'll never hate her. Whatever she says to me, it won't change how I feel. Now I'm stuck all alone wishing she would take me back and knowing she won't. It's pathetic. I can't take you to the family today. I hope that's okay. It's just I'm not up for it after all that has happened."

I shake my head. "No problem. I didn't want to go anyway. None of us did. Are you saying you forgive Tina?"

"She could say that a million times and I would always forgive her. But now she hates me." He buries his head in the space between his arms and screams. It is muffled but it is unmistakably painful. "I'm so weak. I'm half tempted to run crying to my Mom."

"Do you want to hear what I think?" I ask in a desperate attempt to cheer him up.

He lifts his head just an inch. "Why not?"

I grin. "I think there's a way for you to win her back."

That gets his attention for sure, for his head snaps up in a few seconds. "I would die to know how."

"I feel very empowered," I laugh. "But in answer to your question, with me being a girl myself, I know the way they think much more than you ever will. She was hurt so she wanted to hurt you, but she went too far in the moment. She obviously loves you or else your lack of attention wouldn't have affected her so greatly. So this means that she doesn't want to lose you any more than you want to lose her. But the only thing in the way is her pride. She is too proud to admit she was wrong. The only way to get her back is to chase after her, saying that you were wrong and you're sorry. Then she can say that she took you back for your sake and not because she secretly wanted you back anyway, but just won't admit it to anyone. So if you really want to be with her forever, then I suggest you do just that and get over there quick. Did you say she was moving back to Pennsylvania?"

He nods in response.

"When?"

"I don't know; she was getting ready to pack when I left last night, so I suspect that it won't be long before that house is vacant."

"Well you better get going if you want to catch her!"

He sighs again. "I don't think I can. I mean, what if you're wrong? I don't want to be more hurt inside than I am now."

I put a hand on his shoulder for comfort. "I know you may not trust me because I'm so young and you're probably thinking what does she know, but you have to trust me. It's either you sit here and wonder later if I could have been right, or you go after her and have a chance of being happy again. That's your choice."

"I guess you are right. I'll go." He gets up quickly and adjusts himself so he looks agreeable when he pleads for his lover. He places the notebook back in his pocket. I wish I could read what kind of song he wrote in his anguish.

"And if I'm wrong, I owe you forever," I add. "But if I'm right, you owe me forever."

He raises his eyebrows at me, but we snake shake to agree on it. I already have something in mind, but I'll keep it to myself until I feel it's safe to reveal. I'm almost positive I'm going to be correct on in this scenario and will get what I want from it, but if I'm wrong for some odd reason, I don't want to get my hopes up for them to be shot down. He stands there and stares at me for awhile, trying to read my expression and find what he could be getting himself into, but I give no hints. After awhile I have to urge him to go on or he'll be standing there forever and we'll never know if I'm right or not.

"Go before it's too late and she's well on her way to PA!" I yell, and he snaps back to the present moment. He takes one last look at me before taking off in the opposite direction. I watch him run up the jetty, up the steep sandy ramp, and up to the street where his beautiful MX-5 is surely parked. "Hey that rhymes," I add to myself and chuckle. "And I feel good because I just did a good deed for a friend."

I make my way back to camp and relay what had just happened to my brothers. They look hurt when I tell them of what Tina said, and then their reactions become lighter when I tell them of my part in the situation. Matty congratulates me on maybe saving a relationship, and I feel warm inside. "And the best part is," I grin. "We don't have to go see that family after all!"

They both cheer and I join in. All in all, this is a good day. "Did he say that?" Matty inquires.

I nod. "He said he hopes it doesn't make us upset, but he just isn't up for it."

"Upset?!" Kelly exclaims. "We're ecstatic!"

We all laugh at that comment, considering it was what we were all thinking. "I don't think we'll have to go at all either."

This conclusion sure grabs their attention, so I continue, "Well, when Andy and Tina are back together, which if I trust myself at all I must assume they will be, then he will be so happy that he will totally forget about this stupid family. We will get to stay out here with him and maybe if we're lucky, we'll get to meet Tina." I stop to catch my breath after this long-winded explanation.

"I don't know about that," Matty says. He's always the one that prepares for the worst, which it's always good if *someone* is, but most of the time it gets annoying. He just brings me down when I'm excited about something.

I roll my eyes at him to show my exasperation. "We never know anything for sure Matty, but hope is a good thing to have."

"You don't have to get sarcastic with me. I'm just trying to look on the realistic side of things. He cares about us and he thinks that giving us a stable home is the way to show that, so no matter how happy and distracted he is, he's still going to want to show he cares. Therefore, we should keep practicing our plan for the meeting of the family just to be safe."

Kelly and I glare at him. "Fine!" we shout at the same time. He's right *again,* and it makes us mad.

"You'll thank me when we successfully evade the grasp of a fake family," Matty sneers.

"Whatever you say, Matty," I laugh, waving him off like an imbecile.

30

Andy

"You better be right Jenna," I mutter nervously to myself as I pound on the front door of

my house. I ring the doorbell a few times also in case my knocking isn't hard enough to hear. I step back a few inches and wait, my hands crossed behind my back like I'm wearing handcuffs. I try to whistle, but realize after 26 years of life, I still haven't learned to whistle. It's pathetic really when I see little ten year olds whistling whole songs and the only thing that comes out of my mouth is air. Then again, I can barely snap, can't roll my tongue, or anything of that nature. I don't have any common talents.

I stop torturing myself with these thoughts and move on to others. Tina could not be home, she could have left already, she could see it's me and not open the door; so many things could happen that would affect my plan. I feel myself starting to break out into a sweat because I'm starting to panic. The door doesn't open and I don't hear any sign of movement inside the house. I peer into a few of the windows, and the house looks just about how I left it. Still there is no answer. She's either gone or doesn't want to talk to me, and unfortunately I'm leaning toward the latter. I silently count to ten and start to walk away. I'll just tell Jenna she was gone already and I was too late, I think.

I get down the walk and to the top of the driveway before I hear motion coming from the front door. There are clinking noises and the door starts to open. I rush up to the steps again and wait for her to fully open the glass storm door. She's always had trouble with the lock system on it. No matter how many times I show her the correct way to do it, it still takes approximately 6 months for her to open it. I fidget, switching my weight from one foot to another, while she curses and fumbles with the door. Finally it swings open and she has to jump out of the way so it doesn't hit her.

She reappears and glares at me. "I thought I said I never wanted to see you again."

I run my hands through my hair nervously. How do I begin? I wasn't prepared for her to actually open the door. I had convinced myself she wouldn't be there. Now I am stuck and don't know what to say.

"If you're not going to answer, I'm going to go back inside," she states after a long silence.

She attempts to slam the door closed, but I shove my hand in the space before she can leave me out here alone. She ignores it and successfully closes my wrist up in the doorway. I yell in pain and she curses at me. "Get lost Andrew," she screams, her face in the crack in the doorway my hand is allowing.

"My hand is in the door," I inform her, in case she hadn't noticed.

"You're so stubborn," she roars. "Just leave me alone already."

"Think about that Tina. I can't leave without my hand, and my hand is in the door."

She glowers at me through the crack. I give no reaction but a wince of pain as the door continues to dig into my wrist bone. Eventually, she opens the door so my hand can slide through. I planned this time though because when she opens the door, I quickly follow my hand into the foyer. She closes the door behind me and I grin at her.

"Are you kidding me?" she yells. "Why won't you just go away?"

I begin chuckling again, and this time it sounds a bit wicked. "Just listen to what I have to say, and if you still want me to leave, I will."

"I will," she mutters.

"Listen first," I say through my teeth. I hate when she gets like this.

She sticks her tongue out at me and I find that very immature. I ignore it though and begin a speech from the heart. "When I left here last night, I was very upset for two reasons. One was I was hurt because you said some awful things to me, and whether you meant them or not, I never expected them to come out of someone I spent the past 6 years with. Secondly, I realized how stupid I was. I got so used to having you around, that I didn't even realize what a good thing you were. I cried myself silly and was so hurt, and then I said to myself, 'This is a good thing.' Why did I say that? Because if this never happened, I never would have known that I couldn't lose you. I never would have seen that I can't be with anybody else because you're all I want. Loving somebody and being in love with somebody are two totally different things that most people can't tell the difference between, but I don't have to now. I love you *and* I'm in love with you. That's why I'm asking you, no I'm begging you, to forgive me, so I can show you that now that I have come to know this, I will be better than you can ever imagine. Please take me back Tina. Let me be your guy again. Let me live in this beautiful house with you again."

Her face turns from angry that I'm there, to compassionate toward my feelings. "I don't know," she ultimately replies. "How can I know that you're not just saying that and things are really going to change for good?"

"You're just going to have to trust me."

She sighs and places her head in her hands. She's scared to take that chance and I have to show her I really mean what I say. "Look," I say. "Will it help if I get on my knees? I will if you want me to."

She just laughs and I take that as a yes. I lower to my knees and press my hands together to show signs of begging. I look like a dog who wants a treat, but if it works, what can I say? I would literally do anything. I even give her a nice smile to add to the effect.

"How can I say no to you when you're like that?" she asks, exasperated. "This isn't fair."

"That's the point," I laugh. "So what do you say?"

She grabs my arms and pulls me off my knees to a stance. I can't even breathe as I wait for the answer. She bites her lip to keep from smiling, and her eyes rotate dramatically. "I will take you back Andy, but only because you would be lost without me."

"Oh is that only why?" I ask playfully.

She nods, and I laugh and give her a big hug. It feels nice. "Don't tell anyone," she warns. "But I was really hoping you would come by because I was dreading going back to live with my mom. She would have been so happy to see you gone, and I didn't want to deal with her happiness while I was upset. And"-she stalls on this part but finally says it-"I would be lost without you too. What would I do with myself when I've been taking care of you for 6 years?"

"I do my share," I argue. "I clean when I'm upset. But on another note, your secret is safe with me."

"I was going to ask you something. Can I come meet the kids? I have wanted to all this time, but I never had the courage to ask."

"Sure. When?"

"Um, how about tomorrow? If that's okay. I'm not going to Pennsylvania after all, so I'm free."

I crack up at that one. "I'm sure they will be thrilled. I've told them amazing things about you."

"I'm honored."

We then engage in a long, passionate kiss, and I love having her beautiful face in my hands again. I really owe Jenna big after this. She was very right, and I have to give in on my side of the deal. I can only imagine what she might want from me.

31

Matty

We spend the chief of the day messing around in the lake before we spot Andy, returning on his quest for love. He races towards us with an unmistakable smile, and we know the meeting went well. We can't help but share the happiness. Jenna runs up and gives him a huge hug. He skeptically follows through. He once told me about his hugging rule, and that Jenna isn't on that list. I'm glad he broke it; maybe it's the good mood. They embrace and I hear her whisper something to him. Not wanting to be left out, I make my way up to them.

"What do you want," he says softly. "I think I'm a little scared."

"What's going on here?" I ask. There could be many things that Jenna could be up to right now.

They glance at each other and smirk. I'm starting to be a little scared. "Jenna saved my relationship, so I must give her something in return," Andy replies. "And I think I can manage what she requests."

I wait for him to continue, but I have to pull for answers here. "Are you going to tell me what that is?"

Jenna looks at him with pleading eyes, and he shakes his head. "You'll have to just wait and see."

I roll my eyes. I hate when people blatantly keep secrets from me. I like to be part of everything, and even when I'm really lucky, I like being the leader of the groups in which I'm a member. This makes me feel helpless and angry. I stomp off furiously, but Jenna catches up with me. "It's for our own good, I promise you. I just want it to be a pleasant surprise."

I glance at her and turn away. I don't want her to see that I'm upset still. She grabs my face and turns me back toward her. She sees my eyes becoming red. I try to pull away, but she's extra strong today.

"Matty, what's wrong?!" she exclaims.

"It's stupid," I admit.

She pulls me down into a sitting position on a clearing of sand. "It's never stupid when you're unhappy."

"Fine," I sigh. "I don't want to leave here either. I want everything to stay like it is now and never have anything change. Andy is my homeboy. I don't want to lose him or this cool little hide-out we have and move to a house with a new family. I just know it isn't going to feel right, and they'll be trying so hard to make us feel comfortable, that we'll feel uncomfortable. Since we can't have Lauren, Mom, or Dad back, I think it's only fair that we get to keep what we have right now. But I don't know if that's possible, and I'm scared that things will get so bad we won't be able to make it."

I slowly look up at her to study her reaction. Her eyes widen and she yells, "How in the world is that stupid? That's exactly how Kelly and I are feeling too! And I think I just might have fixed that, or at least tried."

She has an evil smile. "Does this have to do with that surprise?"

Before she can answer, we hear a piercing scream coming from deep inside the forest. We know it's Kelly at once and spring into action. We race through the forest in search of him, pushing tree branches and shrubs out of our way. I glance back a second and spot Andy right on our heels. Finally, we find Kelly curled up in a ball in the sand, holding his ears and screaming as loud as he possibly can. I drop to my knees and try to comfort him, but obviously something is really wrong.

"The tree!" he yells, and it comes to me. Mom's carvings! This hasn't happened in so long that I had forgotten all about it. She's communicating with us again. I hope she can give us helpful guidance, because at this point, we need it a great deal.

Jenna and I search around frantically on all the tree trunks for something unusual so it can calm Kelly's mind. We find on a hidden tree there is a small carving with two sentences on it. I trace my fingers over the words and the screaming ceases. Kelly slowly rises and joins us, hands away from his ears.

"This must be it," I mutter. Andy stands back a bit. I beckon him over and he cautiously appears at my side. We all read what is on the tree trunk at once:

Everything will work out how you wish, my loves, but the way you will get there is unusually unexpected. But then again, the journey is always the fun part!!! Love, Mom

We all look at each other in confusion. "What could that possibly mean?" I ask the question everyone is thinking.

"I suppose we'll find out," Kelly replies. That makes us all crack up, but we're still not entirely sure what to expect. But over the course of my life, I can't say I've ever really known what to expect.

32

Andy

Before I leave that night, I inform the kids that a surprise is waiting for them the next day.

They pry me so much that I have to reveal that Tina is coming to visit. They all cheer and their faces light up. I'm glad I can make them so happy. I hope they approve of Tina. I know that's a stupid thing to say. It's just that they love her so much when they haven't even met her, that they may not like her as much in person. I rush home to see her, and she is just as happy to be seeing the kids tomorrow as the kids are. Everything is going so well, except for the fact that she trashed half my stuff that night and I'm in desperate need to go shopping. Other than that, things are great, and I'm so glad that Jenna requested what she did. I didn't want to go through with what she protested in the first place, and now I have an excuse to do what I want and not what's right for the kids.

"Are the kids excited to finally meet me?" Tina asks, putting on her pajamas. "Or haven't you told them about me?"

I laugh at that question. "I talk about you every day. You wouldn't believe how excited they are. It was actually Jenna who saved our relationship."

She raises her eyebrows and climbs into the bed. "How is that?"

I sit down and explain, "She saw how upset I was after you wrecked me, and when I told her what happened, she was mad, but suggested I beg for you back. I wouldn't have come back if it weren't for her, so you can thank her for our future happiness."

"I'll have to remember to do that tomorrow," she laughs. Then her face falls. "Does that mean she had to convince you that you still loved me?"

"No! It's just that I was so scared that you'd say no and hurt me again, that I didn't even want to try. I didn't want to take that chance. It was stupid, and I'm glad she convinced me to come over here."

She leans in and gives me a kiss. "Me too."

"**W**ake up Andrew!" I hear this and roll right off the edge of the bed and onto the floor.

I smack on my stomach, making a large thump, and groan. I open my eyes, and from my position on the floor, I can't see anything. My eyes are blurry without my contacts in, and I have no idea where the voice that woke me came from. "That wasn't graceful, now was it?"

I'm not fully awake, but I'm pretty sure that that is the voice of my father. I flip over onto my back and look up at him. I squint as hard as I can, but I can't make out any details. All I see is the outline of a man standing over me who appears to be holding something.

"One moment please," I mutter, reaching my arm up to the nightstand. I move my hands around aimlessly on the top of the nightstand until they brush against my contacts. I pick them up very carefully and place them in my eyes. That is the worst feeling to me, but I have to do it every day. I look ridiculous in glasses and I'm pretty much blind. I shiver as I accidentally touch my eye. I blink a few times and everything comes into focus. I lower my arm and turn around, so I can see that it is definitely my father standing over me. I look again and I see the thing he is holding is actually a gun!

"Jesus Dad!" I yell. "Stop pointing that at me! You're making me nervous!"

He chuckles evilly. "That's the purpose. You betrayed me Andrew, and I'm not very happy about it!!!"

I stand up in a motion that seems to take a year, all the while keeping my eyes on the end of the gun where the bullet would come out and end my life. "Calm down, Dad. I don't know what you're talking about. No need to get hasty here."

"The hell you don't!" he roars. It's never good when he roars. He shakes the gun at me, and I'm starting to get really nervous. He will do anything when he's angry. He goes completely insane when something sabotages his chances of closing a case and might just shoot his son for fun. I've been meaning to get him to a clinic and watch him get drug away in a straight jacket, but it seems I've had more important things on my mind, and now I might be paying for it with my life. Why do I always end up in these situations? Now I'm going to die helpless next to my bed in nothing but my boxers, and no one will find me until it's too late. I can see my obituary now "Andrew Thompson was more than capable of fighting off lung cancer, but his own father was just too much." I shudder at the thought and decide I better do something about this situation, or I won't be able to think much longer.

I press my back up against the wall and tiptoe along it until I complete a semi circle around him. He watches me like a hawk watching his prey, and when I stop moving, he shoves the end of the gun into my chest. I gasp, my whole body going into overdrive. "Where are you going, son?!"

I try desperately to keep my breathing even. It takes a very deep concentration. I focus on that Tina might still be in the house and I have to stay alive to save her. "Okay look Dad, why would you want to kill me? I'm your only son. The only one that can carry on your legacy. Do you really want to lose that?"

"My son would *never* betray me!" he screams through his teeth. I feel the gun tremble on my chest. So that didn't work.

"What do you want?"

He glares at me. "Show me where the kids are so we can settle this dispute peacefully."

I can't give up everything I've done this summer just because I'm a little fearful for my later existence. I run my hands through my hair, which is starting to fall in my eyes, nervously. I can't stand when it gets like this. I have to cut it so it stands up again. "Sorry, but I don't think I'm going to do that. I've come too far to give up."

That was not an acceptable answer. "I'm already angry. Don't test me. Just tell me where you're hiding the children and this will all be over."

"Yeah, I got that the first time," I sass. "And I'm still not going to cooperate."

His entire face turns so red, it's almost purple. The veins pop out on his neck. I know he's so angry he's about to explode, and when he explodes, anything can happen, such as that gun going off and the bullet piercing through my heart. It's hard to stay calm when you have that thought, but I've had years and years of experience with my father, and I know exactly how to deal with anything he throws at me. "ANDREW! It's over and you can't do anything for them anymore. Just lead me to them and we can act like you tried to fight me off and didn't win. You can still be their hero, but they must get what they deserve. It will be much easier to help me than to fight me. Who knows who could get hurt if you go against me, like poor little helpless Tina." He then proceeds to act out a scene where he pretends to be Tina. He portrays her as fearing for her life. Then he raises the gun to his head and pretends to shoot. He shows her falling to the ground and dying. He finally gets up and cackles. "Oh no, she's gone."

I can't even describe how I feel at this moment. It's a mixture of anger, hate, fear, and helplessness. I can't help myself and charge at my father like a bull. I think I can even feel my face steaming. I start pounding on his chest with all my might, but the thuds are hurting my hands more than him. I try to push him but he only sways back a little and returns to his original position. "Stay away from her!" I yell in frustration. I feel like I'm having a temper tantrum, like a little kid times a hundred. "If you touch her, I'll kill you!"

He rolls his eyes at my threats and slugs me in the stomach. It takes the breath away from me and it's a little while before I regain it. I clutch my stomach and get my breathing even again. The anger returns as I do, and I take that strength I gained to throw my left hand around and punch him right in the jaw.

177

His head snaps back. He gasps. He seems a little shocked as he rubs his sore jaw and twists it around to make sure it still works. He reminds me of a shiftless cow munching on grass, and that makes me want to punch him a second time. I raise my hand to try it, but he stops it. "You're quite a bit stronger than when you were a teenager." I used to hit him all the time when I was in high school and loved it. I have forgotten how amazing that feels.

"I should do that more often," I note.

He glowers at me. "Calm down there. I haven't hurt her"-he pauses to build to the effect-"yet. But I certainly will if I need to. So you choose-Tina or the fugitives?"

I would feel defeated if this was someone other than my father. All I have to do is make him think he has won, and then he makes mistakes. I hang my head and refuse to look at him. "I would do anything for her. I'll lead you to the children," I mutter in disgust.

His face brightens and a little of the crazy fades away. "That's my boy," he says proudly, patting me on the back like I'm eight. This is not the only time I've wished him dead. I can hardly believe I'm related to this monster, let alone him being my father. "You better lead me to the right place, because if I find you tricked me, than things will be much worse than if you cooperate."

"Why would I do something stupid like that?"

He chuckles. "I don't know Andrew, but I think not finishing college made you a little stupider than me."

It takes more self control than I thought I possessed to pretend that doesn't irk me. I stare at my feet and literally bite down on my tongue from saying something back that would make him think I can't be trusted. I know that was a test to see if I'm telling the truth. I fake a smile when I feel I have enough in control to look at him, and he nods to say I passed.

Now it's time to follow through on my plan. "Can you grab my clothes? They're right there in the closet." I point to show him where and he immediately turns around to get them. That is a big mistake.

"You know," he says, shuffling through my closet looking for my uniform. "I'm really glad you came through on this. I would have hated to use my weapon, especially on my junior."

I need to act quickly or else I will lose my only chance. "Whatever," I mumble to show I'm listening and not up to anything. "You know I still don't like doing this." I look around wildly for a large, heavy object.

"I know, but this is the only easy way." He is taking my uniform off of the hanger and I only have a few seconds left. I'm starting to become nervous that I will blow this.

"I guess," I answer absentmindedly. I grab for my alarm clock swiftly so it doesn't make a sound. I rip the plug out of the wall and inch closer to the blind side of my father. I raise it above my head and take a deep breath. This is my one chance.

I scream, "I will never help you in this lifetime!" and hit him over the head with the alarm clock as hard as I can. I hear a crack and he falls to a heap on the floor. My uniform falls on top of him. I place the back of my hand in front of his nose to make sure I haven't killed him. When I feel hot air, I can't help but smile.

"That felt really good," I say to myself. "Now I have to get out of here and warn the kids before he wakes up."

I grab a pair of jeans and a shirt from my closet and throw them on in a few seconds. Then I race down the stairs, grabbing my Chucks on the way, to see Tina sitting in the corner of the kitchen hugging her knees. She shoots up as soon as she sees me, her eyes wide. "I'm so sorry. He had a gun so I didn't know how to stop him. Are you alright?"

"Yeah," I reply, a little out of breath. "But I'm not sure he is."

She gasps. "What did you do?"

"I had to hit him over the head with an alarm clock to get away. I think he'll wake up, but I can't be sure." I can't help grinning again. "It made me feel *strong*."

She stares at me as I wallow in my pride. "Good job. You've just graduated as Hercules." She shakes her head. "Now you need to go rescue the unsuspecting orphans."

I snap out of my little fantasy world and remember I have a limited time frame. "Let's go," I order, pulling on her hand and running to our garage. I throw open the back door and run to my beautiful Miata convertible.

"No," Tina says, pulling back on me. I stop. "What if we have to make a quick get-away? We can't fit us and the three kids in your little baby car."

I have to admit it's true. "Ok, but don't make fun of my car. It's small but strong, like me."

She laughs as we change direction and run toward her Mustang GT. I make it to the driver's side first and she reluctantly climbs in the passenger seat. She doesn't like someone else controlling her pride and joy but she trusts me. I slam the door closed and step on the gas. The car shoots down the driveway with an earsplitting roar from the muffler. I ignore all the stop signs and speed limits, hoping that I won't get stopped. If that occurs, I'll just pull out my badge, which I happen to keep with me at all times, even these ones. I swerve, almost running another car off the road. Finally, we make it to Rehoboth Beach, and I pull into my special hidden parking lot.

"So this is where you disappear to all day," Tina observes.

I pull the key out of the ignition and nod. "This is only the beginning though."

We race out of the car and she follows me into the wooded area where the kid's camp is. At that moment, I feel as if everything is okay. There can't be any way that my father can catch up with us now. With Tina's help, I can pack up the kids and move them to a safer place. Then I will get them with that family while fighting my dad. It is a very dangerous thing to do, but to me it's worth it. This isn't just about defeating my dad anymore; this is about saving those kids and giving them the life they deserve. I realize how much I care about these little people. I would give my life for them. Who knows if I actually will?

33

Jenna

Deep down, all three of us know something is wrong, and I am feeling it the most. Andy told us yesterday he would be here at 10 a.m. sharp, and it's 11. He was going to take us to see the new family, and he was determined to give us a good life. We all knew that. There is no way he would be late for something this important unless something had gone wrong that made him late. My mind can't grasp that he could have just overslept or something simple like that. I can't make myself believe that he's unreliable. He is too amazing, and I can't admit he's not the perfect guy. I can't be disappointed.

My mind automatically goes to the worst thing possible that could have occurred. He could have gotten in a car accident on the way over here, he may not have woken up due to some medical condition, or there was another fight with Tina. What if his cancer is back? I shake that thought out of my head. That can't be. What if there was an intruder in the house and either him or Tina got hurt? What if there was a fire like our house? I decide to stop thinking or I am going to literally worry myself sick. I have some deep love for this guy, even more than an older brother, and if something happened to him like everyone else I've ever loved in my life, I wouldn't be able to keep going like I have before. Dad, Lauren, and Mom are enough for one person to take. I have to make myself believe that he could be just late. I'd rather be disappointed in him than learn of his demise.

Matty sees my pure white face and my uneven breathing. "Relax Jenna. It wouldn't surprise me if he's still sleeping."

I flex my entire body to keep from shaking. "You don't know that for sure and I'm really worried."

"He's fine," Kelly assures me. That's almost funny because I always have to assure him of things. Now he's the adult here and I'm the scared little child.

"I hope so." I feel tears start to come, and I turn my head so they don't see. They don't seem worried or that they even care that much. I can't look like the idiot that is freaking out over what is most likely nothing.

"Hey," Matty smiles sympathetically. He puts his arm around my shoulders and squeezes them. "I would feel the same way if I thought something might have happened to Kristina." Kelly hugs my waist and rests his little head on my stomach. I stroke his hair and it makes me feel better.

Suddenly, a loud roar fills the still air that is definitely not a wave. It sounds like something out of a Fast and Furious movie. "Speaking of Kristina," I comment. "Doesn't that sound like her car?"

Matty's face lights up. "That thing was a beauty."

I have to agree. Maybe it's just a coincidence, but it sure sounds like her car, and there are some sounds you don't forget. The sound gets closer and closer until it hurts our ears, and then it dies away. Something is really strange about this morning.

"That sounds like it's coming from the secret parking lot," Matty notes. "What is such a loud car that could possibly belong to Krissy doing in our hidden parking lot?"

"That is a very good question."

Matty's curiosity gets the better of him, and he creeps away from our camp and into the brush of the forest. I grab Kelly's hand and follow him. I pray it's not the cops, although they wouldn't make such a noise. That would warn us they were coming and we could get away. Maybe it really is Kristina and she has no idea this place is supposed to be secret. She does live a little ways away from here.

Matty stops short and puts a finger to his lips. I have to rock on my heels to keep from knocking him over. We all listen intently and hear the pounding of footsteps approaching fast. It sounds like more than one person, and they are running straight toward us. I give Matty a fearful look and he pulls me to a sitting position. We crawl behind a large bush and try to stay as still as we can, which is really hard when three large kids are trying to fit in a space barely big enough for one small kid. I feel myself shaking again.

The footsteps come so close we can feel their vibrations, and then they stop. I push a little of the bush back so I can see with one eye. There is a guy and a girl standing inches away from where we are hiding, both of them barefoot, and the woman appears to be in her pajama pants. I can only see from the knee down. I pull back and whisper what I saw in Matty's hear so low it is almost a breath. He nods to show he got it all, and I return to my look-out.

"Where are they?" the woman asks. Her voice sounds familiar, but I can't place where I've heard it before.

"I don't know. Their stuff is right here. They might have heard us and hid like I taught them to," the guy replies. I definitely know where I heard that voice.

"It's Andy!" I squeak in happiness. It gives us away, and before I know it, the bush is pulled away to reveal us practically curled up in a ball. He grins at us and we stand up immediately.

"I've taught you well," he says proudly.

I'm so happy to see him that I give him a huge hug. I almost knock him over. "What is this about?"

"I thought you were dead," I blurt out, not wanting to let go. I bury my face in his chest and let a few joyful tears flow. Andy is a little shocked at my reply and inquires why I was wishing him dead.

"I wasn't wishing," I smile through my tears. "This was an important day and I didn't think you'd be late without something awful happening."

"Well, I'm not dead, but something awful did happen. My dad showed up at our house pointing a gun at me. He found out that I betrayed him and wanted me to show him where you three were. I knew I was never going to do that, but I didn't want to get shot either. I, being the smart problem-solver that I am, tricked him into thinking I was on his side, and then when he turned around, I hit him over the head with my alarm clock."

"Really?" I ask in amazement. I always knew he was a superhero.

"Oh yeah! He fell right down and Tina and I raced right over here to warn you guys. It was something right out of movie!"

I pull away a minute to show Matty I was right. "Here that Matty? Something did happen. I wasn't worrying for nothing!" But he doesn't hear me. He hasn't heard a thing since we left our hiding spot. He's too busy staring right past us at the girl, mouth hanging open, completely gawking. He's making a fool of himself.

"Matty!" I yell, but he doesn't respond. It's starting to make me angry. "MATTIX!" I screech, and his head whips around. He despises being called that, which is exactly why I said it. I rely on it to get his attention.

"What?" he growls.

"What are you doing?" I can't see the girl past Andy, or else I would have been able to answer that question on my own. "You look like an idiot."

"Krissy," is all he can whisper.

I don't understand. "You gave her a nickname? Come on, that's embarrassing. And why are you bringing her up anyway?"

 "Wait, who's Krissy?" Andy asks. He's more confused than I am.

I roll my eyes. "Some girl we met that Matty is secretly in love with."

"Shut up!" Matty yells, pointing straight ahead. "She's right there!"

Now I am really lost. That isn't possible. I shift a little so I can see past Andy, and I gawk the exact same way Matty did. There, right in front of me, is Kristina in her pajamas with her hair messily put up into a ponytail. She smiles widely because I just announced my brother had a crush on her. I could hardly believe my eyes. I blink a few times to make sure I'm not hallucinating, but she still stays in the same spot. But, if she really is there, then why?

"Well, fancy meeting you here," I almost laugh.

She giggles too. "Well I just learned a lot."

I turn to Matty. "Sorry about that by the way."

He glares at me. Oh well, it's bad to keep things like that inside. I'm just surprised she didn't know already, with the way he turns twenty shades of scarlet every time she speaks. I hope I don't do that with Andy. It just occurred to me that I might. At least he knows why. It's out there. He's gorgeous and that's just that.

"You guys know her?" Andy questions.

"Of course," Kelly chimes in the conversation. "Do you?"

Andy looks as shocked as we are. "This is Tina."

All three of our mouths drop open at the exact same time, and they stay there for at least a minute. I'm the first one to gain my composure. "No way."

"I'm not lying." He puts his arm around her to prove that point.

"So that's why I heard her car," Matty whispers.

Kelly adds, "Now *that* is ironic!" He makes us all laugh. I can still hardly believe it. I had pictured the amazing Tina as completely different from Kristina, when all this time they had been the same person. I admit I should have known. The pieces were all there to put together if I would have thought about it a little bit. I guess the thought never crossed my mind, even though they both talked about the same house and Andy said Tina was a teacher. And the kicker was Tina was the last part of Kristina. I laugh to myself thinking of how small the world we live in is.

The next thought that comes to my head is how much I liked Kristina since the first time we met. She was beautiful and nice and plain amazing just like Andy. My heart warms. With how precious Andy is to me, I couldn't take him being completely in love with any lesser of a girl. If it's not going to be me, which I must admit to myself it never will be even though it hurts, I would want it to be her.

"OH!" Andy yells suddenly. "All this confusion made me totally forget we're all being chased by a mad man!"

Tina jumps into action yelling, "Pack up all your stuff as quick as you can. We're going to escape in my Mustang."

That is a very appealing thought as I shove all my belongings into a bag. Matty and Kelly do the same with Andy and Tina helping us out to make it quicker. We throw the loaded bags over our shoulders, taking one last look to make sure we haven't left anything important. I feel for the ring on my finger and peer over at Matty's hand to see he is still wearing his too. We are about to run when Kelly cries out.

"I can't go!" he screams, and we all stop to question him. "Salamander is gone!"

A sinking feeling appears in my stomach. "Where did you leave him?"

"I don't know," he replies, panicking.

"We have to go," Andy reminds us. "We've wasted too much time already." We all agree with him, but Kelly doesn't want to hear it.

"I'm either going with Salamander or staying here until I find him." He sits down and crosses his arms to show his protest is real.

We don't know what to do. We have to leave, but it's clear that Kelly is not budging. "It's over there," Matty informs us, pointing to a far away tree where Salamander is hanging by his foot. How he got there, I will never know. Boys don't take care of anything, even if they love it dearly.

"Go get it," I order Kelly and he shoots up screaming for Salamander. We catch up with him and run as fast as we can, hoping that we have enough time left.

We make it to the car, just at the edge of the forest, and throw the bags in the trunk. They just fit. Andy unlocks the door and begins to open it. We believe that we can make it, that we will escape and be safe in a short amount of time. But the click of a gun very near our heads rips that belief away from us and stomps on it. We all turn around slowly to see Andy's dad, or "cocky cop" as Matty would call him, standing in front of us with his gun. There are a few other cops behind him that I don't recognize for back-up. We're too late.

34

Andy

"**M**Y head hurts Andrew," my father states condescendingly. He almost laughs when he says it. He has one hand on where I hit his head and one hand on the gun he's pointing at me, and he's chuckling to himself. That's how I can tell this isn't going to be good. He only gets this way when he's so angry he's gone off the deep end, even more than this morning. He has finally lost it right here, and the danger that comes with that is unimaginable. The first thing I think of is that I have to get out of here alive along with the kids and Tina. Then I wonder if that can really happen. He's come here to shoot someone, and if that person has to be me, so be it. I never got what I wanted in life. But at least I will die a hero. Still I must try to get out too. My death would hurt a lot of people. I learned that when fighting cancer.

"Sorry about that," I say innocently. "I tripped and fell on you."

His smile fades away and I think I hear growling. Jenna glances at me in fear. I shouldn't have said that. "Cut the crap! We both know you were trying to be the hero in the movie, killing the villain in the hopeless situation and taking off to rescue his innocent little people. Bravo!" He claps a few times, and Detective Morgan, Cox, and Jones standing behind him start to get uneasy. They are starting to see the crazy side of him that I've known all my life.

"Okay, you're right," I admit. "But don't think you've won. You may have found us, but I'm smarter and faster than you, and I will get us out of this."

He raises his eyebrows. "Are you trying to convince me or yourself? Because I know for sure that I have won and you cannot change that. It was a fun game and you put up quite a fight, so I must give you credit for that."

He's starting to make me angry again. I hate when he gives me that taunting tone, like I'm this little helpless boy and he's going to decapitate me with his dictator ways. Even though he may be correct in that I see no way I can beat him this time, I can't let him see my defeat. The only way to get out of this is to fool him with fake confidence.

I start to say something back, but he won't allow me. "The game is over now. Even though you fought hard and gave me quite a challenge, I have still come out on top, like always. Now let's admit that rationally. There's an easy way to admit defeat without anyone getting hurt. Just hand over the kids and we will all forget you've betrayed us. It will be like this summer never even happened."

"How many times do I have to tell you, I will *never*, do you get that, *never ever*, do that. After all the pain you have put me through and all things you have made me do so I live my life how you want me to, the last thing I want to do is help you. In fact, I'm going to keep going against you until you are finally beaten. So that means no, I won't hand over the kids. Sorry, no can do."

This time he really does growl. He bares his teeth like a wolf ready to attack and growls from deep down in his throat. I can hardly believe he's a grown man at this point. "Andrew, fine you won. You really did. You successfully tricked me for months and made things difficult for me. You can tell everyone you finally got one over on me, but you must hand over the kids. They broke the law and they deserve to be locked up for it, plain and simple. Don't make this about you and me anymore. Just give me the kids and no one gets hurt."

"OVER MY DEAD BODY!"

"That's it. You just brought violence into this." He turns around and orders, "Jones, grab the woman so I can shoot her."

I go ice cold once again. I wish I would have talked to Jones. Now she thinks I hate her and has no reason to go against my father. I look to her pleadingly.

"Tina?" she asks him, catching my eye. "I don't think I can do that."

My dad's eyes widen in fury. "You're taking his side now?! Just because of a little crush, you're going to go against the law and risk losing your job?! And why wouldn't you want to kill her so you can have my son all to yourself? I see you get something out of this too."

My heart thumps so loud I'm sure everyone can hear it. I swear the blood has stopped short in my veins also, and I'm having trouble breathing. I keep my composure to keep that confidence thing up, but it is so hard in these kinds of situations. If my dad is good at anything, it is persuasion and getting into people's heads so they do what he wants.

"He'll never forgive me if I go and do that. No." I look over to her to show her that I'm forever grateful, but she doesn't see me. The gun is pointing her way and she is rigid.

"Get out of here before I shoot you," he yells, spit flying out of his mouth. It almost looks as if he has rabies. Jones looks at me one more time, almost like she is contemplating grabbing me and running so this isn't the last time she sees me, before disappearing into the woods. She isn't that bad after all. She's just hurt. But I have no time to think of that now. I still have an armed crazy man positioned in front of me.

The gun moves back over in Tina and my direction. "Now that we have gotten rid of the weak, let me have the kids."

"It's still no," I reply calmly.

He stays calm too. He shakes his gun a little, dangerously close to Tina, to remind me he still has it and says, "If you're not going to help me, I guess I will have to get rid of you. You know I will do anything for my job, even if that means going through you." Then he laughs evilly.

I gulp and begin my speech. Somehow I knew it would come to this. "Go ahead Dad, shoot me. Just end it all. I was never what you wanted anyway. You dreamed of having a son who would be a carbon copy of you, some crazy crooked cop who messed up the lives of everyone he was around. But out of some miracle, I didn't turn out like you. I was the opposite. I was a good guy. I didn't want to hurt people, I wanted to help them. I wanted to start a band that made music that inspired people and made them feel better about themselves. I wanted to interact with people all over the world and see from all kinds of different points of view. I thought I could get through tough times with my music through my entire life, but you took that away from me. You wanted me to be something else so bad that you used force to make me be like you. I had to go to college, quit my band, become a lousy cop, and follow you around on your stupid cases, which most of the time had priority issues much like this one, out of fear for my life. I went through cancer thinking my life was a waste and that I had to change things, but still you threatened me and still I gave in to the fear. But now I see that I need to stop this vicious cycle. I need to go against you and live my life like I want, before I lose my chance. This 'helping the kids' thing started out as my way of doing that, but now it's more. There's still the thrill of finally defeating you, but these kids mean something to me. They mean a hell of a lot more than you do, and I would give my life to keep them away from you. Same with Tina. So shoot Dad. I want you to shoot because I'm never going to give you the kids. Get rid of me now so you don't have to deal with a son you never wanted anyway. I see it as you get something out of this too." I put my arms out as far as they could go so they are shielding Matty and Jenna on one side and Tina and Kelly on the other. I close my eyes and brace myself for an end. I hope it will be quick and painless.

"If that's what you want. Last chance to make this peaceful."

I shake my head, my eyes still closed. I can feel a tear run down my cheek, and I have to fight to keep from running out of there and letting the kids fight for themselves. I really don't want to die after all I've been through.

There is a long silence, and then I hear a click. I don't want to see his angry face right before he kills me. Instead I think of all my good times over the years. My childhood years when my mom taught me how to cook, my high school year when I showed up for band practice in Ryan's garage and we signed up for the musical talent show, which was the biggest event of senior year in my school, college where I met Tina, hearing I was cancer free after a year and a half, when I showed Tina the amazing house I bought her and she excitedly agreed to move in with me, all the family get-togethers where I usually ended up rolling on the floor in laughter afterwards, and especially this summer. I don't think I've had so much fun in my life as I have had in the last three months or so. These kids showed me what it's like to have fun again, to live again. I would like to die this way if I have to die. At least my head is full of good things.

Then I hear a crack and the skin on the right side of my chest, almost symmetrical to my copyright branding on the other side, rips open. I feel warm blood pour out down my stomach. It feels like I got stabbed by a foot long dagger from a running person. My brain shuts my body down, making it numb so I don't have to feel this anymore. I try to fight that feeling to stay alive, but I'm too weak. The pain is so intense, my body can't take it and my legs give way. I fall to a laying position on the sand with a pool of my own blood forming around me. I tilt my head toward the kids and Tina in a final plea for them to save me, but things have gotten so blurry that I can't see their faces. The forest starts swirling around and I know I can't hold on any longer. Finally, the world goes black and swallows me up.

35

Jenna

I feel my heart stop, literally. I stand there unable to move an inch. I can't breathe, and I can't feel my body. I just stare at Andy's crumpled body on the floor, dying, in complete shock. I see him look over at me, helpless and in pain, before his eyes close and his head falls. A stabbing pain I have never felt before shoots through my entire body, like I've been shot myself. All the sound fades away and all I can see is him. The crazy distorted face of "cocky cop" disappears into the darkness, and Matty and Kelly get swallowed up also. Everything goes silent and dark, and I feel like I'm at a comedy show where everything is black except the spotlight on the comedian. Tina comes running up to him in slow motion and falls on top of him, crying hysterically. She pushes her hands down on the wound on his chest, trying to apply pressure, but is in so much shock that her hands keep slipping. Cocky cop steps into the spotlight to step over his body and then disappears again. The other cops do the same, except for the girl that ran into the woods earlier and must have run back when she heard the shot. She stoops by Andy's side and runs her fingers through the blood in the sand, shaking uncontrollably. Tina yells something at her that I can't hear, and the woman cop springs into action, grabbing her phone. The way she yells into it shows she's panicking too. It's clear she cares about him almost as much as Tina. I continue to stare until I feel someone pulling on my arm. My arm is being pulled so hard I'm almost falling over to that side, but still I have no reaction. I just move from side to side as I'm being pulled and continue to watch the silent horror movie on the ground in front of me. Tina looks up from Andy to me and screams something to me, but I can't hear it. I can't feel anything at this point, not even that stabbing pain. I go numb as I watch this amazing guy that I love so unconditionally being ripped away from me, just like the others. I'm in such a deep state of shock, I'm about to fall down and die next to him.

Tina gets up and runs toward me. She shakes me like a doll by the shoulders, but I stare right through her to the spotlight. She lifts my chin so I look her in the eye, and I see they are puffy, red, and just plain petrified that she's going to lose the love of her life. She mouths the word 'run', and something clicks in my head. The sun of the early morning shines around me again, and the many sounds of the world reach my ears again. I hear a lot of screaming and crying and a gruff yell that seems to be an order from cocky cop. I hear Matty screaming at me and Kelly squealing. I look over and see the panic all over Matty's face as he tugs as hard as he can on my arm. One of the cops is trying to get a hold of Kelly. He is squealing and twisting out of his grasp. I turn my head once again and see the woman cop ushering over the people coming out of the ambulance with a stretcher. The sirens blare and more screams erupt. A shrill shriek from Kelly surpasses all the other noise, and my head snaps around. The cop has taken Salamander and is using him as a way to trap Kelly. I let out a gasp as my regular breathing and heartbeat returns. I can feel my body, all the way down to my feet, again and shake Matty and Tina off me to run toward Kelly.

"Give that back, now!" I scream, throwing a semi-strong punch to the cop's side. I'm so angry and upset at this point, I want to hurt someone. I want to hurt them like they hurt me over and over and they hurt my Andy.

He looks down at me, a little surprised, and laughs. "How are you going to make me?" He pulls out the hand-cuffs and shakes them in my face. "I've got this against you."

"You're the meanest person in the world! My daddy died when I was one and this present he gave me is all I have to remember him by, and you want to take that away for your stupid job!!! I hate you! I hate all of you! You killed Andy!" Kelly screams, tears pouring down his face. He throws punches wildly.

The cop, whose name is Detective Morgan apparently, smile fades away, and he lowers the hand that is clutching Salamander. He has a sad face on, almost as if he understands what it's like to not remember one of the most important people in your life. He extends his hand out to return Salamander to Kelly and Kelly reaches for it. At the last second, Detective Morgan grabs Kelly's arm and pulls him back. He holds Kelly by the waist and attempts to hand-cuff him while Kelly punches and kicks him in the stomach.

A wave of red fury boils up inside me like a volcano just erupted. "You're a soulless jerk!!!" I run into him as hard as I can and knock both him and Kelly over. I wrestle Salamander away from Detective Morgan, while Kelly rolls away from us as soon as Detective Morgan loosens his grip. I worm my way out with Salamander and give Detective Morgan a good, hard kick before Kelly and I run off. I laugh to myself as I hear him groan in pain and defeat from a thirteen year old girl. Well, I will be fourteen in two short weeks.

We look around for Matty, and I spot Andy being pulled onto the stretcher. I fight going back into shock again. My brothers need me. Matty shows up behind me. "We have to run now Jenna!"

I turn around to look at him a second before watching Andy again. Tina catches me staring again and walks over. "You have to go," she tells me. "He'll be fine. If I know anything about him, it's that he doesn't give up easy and is a survivor, so there's no way he's going like this. You need to save yourself because it wouldn't be very fair to let yourself get caught after he took a bullet for you." I study her a second to see if she's telling the truth. I don't want to see that she is just as scared and uncertain as me and is just trying to get me to save myself, but that's exactly what I see. I feel like I could vomit.

"Make sure he is alright. Do that for me."

She nods. "I will, now go!"

I take one last nervous glance at the ambulance and run after Matty, with Kelly holding my hand. We don't look back as we race through the forest, pushing branches out of our faces. We pass our camp and reach the clearing with the lake. We try our best not to slip as we move fast across the rocks and to the big trees on the other side of the clearing.

"Behind that tree!" Matty orders, pointing to what has to be the largest tree in the forest. We drop to our knees and crawl behind it. I press my back against the trunk, facing the opposite direction of the lake. Kelly climbs in my lap and we both sit silent and still. Matty sits next to me, with half of his face looking past the tree so he knows if someone is coming. I close my eyes and rest the back of my head on the tree trunk. I am exhausted from all that has gone on this summer, and I use this little bit of time to break down. The tears fall profusely and my whole body shakes as I think of all that I've been through. At this point, I'm not sure the tragedy will ever end. All I want is a life like a normal kid who goes to school and hangs out with their friends on the weekend. Matty and I should be celebrating our birthdays without the burden of having to take care of our little brother and having to fight everyday for our survival and freedom. We should have a house and a bed and clothes and somewhere to cook food. We should have some sort of guardian, but instead we're stuck living in the woods hiding from a lunatic cop who wants to arrest us as a way to get publicity. I shouldn't have had to go through losing my sister, my mother, and my father. I shouldn't have had to watch my house, along with everything I knew in my life, burn down to the ground. I shouldn't have had to steal clothes and hide in my grandmother's house from the cops. I shouldn't have had to live in the woods hidden behind the beach. I shouldn't have had to worry that I would get killed or arrested every day of my summer. I shouldn't have had to go through all these things, but I did. Life isn't fair and I got the short end of the stick over and over and over again. The only good thing that came out of all this was Andy. He was so perfect and amazing, and he loved us so much from the minute he saw us, that he risked his life for us. He gave us everything to make us still feel like regular kids and tried so hard to keep us happy. He was the closest thing I had to a parental figure and I clung to him. And now I have to watch him get shot and then leave him while he could possibly be bleeding to death. He can't die. He can't die trying to save us. The world can't lose such an angel because of me. I can't take any more crap in my life to deal with. Can I just win for once?!

"What?" Matty whispers.

Did I say that last part out loud? "I didn't say anything." At least I didn't mean to say anything.

"I think you may have."

I stare at Matty. That didn't sound like him, but it had to be. He stares back at me, just as confused. I look down at Kelly and he is staring wide-eyed to my left side. I follow his gaze to a pair of shoes, then up to the cop uniform, and up to the twitching angry lunatic face of Andy's dad, pointing the same gun he shot his son with at us. And he looks like he would have no problem pulling that trigger again.

Matty stands up before I can even react to what I'm seeing and walks toward him until he's two inches away from the end of the gun. I want to tell him to stop, but I don't have any breath to even form words. I just watch, holding Kelly tight, as there is a stare down between my brother and "cocky cop".

"You are a crazy psycho lunatic and I hope you burn in hell," Matty says through his teeth. I can hardly believe this. It's almost as if he's asking to be killed. Maybe he has finally given up like I'm about to at this point.

Andy's dad tilts his head to the side like a dog and smirks. "You want to be a brave little boy, now don't you? You remind me so much of my son. You want to be courageous and rebellious against me, and it only ends in pain. No one can defeat me. I have no conscious, and I think if Andrew dies, that is a weight off my shoulders. I don't have to deal with his nonsense anymore or my wife saying how we should really try to like each other because we're family. She *always* takes his side because he's her momma's boy and I'm tired of it. So if I killed him, it would be a good thing. Maybe then she would love her husband more than her son like she is supposed to, and he won't disappoint me anymore." Then he starts cackling like a witch. I don't think I've ever been in contact with anyone more insane and dangerous. I thought these kinds of people were only in movies or locked away somewhere in a straight jacket where they can't endanger anyone.

"Stay here," I whisper to Kelly, sliding him off of my lap and joining Matty. I stand by his side proudly. Before I know it, Kelly has squeezed in between us.

"I thought I said to stay where you were," I hiss at him.

"No. I want to be brave and awesome like Andy too." I can't help but smile at that comment. That he is, and we're standing up not only for ourselves, but for him too, and all he's done for us.

I nod to tell him it's okay to stay. We all turn around and face the gun again. It's a very scary moment, but somehow I feel safe next to my brothers. I feel like somehow, somewhere we're going to be okay. Things are going to get better.

"Oh, so you all have a death wish, I see. I guess I can grant you your wish while my gun is still hot." He blows on the end of the gun and chuckles to himself. "Wouldn't you like to kill more bad people who try to go against your master?"

I glance at Matty and he rolls his eyes. Now he's talking to his gun like it's his pet snake.

"Go ahead and shoot us," Matty replies. "We don't have a death wish anymore than Andy, but we are just like him. We would rather die good people than live on to end up as screwed up as you, someone who kills people for the fun of it and messes with anyone's life that can help you get what you want. I don't want to be like that. I want to be shot and killed long before that happens."

"Perfectly said," I add in agreement.

He shakes his head. "No, I won't kill you. That's too easy, not what you deserve. Instead, I'll have you all rot in jail and think to yourselves what you're lives could have been, if only you weren't orphans. How does that sound?"

Have you ever hated someone so much you fantasize about them suffering? Well, that is the only way to explain the way the three of us feel about this man. It is such an intense feeling, I have to use all the self-control I have in me not to take that gun and shoot him right there. I'm sure Matty is doing the exact same thing. I can even here Kelly growling as he digs into Salamander with his fingernails.

Andy's father turns us all around with such a force that we can't possibly escape, and hand-cuffs us. Detective Cox and Detective Morgan, looking still a little winded from our previous encounter, come to help. They each take one of us by the shoulders and push us towards the exit of the forest. Detective Cox squeezes my shoulders and I cringe. I hate strangers touching me. I throw my foot and kick him in the knee as a last attempt to be free, but all it does is make him angry and push me harder into the back of the cop car next to my brothers. Kelly looks really scared and I try my best to comfort him. Matty just looks defeated and I know there's no helping that. He feels like he failed us when that's not true in the least. We all tried our very best and continually helped each other, but they were just too much for us. But somehow, sitting there, I still have the feeling that things are going to work themselves out, and we aren't doomed after all. Just like I can feel when something big and bad is about to happen, I feel when something big and good is about to happen. I hope I have that feeling because it's true.

36

Matty

I finally went and did it. I failed my family. It was my job to keep my sister and brother from this fate, and I just couldn't do it. I wasn't man enough to get us out of this, and now we're going to be stuck in jail forever. We're never going to get what we want from life just like cocky cop said, and it's entirely my fault. That is a depressing thought to have while sitting in a jail cell with concrete walls on three sides, long, thin metal rods on the fourth, and a cold, concrete floor beneath my feet. My shoes are in the bag in Krissy's car, so I have to sit with my feet under me so they don't freeze touching the floor. First of all, I wonder why the floor is so cold when it is only the beginning of September. Secondly, sitting on my feet hurts because I have to twist my ankles to balance myself and the bed they're pressing against is like a hard plank of wood. Why is this mattress so unbelievably hard, like it's not a mattress at all and just a fake-out? It is a perfect rectangle with a white sheet overtop of it and a hard, white pillow resting on one end. There are two bunk beds in the tiny room, so there are two beds on the right and left sides of the room and about a foot of floor space between them. The walls are completely white and blank, along with the ceiling. This is worse than what I imagined jail to be like, much worse. Probably because cocky cop got to choose the lack of amenities.

I look across the room to where Jenna is in the same position on the opposite bed, or wood table with a sheet over it. She gives me a longing look, like I'm supposed to know how to get us out of here and to safety. Honestly, I wish I could give that look to someone to take that responsibility off of my shoulders. But I'm the leader, the protector, and I have been since the fire. It's my job to make everything right for my brother and sister, whether I like it or not, and I failed my job. I no longer have a great plan to get us to safety. My luck has run out, and I begin to realize that that was all it had been all along. I wasn't some great leader who always knew what to do in tight situations; I was just lucky and now I'm not. And that makes me even more depressed.

I can't bear to look at Jenna any longer, so I look above her to see Kelly curled up on the top bunk. He's so scared that he's going to fall off that he doesn't move a muscle as he hugs his knees, lying on his side, and tries to even his breathing. Tears fill up in his eyes, but he blinks many times so they don't fall out onto his face. He's trying to be strong like his big brother, but what he doesn't know is that I wish I could cry too. In fact, I'm trying hard not to cry. My mom and dad always used to tell me that it's okay for boys to cry, but I don't think that applies to this situation. I know if I let out those much needed emotions, than that will show Jenna and Kelly that there is no hope left. Even if it's true, I don't want them to know it.

I decide I can't look at either of them, and I don't want my mind to even go near the thought of Andy in a morgue because of me, so I avert my gaze to the only side of the small room without a drab wall-the one with the iron bars. They are evenly spaced like they should be, and I busy myself trying to estimate how big the space between them is. When that hurts my brain, I look through the spaces and see a guard glaring at me. When cocky cop left us here, he told the guard not to take his eyes off of us. "They have a tendency to try stupid things," he had said, and had patted the short, fat guard on the back and cackled. The guard took the orders quite seriously, most likely because he knew the insane chief of police was gun happy today, and really never took his eyes off of us. No, I take that back. He never took his eyes off of *me*. He is not worried about the scared little 7 year old or the girl whom he underestimates her strength. He is only worried about me, thinking I am the largest flight risk. I'm sure I don't look the type that would grab him by the neck and bang his head against the bars so they split in half and I can escape like a ninja movie, but maybe he thinks if he takes his eyes off of me, I'll make some kind of contraption that will aid my escape. I've got that first glance sneaky smart look about me, so I'm told. Looking at this guard, a thought occurs to me. Messing with him will cheer up my siblings, and when we're all happy, we think better.

A smile spreads across my face, and he continues to glower at me with a straight face, arms crossed over his pudgy chest. I raise one hand and wave vigorously at him, still holding the smile. That ought to annoy a guy like him. His expression grows angrier and I can't help but chuckle. "I'm waving to you," I inform him, rather loudly.

No response. I hold up one finger and rip the sheet off the bed above me. I place it carefully on the floor and step down. That way my feet won't freeze off. I swagger over to the iron bars, still smirking, and hold a bar with each hand. I place as much of my face as I can possibly squeeze through the space between two bars, and stare right in the guard's face. "Hi!" I scream.

"Back up kid," the guard grumbles. "Unless you want trouble."

I laugh and hear snickers coming from Jenna also. "Not until you say hi to me. I was waving back there and thought you couldn't see me. I got close so you would say hi."

Now I hear Kelly laughing too. My plan is working. The guard just stares at me like he wishes I could turn into a chocolate glaze donut that he could pull through the bars and eat. "Hi," he mumbles, almost silently.

I put my hand up to my ear. "What? I can't hear you."

"You heard me."

I shake my head. "No, actually I didn't." I turn around to Jenna and Kelly, trying to hold back a laugh. They are doing exactly the same thing. "Did you hear anything?" I ask them.

They shake their heads immediately in response. "Not a thing," Jenna snickers.

I turn back to the guard and shake my head again. "They didn't hear you either. You see, your mouth is moving, but no sound comes out. You should really get that checked out."

His face grows as red as a beet in five seconds. His embarrassment only makes us laugh harder. "You should really get your blood pressure checked too if your face gets that red that quick. With your weight, that could be a real problem in the long-run." I can barely get it out before I burst out laughing so hard that no sound comes out, just air. The guard's hand rises to touch his face, and he looks quite hurt by my comments and our laughing. I would feel bad if this weren't the only way to make us happy while stuck in jail for what could be a very long time.

When we have laughed so hard that all our chests hurt, the guard regains his angry, serious face. "Ignorant teenager," he grunts. "I will never have kids because they become teenagers, and I hate teenagers. I'll be sure to tell Chief Thompson what you have done son, so you can get the punishment you deserve from him."

I raise my eyebrows. "Oh is that so? You're gonna cry to your chief because you're not man enough to deal with me on your own?"

"I could very easily deal with you, but I figure that Chief Thompson will do it more effectively," he answers. "And by effectively, I mean painfully."

Before I can come up with a witty comment, we all hear yelling coming from down the hall. The guard's head snaps around to see what's going on, and I stand on my toes to try to see if I can see anything at all. Someone calls to the guard, but I can't make out what they say.

"I don't think Chief Thompson's gonna like that very much." He shakes his head. "I know, but we're dead meat if we let that happen. You know that."

This is almost as frustrating as trying to figure out a phone conversation from what someone is saying on one end of the line. "What's going on?"

"Fine," the guard says to whoever he is speaking to, completely ignoring me. "But I'm going to say it was your idea."

I crane my neck to see who is making the following footsteps. They are hurried, and before I know it, Krissy is standing right in front of me, breathing heavily and red in the face. Her eyes look tear-stricken and puffy. Jenna jumps up off of the bed in two seconds flat when she sees her. She had been worried about Andy sick all day and now we were finally getting some answers.

"Tina?!" I ask, very surprised to see her here and not in the hospital.

"Hey Matty, Jenna, Kelly."

"How's Andy?" Jenna pries before Krissy can even continue.

Her face looks worried, and she takes a deep breath. "They had to take him into surgery to remove the bullet, and he's still not out. I was going to worry myself sick waiting in the waiting room, so I thought I would do what he would want-to try my best to get you guys out of here."

"But how?"

"Well, I thought maybe I could post bail, but I don't think crazy Andrew Sr. is going to allow that. I have to do something though."

"He has to let us out," Jenna cries. "That's the law."

"And he's the chief of police," I remind her. "So he can keep us in here if he thinks we would endanger someone. Even if it's not true, he has a good way with persuasion."

Jenna starts to panic. She would do anything to get out of here, which means she is going to start thinking irrationally. "That's not fair! I have to go see him!" She pounds on the bars with both fists and bangs her head on one of them. I can tell by her breathing that she is starting to cry, even if she doesn't want me to see. I guess messing with that guard was all for nothing.

Speaking of the guard, he is watching and listening the entire time, and I forgot he was there until right now, when the guy who he was speaking to earlier rushes over. Our conversation ceases, and both Krissy and I look over to see what is happening. Even Jenna lifts her head just a little so she can see without me noticing her tears. She must really love this guy. I mean I do too, but she feels something much more than I ever will. I suppose that is how I would feel if something like this were to happen to Krissy-where she might be dying and I'm stuck here worrying and not being able to do a thing. That helplessness feeling can break anyone.

But back to why the desk guy came rushing over. He is also quite fat and short and waddles over so fast his head is literally moving from side to side like a Weeble-wobble. I let a little air escape my nose at the sight of it, but no one notices.

"I can't get a hold of Chief Thompson," he grunts in an impeccably deep voice. It makes the gray mustache, which curls up into points near the sides of his nose, flutter a little way away from his upper lip. The rest of his face looks red and flustered, and the bald spot on the top of his head, where his gray hair seemed to give up on, looks the reddest.

The guard's face goes pale and blank with fear, his eyes widening. "Why not?"

The old desk man throws his hands in the air. "I tried calling him many times to let him know that his kids are getting a lovely young visitor, but he's not picking up. He *always* picks up, especially when it's an important work matter! Do you think something could have happened to him?"

"Oh, don't jump to conclusions like that. He most likely is just busy." The guard says the words but you can tell on his face that he is trying harder to convince *himself* than the man to which he's speaking. I steal a glance at Jenna, and she gives me a sly smile. Maybe by some stroke of luck, something did happen to "cocky cop", and we are going to get out of here after all. Things are looking up.

Krissy places her hands on her hips. "Well, you can't just leave me standing here. I have the bail money and you have to let me give it to you."

The guard and the Weeble-wobble stare at each other nervously. They don't want to upset their boss, which is completely understandable, but it is the law to let Krissy post the bail. I feel Kelly's soft hair push under my hanging hand as we hold our breath, waiting for an answer.

The guard looks away first and sighs. "We have to let them go."

Weeble-wobble's eyes widen. "What do we tell Chief Thompson? He'll strangle us both when he sees we let the kids he worked all summer to capture go that easy."

"Yes I know this, but what can we do? The law is the law and he wasn't around to stop us. We'll just tell him we couldn't get a hold of him and that should get us out of dying."

"But not getting beat nearly to death," Weeble-wobble mutters. The guard gives him a warning look that seems to say 'don't let another comment like that slip or we're both definitely dead.' Weeble-wobble ignores it and puts his arm around Krissy's shoulders. He pushes her back to the desk, only escorting her, but I jump to the defense immediately. That dirty old man better keep his hands right where they are-on her collar bone-or when I get out of here I'm going to be the one to strangle him, before cocky cop can even get to him. I smile evilly at that thought.

Jenna shakes me. "Cool it Mr. Testosterone."

She shakes the thought out of my head and the smile fades. "Shut up. You were the one crying over Andy just a few seconds ago. And you know you would like to see me beat the crap out of him."

She chuckles and I continue, "Andy would want me to protect his girl in his absence."

She rolls her eyes, almost playfully. "And I'm sure that's the only reason you're getting all defensive."

"So what if it isn't?"

Before she can reply with a sarcastic comment, the guard sighs so loudly I think I feel the room shake a bit. "Hurry up Gordon; I can't take much more of this senseless banter!" A laugh coming from the weeble-wobble echoes in reply.

I have an idea. "Hey guard, let me see your hands."

"Oh no," Jenna whispers and the guard's head snaps around. He glares at me again and grunts, "No."

"Please, let me see them. I promise I won't do you any harm or use that to make some kind of unneeded getaway. I just want to see them a moment."

He raises one eyebrow in suspicion. "Why?"

I huff. "I can read people from what their hands look like, and I think you'll be a fun victim at the moment."

He huffs three times louder than I just did and shoves one thick hand through a space in the iron bars. I grab his wrist and twist it a little so I can get a better look. I can feel him trying to pull away, completely untrusting of me. I don't let him though and examine his hand thoroughly, all the while making comments such as 'hmmm, that's interesting.' Every few seconds, I look out of the top of my eyes to see how nervous his expression is growing, then return to my observations. Finally I let his hand go, and he jerks it back through the bars immediately. He checks it out to make sure I didn't put some curse on him, and then looks back at me. "So?"

I give him a surprised look. "You really want to know?"

"Well, I didn't let you examine my hand for ten minutes just for the hell of it."

I back up a little, raising my hands almost as if I'm surrendering. "Wow there tiger. No need to get sassy with me. It's just not a good prognosis and I was making sure you were ready for it."

"Just tell me kid!"

I smirk. "First of all, you chew your nails, which mean you're a nervous guy. Maybe it's your job or maybe it's because you're still alone and you're getting old, wondering when your parents are going to finally kick you out of their basement."

Jenna bursts out laughing so hard that a little bit of spit flies past me. The guard's eyes widen, and his face grows red again in no time. I continue, "You don't have any freckles, which means you don't go out in the sun very often, unless of course you wear gloves in the middle of the summer. That leads me to my next observation, which is the skin on the bottom of your thumbs is wearing down. The only reason for that obviously is that you play a lot of video games, which would explain your lack of sun exposure. There is lots of dirt under what remains of your rigid nails, meaning you either don't wash your hands very often, or you scarf down so much food that it overpowers the washing. Finally, your fingers are so chubby that there is little chance that you excel at playing a musical instrument."

He just stares at me in disbelief. "This is where you say, 'How did you do that kid?'" I add.

"I'm not going to do that because none of that is true. You just took random guesses, and that is all wrong. In fact, everything is the opposite of what you said." His voice is shaking as he says it, and I can't help but smile mockingly.

"You keep telling yourself that," I say. "But between you and me, I always believe what I observe, not what someone tells me."

His face turns from red to a dark hue of purple. I begin to fear that he is going to suffer from a heart attack, so I turn to Jenna. "When are we getting out of here? I feel bad for revealing the brutal truth about this poor soul."

"It is *not* the truth!" the guard shouts, but I ignore him. Krissy and the other cop come walking back down the hall. The cop puts a key in the lock on one side of the iron bars, and I hear a much needed click. Jenna, Kelly, and I all breathe sighs of relief as the cop says in a reluctant tone, "You're free to go." Krissy's face lights up as I push past the guard on my way out of the cell. Jenna and Kelly follow, and the cop places our clothes and belongings that he took when we got here in our hands. I forgot to mention we were wearing orange jumpsuits this whole time, so it is quite a good thing to see something of another color. Krissy puts her arm around our shoulders, making me feel warm inside again. I start to feel bad for the guard I picked on, so I turn my head and look back at him. He looks at me, embarrassed, and I know I was right at most, if not all, of what I observed. I am very good at reading people through their hands, courtesy of my father, and sometimes it hurts for people to hear from someone else what they can't admit to themselves. That's why I don't do it often-only when necessary, and he deserved it for being such a jerk to us the entire day. Yet, I still feel awful for making him so upset and embarrassed.

"It's never too late to change your hands," I say, giving him a sympathetic half smile. He nods, showing me he knows what I mean. I also take it as a thank you for showing him the truth. I turn my head around and look at Krissy again, then to Jenna and Kelly. Only Andy is missing in this picture, and somehow I feel like once we retrieve him from the hospital, we can never be ripped apart again. But still the question looms, what happened to his crazy and dangerous father?

37

Jenna

My heart won't stop beating a million miles per second as we enter the hospital. Andy has

to be okay. He has to make it out of surgery; there is no other option. I can't live without him any more than I can live without Matty or Kelly. And now I'm beginning to think that Tina is making that list also. I can never repay her for getting us out of that jail cell so we can come here. I thought I was going to die from worry sitting there not knowing what is happening to him, but now we're here and I feel even worse. I refuse to hear bad news. I squeeze Matty's hand as we get to the waiting room, and he gives me a reassuring look. I feel tears spring in my eyes, and I tell myself not to cry yet. Tina tells us to sit and wait until the doctor comes out to give us news, but I have an idea of my own. While Matty positions himself in a seat next to Tina, obviously hoping to comfort her in troubling times, and Kelly sits on his lap with Salamander, I walk myself up to the desk. The clerk in blue scrubs turns to greet me and smiles brightly. "How can I help you young lady?" she asks.

I smile back politely. "Yes, do you have Andrew Thompson's belongings?"

"I do. And who are you?"

I'm pretty sure you have to be family to do this kind of thing, so I improvise. "I'm his sister, Jenna."

She raises her eyebrows. "Really?"

"Half sister," I correct. It has to be true in a way if I feel like I am. That thought makes me confident as she stares at me suspiciously awhile, hoping to break me. I continue to smile and she nods.

"What do you want them for?"

"I want his shoes. It's a long story, but having them while he's in surgery means a lot to me."

"Okay, just a moment." She turns around and kneels down on the opposite side of the desk. She pulls out a box, searches through it a moment, and retrieves his beat up black and white Converse. My heart warms thinking of when I first saw that pair of shoes. It feels like so long ago, but just yesterday at the same time. She hands them over the counter to me and I grasp them.

"Thank you," I whisper. I turn away before the tears I've kept in the entire day pour out. I hold the shoes by the shoelaces in my left hand so they bang against each other as I walk in a rhythm. I make my way back to where my family is sitting and take a seat beside Matty. I sit with my knees against my chest and my arms wrapped around my legs. The shoes rest against my stomach, so I can just feel them pressing against where my heart is supposed to be. My breathing moves them back and forth as I rest my chin on my knees and cry. I think of all the good times we had this summer and how almost all of them included Andy. Those good days can't be over. Even if Andy makes it out of surgery and is fine, I can't bear to think that our original plan will play out. I want him and Tina to be a permanent part of my life, and I think I deserve to get something I want for a change. As all the thoughts run through my head, Matty pries himself away from Tina to hug me from behind.

"He'll be fine and you know it," he assures me. "If he can survive cancer and a life with his father, this is a cake walk."

"But what if we lose him anyway?"

He's silent a minute, thinking about what that question means. "I'll make sure that doesn't happen."

I twist my head a little until I see his expression. He doesn't look at me. Instead, he looks over my head like he's thinking hard. I know that far-away look, and most of the time it's when he doubts himself. "How?"

"I don't know yet, but I will do anything to make sure this isn't the last time we see him. I've failed in everything else I've tried to do for you since Mom died, so I must do this right. It is my duty to protect you and Kelly and make sure your lives are at least bearable now. I haven't done my job very well up until now, judging on that I landed us in jail, so now I'm going to do better."

He is making my heart hurt more than it already was. I knew he felt pressured to be our guidance, but I didn't know he felt this bad about what he did. "The choices you made for us were the best you could with what we had to work with. I admire you for the courage you had and still have. So don't feel bad, because you didn't fail us by any means. There is no possible way we would have made it through the summer without you. I would have been rotting in jail for months by now if it weren't for you. You are a fantastic leader, and I believe you when you say you'll make sure Andy and Tina stay in our lives."

One side of his mouth curves up a bit to show a weak smile. I see his eyes brighten to a slightly lighter blue, and that makes me feel like I did something good for him just now.

"Thanks Jenna," he whispers. "That helped. You're a good twin."

I chuckle. "So are you, even when you're annoying. And Kelly is an awesome little brother."

He nods in agreement. We sit in silence for awhile until we see the doctor walking quickly towards us. Matty releases his arms from me and stands up. I take a place beside him with Tina on the other side of him and Kelly in front of me. There is a nervous air swirling around us. I even hold my breath as the doctor stops in front of us. She is much taller than me and is built very muscular from what I see underneath her purple scrubs. She has her hair up in a scrub cap with little yellow ducks, and I can see pieces of her dirty blond hair falling out on her forehead. I can't read her expression as she looks at us with her bright turquoise eyes. Just say it, I think, to stop this feeling of uncertainty. Whatever *it* may be.

38

Andy

There is a very beautiful woman in purple scrubs standing over me when I open my eyes. I look around and notice I'm in a hospital bed with tubes connected to me and machines clicking in my ears. It brings back memories, making me a little uneasy. I guess that means I survived my father shooting me though. I have no idea what happened to Tina, Matty, Jenna, or Kelly though. They could be dead or trapped in jail or being tortured for all I know while I lie here helpless. I feel panic wash over me, and it takes everything I have not to knock the doctor down and run out of the hospital full speed. But something tells me that would not be the logical thing to do, considering I don't even know if I'm capable of standing up, let alone running full speed, and I might drop dead trying. Instead, I try the safer approach and speak to the doctor.

"Is anyone waiting for me?"

She turns toward me, and I see turquoise almost as gorgeous as Tina's. "You're a fighter, and I think it's because you have an array of visitors outside waiting for you. There's a very pretty woman with two teenage kids and a little kid. She was on the phone with what seemed to be your mother and sister. They are well on their way also. From what I can see, you are well loved."

I can't hold back a wide smile, I am so relieved. I can barely believe my luck. I start to think maybe I really died and this is heaven. "They are really all there?"

She nods. "If what I mentioned is all to you, then yes."

"They're not in jail? I didn't fail them! I didn't get shot for nothing!"

She raises her eyebrows and laughs at me. I'm sure what I'm saying is sounding like babble to her, but I am so happy and excited that I can't keep my mouth shut. "I have no idea why they would be in jail, and I'm sure I don't want to know, but they aren't unless they have the capability of being in two places at once. And you're alive and so are they, so I can't see why any failure would be seen here. So no, you didn't get shot for nothing."

Excitement washes over me. I need to see Tina right now. "Can I see them?"

"I would suggest you see one at a time because I don't know if you can handle the whole crowd in your condition."

I nod. "What is my condition exactly?"

"Gunshot recovery," she replies, bluntly. "But I'm almost positive you will fully recover. I'm that good."

I laugh a little and it makes my chest hurt, just like when I laughed while possessing a tumor in my lung. I like her attitude. "I'm lucky. I was preparing to die when my father shot me. Now I'm alive and get to get out of this hospital, and everyone I was trying to protect is completely fine. I couldn't ask for much more."

Her expression becomes shocked. "Your father did this?"

I bite my bottom lip nervously. "I said too much already. Can you just go out and get Tina for me? I need to see her first."

She turns and walks out of the room without another word. I should really think before I say things. I have that problem when I get excited. I just keep babbling until I say too much and get in trouble for it, just like my mother. But I can hardly believe this. Where is my father to cause all the trouble that I expected? I thought for sure that if I ever did wake up again, I would lose the kids. They would be doomed to jail forever and my beloved Tina would be injured in some way or another. Many others would have fell victim to my father before he would let any of them get away. And even if they did get away from him, he would know they would be coming here to visit me. Matty would be smart enough to realize that even though he wanted to bring Jenna here, it was not safe, and it is his duty to protect his siblings first. No matter how things went down after I fell unconscious, there is no logical reason why they could all be in the waiting room, in plain sight, acting as if nothing happened. Maybe if I talk to Tina, a few things will be cleared up.

"Why the solemn face?" Tina asks as she walks in the room. That face to which she was referring disappears as soon as I see her. The smile I had when the doctor told me that I had a group of visitors outside reappears, and I open my arms wide to greet her.

"Are you too fragile to hug?" she asks cautiously.

I almost laugh. "I'm not going to shatter if that's what you think."

She rests her head on my chest and her arms on my shoulders. I wrap my arms around her and stroke her hair with one hand. I want to keep this moment forever, just holding her and forgetting all that has happened, and something tells me she feels the same way. "I can't tell you how sorry I am." Her voice is muffled, and I'm not sure if she's crying or not.

"For what?"

"For saying those things the other night. I was just scared that I was going to lose you to your mission with the kids. I was having a jealous fit, and I went way too far trying to make you see that it was hurting me. I hope you know I didn't mean what I said about…" She cuts off, and this time I'm positive she's crying.

"Hey," I say sympathetically. "I know you didn't mean that about my cancer. It's one of those things that you say that you wish you could take back. I'm not innocent in that category, trust me. It hurt to hear you say that, but I love you so much that it didn't even matter by morning. All I wanted was for you to forgive me, and it didn't even cross my mind to be angry at you."

She lifts her head a little so I can see her tear stricken face. "I don't think there's any better than you out there, and I will forever feel awful for saying those things, no matter how many times you assure me that you're past it."

I'm not sure what to say to that, so I change to the subject of why I'm so confused still. "The doctor told me that Jenna, Matty, and Kelly were out there with you. I missed a lot, didn't I?"

She nods. "Oh yeah. Your dad captured the kids, even though they tried desperately to get away, and put them in jail the entire day. I waited here with you, figuring there was nothing I could do unless I wanted to be shot also, until they said you were going to be awhile in surgery. Then, I thought to calm my nerves that I better go do something to help them. I found them messing with the guards, but your dad was nowhere in sight. I posted bail, and we came here and waited until the doctor came out and told us that you wanted to see me. No one, even the guards in the jail or any of the other cops that were working with him to take the kids down, has seen your dad since he captured the kids. He's missing in action, and I think that's why we were able to get away with as much as we have. It's a mystery."

My brow furrows as I think of where he could possibly be. That makes sense as to why the kids got out of jail so easily and are now waiting to see me, but why? He wouldn't miss the chance to mess with me and the people I love for *anything*. There's no way he would just go missing when there was all this "fun" to be had, unless something went terribly wrong. Something that he would never have guessed would happen to him that out tricked him and made him disappear just like that. This was definitely out of character, and I almost feel like it's my job to figure out what became of him.

"What are you thinking?"

I look back down to her. "This is odd and not like him at all to miss something like this. Something must have happened to him, but I can't, for the life of me, guess what."

She shrugs. "Maybe we're not supposed to. Maybe it's just a miracle and we have to accept that."

Something about the way she says that makes me have an idea as to how that miracle happened. I think back to the sequence of events before I was shot, and what Tina told me happened when I was under. I piece things together in my mind and see an obvious answer for why my father disappeared and where. I have a very good idea to who the perpetrator of this event is also-someone he would never expect to prevent him from finishing his job. The only thing that doesn't make sense is why they would do it. Based on what I know, I see no logical reason unless, of course, the obvious isn't really the obvious at all.

"I don't think so. I think this was no act of God, and I have a way to figure it out. Can I see Jenna?"

She looks up at me, a little surprised. "Are you worried about your dad?"

"No, I'm worried about the person who abducted him."

39

Jenna

I place the Converse gently on the chair I was sitting on and rush toward Andy's room. I

push past Tina, unbelievably excited to see him. I thought I was never going to see him again in the woods, and now here I am. Things worked out for once, and I can't explain the happiness I feel. I haven't felt this way since I was part of an embrace in the house I will never see again with my loving mother. I thought I never would feel this way again, and it gives me unseen hope. I enter the room and his face lights up. I ignore the hospital bed, tubes, and clicking machines, and just give him a hug. He seems genuinely happy to see me, and that warms my heart.

"I thought I'd never see you again," he says as I take a cross-legged position on the end of his bed.

"*You* would never see *me* again? I thought you were dead!"

"I was sure my father would have been torturing you in jail by now, but here you are, right in front of me, perfectly safe. And Matty and Kelly are still waiting for me. How did this happen?"

I raise my hands to show him that I'm just as puzzled about that. "All I know is that I spent the day in jail and got bailed out by Tina. Your loony father was nowhere to be found the entire time. Frankly, I think that is a great thing!"

"You don't care where he is?" he questions me suspiciously.

"If we're not in danger, then no I don't."

He smirks. "Then you won't want to hear that I know where he is and with your help we can finally bring him down?"

"What?! That is a totally different scenario."

He shrugs. "Oh well, you don't care."

I huff. "I do care okay! I care a lot about bringing him down!"

"You sure about that?"

"Yes."

"Really?"

"Andy, just tell me!"

"Okay," he laughs. "From what Tina told me, I think I know where my father is and who he's with. But I need you to clarify it."

"And?" I'm getting a little impatient here.

"No one in the police station or jail knows anything about his whereabouts?"

"The two guys in the jail were flipping out because he was missing. I have no idea about the police station. I wasn't there, but I believe the guards in the jail would have called the police station first to ask if they had seen him."

He nods. "Okay, so that means you haven't seen any of the cops that were with him when I shot? The ones that are part of his team?"

"Would they be the same ones that were looking for us at our grandmother's house?"

"Yes, minus me."

"Then no. I beat one up to get his hands off of Kelly and that was the last time I saw any of them."

He laughs. "Nice going. I wish I could have been conscious to see that go down."

I feel myself blush a little. "It had to be done, and I'm tougher than you think. I could take you down too if need be."

He raises his eyebrows almost as if to mock me, and I raise a fist to show him that he's in a vulnerable position right now and to quit making me mad. "Okay, I believe you. I just want to know how you were able to get my shoes when you're not family."

"How did you know about that?" I ask, taken by surprise.

"Some things I just know," he replies mysteriously. He gives me a sly smile so I figure I'm not going to get an answer to that.

"I told the clerk you were my brother."

He bursts out laughing and my face gets hot. I don't see much that's funny. "Your brother that you think is hot?"

I look down in my lap to hide my embarrassment. "Yes," I mutter so quietly that I can barely hear it.

"Don't you think that's a little disturbing?"

I put my head in my hands. I know if I look at him now, I'm going to die. "You're not my real biological brother like Matty or Kelly, so not really." It's muffled because I'm talking through my hands, but it seems far better than trying to look him in the eye and say that.

I can hear him laughing at my response, but I pretend I don't. "Whatever you say Jenna. Just so you know, I'm still flattered."

I can't take this anymore. I lift my head and look right at him. "When are you going to tell me where you think your dad is?"

"I'm not. I'm going to show you."

I throw my hands in the air angrily. He backed me in a corner and I have no way to defend myself. I hate when this happens. I jump off the bed and begin to walk out of the room, even though really I don't want to leave. I want him to stop me.

"Jenna!"

I turn around at the door. "What?"

"I was just messing with you because I'm glad to see you. No need to get all worked up and angry."

"You told me you were going to tell me how to bring down your father, and now you won't. I have a right to be angry."

He runs his hand through his black hair until it sticks straight up in a Mohawk and sighs. "I know that's not what you're angry about, but sorry. I just thought that what I know would have a greater affect if I showed you than if I simply told you. We can have one last big adventure." He smiles, knowing I can't resist a fun adventure any more than Matty.

I roll my eyes. "I'll go get Matty. He wants to see you."

I start to walk out the door a second time when he stops me again with a "Wait!"

I spin around on my heels. "What is it this time?"

He points over to the counter under the window in the room. The last rays of the sun before it sets shine on a little green notebook with a pen resting on top of it. There are papers sticking out of it in all directions and the front cover of it is filled with little doodles and is half falling off the rings. I walk over to it and move the pen so I can pick it up. It is heavier than I thought it would be, and I almost drop it. I catch it before any of the papers fall out and skim through it. Every paper seems to be ripped or crumpled in some way and has shaky handwriting filling up almost every line. It's a big version of the little one he keeps in his back pocket. Other loose papers have little pictures of random things or little notes that make no sense to me. This is worse than the writing folder I used to keep before it went up in flames, but I can understand that everything must have some significance. "Is this yours?" I ask him when I'm done snooping through it.

"Yeah, I know it's a mess, but that's the best way I work."

"You write?" I know he scrawls some poems, but not anything this dedicated.

"Songs," he replies. "Whenever I get inspiration, I put all my ideas in the little notebook you saw. Then I transfer it all to here."

"Wow. Can I read any of them?"

He shakes his head. "It's a surprise. I'm waiting to share them with the world all at once."

I put it and the pen in his lap and smile. "I can't wait until that day." This time I really do walk out of the door without any interruptions. I stop at the glass pane in the wall that separates the hallway from the hospital room. I see him bent over the notebook, quickly scrawling something on a blank page in the notebook. He is completely unaware that anyone is watching him, and that makes me more comfortable doing it somehow. This is when I realize how much I really hate his father-the man who kept him from his dreams. I want nothing more than to get rid of that guy for good. He should be locked up in jail so Andy can be all he wants to be. I know now that the day he finally does get to share his music with the world will be a beautiful day, and I hope it's sooner than any of us think.

40

Andy

After a short chat with Matty about the happenings in the jail cell, my plans of getting revenge on my father once and for all, and reassuring him that all that happened today is my fault and not his, my mother and Stacy rush into the room screaming and totally ignoring the one person at a time rule. My mom is a very emotional woman, and the thought of her miracle son almost dying by the hand of her husband is too much for her to handle. She squeezes me into a hug so hard, all the breath I had escapes me, and my shoulder is wet by the time she's done sobbing on me. I try to reassure her that I'm going to be okay and there's no need to worry about me anymore, but she won't listen. She's too busy telling me how scared she was when she got the call, and that she came right over here as fast as she possibly could. She tells me that she's glad I was so far away because although she was worried sick the entire ride over, at least her hands had been busy, when if she would have been waiting with Tina in the waiting room, she most likely would have fainted. Then she proceeds to inform me a million times how much she loves me, and she doesn't believe my dad could ever do such a thing to his son, and that he deserves to pay. Stacy suggests that he be hauled off to the insane asylum because she knew all along that that's where he should be. I can't help but laugh and agree at that statement, and my mom stops screaming and crying and talking a mile a minute to join us.

"Andrew, how did you ever get yourself into this? You always get into fights with your father, but I never dreamed something like this would happen. What got into him? Did you instigate, or does he just have evil hidden in him? I always thought he was a little off, but didn't think he was capable of shooting his own son. And he shot to kill, not just to injure, but luckily you're stronger than him. I always thought that when it came down to it, you would be able to beat him. You had stronger beliefs, even though you were much smaller, when all he thought of was work. I hope you get away from that horrible job he made you get and go after what you're really good at, which is music, and don't think I don't know you're talented. Mothers know these things, so do what yours says and start a band already, unless you want to be a solo artist, which is totally okay also. I just want you to achieve your dreams, and did I mention I was filing for divorce? That way that horrible man I married won't get in the way of what you or Stacy wants anymore. I'll make sure he doesn't try to get back in our lives either. I'm just as strong as you Andrew and..."

Behind her Stacy ties an imaginary rope around her neck and pulls upward. She pretends to die, and I try my best not to laugh, but I can't. She is depicting exactly what I was thinking the entire time my mom was talking. I'm used to her constant babbling, stringing together topics that don't really go together when she thinks of them, but she's on overdrive today. She stops talking when she sees me laughing and snaps her head to Stacy. Stacy immediately stops what she was doing and looks innocent. She is always the one that gets accused of everything from eating the last cookie without permission, to sneaking out of her bedroom window to go to a party she's not allowed to, so she's an expert at looking innocent. My mom looks from her, to me, and back to her again suspiciously. That makes me laugh harder.

"Okay, what is so funny?" my mom asks.

"You," I answer, when I can catch my breath. "You're talking so fast and about so many things that it's impossible to follow you. Calm down."

She sighs. "Did you catch any of it or do I have to start over?"

"I think I got the gist of it," I say, panicking. I don't think I can take it if she starts over. "You don't know what happened to Dad. You think I'm better than him and that I should follow my dreams of a music career. You are filing for divorce so you don't have to live with the poison Dad inflicts on all of us anymore."

"Okay, that's pretty much what I wanted to tell you."

"See how much less painful that was without so many words?" I ask, laughing again.

"Oh shut up!" she exclaims, playfully punching me in the shoulder. "You know I get all worked up when I'm scared."

"There's nothing to be scared about. I'm fine and Dad's nowhere to be found. Although I think I know where he is, and before long, he will get what he deserves."

That sparks Stacy's interest. "What are you saying?"

I smirk just like I did when Jenna had the same reaction. "You'll see soon enough." They both stare at me awhile but let it go. I'm stubborn when I want things to be a surprise, and they know that better than anyone.

"If Mom was as frazzled as she was, I can imagine what Tina must have been feeling," Stacy finally says. "She said on the phone she was there when you got shot."

I nod. "She was part of the reason I got shot. She was upset, but she knows now that I'm going to be okay. She's great."

Stacy rolls her eyes at my last comment. She's always been more of an older brother to me than sister. When normal sisters would have found that really sweet, she finds it disgusting. She'd rather have her ogre of a man grunt at her and her kids. She could do a lot better, but I know if I tried to tell her that, she'd call me a pansy, so I don't try. I have my own issues to deal with first.

My mom opens her mouth to give me another lecture like she does frequently on the phone, but I raise my palm to stop her. I know exactly what she is going to say, and I smile. "You will never have to say that again."

She looks stunned, obviously not expecting me to say that. "What does that mean?"

"What were you going to say to me?"

"I was going to say, if she is so great, then you should finally settle down with this girl, but you rudely interrupted me with a comment that made no sense."

All I do is keep smiling, making her think about this. Stacy's eyes widen, being the first to understand. "You're not!" she almost protests, and my ears get hot.

"I am."

My mom looks even more confused. "You are what? I'm lost again."

Stacy laughs. "You're always lost, but this isn't that hard to figure out. He's going to propose to Tina."

Her head snaps around, and she looks at me for reassurance. When I nod, she erupts into a fit of squeals. She hugs me, then Stacy, and jumps up and down as Stacy and I watch. "Finally, my boy comes to his senses!" she exclaims happily.

I blush and she asks, "What made you change your mind?"

"Well, almost dying for the second time made me see things a bit clearer."

She rolls her eyes in exasperation. "So my constant pushing you toward the idea had no affect on your decision whatsoever?"

"Not really."

"Not even a little bit?"

I laugh. "Okay, maybe a little, but mostly it was my decision."

"Well it is a good one," she says, hugging me for the third time in a half hour.

"Can I talk to you alone a minute?" Stacy asks me when my mom lets go.

I nod, and my mom takes that as a cue to leave us alone. She reluctantly walks out of the door, telling me that she will be back in no more than ten minutes. Stacy has to pretty much push her away before she can shut the door. When we are alone, I say, "Don't try to talk me out of it because it's not going to work. I made my decision because I love her, and I'm going to spend the rest of my life with her no matter what you say."

"I wasn't going to try to talk you out of it," she says, making me feel bad for thinking it. "Congratulations on that, but I wasn't going to talk to you about Tina at all."

"Then what is it?"

"I know you're going to be all surprised, but don't say anything smart, okay?"

"Yeah, spill."

"When Tina called me and said you were in the hospital and could die, I felt really awful. I felt like all I did was pick on you your entire life, and you would die thinking I was a horrible sister. I'm sorry for not being nicer to you, and I'm going to quit smoking. I only did it to try to prove to myself that there was nothing to be afraid of because I was afraid for you. I love my little brother, and I don't want him to die. I want him to love me too and to want to spend time with me. I know you love my kids, and you hate Randy, and you think that I should do better for me and Spencer and Tanner, but he loves me. It's better than I've done before. I'm starting to sound as emotional as Mom, so I'm just going to get to my point. I don't want you to resent me anymore. I failed as being a sister, and I want to make it up to you." She stops and stares at me nervously, trying to read my expression.

"I don't resent you. You're my sister and I love you. You've always been a bit abrasive, and I hated the way you taunted my cancer, but you've always been a good sister. Randy is a little rough, but as long as he loves you the way he should, then that's good. So stop being hard on yourself and just be yourself."

She smiles. "I think your love with Tina is really sweet and I like her."

"So you are a girl," I joke. She attempts to hit me, but I block it.

"No one will know we had this conversation, okay?"

"Oh, will it ruin your reputation?"

She glares at me and I laugh. "Fine, I won't let anyone know you have feelings."

"Honestly, I feel bad for Tina. She has to put up with you for the rest of her life."

"Sure you do," I simply reply, and it sets her off. There is nothing better than messing with a brother or a sister. Nothing at all.

41

Matty

I have no idea where we are going. The trees rush by us in a blur of green, we are driving so fast, and it is making me sick. I have to tilt my head back, look through the tee tops, and breathe in and out slowly to ward off the nausea. The blue sky, with its few puffy white clouds, seems to stay completely still, and it gives me a peaceful feeling inside. When I was Kelly's age, I used to tilt my head back while standing in the back yard and look at the sky for hours while walking slowly in a circle. I would completely forget the world, and it felt so nice. No one could get my attention until I decided I was going to go inside, and that was usually when the stars came out and there were no clouds left to see. To me, the contrast between the baby blue and perfect white was the most beautiful thing I'll ever see. If I were a painter, that would be the thing I would paint first. I think that is why looking at the sky right now calms me, and all traces of car sickness disappear. I forget about all that is happening in the present and sing songs that all the words to are imprinted in my brain. I don't even realize that Jenna is staring at me the entire time smiling; she tells me that later. The next thing I know the car is jerking to a stop, and my view of the peaceful sky scene turns to the dark gray leather front seat of the Mustang as my face slams into it. It's quite a surprise, but I get over it by rubbing my nose a little and snapping back to reality.

"This is it!" Andy yells, and I remember I'm in Krissy's Mustang GT with Andy driving, Krissy in the passenger seat, and Kelly and Jenna both to my right. I was told while entering the car that we were going to find cocky cop and bring him down for good, but I wasn't allowed to know where exactly our destination is. Judging on what Andy just yelled, I would say we are there now.

Andy throws open the door and jumps out of the car. He disappears for a few minutes, leaving us silent in the car, and then returns. He beckons for us to come out, and I follow Krissy and my siblings, still in a little bit of a daze from my abrupt return to Earth. For the first time, I actually look around at where the car stopped. It's a field out in the middle of nowhere with long stalks of brown grass blowing in the soft wind. I look around, but other than a large red barn set a football field or so away from where we're standing, that is all I see for miles. The car is positioned on a narrow dirt road that you wouldn't be able to spot unless you were looking really close. The bright orange Mustang GT, with its racing stripes, looks quite out of place in this barren land, and it brings a smile to my face. The rest of the group begins walking toward the barn, and I assume that is the reason we are here.

"Is your dad in the barn?" I ask. If not, we'll never find him here. Although it would be hard to hide, there is so much open land that it would take forever to search it all. How come I've never seen this place? I've lived in Delaware my entire life, and I have been to almost every inch of it. Unless this isn't Delaware at all. How long had we been driving? I can't remember anything after a few minutes when I started staring at the sky to calm my sickness. We could be halfway across the country for all I know, and I thought I was always alert. I don't get an answer from Andy or anyone else for that matter, so that makes me feel worse. Great, now I'm nonexistent.

I keep my mouth shut until we reach the wide entrance of the barn. The barn is six times bigger than it looked from the car. I have to tilt my head all the way back to see the top of it now. It looks like one you would see in a little kid's book where they show that "Pigs and Chickens live in big red barns!" The enormous doors are swung inside, so there is an opening to just walk through. The inside is covered knee high with hay, and along the sides and back are different levels with more hay and crates. It looks as if no one has used, let alone even gone near this barn, in at least half a century. Personally, it is giving me the creeps.

"Um, why are we here?" I ask, hoping this time someone will acknowledge my presence. I have no luck though, and everyone just keeps staring inside. "Hello, am I a ghost now?"

Andy replies by walking forward into the barn. His feet sink in the hay, but he keeps marching on, looking straight ahead. Krissy follows him and Jenna picks up Kelly and joins them. They are like a line of robots, and I feel like I'm the only one human. Should I run away and save myself?

"I am not going in there," I protest, shaking my head. "No way. Someone could be hiding in there and jump out and kill us. We've been through too much to die here. Or even if it is vacant in here, brown recluse spiders love dark, wet places. That's most likely how under the hay is, and one bite will make you lose limbs. This place really looks like no one has been in it in a very long time. There's no use looking; I know for a fact that cocky cop isn't here. Even though he's crazy, he would pick somewhere more practical to hide. He doesn't have a death wish and neither do I, so I am staying right here, and I suggest you do the same. Come on, you can't leave me here. Someone say something!"

I feel like I'm going to cry. I think I really am a ghost. Something must have happened during my absence in the car, and now I'm invisible. Andy turns around and looks straight at me. My face brightens and I blink several times to keep tears from surfacing. "Will you please shut up?" he says.

I can't help but smile. I'm okay; I'm just being ignored. That's better than being a ghost stuck in the world of the living where no one can hear or see me. "So now you say something to me? You had me thinking I didn't really exist. I was about to cry and all you can say is shut up. Someone please tell me what is going on!" My voice is getting really loud, and it echoes throughout the entire barn. Andy's face gets twisted and angry as he violently brings his finger to his lips. Krissy and Jenna glare at me also, and I'm not sure what I'm doing wrong. I hate being confused and out of the loop.

I throw my hands in the air. Jenna sees I really don't know what is going on and puts down Kelly. She points at him silently, telling him to stay right there. She runs through the hay as fast as she can while sinking. She comes so close to me that our faces are inches apart. "Did you not hear a word Andy said in the car?!" she hisses.

I pull back a little and shake my head. "I was lost in my little sky world trying to fight throwing up all over the place."

She sighs heavily. "Well, he told us not to talk after we left the car, especially when we got near the barn, unless it was absolutely necessary, because that would defeat the whole purpose of coming here to catch his father off guard. We need to be completely silent if we want to bring cocky cop down, so you do exist. We were ignoring you because we were hoping if we stayed quiet long enough, you would get the hint. So stop freaking out and come with us, quietly."

I nod once to show I understand and mouth the words "thank you for explaining". She gives me a thumbs up sign and runs back to Kelly. I'm still afraid of all the horrible things that can happen in here, but I have to come, so I might as well cooperate. I step carefully in the hay and shrink a couple inches as it swallows me halfway up my calves. I take a few more steps until I'm sure I'm not going to die, and then I move more swiftly. I make it to where the rest of the group is and stop. They stare at me for a little while and then turn around and keep going. I reluctantly follow, looking around me to make sure no one is going to pop out at me. I look behind me and see that the barn door didn't swing shut on its own and lock us in, so I figure this isn't going to be a regular horror movie.

We walk in silence, the sound of the hay crunching beneath our feet, our breathing the only sounds that can be heard, until we reach the other side of the barn. It was a twenty minute walk at least; the barn is unexplainably huge. It's one of those things you have to see to completely understand its magnitude. At the opposite wall from the door, there is a tiny little door. I have to squint to see the keyhole but Andy obviously knows all about this place. If I could speak, I would be asking nonstop questions. My love for adventure makes me unbelievably curious in a place like this.

Andy retrieves a small key from his shorts pocket and places it carefully in the keyhole. He twists to the right and then to the left, and I hear a small click. He pulls on the door and it swings open, flooding the shaded hay with a square of light. The opening looks just big enough for me to climb through, but I'm not so sure about Andy. He's not very big, but he's still a 26 year old guy. We all look at each other, wondering what we are supposed to do know. This not talking thing is killing me.

Andy motions toward me and points to the opening. I shake my head in response. There is no way I am going into that strange place first. I could get shot or eaten or stabbed. I don't even want to be in this barn in the first place. Andy glares at me and points violently toward the door. I keep shaking my head, starting to give myself a headache. I look over to Krissy and she gives me a pleading look. "For me," she whispers almost silently. I look to Jenna and she is giving the same look. God, these people really know my weaknesses. I throw my hands in the air and drop to my knees. I start to crawl through the hole and peer back at what is now my family. I give them a small wave and their smiles show a hint of concern. I crawl through and am almost blinded by how much light is in this place. I rub my eyes and sit there until they adjust. I open them slowly and look around.

The walls are exactly the same as the barn, and it is the exact same size, almost to the point that someone made a replica of the barn and plopped it right next to the original. The only difference is that this one doesn't have a roof. The walls come up, curl inward a little, and stop, leaving a large circular opening. I can see the blue sky with the white puffy clouds straight up through the opening, and I sit mesmerized for a minute. The sun shines in and warms my face. I sit there on my knees and raise my arms toward the sky in happiness. I could stay here all day, but a rock hits me in the side, reminding me that is not possible. I turn my head around and see Jenna's face poking through the opening I crawled through. She beckons to me. I walk on my knees toward her.

"You're supposed to tell us if the coast is clear," she hisses.

"But the sky is so beautiful."

She rolls her eyes. "Can I come?"

I look around me and everything seems quiet, so I nod. She crawls through the opening and waits until her eyes adjust, just as I had. Kelly follows her and does the same. They both look around and have the same reaction I did at the beautiful sky. I smile. "It's gorgeous, isn't it?"

Jenna picks up the rock she hit me with before and hits me again. I can't help but cry out and Andy's head appears almost immediately. He glowers at me and I smile meekly. His head disappears and Krissy's takes its place. She squeezes through the opening and follows suit on the actions of entering the replica barn. Andy attempts to get through, but his shoulders are just a little too wide and his back is too tall. He curses under his breath and pushes as hard as he can. That bad move gets him stuck in the opening and he can't get out, let alone in like he wants. Jenna's face becomes very worried, even more than Krissy's. That gets to me. I mean he's a good guy, but I just don't get what the strong attraction is; I'm much better looking than him. Not that I care who my sister likes as long as he doesn't hurt her, but Krissy too? My Krissy? She's much older than me, but I still see her as mine. Why does this Andy guy, with his tattoos and pierced eyebrows and total lack of muscles, get the most amazing girl on the face of the planet, while I'm here watching? Jenna and Krissy run over to help pull Andy out, but I stay put. Maybe if I just leave him there, Krissy will see who is better for her and we can run away together. I can't help but grin at that thought. For the third time, I get hit with a rock, this time in the side of the head. I scream at the top of my lungs and slap my hand against my mouth. We all listen and after a minute, when everything seems quiet, Jenna grabs my arm and drags me over to the opening. I get hay in my hair and some of it pokes me in the eye. I pull my arm away from her and wipe myself down. After I get my bearings, I shoot her an "I will kill you if you pull that one again" look.

"Grab Andy's arm," she orders. I don't want to look like a total tool in front of Krissy and lose any chance I might have with her, so I do what my sister says. "One, two, three, tug!" Jenna whispers loudly and we pull as hard as we can. Andy tumbles head first through the opening and almost knocks me over. He gets to his knees and smiles.

"I'm okay," he assures us, shaking hay from his hair. I think I see Jenna drool a little, and I use that as my turn to throw the rock at her. It hits her square in the right shoulder, and her head snaps around so fast I would have thought she'd get whiplash. I imitate her face while watching Andy shake his hair and grin. Her face turns bright red, and instead of trying to hit me as usual, she looks down at her feet. This is unusual behavior. What is with this guy? I just shake my head and let it go. We all rise to our feet and start searching the replica barn from top to bottom. The whole place seems as empty as the last one we were inside. I look behind a pile of hay to make sure some rabid animal isn't hiding and hear a click, sounding much like cocky cop's gun. I turn around to see a masked person holding Andy by the throat and pointing a gun toward his head.

T his is when I start to feel really bad for all the things I thought just a few minutes ago of

Andy. After all the things he has done for us-bringing us food, saving us from being arrested, giving us a shelter, giving us a parental guardian, bringing us clothes and other necessities, protecting us from storms, providing us with a fun summer despite the circumstances, giving up time with the love of his life for us, getting shot for us, betraying his own father for us, giving up his paying job for us, and just plain loving us when we thought there was no one else in the world that did-I go and repay him for all that by having a childish jealous fit? Just because I have this enormous crush on Krissy, doesn't mean that I should betray Andy. He loves me and I love him. I must admit I have no chance with Krissy, no her name is Tina. Part of accepting that she is Andy's because they love each other and belong with each other is calling her by her real name, not some pet name I came up with out of a fantasy. Reality check Matty-never gonna happen! I am so stupid for thinking that there was any chance, and then going as far as hating Andy because he was supposedly stealing my time with my soul mate. I am ridiculous, and yes I love Tina, but I will stop letting her get to me. Jenna can easily have those weird feelings for Andy and still think of Tina as a sister. Why do I feel like I have to go and have a fight to show who is dominant? I feel awful for thinking those things and decide to never think them again. And the only way to repay Andy for what he has done for me and for thinking those things is to save him now. I must man up and do my duties.

Before I can even think any further, I am charging toward the armed perpetrator at full speed. Jenna yells to stop, but my legs keep going. I feel like I'm gliding across the hay as Andy and the masked gunman come closer and closer. I throw a diving tackle toward them, and the three of us end up in a tumbled heap, half covered in hay. Jenna, Tina, and Kelly come charging toward us, throwing the hay away as fast as they can. I pop my head through an opening and stare down at Andy who seems to be just fine. I look over to the gunman who really isn't a gunman at all. The mask has fallen off and I see that I recognize the woman as Detective Jones.

"What are you doing here?" I ask when our eyes meet. "And with a gun no less." Andy looks just as surprised as we wait for her to answer.

She sits up and brushes the hay from her face and neck. She smoothes her hair and says, "Sorry about that. I thought you were someone else."

I look back to Jenna and she raises an eyebrow at me. "Can you please tell me why you just attempted to kill me," Andy begs. "That remains a mystery."

She laughs. "I really didn't mean to. I thought you were one of your father's goons. You know I would never hurt you." She looks at him just a little too longingly and forces him to look down in embarrassment. Seriously, I think again, is there something I'm not seeing that all these women do? I thought women and girls liked straight-laced, well built guys, but what do I know?

"And I ask again, what are you doing here?" I had to break the silence.

She looks to me. "Are you Matty?"

I nod and she continues, "Then I know I can trust you. I have Andrew's father around back so he can't cause any trouble. A long time ago, when I was young and stupid, I ended up pregnant and gave birth back here in this abandoned barn. No one found me, and I thought this place would be somewhere perfect for hiding him. I was hoping that I could get him carted off to an insane asylum, and I was halfway there, when I heard a scream and panicked. I grabbed my gun, threw on a ski mask, and crept in here to see what was happening. It turns out I can't see very well through this thing, so all I could make out is outlines. I thought the safest thing to do was bet it was someone I couldn't trust, so I grabbed him and held him hostage, hoping someone would tell me who you guys were. Next thing I knew I was face down in the hay over here."

My eyes widen. "You have cocky cop?"

She seems surprised that I would call him that, and it takes her a few moments to put two and two together. "Yes, I do. I can bring you to him if you want."

"I knew you would bring him here," Andy comments. "I would have bet my life that I would find you in this barn with him." I look over to Andy and can tell he knew all about her past with this barn and that she would do what she did. I wonder if they were once friends in the police force.

"I did it for you," she smiles, her cheeks flushed. I must admit, she does look a lot better not in uniform and with her dirty blond hair falling over her shoulders, but she is no match for Tina. I see Tina's face becoming concerned and territorial, like she is ready to pull some hair out with one wrong move toward her man.

"Take us to him," I order, ending that uncomfortable moment. Andy helps Detective Jones, whose first name happens to be Tamara, up, and we start walking. Tamara leads us through the back door of the barn and around a corner. I spot cocky cop tied to a chair with tight rope, gagged, and almost succeeding in tipping the chair over. We all can't help but laugh at the sight of him. It feels great to see him as the vulnerable one for once.

He squirms even more when he sees us, in complete rage. Andy goes right up to him and holds the chair still. "Dad, you need help. You've needed help for awhile now, but you wouldn't take it. Now we're going to force you so you can get better and be a real father for me and Stacy. We lost many years with you, and this is the right thing to do, whether you want it or not. I love you, and that's the only reason I'm doing this." He gives him a huge hug and pulls away. I totally did not expect *that*. I thought they hated each other and that was the whole reason they were fighting over us. Maybe all along it was just a father who couldn't control himself due to mental illness, and a son who just wanted his dad to be better. It makes me miss my own dad more, and I feel tears spring in my eyes. I choke them down though because it's not over yet. I still need to be strong for my family.

42

Andy

We spend the next few days in Pennsylvania making sure my dad gets settled into the

mental hospital and doesn't kill any of the nurses before they even try to help him. I hate having to drag the kids around to all different hotels as we search for the best hospital, but it has to be done. Though none of the places we stay are five star, most of them being run-down, the floor being cleaner than the beds, and sometimes we just sleep in the car, very cramped with all our belongings with us, the kids make no noise of complaint. I think they are as glad as I am that my dad is finally getting the help he needs and won't be running around ramped looking to either put them in jail or kill them. I can only hope that the doctors can fix him so he can be a loving dad like Stacy and I have always needed. My mom needs a non-violent, not bi-polar or psychopathic, caring husband after all these years. And most of all, Tina won't be a target to his anger towards me constantly. I know deep down that I'm doing the right thing for all these reasons.

During all this time, Detective Jones, who now has become my good friend Tamara, has watched over my father in the barn. She has made sure he has had his necessities but hasn't tried to escape. She hasn't made any complaints either, which surprises me. The Detective Jones I knew would have been chewing my ear off for making her do this for me, but I guess something changed. Seeing this barn where she had seen her only child for the last time before giving him to foster care, made her become Tamara, and she is more than willing to help me do the right thing. Maybe all this time she didn't really hate me the way I really didn't hate her. Maybe her secretly loving me just caused a lot of hard feelings that we couldn't get past. Or maybe my most recent near death has made her realize there is no reason to hate me. Who knows? All I care about is that I have made a new friend, and she is a really excellent, for life, one.

Today we finally found the perfect hospital. It's just a few miles from the house I grew up in where my mom still lives, so she can go and see him with ease if she chooses. Right now she's still pretty mad at him for shooting her son, which is very understandable, so I don't think she'll go see him for awhile. Maybe he needs the alone time to contemplate all the choices he has made in his life. The hospital will give him a little room to himself, the medication he needs every day, the best doctors and nurses to make sure he controls himself, a group talk where he can interact with other people with the same problems, and a daily therapy session. He will most likely resist all this at first, but I'm pretty sure they can handle him, and what harm can it do? The doctor that gave me the tour of the hospital said she expects my father will be able to get out of there within a few years. Whether that is true or not, I have no clue, but all I want is for something to be done to try, at least.

I leave the hospital feeling the sun is shining a little brighter. I take a quick drive to the barn with Tina and the kids and tell them to stay in the car as I go and tell Tamara the news. I jog through the field and through the hay in the barn to the back entrance. I drop to my knees and poke my head through the little opening to the hidden room. I give a small knock on the wall and Tamara appears within seconds. She helps me through the opening, and when I get my bearings again, she looks at me quizzically. I haven't been here in two days, the last time with no good news, and I know she is hoping that things are different this time around. I smile because I love giving people what they want and I'm about to do just that. Her face grows relieved, her smile reaching up to her eyes.

"Finally," she sighs.

I nod. "It's perfect, and I knew it had to be for my dad. They want us to bring him in as soon as possible."

"He's around the back eating lunch right now. I had to tie him to the chair again because he was mapping out an escape route. I almost lost him today so you came just in time."

A sinking feeling rises up through my body just thinking about all the trouble that would have caused. I have a sudden urge to go see him just to calm my nerves. I stand up and walk around through the door to the back of the barn. I spot him with his waist tied to the back of the chair with a thick, light brown rope. He is leaning over a little picnic table, shoveling a sandwich in his mouth with his gigantic hands. He stops for one second to look up at me, and then returns to eating. Tamara appears before me and takes the food away from him. He cries out, "What are you doing with me now? Am I finally leaving this barn? I feel like some kind of pet chicken to you two."

As Tamara unties him from the chair, I start to feel a little bad about the way we have been treating him the last few days. He has been told when he can use the bathroom and eat and when he has to be awake and sleeping, all the time being watched. His only free time is in the barn, where either one of us can see him. Other than that, he is always tied to a chair or the wall of the barn. He's like some kind of animal that is being trained, but it's inevitable. He has to be watched at all times or he'll try to escape, and the only way to get him help is to force him. Putting him in a care facility makes me feel a little better because they have security cameras that watch him instead of having him tied to something like a dog in the backyard.

Tamara nods to show me that I should take one of his hands to lead him to the car. I don't move my hands though; I just look from her, to my dad, and back. Is this right? Should I really be doing this, I ask myself. I thought it was what was best for him when we still didn't have a hospital, but now that he is about to go, I'm second guessing myself.

As if reading my thoughts, Tamara says, "It's still the best thing Andy. You'll thank me for telling you that when you have your dad back."

I reluctantly take his other hand and walk all the way around the side of the barn to avoid trying to fit him through the tiny secret door. I still can't help but wonder one thing though. I have known my dad to be the way he is my whole life. What if he is different when he is no longer mentally ill and doesn't love any of us anymore? Not that he really showed that he did before, but at least I knew deep down that he felt something for my mom, my sister, and I. What if when he is helped, he is such a totally different person that he isn't really my dad anymore? I'm doing this to get my dad. What if I lose what I still have of him? I try to shake all these doubts out of my head as we drive to the hospital and drop him off, but there is still some lingering. As we hand him over to the doctors, they reassure me that he will be well taken care of and I will be able to see him at almost any time I want. I say my goodbyes to him, but he just glares at me. I hear screaming coming from down the hall and know it's time for me to leave. Tamara and Tina walk me out, and I feel strangely apathetic, like nothing in the world matters much now. I know it's probably the fear, but I zone everything out and sit in my empty mind. I need to go home now and hope that God takes care of my father for me.

I start to feel better after a few hours of rest in the car. Tina offered to drive the mustang and Tamara her SUV with the kids in the back so I could sit in the passenger seat next to Tina, in complete peace. I lean my head against the window and stare at the road moving past underneath the tires. You might think I'm depressed, but I have no sadness in me. It's totally different, almost like the world stopped turning and everything is just on pause. I have no cares or worries and don't want to do anything but rest and look through something, not thinking. You may never have had this feeling, but that's the best way I can try to explain it. It's one of those things you have to experience, and once I get my few hours on the drive back to Rehoboth of nothingness, I am virtually back to normal. I remember my responsibilities and the things I have to still do before my deed is done for the kids. And, of course, that question I have to ask Tina. I have a perfect plan for that and a grin reaches my face thinking about it.

Tina laughs as we pull into the driveway. "Hey, you're finally back on Earth! You lost all expression for so long that I thought you were gonna be lost in Andyland forever."

I roll my eyes at her comment and hop out of the car. Tamara's car pulls in behind us and the kids get out with all their belongings. I told them they can stay here a few days while I get things sorted out and they happily agreed. I grab the bags from Jenna and Kelly, but Matty and his pride won't let go of them, even though he is almost falling over. I know the feeling though so I don't say a word. We make our way up the long driveway and the walk to the front door. By the time I get the door unlocked, Matty's bags fall through the opening and Matty falls over on top of them. We all laugh and he springs to his feet, his face red with embarrassment.

"Are you *positive* you don't want me to take those for you?" I ask teasingly. "I don't want you to get seriously injured."

He glowers at me. "No, I can handle it. I'm not a total wimp."

"It's okay," I assure him. "You haven't had a nice big, hot meal or a good night's sleep in a long time. You aren't as strong as you once were."

He stares at me, not sure what to do, and reluctantly hands over the bags. I toss Kelly's light bag to Tina and take Matty's in my free hand. We trudge up the stairs slowly, and I lead Matty to his room first. He takes a quick look around and sees the television, the video game chair, the nice bed, and the ping-pong table, and I'm pretty sure by that point, he never wants to leave.

"This is unbelievable!" I smirk at his comment and add, "Yeah, this was my game room and I'm giving it to you for now, so treat it with care."

He nods with a huge smile engulfing his face, "I will for sure." He flips on the TV and plops himself down in the game chair.

"I think we lost him for the day," Jenna laughs.

"Agreed. Now it's time for your room."

I walk across the hall and open the door. The light from the wrap-around windows almost blinds us. The room is light and cheery like I wanted. The pink bed with the canopy and the fuzzy green chair with pillows everywhere is what Tina said a young teenage girl would want in her room, so I let her handle it. The thing Jenna gravitates toward is the desk with wood finish that reaches up to the ceiling. It has a chair that rolls and spins around next to it and my old laptop, which is still in very good condition, sitting on the top. I even threw in a notebook so she is all set for achieving her writing goals. If it was up to me, they would be staying in this house for a long time, so I got amazing rooms together in the hopes that I will get my way.

Jenna runs her hands along the laptop. "This is mine?"

I nod. "It's no big thing. Every writer needs their own laptop, so I figured I should put one in your room. Just as long as you promise to write really good ideas down in here. But don't spend *too* much time so at least I get to see you."

"Of course! Thank you so much! I never had my own writing space before. This is the first step to my dream coming true."

I shrug. "Well I guess you'll have to thank me first when you get your Newberry Award then."

"You know it." She sits down in the chair and puts her hands on the home keys. She presses a few keys, but the laptop is shutdown, so nothing happens. "This feels right." Then her face falls to the point it almost looks pained. "Too bad it's only temporary."

I look her in the eyes and say, "I'm gonna fix that. I didn't forget our deal."

I walk down the hall a ways with Kelly and show him his room. Tina is already in there unpacking his bag. His room is smaller than the other two, but the same goes for him, so it works. It has a nice green bed, a green dresser, and green walls, obviously his favorite color. A mountain of stuffed animals is in the corner, some new and some from our childhoods, and there is an exercise ball next to them. He immediately runs and jumps on it, and I know it was the right choice. If I know anything about this kid, it's that he loves bouncing and jumping-anything that involves being momentarily airborne. He bounces up and down multiple times with Salamander in his hand, laughing hysterically.

"What a simple kid," I mutter to Tina.

She laughs. "You can say that again." She walks over to him. "Hey Kelly."

He stops bouncing for a minute and looks at her. "Yeah?" He's still giggling.

"Look what is on the table next to your bed," she says, pointing in the direction he should look. "It's a boom box so you can play your music as much as you want without having to ask Jenna. And I got you a CD that I know you'll enjoy to play in it."

"Wow! Awesome! What CD?!" He hops off the ball and bounds over. Tina kneels down to his level and hands him the CD she picked out. She told me she was going to get him one when we were bringing this boom box that we never use upstairs, but I didn't know what one. I step over to see just when Kelly grabs it and jumps up and down.

"Look Andy!!!" he squeals, jumping in circles toward me. "It's Cradlesong! I wanted this one really bad!"

I take the CD from his hand and see it is Rob Thomas' new CD. I should have known that Tina would remember he requested that to her when she was driving them here for the first time. I hand it back to him, and he rips it open and puts it in the player. The song that plays on the radio all the time comes on, and Kelly turns it up and starts dancing around and singing it, eyes closed the entire time. I can't help but smile, and Tina is beaming at his reaction to her present.

"Sing Salamander! Such pretty noises and symbols!"

Matty and Jenna come running in to see what all the noise is about. "You got him a boom box and that CD?" Jenna asks.

Tina nods and she laughs, "We will never have peace in this house now!"

They start dancing along with Kelly, and as I watch them, I start to see just how skinny they look. They haven't had a hot meal in months and are starting to resemble the contestants in Survivor. When the song ends, I ask if they want to go out to get something to eat.

Matty's face lights up. "*That* would be heavenly." Jenna and Kelly nod their heads in agreement.

"I was thinking I would get that response. You three are looking a bit sickly."

Jenna's eyes widen. She pushes past everyone to get to the bathroom. Matty and Kelly follow her. They all look at themselves in the mirror and realize all the devastation that has occurred on their bodies.

"We look like walking skeletons right now," Jenna gasps.

Matty nods. "Yeah, I don't think I've ever seen any of these bones in my face before."

Kelly pulls at the skin on his face and frowns. He pulls off his shirt and stares at himself in the mirror. So do the rest of us. He turns around in a complete circle. "This isn't good."

"Poor Kelly!" Jenna cries. His ribs are jutting out, his back bone is sticking out like a stegosaurus, and his arms look like sticks coming out of his softball shoulders. It almost reminds me of a smaller version of myself when I was sick, weak, and not eating because all I did was throw up. I shake my memory from my mind as quick as it comes.

"Haven't you been feeding this boy?!" Tina asks, shocked.

"Yes, I guess his little body can't take eating so little and having so much activity."

"Well, we need to get them to a buffet. How does that Chinese food buffet down in that shopping center on Route 1 sound?"

All three kids cheer for that one. Tina laughs and says, "Well then I guess it's agreed that we are going there, right A?"

"Um, you can take them. I think I'm gonna pass."

"Why?" they all ask at once.

"I have something that I need to take care of before my stomach is ready to eat." I have a stomach that changes with my mood. If I'm worried about something, sad, angry, or know someone else is upset with me, there is no way I can eat, and right now my stomach is flipping around in worriment.

"Come on, it's gonna be no fun without you," Jenna protests. "Please come."

I shake my head. "No I can't. You get some food, but not too much to make yourselves vomit. When you get back, I will be finished with what I have to do."

Tina looks at me, trying to read my expression. "What are you doing?"

"I'm going to go make sure that the kids get what I promised," I whisper to her, while giving her a hug. "Make sure they get their nutrition. I'll be back in a few hours, hopefully."

"And what do I do if we get back and you aren't here like you said?"

"Entertain them, keep them happy." I pull away and start to walk out the door. "Thanks. I'll be back soon!"

"Be careful Andy," she calls after me. I hear Jenna say, "Yeah, please be careful with whatever you're doing." I don't think she wanted me to hear it, but I did, and I smile as I rush to my Miata. I have a heavy heart at the moment, knowing that what I want could very easily not happen.

I feel very awkward standing on the doorstep of a house that I have only been in once. The last time that I was here was with my father on business, and it's crazy to think of how things can change in one summer. The house seems very inviting in the light, much more than in the dark. A forest of trees surround three sides of the house, and the grass is covered in crunchy, brown leaves. It seemed almost haunted the last time I was here, but now it just feels like a house I know very well and love. The task ahead gives me anxiety though, and I am very close to turning around and running away as fast as I can. I don't want to hear no at this point, and I am scared to death I will. I have only wanted two other things this much in my life, a music career and my dad to accept me, and so far I've had an extremely bad track record. I can't have the kids taken away from me after all this time. I made too many promises and I've grown too attached. I can only hope and pray that this woman forgives me from my intentions on my last visit, even though I was only trying to help by accompanying my father.

I take a deep breath and look up at the enormous house towering over me one more time. It's gray all around with the bright pink door that looks me in the face right now. The wind rustles in the trees and birds chirp. The quiet makes me more nervous. I knock on the pink door very lightly. I can barely hear it and I scold myself for being such a wimp. I rap on the door very hard and aggressive this time and have the urge to hide again. I know that will only make things worse though, so I stay and run my hands through my hair anxiously. My hands are shaking and I struggle to keep my breathing even. What is this about? I never have panic attacks like this, but here I am looking like an idiot. How am I ever going to perform in front of thousands of people like I want to if talking to one elderly woman gives me this much of a reaction?

The door swings open and I jump. I was so busy giving myself a mental lecture that I forgot that someone was going to answer the door. Laura Thornton appears in the doorway in gray sweatpants and a gray t-shirt. She's looks much older than when I last saw her, and the worry in her eyes gives me the reason why. For a second, I think she's going to slam the door in my face, but a warm smile reaches her sad eyes. I breathe a sigh of relief and give a weak smile. My first worry of her hating me is proved to be just over thinking, and I feel like I might actually accomplish my goal.

"I remember your face. The rest of you looks so different that it took me a few minutes to register why I know you."

My smile grows stronger. "I can see why you would say that." I turned from the clean cut cop to my more wild self in jeans and a button down shirt. I also lost a pound of hair gel in the process, and my black hair dye faded a little so it's more dark brown. Come to think of it, I've changed greatly as a whole, not just my looks.

"So what brings you to my humble abode?"

"I have something important to ask you. It can't wait any longer."

Her eyes widen. She steps aside and motions for me to come inside. "By all means, come in then."

I step past her and into her living room. Once again, I get a better feeling than I did when I was here in the dark. There is a large pink couch in the middle of the floor that almost seems to call my name. I sit down and sink in it a little. I feel my face light up and Laura laughs at me.

"I see you enjoy my couch."

I nod. "It's a nice couch."

She sits in a chair across from me and looks me up and down. "You seemed awfully serious when you said you have something important to ask me. I can't imagine what it could be."

I draw in a deep breath and begin what I practiced to say at this point. "Well, you may not know this, but I've been taking care of your grandkids since they left your house. I knew they were here, and I actually found them in your crawlspace, but I said all was clear because I was on their side, not my father's. So I let them go, and when we finally caught them on the beach, I told my dad I would take care of it. When he left, I hid them. I told my dad I lost them, but really I came back every day to the same spot to give them food and clothing and other necessities. I also steered the case away from that area nonchalantly when my father talked of looking there again. I told him that I was on sick leave, and since it wasn't very unbelievable that I had pneumonia with my fragile lungs, I could have time to help the kids."

The entire time I talk, Laura nods, listening intently. "So you're telling me, you were secretly betraying your father by sabotaging the case against my grandchildren. I definitely did not see that coming."

"Yeah, no one did until my dad figured it out and shot me."

She gasps. "Oh my goodness, are you okay?"

"Oh, don't worry, I made a full recovery. I was trying to protect the kids from my crazy dad with a gun and ended up getting in the way of a bullet. Next thing I knew, I was in the hospital and the kids were in jail. But my girlfriend Tina bailed them out and my father was nowhere to be found to keep them from being released, so the charges are no longer applicable. It turns out one of my ex-coworkers, meaning that I am no longer a police officer at this point and living off money that we already had, what Tina makes, and checks in the mail from my mother, had my father held hostage in an old vacant barn where she had some history. We got him sent to a mental institution because I always knew he needed help, and your grandchildren are currently living in my home." I feel like I'm rambling on like an idiot, so I pause a moment.

"Wow, you're hard to follow."

I laugh nervously. "I'm my mother's boy. I talk a lot of useless nonsense when I get anxious." Come on Andy, I yell at myself. She's going to think you're a lunatic and not let her grandkids live with you. Telling her that your dad is in a mental institution and you're currently unemployed is one way *not* to get custody. I always tease my mother for babbling on and on, but it turns out I'm even worse. I should just leave now, but I can't be that much of a coward.

"What is there to be anxious about? I certainly should not make you anxious. I'm just listening to your soap opera of a life and waiting for what it is that is so important."

"Okay, I'll get to the point," I laugh. "I wanted to ask you if you would turn over your rights as guardian of the kids to Tina and me."

I watch as shock spreads across her face. "That is quite a lofty request. I was going to take the kids until they were taken from me by the law. This whole dramatic scene is all due to your father going overboard. It ruined what chance the children had at a normal life after the fire and left me with many sleepless nights. I mean, I am unbelievably thankful to you for helping them survive and taking a bullet for them, but you must understand they are all I have left. The rest of my family has died out on me slowly, and without them, I have no one left in this world. I can't just hand them over to you."

This is exactly what I was afraid of, but I must plead my case. "I understand. Hear me out for a minute though and let me explain some things to you."

She nods and I continue, "I came into this just to get revenge against my father. He had always thought I was worthless because I didn't want to join him in the law enforcement and wanted a music career. It made me an angry, rebellious teenager, and I finally had the chance to ruin something that was very important to him, like he did to me. If I didn't get my dream of starting a band because he threatened me into becoming a detective, he wouldn't get to close this important case and make a good image for himself. That was it, but something changed along the way. I realized the kids were more than just tools to get to my father; they were people. They had stories, hopes, dreams, likes, dislikes, and were grieving for lost loved ones. They lost their parents and older sister, their home, and all of their possessions, and now they were facing a life in jail. They clung to me and it made their day to see me. They felt okay telling me things that they were thinking and feeling and felt like everything was going to work out when I was around. And somewhere along the way, I needed to see them to get through a day. I felt like I had some special connection with them. In just one summer, I loved them like they were my own children, and the thought of losing them sickened me. They love me too, and I can see they're as scared to death that we will be separated as I am. They changed me for the better. Three months ago, I was full of hate and fear-I thought settling down, getting married, and having kids would ruin my life. Now I'm about to propose and am asking for legal guardianship of three kids. I feel like I'm finally going to turn my life around so I can get where I want to be. Something happened, something very good."

She closes her eyes and sighs. Then she opens them again and looks up at me, a single tear rolls down her cheeks. "Your time has come. This was the summer that you changed from an immature boy to a man. I can see in your eyes that what you say is true. You and my grandchildren need each other, and I wouldn't be able to live with myself if I were to separate you. I will call my lawyer to get the papers so I can sign over my rights. Promise a few things first though please?"

I can't hold back the smile that is overtaking my face. My eyes light up and my heart starts pounding. "Thank you so much! You have no idea what this means to me! I will promise anything at this point!"

"There are conditions here, so listen carefully. First off, you better know that this love with Tina is true, and that you are ready to be married, because the last thing those kids need is to go through a divorce. You have to act like parents and work things out to benefit your children. You need to understand that you have a responsibility other than yourself now, and you need to be dedicated to them. Teenagers are hard, and you need to help them through rough times, and Kelly is a strange boy who needs extra guidance, especially after all he's been through so early in his life. No matter what is going on in your and Tina's lives, they come first. To be a good man, you must succeed as a father and a husband."

"They mean everything to me. I will stop at nothing to make sure they are loved and happy."

"Good. Mackenzie, my son, and I got in so many arguments over his life choices. We screamed at each other and hated each other at times, but no matter what, he was my son, and I loved him. It took very long for him to grow up, but I was there throughout it all to guide him. Parenting is the hardest thing you will ever do, but it is well worth it in the end."

I nod. "I understand all of that. My own mother used to tell me all the time that I needed to be careful in life. I needed to be completely ready for the responsibility of parenthood before I fell into it. No matter how hard it will be, I will do it because they deserve it."

She grins. "I believe you. One more thing. You need to live somewhere where I can see them on holidays and birthdays and any time when I want to be a grandmother and spoil them."

"Of course! You can see them whenever you want. I wouldn't even think of cutting them out of your life or vice versa."

"Well then they are going to be yours very soon."

I jump up and give her a hug. That's another thing that has changed in me. I think my hug rule is ridiculous. If someone deserves a hug, no matter who they are, I'm going to give them one. I had too many rules before, and I think with them gone, I'm going to be a better person. She almost falls over in the chair when I hug her and we both laugh. "Thank you, thank you, thank you!" I say over and over like a little kid who just got the most amazing Christmas present in their life.

"You're welcome! For goodness sake, calm down. You almost killed me!"

I let go of her and step back. "I'm sorry. I just couldn't contain myself. I thought you would never let me, being some stranger, take your grandchildren, no matter how much I tried to persuade. I thought I wouldn't be able to do that for them, but it turns out good things can actually happen for me! One dream wasn't crushed for once. I'm so happy and excited that I'm about to burst!!!"

"Well your happiness is contagious. I trust you with those kids because you are very much like my son. I could swear you are a Godsend replica of him for those children to be able to carry on in their lives. I can see in your eyes that you've been through a lot and you're ready for this."

I nod. "Yes, I never did get that music career, my father is clinically insane and was mentally abusive, I love my sister dearly but she has always picked on me, I almost lost the love of my life, and I'm a 3 year lung cancer survivor. I'm more than ready for good things."

"Well, when you get your first album out, let me know, and I'll be one of the first to buy it."

"Really?"

"I wouldn't say it if I didn't mean it. And I expect an invitation to those upcoming nuptials of yours." She winks teasingly.

"You bet." I glance at the clock on the wall and notice it's getting late. Tina and the kids are most likely long home by now and waiting for me. Tina is probably doing her best to entertain them, but they still want me to come back. I'm putting a lot of pressure on her, and I know I need to get back. "My family is waiting for me. I really need to get back to them and it's a long drive." It feels strange, yet good to feel the word family on my tongue. I want to use it a lot now.

She gives me two thumbs up signs. "Good man. Now go! I will be seeing enough of you later on."

"Okay, thanks again," I say, rushing out through the door. I jump in my beloved Miata and pull out of the driveway. I see Laura standing in her front door and wave goodbye. She waves back, a colossal grin engulfing her face. I step down on the gas and scream. I have never felt this free and happy in my life. For the first time, I'm not afraid of the future, I'm welcoming it. For the first time, I feel like I will get everything I ever wanted in life. That feeling can be described by no words, no matter how hard I try to form the right ones. Now all I have to do is propose. Oh boy.

43

Jenna

"Why isn't he back by now?" I ask Tina for the hundredth time, along with 'Where is

he?' and 'Will he be back soon?' I can see she is getting very annoyed with me because she doesn't know any more than I do, and she continues to tell me that, but I can't help it. I'm anxious beyond belief, like when I wait for someone to answer an important email, or when I sit outside by the mailbox, waiting for my Amazon box to arrive. I tap a beat on my thighs and try to calm myself down by reciting song lyrics that are engraved in my brain. That just makes me think of him more and what kind of music he writes. I like rock, pop, alternative, and punk rock the most, and he seems like he would fall into one of those categories. There's no way it's country, and I don't find him capable of writing rap. I hope it's not heavy, emo rock either, although he's too sweet for that. Who cares? I would listen to it, whatever it is. That makes me wonder where that notebook I saw in the hospital is now. I would like to sneak a glance at that.

"Who are you talking to Jenna?" Matty asks. He leans over in front of my face and looks at me like I'm crazy. I have no idea what he's talking about, so I just stare back. Tina and Kelly are looking at me too, so I know they must all be thinking something I'm not.

"I asked Tina a question."

Matty chuckles. "And obviously didn't wait for an answer. She told you that she thinks he'll be back soon, but you were too busy whispering something to yourself and staring at the wall like someone was there. We thought you were part of one of those horror movies where the ghost possesses you."

Oh. All the thoughts that were running through my head were coming out very quietly through my mouth. I'm usually pretty good at keeping them inside but when I get really worried or happy, I lose my self control. They come exploding out and I start rambling to myself. I accepted it as a little quirk of mine and don't try to stop it unless I'm somewhere that I could get humiliated. Now would be one of those times. Oh well, I'm just vocal and everyone will have to deal with that.

"I'm allowed to talk to myself. I'm worried." I shoot him a 'shut up you idiot' look and he shoots one back.

"You always talk to yourself. I always hear it coming from your room like you have a friend in there. That's normal for you. This was different. You were distant and sounded like this." He then tries to imitate me, but sounds more like a leaky tire.

"I was thinking about things, so stop trying to look cool in front in Tina."

His face twists and I can tell he's embarrassed. He takes a few moments to think of a comeback and says, "What are you thinking about, your dream lover?"

I draw in a quick breath and glare at him, eyebrows far down over my eyes. "You don't know what you're talking about. He's like a brother to me, and for all I know, he's out fighting ninjas in the woods. I have a right to be a little worried."

He rolls his eyes. "A brother? Sure." He drags out the word sure way too long. It gets under my skin. I'm only a little bit lying on that one, but he doesn't need to call me out. He just wants to impress Tina and make her think he's the cool twin and I'm the pathetic one. I am a little pathetic, I must admit, but he's no cooler than me. He's a science nerd who's obsessed with time, and I make up stories in my head and sometimes talk to inanimate objects. We're tied.

"I mean we all know you're jealous of Tina," he instigates. "And there's always been something a little off in your head that you crush on older men instead of boys like you're supposed to."

"Older guys are better because they have an equal maturity level as me, unlike little boys like you."

His cheeks, nose, and even the tips of his ears grow tomato red in split seconds. He is fuming, but he started it, so I was forced to hold my own. "I'm older than you!"

"Ha, and those three minutes make so much of a difference!"

He intertwines his fingers and stretches out his arms so they bend back. There is a little crackle, and if I wasn't so angry, I would have thought it was funny. He thinks he's so tough, but he has a lot to learn. "It does. And plus, Andy looks just like Dad so that's even weirder."

My eyes widen and I hope he sees flames in them. "How dare you bring Dad into this?!"

He shrugs. "I'm just saying you're a bit incestuous."

"I am not!" I roar. "They are two totally different people and you know it! You're being a real tool!"

He cackles, throwing his head back and clapping his hands. "I can't believe my sister has incestuous wishes," he adds under his breath. He's too scared to say it really loud because he knows I'll hurt him, but it is just loud enough for me to hear it. No matter how loud it is, he pushes me over the edge, and I jump out of my chair in a flash. He must have been on high alert, knowing my reactions so well, because he is running into the next room as quick as I get up. I chase after him, screaming, and I hear him laughing. I dash through the entire downstairs a few times, rooms rushing past me in a blur. I dodge furniture very well for not knowing the place by heart. If this was our old house, I would have caught him by now.

I stop in my tracks at that thought. Flashes of the fire, the gaping hole in Matty's room where the lightning had struck, and firemen carrying Mom and Matty's limp bodies out of the house and into the ambulance fill my head. I feel the warm summer night again, the rain on my face, the sirens blaring, Kelly screaming. I feel the smoke in my lungs again; the white, red, yellow, and orange flashes of flames seem right in front of me again. I stand in the middle of the kitchen in silent pain, real tears streaming down my cheeks. My body quivers a bit, but other than that, I make no sound. I flash back to the hug Matty, Kelly, Mom, and I shared before Mom... My heart feels like it's going to explode. I hear Matty screaming for me, asking if I am alright from another room. I don't respond. I drop to my knees, propping myself up on my toes, and hold the sides of my head. Matty comes running in to see why I stopped chasing him as I silently weep. He kneels beside me and asks me what's wrong, panic filling his bright blue eyes. Tina and Kelly come in after him, saying things that I neglect to hear.

"I was just messing with you Jen. You never liked a guy before, or at least I didn't know about it, and it's my job to tease you. He's a cool guy, and you're right, he's not Dad. I'm sorry. Please say something so I know you're okay."

I look into his eyes and wrap my arms around him. He pats me on the back and I whisper into his ear, "The fire shouldn't have happened. Mom shouldn't have died. Dad and Lauren shouldn't have died either. We shouldn't have lost our home, and we shouldn't have gone to jail. Andy shouldn't have been shot and almost died. We shouldn't fight; we're all we have left."

"I know. I'm sorry." I feel someone's arms around my shoulder blades, and I turn my head a little to see it's Kelly. I smile at him and he says, "Don't be sad Jenna."

I let go of Matty a moment to give Kelly a kiss, and then turn back. I pretend Mom is there with us too, and I know they are sharing that thought. We are well fed, have people who love us, the cops aren't after us anymore, and with any luck we'll have a new home, but most of all, we have each other. And we won't ever be separated, at least not in spirit.

 fter we've all calmed down, an uncomfortable Tina requests that we play Wii. She says

Andy's nephews love to play it when they're here, and that they have some pretty good games. I feel bad that she was sort of left out of our little bonding moment. That must have been awkward, but soon enough she will know us well enough to join in on them. Another thing is I didn't know Andy had nephews! I knew he had a sister, but he didn't talk about her much. Certainly not enough to tell us that she had kids. I wonder how old they are and why they couldn't be girls. I've always liked hanging out with boys more than girls, mostly because Matty always had friends over and they became my friends too, but I need some girl time too. I used to take out the girl stuff on Mom, but now I have no one. I'm surrounded by guys, and I don't know Tina well enough yet to share things with her. If I'm going to have surrogate cousins, why couldn't one of them be a girl near my age whom I would get along with? Oh well, I should be grateful that I have surrogate cousins at all. I never had cousins at all. Dad was an only child, and Mom's brother Slade is off somewhere we don't know, most likely getting into trouble.

We decide to play Wii sports and beating everyone in tennis matches and getting multiple homeruns in baseball takes my mind off of things for awhile. It's much needed therapy, and my brothers seem to be having a good time too. I feel much better after letting some tears out as always. I get that cleansed feeling, like I've washed away all my worries for the day and there's more room for good things. I have the sudden urge to want to go do some of my acting though. I haven't done acting for my stories or written anything for a very long time, and I'm starting to feel deprived. I hope I haven't lost my imagination, although I don't know if that's possible. Maybe it's possible to forget how to form sentences too, or type on a keyboard, but I think that's like riding a bicycle so I doubt it. I wish my life would just work itself out, so I can do normal things like I used to do. You know it is bad when you realize you took forming sentences for granted. I laugh to myself, glad that I still have my wit.

I hear the sound of a car pulling in the driveway, something I'd become accustomed to, considering my old room was above the garage, before anyone else. I drop the Wii controller on the couch and run to the back door at lightning speed. I fling open the door and jump to the floor of the garage, completely skipping the steps. I skip putting on shoes too and catch the big garage door just as it is going up. The beautiful red Miata pulls in next to me and I wave, a huge smile taking over my face. Matty, Kelly, and Tina appear behind me as Andy opens his door and gets out.

"What took you so long?" I ask, unbelievably excited to see him. "We thought you got lost in the woods while trying to fight those ninjas."

His face looks puzzled and I almost laugh. "What?"

"Don't worry about it," Matty replies before I can. "She's stranger than usual today." He grins and peers at me through the corner of his eye to see if I was irritated by the comment. I'm too happy at this point to care what he says, so I just laugh with him. I am strange and proud!

"I won't ask then," Andy chuckles. "You won't believe the news I have for you four."

"What is it?" we all ask in unison. He pushes past us and opens the back door to get in the house.

"Come inside and I'll tell you." There's a stampede to get inside at that point. I almost step on Kelly and swoop him up, arm under his stomach, to make sure Matty doesn't. He squirms and laughs as we run together into the family room, where a game of bowling is paused on the TV screen. I sit him on my lap on the couch and notice he is getting bigger and heavier. He used to be as light as a feather when he was a toddler, but now he's almost eight and is putting much more pressure on my little legs. Matty plops down next to me, Tina sits cross-legged on the carpet, and we all wait patiently for Andy to settle himself and look back at us.

His grin is overbearing, and I can't wait to hear what he finds unbelievably good news. It could be anything. My mind races with the possibilities. All I know is that I need really good news at this point, and I'm hoping it's one thing in particular.

"Well, while you four were enjoying the buffet, I was taking care of very important business that affects all of us." We all lean in closer. I stroke Kelly's hair nervously. He loves it, so he doesn't mind.

"So you weren't fighting ninjas?" Matty asks so quietly that only I can hear it, and we both crack up.

Andy ignores us and continues, "I went to your grandmother's house."

My eyes widen. I look back at Matty and see he's sharing my surprise. So that's why he took so long. He had to drive all the way to Grandma's house in Pennsylvania, take care of whatever business he had with her, and drive back. I wonder what he could have wanted to see Grandma about. The only time he had ever been to that house was on his police mission, before we met him, when he saw us under the crawlspace. Grandma probably thought he had quite the nerve, and I can imagine she had a few words to say to him. Although, if he told her what he did for us, she would quiet down real quickly.

"How is she doing?" Matty inquires. "We had to make a quick get-away and didn't get to say a proper goodbye."

"I'm sorry about that. I did all I could. And she is doing great actually, but of course is worried about her grandchildren. She welcomed me into her home warmly, despite the circumstances in which I was in it last."

That's a surprise. Maybe it was the fact that he looks and acts so much like what I remember of Dad, and she trusted him automatically. He seems to have that affect on the Thornton family. "What were you talking to her about?"

He holds his hand up. "I'm getting there. I told her our story. How the last time I was there, I pretended to be her enemy to trick my father, and that I really was on her and your side. I told her about how we bonded and how I made sure you were safe over the summer. I told her about how my dad shot me and put you all in jail, but a fellow detective kept him under wraps so Tina could get you released and I could recover. I told her we put him in a mental institution, and then I told her about your living situation." He stops there and looks down. My heart starts pounding as I realize what he was there to talk to her about our deal. What did she say? I fight not to become panicked.

"She told me that her grandchildren are all she has left and she needs them in her life. I understood that, and I told her I need you too in my life because what started out as a mission of revenge, turned into me loving you three unconditionally."

I can't help but smile. That is so sweet and cute and I love when guys get like that. I'm also quite glad that he feels the same way about us that we feel about him. "Did she change her mind?" I can't take the suspense much longer.

"She better have! I love Grandma but I want to live here!" Kelly cries out. I squeeze his shoulders to tell him to calm down until we know what is really happening.

Andy's face lightens as he relays the news, "You will be living here permanently as soon as your grandmother signs over her rights to Tina and I. She said you have to visit her on holidays and birthdays so she can still do her grandmotherly duties though, and I said I wouldn't think of not letting her. So yeah, you're my kids now."

My heart soars at that moment. I never thought things would work out this perfectly, but somehow they did. Life seems like it will be okay after all. Living here with Andy, Tina, and my brothers and being able to visit the beach anytime we want while still being able to visit Grandma on special occasions! Could I have asked for anything better with what I had left? I figure I couldn't have, so I become very grateful. It was well worth the wait and the fight with Matty for this heartwarming news.

"Really? You're not joking?" Kelly asks. He has one eyebrow raised in a skeptical way.

We all smile at him. "Why would we joke about something like that?" Andy replies with a question, and Kelly agrees that we aren't all that mean to do something like that to him. I ruffle his hair so his bangs stick up off his forehead, and he laughs and does a somersault, ending up with his head in my lap.

"I think this just made our entire summer," Matty adds as Tina runs over to give Andy a hug. She whispers "mission accomplished, good job" in his ear, and he thanks her. Matty raises his elbow up over the arm of the couch and jams it into my side. I glare at him. He silently points and laughs. Brothers, I swear, they were made to annoy their sisters.

I figure I need to avert the attention back to me before I have a jealous fit, so I playfully ask Andy, "Does that mean I should call you Daddy?"

He pulls away from Tina to answer me, making me feel a little better. "No, I think you should just stick with hot non-biological brother." He winks at me, and I get the same feeling I did when this was last discussed-like I'm going to die of mortification. Matty obviously thinks that is the most hilarious thing he has ever heard because he literally rolls on the floor laughing. I roll my eyes at him and hope that my face doesn't look as red and burning as it feels.

Matty stops rolling long enough to see my reaction and erupts into another fit of laughter. He manages to get out, "Now she's all hot and bothered. The wink sets her over the edge," in between his sputters. There goes my hope that I'm not twenty shades of scarlet.

"You're so funny Matty," I mock. "Har har har!"

"I know, right?" he yells, very proud of his comment.

I have a bad foreboding that this will be brought up in the future if I'm going to be living here. Matty certainly won't let this go and Andy will egg him on, making it worse. I guess that's the price I have to pay for such an optimistic outcome. I must say though, as much as it's humiliating to sit through Matty's comments, so much that I want to run and hide in a corner somewhere, I do like the attention. Life would be severely boring if I wasn't forced to laugh at myself every once in awhile.

Exploring a house has always been one of my favorite pastimes, so I am more than happy to have time to myself to wander through the different rooms. I have already seen the family room, kitchen, dining room, living room, foyer, and caught a glimpse of the sunroom, and they seemed pretty normal. I hope that the doors that are always closed lead to secret rooms and the winding staircase leads to a new world. That is highly unlikely, but I can't help but wish. I have always wanted to be like one of those kids in fantasy books and movies who move into a new house and find a secret passageway that leads to a whole new world with mysterious creatures that become their best friends. I would keep it to myself and visit them everyday secretly. Eventually they would convince me to live with them, and I would leave my other life and become a mysterious creature myself. My disappearance would become the great mystery of the town for years to come, but no one would ever figure it out. I just disappeared without a trace and no one would ever find me, while meanwhile I was queen of the new world for the rest of my long life. Hundreds of years later, a new family would discover the secret passageway in the house and wouldn't believe their eyes when they found me there. They wouldn't be able to tell anyone though, or else I would drag them away to the dungeon. Oh what a life. I should really write about this. That would make a really good book and maybe I could be famous from it. At least if it didn't really happen, it would be a story shared with everyone.

Anyhow, I search the house now, hoping that I will find something I hadn't found in my house, Grandma's house, or any of my friends' houses-somewhere just for me that I can hold close to my heart forever. I peer through the closed door on the side of the family room and see a small room with computers and office supplies in it. That doesn't interest me, so I close the door again. I look through the other doors and find a pantry full of food where our summer food supply must have come from, a laundry room, and a small bathroom. I run full speed through the dining room and living room to the foot of the spiraling staircase. I run up it, feeling like I'm running in circles, and reach where Matty's, Kelly's, and my room are. There is another room that has a closed door halfway between Matty and Kelly's rooms. I open it slowly, making it creak. It looks like a normal bedroom, except much larger. There is a bathroom on one side of it, and I gulp as I realize that it must be the room Andy and Tina share. I don't want to see anymore, so I close the door. All that is left upstairs is a bathroom that I have to share with my brothers, and I find myself very disappointed. I don't want to live in a house without at least one special room.

I trudge back down the spiral staircase and through the foyer to the family room. I fall down on the couch and lay down, staring at the white ceiling. I hear a faint music sound and smile. At first I think maybe Kelly is playing something or it's just in my mind, but then I realize it sounds like its closer and outside my head. I hop off of the couch and follow the sound the best I can. I find myself back in the office and realize I should have looked closer in that room. I find a door on the opposite side of the room, one you can only see if you really enter the room and look. I press my ear up against it, and I'm positive the music is coming from the room. I twist the knob as slowly as I possibly can and press open the door. I hear a small click, but the music doesn't stop. It gets louder and sounds like a piano. I step in and instantly see it's a music room. There are a few different guitars propped up against the wall, a banjo, a drum set, a violin, a trumpet, and a switchboard in the corner. I look up at the walls, and they look like someone threw different colors of paint at them and let it splash wherever it may. There are black music notes of all kinds covering the other white spots on the wall-whole notes, 4th notes, beamed 8th notes, 16th notes, flat signs, sharp signs, staffs, rests, G clefs, C clefs, etc. I could stare at them forever. I finally tear my eyes away and turn a corner in the colossal room, my feet feeling nice on the plush, light blue rug. I stop short when I see a black baby grand piano in front of me with Andy sitting at the bench in front of it. His fingers glide across the white and black keys, making beautiful music, and he looks like he belongs there. Luckily his eyes are closed and his head is bobbing to the music, so he doesn't see or hear me. I step closer until I am standing right behind him. I see his notebook lying on the top of the piano, and I peer at it. Words are scrawled on all sides of one page, some crossed out, and some with notations above them. On the next page, there is a hand drawn music staff with notes all over it and other music signs. It is absolutely enthralling. I can't comprehend how someone could completely write all the music for all the different instruments *and* the lyrics for a song and make it sound so good. It's a gift I wish I had.

I'm so busy looking at the notebook, that I don't notice Andy has stopped playing and has turned around. I jump a little when I see him looking at me. "I didn't mean to intrude," I apologize. "I was just exploring the house and heard the piano."

"No, it's okay. I was just doing some writing. Do you like the room?"

I nod. "It's amazing. Much different than the rest of the house."

"That's because I designed it myself," he says, leaning in closer to whisper. "Tina's style tends to get a little boring. I prefer the wild colors and the uniqueness of the set-up."

Looks like I found that special room I was looking for so hard. I feel like I'm going to gravitate to this room most of the time I spend here. I agree with Andy about the wallpaper, and all the instruments amaze me. It looks like a music studio built right into a normal home. "Did you do the walls yourself?"

He grins. "You know it. Ever since I was a little kid, I always wanted to throw paint at the walls. It was an exhilarating experience that made me feel wild. Then I added all the symbols because there were white spaces. And, of course, I couldn't resist these rugs."

"Wow, I love it. It really shows your wild child side."

"That's what I am at heart," he laughs, tapping his chest. "Wait until you see me on stage. I'm going to jump off the stage and into the arms of my fans."

I can't help but crack up at that. That would be quite a sight to see, and I'm positive he would do it. "I can't go through life without witnessing that."

"Then it's a promise." His mischievous smirk is extremely cute.

I suddenly feel a little uncomfortable and look around at the instruments again. "Do you play all these?"

"I don't, but I can."

My eyes widen. "How do you even begin to learn all of these?!"

"I started to mess around at the piano at three, so that's where I started. I had it mastered by third grade, and then my grandfather taught me the violin, which I learned by ten. I took band in sixth grade and learned trumpet, but I'm not that good at it anymore. Then I transferred to drums until ninth grade and was the main drummer in the high school band. My dad had a drum set in the house from when he played as a kid, so I practiced throughout my life and never lost the ability to play. That"-he motions to the drum set in the corner-"is the same one because my mom thought I would use it more. Also in high school, I took a class on guitar as one of my electives and was a pro at that by the time I graduated. I wanted to take advanced piano because I loved it so much, but I got made fun of for being one of the only guys in the class. They said only girls and feminine guys played piano, and if I wanted to prove my manhood, I should be in guitar with them. I don't know why I listened to them, because later I found out that the girls thought that the piano playing guys were hotter than guitar guys, and the guys only said that because they were threatened by me." He shrugs. "I guess I benefited from the experience though because now I excel at both piano and guitar."

I roll my eyes. "Never listen to teenage guys. They are just as vicious and jealous as the girls; they just don't show it on the outside as much."

"So I learned. Oh, and as for the banjo, my roommate in my freshmen dorm played it. I thought it was the coolest thing, so I made it my goal to learn it by the time I graduated. Of course, I never graduated, but I still know the basics."

"So basically you've been playing music since you were three?"

"It's my passion, and I still can't get enough. I've been writing music since I was your age, but it's better now."

I feel like I understand him, being that I have a passion of my own, and my heart is warmed. Now if only I could backtrack his age to mine so I can become his love instead of Tina. That would be such a dream and thinking about its impossibility takes all the warming away from my heart and makes it ache. I finally found a guy who was as perfect as the book characters I write, and I can't have a shot at him. Is it possible that there is another like him out there for me? I know he can't be duplicated, but maybe someone can overpass him. I shake my head at that thought. Nope, the bar was set too high. Now I'm going to end up alone because no one will be as good as him. I'm going to end up writing in a dark basement all alone with five cats-an old woman who was never loved because she could never find an amazing guy like her surrogate father, or her real one for that matter. I'm going to die alone and sad, and my books probably won't even be published because no one will like the writings of someone who's so depressed. I have to hold my breath so I don't start hyperventilating and crying.

"What's wrong?!" Andy asks, panic in his voice. I realize that my face has suddenly gotten sullen, and my eyes have filled with tears as he has been watching me. I feel even worse because now I made him feel helpless, when it's not his fault that I think and worry too much.

I squeeze my eyes shut tight until the tears fall out of them and wipe them off my cheeks. "I'm fine. My mind was just racing; it happens. Never give up on that dream because it's really sad that you have been kept from chasing it all these years."

"Is that what you're crying about? Because I'm chasing it now and I'm going to get there before you know it. I definitely have the talent and the potential. And if you don't think you're going to be a writer, you will, because you have talent at that. I can tell by your personality. Please don't cry."

"I know. I'm just an idiot. An over thinker. Don't get all panicked because it happens without warning." I don't want to tell him that that was only part of why I was getting upset. It was mostly because I'm stupidly in love with someone that is *way* out of my league and am afraid that I will never love anyone else like this. I can't push those words out for the life of me. I decide the best thing to do is change the subject so I don't get upset again and have to tell him what's really going on inside my complicated head.

"So what were you writing when I came in? Can I see it?"

He examines my face for a moment to make sure I'm not going to break down right there, and his face grows relieved. "It's sort of a secret."

I lower my eyebrows. "I'm very trustworthy. Much more than Matty or Kelly will ever be."

"I know. I just don't know if you can keep this big of a secret."

"Ha," I wave my hand in the air as if to blow off that statement. "I can keep any secret, unless you committed a crime, but even then I would probably still keep it for you."

His face becomes a mix of laughter and disbelief. "No, I didn't commit a crime and I'm a little insulted that you think I would. I'm not that much of a wild child. This is a different kind of secret." He gets up from the piano bench and picks up one of the guitars that are leaning against the wall. He shakes it until a small square box falls out into his hand. He sets down the guitar and walks back over to me, moving the box around in his hands. I have a sinking feeling because I'm pretty sure I know what's coming.

He sits back down and opens the lid to the box so it sits open. A beautiful, glistening diamond ring stares back at me, and I can't help but gasp. It's a gold band with a pear cut diamond in the middle. The diamond has diamond chips surrounding it, and it has to be one of the most beautiful things I've ever seen. I stare at it, mesmerized. "Wow, that's gorgeous," I whisper.

"Yeah I hope Tina thinks so too. I had to do this all without her ever having a clue so she'll be blind-sided."

"You're proposing?" I half ask, half squeal, even though I know the answer.

The panic reappears on his face, and I can tell he's scared to death to do it. "Yes," he replies, in a very small voice.

"And you wrote a song to go with it?"

He nods. "The plan is to get her in here so I can play and sing the song. Then once she is really confused at why I'm doing this, I will kneel down with the ring and ask her to be my bride. Then I expect a very surprised, yet very excited yes."

I give him my best, 'that is the sweetest and cutest thing I've ever heard' face, but he still looks unsure. "What if she says no? I mean, I don't think she will, but she said some things to me that night we had the fight. I don't know if secretly she means them and is just with me out of pity. She always wanted to get married, I didn't. I thought that you could love someone and not have to make a big production out of it in a wedding. I thought a lot of stupid things, and almost dying for the third time made me figure that out. I told her that. She accepted it, but that was still part of our fight. She was sacrificing every girl's dream of a big white wedding for me, and it hurt her. I want to surprise her with this so she's stunned and ecstatic."

"And you will," I assure him. "She wouldn't stay with you if she wanted to get married and knew you didn't, if she wasn't in love with you."

One side of his mouth turns up in an attempted smile, but he's too worried for it to reach his eyes. "I only want to do this one time. I don't want to screw it up."

"Then practice on me. Since I'm a girl too, I'll tell you if she's going to like it or not." And I get to pretend I'm a princess with the most amazing guy in the world proposing to me in song, I add in my mind.

"Okay, but be honest." I nod, and he props the music written in his notebook in front of him. He places his hands on the piano, takes a deep breath, and starts to play. A wonderful harmony fills my ears, and I sigh in contentment. He starts singing, and I realize I've never heard him sing before. He has a unique yet soothing voice, the kind I could fall asleep to in minutes on the nights I toss and turn in bed. Between the piano and the actual words he is singing, it has to be the sweetest song I've ever heard. He sings about how he didn't know how much he needed her until he was faced with losing her, that she helped him through his battle with lung cancer, and that he was so stupid for thinking that there might even be a chance that anyone more beautiful inside and out even existed. He looks up at me every once in awhile, in between looking at what keys his fingers are pressing, and the music in the book, and for those moments I pretend he's singing to me. I get a glimpse of how lucky that girl really is, and she better know it.

He finishes with a "what I'm trying to say is, I'll love you forever and always" and a little piano solo. Then he takes the box in his hands, kneels down in front of me, and opens it, revealing that stunning ring. "Will you be my beautiful, blushing bride?"

Before I can answer, he stands back up and closes the box. My dreams are crushed again. "So?"

I shake my head. "You are such a fool for thinking any girl could ever say no to that! *I* was about to marry you!"

He laughs, looking very relieved. "That is very good. Why is it that you are always playing the part of the mature adult reassuring me and giving advice?"

"I'm very mature and can read people exceptionally well. It comes with the writer's personality. And you help me too so don't worry."

"That's definitely true," he agrees. "You're more mature than most of my friends."

I laugh. "It's hard going to school when you feel like you're in a class full of immature idiots." I look back over at his notebook, still as curious as when I first saw it. "And what I want more than anything is to take a look at that notebook."

He laughs with me, picking up the notebook. "I was always the immature one." He places the notebook in my hands, and I realize it's gotten heavier than at the hospital. It has a very large number of loose papers shoved in it, so much that I can't even locate the pages it came with, and I suppose that weighs it down. I open it with care as to not let anything fall out of place. He watches me with his baby. I flip through all kinds of different things-lyrics to songs, music notes for all the different instruments, sketches he drew of album covers, lists of possible song and album titles, and even lists of possible band members and what they would do for his band. It's all enthralling to me, like taking a trip through his mind. I didn't get to look at it this thoroughly the last time.

I stop flipping when I come across the lyrics to a song titled "Jenna Dear". I flash back to when he caught me doing my acting and started writing something down. All this time he was writing a song for *me*! My heart soars; I'd always wanted to be the basis of one of the songs that I listen to and love.

I don't get a chance to read it before he claps the notebook shut in my hands. "Hey!" I protest, "I was about to read that!"

He pulls the notebook out of my hands before I can hold on tighter and holds it under his arm. "You're not allowed to read it."

"Come on! You're gonna kill me!"

"You will know of it when I want you to, and no sooner."

I give him my best puppy dog face, trying to make myself cry again, but he just stares back at me, very triumphant. He's not going to budge on that one no matter how much I plead, and we both know it. I let out a huge heaving sigh. "Fine. I'll just die of curiosity. They will make a new saying-curiosity killed the teenage girl." Then I walk out of the room, head held high, and up the staircase to my bedroom. It feels nice to call it my room, and I know I can because the papers were just signed yesterday. I power on the laptop, open a new Word document, and title it "My Surrogate Father Andy". The first line reads, "I don't know how, but the worst summer of my life and the best summer of my life were the same." If he can write a secret song about me, I can write a secret heartfelt book about him and what we've been through in the past couple months.

44

Andy

I don't think I've ever sweated this much in my entire life. I'm not really into sports, so I never broke a sweat in gym class, but my dad made me do all kinds of vigorous activities to make sure I was ready to be a detective. I used to practice with my band in the hot garage too, not to mention the shows we put on for friends and the school. I jumped around like a lunatic, that being one of my favorite things to do, and I really needed a shower after that, but it doesn't even compare to right now. I rub my clammy hands together to keep the blood flowing to them. I continually have to re-spike my hair up because it keeps falling down and sticking to my forehead and the sides of my face. I'm glad I use permanent hair dye or it would be running down my neck about now. Why do we sweat when we're nervous anyway? Maybe it's because my heart is beating a thousand miles per minute and making my whole body go on overdrive. Did I take my ADHD meds today? I start to freak out thinking that's why I can't keep any part of me still for more than two seconds. I start pacing across the room, bang on the drums for a minute, and then sit back down on my piano bench.

My stomach hurts, but I couldn't keep any food down this morning, so it's no use trying to eat. I pull off my t-shirt and look down at myself. I'm relieved that I don't look extremely skinny, just moderately skinny. I look at my colorful tattoos and suddenly want to get another one farther up my left arm. It looks too bare. And maybe the right one too so they match. I trace around the copyright sign on my chest with my finger a couple times and shoot to my feet again. I stare at the clock and see I still have two hours to go. The hands seem to move a lot slower than they usually do. I try to make them move faster with my mind, but I obviously don't have that skill. I figure that I need something to keep my mind from racing so much so I head upstairs to my bedroom. A huge clump of black hair falls in front of my eyes again, and I'm very close to cutting it all off right there. I fill the sink in my bathroom with water and dunk my head in it. After thirty seconds, I fling my head back as hard as I can. Drops of water cover the walls and wet the floor. I stare horrified in the mirror as I realize I caused my hair to part in the middle of my head and fall over my ears.

I run down to the office, grab the large scissors out of the cabinet, and return to the bathroom. I try to push my hair off my ears, but it keeps falling down. It looks worse than when it's gelled. I try to remember the last time I cut it, but all my months are blurring together. June or July maybe? Either way, it needs it before it gets long. Long hair and I don't mix, unless it's blond, and there's no way I'm getting it back to the blond it was before I dyed it. If the black gets long,

I'll end up looking like an Indian woman, considering my lack of muscle tone. I look at my arms and think they look a little bit too much like colorful twigs right now. I panic, thinking I won't be able to carry my bride. Maybe I should try lifting weights, although I'm sure I will end up dropping them and crushing myself.

Jesus, I really do need more ADHD meds. My mind can't focus on one topic for the life of me. I need to deal with this mess on my head. I hang my head down so I can see it all. I brush it off the back of my neck and my temples until it all hangs loosely in front of my eyes. I start with the front and cut off all the bangs until they are short enough to stick up in spikes. Then I move to the back where I snip until it falls nicely into a point at the center of the back of my neck. I smooth it down there and into the start of sideburns in front of my ears. I run my fingers through the top until the hair on the sides of my head are smoothed down, but the top is a faux hawk right up to the bangs. I shake my head a little so the spikes intertwine into each other. I brush the stray pieces off of my face. I look back in the mirror and smile. Much better.

Little clumps of jet black hair lie on the floor, twisting in all directions. It kind of reminds me of a mix of spider legs and a black shag rug. I retrieve a dust pan from the kitchen and sweep it all up. I take a clump off the pan and rub it between my thumb and forefinger. It feels as soft as a kitten, and a let out a little 'aw' as I think of stroking a tiny black kitten. I've always been a cat guy, a sucker for a little kitten looking up at me with its cute little eyes. I dispose of the fake kitten in the trash and decide to take those pills, since my mind has been bouncing all over the place.

I stare at the clock again, only one more hour. I recruited Jenna to get everyone out of the house and then get only Tina in at exactly 2 p.m. Even though she's still mad at me for not showing her the song, she still agreed. She begged to go to the boardwalk, and Matty and Kelly were more than willing to join her. I said I had business to attend to and convinced Tina that taking them would be a great bonding time. I could tell she was very annoyed with me for bailing out on her, especially because I didn't tell her exactly why. I'm hoping that it will be all worth it and she forgets all that when she comes back and finds what I'm really up to here. I have a feeling that I'm going to make it up to Jenna too, due to the fact that she thinks I'm being so awful for not telling her what the song I wrote about her said. I just wrote a few things down when I was watching her sometimes and put them together. The plan was to surprise her with it, and I didn't want to ruin that. I have something in mind that I can do for both her and Matty though.

That reminds me! I take out my cell phone and take a deep breath as I search through my contacts. I place the call and fight the urge to hang up. "Hello?" Tina's mother's voice asks.

"Hi Jean. It's Andrew," I reply nervously.

"I haven't heard from you in awhile. Is something wrong?"

I shake my head and realize she can't see me. "No, no. I wanted to speak to Jon actually."

"Oh okay. Hold on." I hear her call him and then footsteps.

"Hello Andrew. Is there something you need?"

I hadn't thought how to really ask this and I'm starting to think I really should have. He's always been a hard one to please, the kind that thinks no one is good enough for his only daughter. He thinks the tattoos, piercings, and dyed hair means that I'm a bad person and frowns upon the fact that I would have rather started trying to make my way in the music business out of high school than go to college. His tone is disapproving even now, and I don't think I can handle it if he rudely denies me now.

"Yes, and it's very important," I finally manage to get out.

There is silence on the other end of the phone and I worry that he hung up on me. "Speak boy! I have things to do with my life."

I jump a little. I can already tell that he's not going to take this well. "I wanted to ask you for your blessing-for you to tell me if it's okay if I..."

"Oh no," he grunts, cutting me off. "I worried this day was coming when you wanted to marry my Kristina."

"Worried?" I squeak.

He cackles in my ear. "Well at least I know that you won't abuse her because I'm sure she can take you. And you better live close because I may need to come over to help you open your applesauce." He barely gets the last part out because he's laughing so hard.

I feel like saying 'oh thanks, you'll be a great father in law', but I'm afraid he really *can* come over here and snap me in half.

When he finally stops laughing, he says, "I'm sorry kid. I just have so much wit sometimes that I can't keep it to myself. Although you're not the kind of guy I would picture my little girl marrying, she loves you. So yes, you have my blessing. So stop freaking out and make it special because she deserves it."

I close my eyes and let out a sigh of relief. "Thank you. I created a musical piece so it will be special."

"Good." I hear Jean asking what's going on, and he tells her to give him one moment. "You done with me now?"

"I also wanted to ask you if you and Jean were free next weekend. I'm planning something that I want you to be a part of."

"One moment kid," he replies. He asks what they're doing next weekend, and I hear that there is nothing planned. That is what I wanted to hear. "Nothing, what are we doing?"

I answer, knowing that with the next couple calls, I will be saying this very often. It's important to me so I hope that I get everyone to come.

I pull my eyebrow out and stick the point with the silver ball on the end through the hole. I twist the other silver ball on the end so it stays and do the same with the other eyebrow. They really compliment my dark hair and bright blue eyes, and I like the way that looks. After making the phone calls I had to, I'd changed my clothes and sprayed cologne on my shirt. I hope it's not too much. My mom always used to get on me when I was teenager that I smelled like I took a bath in it, and it was giving her a headache. I never had a really good sense of smell, so I hope that doesn't get to me in this situation. Then I trimmed my soul patch, getting rid of any kind of stubble around it in the process, and made it look nice. Now I make my way down to the music room again, carrying my notebook with me under my arm. I sit myself down at the piano bench and don't feel nervous anymore. I feel ready. I had a good turn-out on the phone, and now I only have minutes before Tina will return. I feel like I already waited too long to do this, and I'm more than ready. I open my notebook up to the song I wrote for her and run my fingers along the white, shiny keys of the piano.

At that moment, Jenna comes running in the room. "You ready?" she asks, breathless. "You better be because this was much harder than it sounded."

I nod. "I'm more than ready."

"You could have texted me then so I didn't have to pretend I was interested in boardwalk crap!"

"Sorry," I mouth as I hear the rest of the family file through the back door. My stomach does back flips, and I'm pretty sure it's no longer in the correct position. I take deep breaths to try to calm myself down and think of how this is definitely going to be worth it.

"Good luck," she whispers, smiling. "I'll be back in when you tell me all is good."

"Thanks so much. Keep Johnny with you."

She nods and runs out to the family room to stop them from coming in here. "Where's A?" I hear Tina ask. Her voice makes me even more nervous. I bounce in the bench a little.

"He's in the music room," Jenna calmly replies, no hint that she's keeping something from them. "He wants to talk to you. Matty, Kelly, do you want to head outside and try to fly that remote control aeroplane?"

I hear the back door open and close again and then lone footsteps. "A? Jenna said you're in here?"

"Yeah, I need to show you something." My heart is about to explode through the front of my chest, and I take more deep breaths. Tina appears around the bend of the wall and looks confused as she sees me sitting at the piano bench, looking quite fresh. I smile and motion for her to sit on the chair near where the guitars are set up so I can look at her periodically as I play. She sits and waits for me to say something about why she's here.

I take one last deep breath, close my eyes a moment, and begin playing the song. Here goes nothing, I say to myself. It really is nothing. I can do this, I've been doing this since I was in elementary school, and this is nothing different. I play and bob my head so I don't lose the beat. Then I start singing and glance up at her. She looks surprised. She hasn't heard me play and sing my own songs since I got sick, and this is very sudden. I realize just how much I miss it.

I pour my heart out right on this piano; everything that I've ever wanted to say to her just floods out. Everything from the first moments I talked with her in our campus apartment, to how she helped me through my cancer, to when she started living with me in this house, to when she became the only person who supported my music career in my life, to how I felt when I almost lost her, and how the third time I almost died put everything in perspective. My rules about life and love just fall away, and here I am now facing everything I was afraid of with courage. I sing to her everything I love about her and everything I can't live without. I even mention Laura's saying of how I had the summer where my boy self turned into a man. When I glance up at the near end of the song, I can see her eyes are filled with tears. I end with the most perfect last line I've ever written, "What I'm trying to say here is I love you, and don't you ever forget it because nothing in this world will ever be truer."

I take my hands off of the piano and pull the little black box out of my pocket. She stares at me in disbelief as I stand before her with the tiny box. I smile warmly and say, "I wrote that song because I have trouble telling people what I feel face to face. I write so people can read and hear the lyrics I write, but it's easier because it's not direct. I can look at my piano when I get uncomfortable. I needed to tell you all of this because I changed my mind about a lot of things, and this was the only way it was all coming out of me. I really did change this summer for the better. I'm going for my dreams, I'm not dwelling on my past, and I stopped making stupid rules for myself because I was scared of life. I want to live in this house with you until I'm all old and ugly and take care of Matty, Jenna, and Kelly. And one day in the future I would like to see a mini version of me running around, if you would. So before I run away in fear you'll bring everything crashing down on me, I have to ask you-will you, Kristina Lynne Welsh, be my beautiful blushing bride?" I kneel down to one knee and flip up the top to the box. I swear the ring glimmers in Tina's eyes.

She stands there, mouth wide open in a smile, taking it all in a moment. She's definitely in shock, and I silently tell myself good job for pulling that one off. I'm glad my appreciation gift to Jenna for helping me, and the boys for cooperating, is beyond amazing. They will be thanking me for asking for their help. I laugh out loud a little at that one. My laugh snaps Tina out of her shocked state, and she starts squealing and jumping up and down.

"Yes, yes, yes, oh my goodness yes!!!" she screams through a few squeals. She stops jumping and runs right to me, tackling me into the ground. We tumble across the floor and she ends up lying on top of me. I wasn't expecting that. I feel a little squished, but I can't say I don't like it.

"Wow," I laugh. "I figured you would happily agree, but I didn't know I would get this much of a reaction!"

"How could I have any less of a reaction?!" she asks, a little out of breath from all the jumping and squealing. "We had a fight and I kicked you out of the house because you weren't willing to marry me, and here you are blind-siding me with a proposal. You can't even fathom how happy I am right now. I'm so elated and am on cloud nine right now. I feel like a little girl who just got asked to the dance by the cutest boy in school! I'm the luckiest girl in the whole world. I can't wait to make everyone jealous with my fiancé!"

"And I thought you were going to say no."

She cracks up at that one. "You're not getting rid of me that easy. In fact, you're not getting rid of me at all. You made yourself extra cute for this too. I love your haircut, this length is the best, and I haven't seen your eyebrow rings in forever!"

"Well I thought I had a better chance if I cleaned myself up."

"Oh," she raises her eyebrows. "You thought that the excellent piano playing and the singing wasn't enough?"

"You can never be too sure."

She lets out another squeal. "You're such a sexy beast. No one can resist you." She kisses me and our tongues brush against each other. Life can't get much better than this. I slide the ring on her left hand, and the entire world feels like it's finally revolving correctly on its axis-that all the stars are aligned on this day and we're a part of them. If I feel this way now, I can't wait to know what I'll feel like on my wedding day, and when I finally jump off of that stage into a screaming group of my fans. In this moment, I feel like everything I've ever wanted is just within my reach.

She jumps to her feet and runs around in circles, obviously not thinking too well at the moment. "I have to call my mom! Where's the phone?"

"Left pocket as always," I grin. She bursts out laughing and rolls her eyes, exasperated with herself. She dials the numbers, fingers shaking, and jumps up and down in a circle as she waits for an answer. Two girl things I notice at this moment-they always jump and squeal when they are really excited, and when something big happens, they always contact the closest female-mother, sister, or best friend. I'm not about to burst her bubble and let her know that if her parents communicate at all, her mom already knows what she is calling about. I am content with just laying on the floor watching her, feeling like the luckiest guy in the entire Virgo Supercluster that she's mine. Wow, I actually learned something from Matty's space banter.

45

Jenna

Andy said he had something big planned for Matty and my birthday. He said retiring from the year of baby teenager is a big deal and deserves a big celebration. I said I would have to agree, considering all we've been through in that year, and the fact that we ever survived it all. This is just days before that, and we decide that since we'll be in Rehoboth for the actual day, that visiting Grandma for our "fake birthdays" will be a nice thing. We haven't seen her since we had to run away in the middle of the night and hide in the crawlspace. It seems like so much has happened since then. We didn't even know Andy then, we thought he was against us, and now we live with him and love him as family. That really shows that even though time seems to be so short, so much can happen and change. To add to that, I can tell that I'm not the only one who is glad to see Grandma without the tension of being caught.

The car ride up is a good time, one of the best car rides I've ever had. Kelly brought his ever-growing collection of albums, and we rock out to everything from the country side of Lady Antebellum and Taylor Swift, to the pop side of Lifehouse and OneRepublic, to the rock side of Kings of Leon and Matchbox Twenty. I love it all, my favorite being The Fray album, and I can't stop laughing the entire time. Andy gets us all dancing in our seats, and Matty looks completely ridiculous. I decide that I will definitely be stealing all Kelly's music for some listening on Johnny. It will be difficult because he protects his music with his life, but I will have to do it. I don't have the money like he does to get all that music. I don't know how that kid does it, but he always seems to have a stack of money like in one of those rap videos, no matter how much he buys. He holds it close to his chest and looks up drooling at the collection of CDs in any given store. Then he's happy for the rest of the day, sitting cross-legged on his bedroom floor, eyes closed, and rocking his head slightly as his boom-box plays. In just a few days, he knows the entire album by heart and is singing around the house and tapping beats on the furniture. Needless to say, he is the happiest of us all on the car ride and seems almost pouty when Grandma's house comes into view.

We all hop out of the car, still laughing, and stretch. Three hours of sitting, moving around, and dancing will make your entire lower body numb, and it takes a few moments to remember how to keep your balance upright against gravity. I walk shakily up the rocky driveway, extending my arms out until my elbows ease up and crack. The wind rustles through the many trees, and it feels chilly against my skin. I remember the downside of the arrival of my birthday. The end of September turns summer into fall, which will soon turn into winter, where I have to stay inside, wear coats, and shovel snow. I hate my hands, feet, ears, and nose in the winter because due to my bad circulation, they turn blue and numb and it's annoying. It hurts insanely bad, and I welcome Kelly's birthday, March 20th, the first day of spring, with open arms. Hopefully the summer this year will be less dreadful and emotionally taxing.

"Don't you hate what time of year our birthdays are in?" Matty asks, rubbing goose bumps off his arms.

I laugh, thinking we must have twin telepathy or something. "Very much."

Kelly runs ahead of us, singing something about houses set back in forests and the ghosts that live in them. I only catch a few of the words because as he gets farther away, the wind takes his voice in another direction. He jumps up from the bottom step to the top one, landing with a thump on the welcome mat outside the front door. He pounds on the door with both the pinky finger ends of his fists and runs in circles around the top step as he waits for Grandma to answer. Matty starts to run after him, but stops and turns around to wait for me to do the same. I shake my head and keep walking.

He starts jogging backwards. "Come on so we all can be there when Grandma's at the door. It's a surprise for *our* fake birthday visit, remember?"

I let out a loud drawn-out sigh to show him that I really don't want to, but I will because he wants me to do it. "Fine." I'm tired from the car ride and feel like I'm getting cramps, but I push myself to run with Matty. We make it to the bottom step just as Grandma opens the door and smiles wildly at the sight of her youngest grandson.

"Kelly baby!" she says, kneeling down a little and throwing her arms out at him.

"Hi Grandma!" Kelly replies excitedly. He jumps up into a hug with her, and she picks him up and squeezes him. She props him up on her hip and kisses him on the top of his messy black hair filled head. Then she spots us and lights up again. We run up the steps and embrace her on the side that Kelly isn't. She wraps her free arm around us and gives us both kisses too.

We pull back and she says, "What a pleasant surprise! What brings you here?"

Before we can answer, Andy says, "They wanted to see you for their birthday, but they couldn't make it on the actual day."

"Oh, that is completely okay. Thank you so much for bringing them." I think I see her smirk at him, but maybe I'm seeing things. He nods and leads Tina up the steps. Grandma pushes past us and gives him a small hug, and then moves on to Tina. Tina's diamond ring glints in the afternoon sunlight, and it catches Grandma's eye quickly.

"Oh my, that is quite beautiful," she marvels. She winks at Andy, and he smiles and blushes a little. She must have known what he was up to beforehand like I did. Something tells me when he came up here to discuss the custody, she gave him a wise talk about the things that are going to change in his life. I wonder if that's what she and Dad were like when he was young and about to marry Mom. From what Mom had told me, Dad and Grandma were very close. He was her only son, her only child, and the only thing she had left of her husband when he died. Dad was only ten and they stuck together. It was Laura and Mackenzie against the world, and he always told her that when he grew up, he would touch the world with his music. Everyone would listen, even Grandpa, and when he reaped the profits, he would buy her anything she ever wanted and get her front-row tickets to all his shows. They were everything to each other, and as he got older, he would come to her for advice about the struggles of life and being a teenager. He had his times when he was an immature boy and screamed that she didn't love him because she didn't buy him what other rich mothers bought their kids, and she screamed back that he didn't appreciate all she'd done to get him to where he is. He would storm out and not come back all night, and she would refuse to talk to him at points, but they got through it. She helped him through his first heartbreak and the constant rejections of the music business. Even when they hated each other, they loved and supported each other.

Grandma was the one who got him to the point where he succeeded. She was the one who screamed the loudest when he got the call that he was chosen to open up for a band at an intimate setting. She was the one who threw him a party when he finally got a record deal and started producing his music. She was first in line to buy his EP, which sadly can't be bought anymore. He had to give up all that when he started his family. She was the one who gave him the much needed advice about how to win over Mom and beamed at his wedding. She was the first one there to welcome Lauren into the world and moved in a little while to help take care of her. She was the first one to send little boy and girl outfits to celebrate the birth of her son's twins-Matty and I. She was the one who let him cry on her shoulder after they got Lauren's diagnosis, and then helped Mom and him pick treatment options. She bought Kelly his music swing when he was born so that he could fall asleep to some good music in his little baby swing. She made sure Lauren's last months were fantastic, and that the rest of our family was able to get through the fact that it was her last months.

When Dad died, she was beyond devastated. She couldn't move for months and broke down in a crying heap at his funeral. I remember feeling young and helpless as I watched Mom and Grandma struggling to cope with the fact that not only had Lauren died, but Dad had gone with her. I remember her saying that her chest ached like someone had stuck their hand through it and squeezed the life out of her heart. I know she doesn't feel exactly the same as she did all those years ago, but I'm sure her chest still aches. Her eyes always have a little underlying sadness, and even a little disbelief, as if she still doesn't want to accept that her son died before her. I almost feel bad about living three hours away because she has to live alone and doesn't get to hold on to us closely-her last little bit of her Mackenzie. I don't care how long the drive is or how numb I get, I want to visit her as much as I possibly can, and that will be a lot when I can drive.

I feel my chest start to ache as I twist the ring Dad gave Mom around my finger. I barely hear Tina rambling on happily about how Andy proposed and what she is planning for the wedding. Instead I feel Dad holding his kindergarten daughter as he tucks her into bed the very last time. I feel him telling her he loves her more than the sun loves to shine on her face, the wind loves to blow her hair, the stars love to twinkle in her eyes, and the moon loves to smile at her. I feel him kissing her on the top of her head and telling her he wants to protect her longer than gravity will keep the universe in orbit, and that he will even if he has to give everything for it. I remember him turning out the light and blowing her one more kiss before he closes the door. I remember her closing her eyes and listening as his footsteps move to his son's rooms. I remember her waking up hours later to the whipping winds of a snowstorm and the sound of her parent's voices screaming at each other about her sister. She hops out of bed and runs down the hall, her twin brother by her side, and they both crouch behind the wall. They hear their mom cry as their dad and older sister leave into the night for the very last time. And then they hear the call that it was indeed the very last time, and that their dad would never tuck them in again, or tell them he loved them, or give them wise advice, or sing to them when they were scared. I remember being that little girl, clutching a rose, and reciting my Daddy's last words to him and my sister as I look down over two gravestones.

I walk like a zombie after the rest of my family into Grandma's house and sit on the comfy, bright pink couch. They talk around me as I continue to stare down at my ring and touch it. Andy and Tina go into the kitchen awhile and make us all some lunch, even though Grandma insists that she is very much capable of making it. Grandma grabs my hand and squeezes it, making me look up at her. She smiles warmly at me, and I try my best attempt at smiling back, starting to feel like I can't breathe.

"What's bothering you sweetheart?" she asks, looking me straight in the eye and whispering so no one else can hear. I look around and see that no one else is even paying attention. Kelly is dancing around and singing on the other side of the room, and Matty has migrated into the kitchen to see what he's getting to eat.

I look back to her and touch my ring again. She knows what I'm thinking without me having to say it. "You're thinking about your Dad and Mom and Lauren?"

I nod slowly, refusing to look at her again so I don't cry. "I didn't know it was possible to miss and love people this much," I say so softly that barely I can hear it.

"Me neither," she whispers back. She grabs my face with her hands and kisses me on the forehead. "I have something I need to show you and your brothers. I think maybe you need to see it before we celebrate your birthday. It may make you feel better."

I look up at her again. "Okay." I squeeze my eyes shut tightly to keep the tears from coming out and stand up. I make my way into the kitchen and grab Matty. He turns around and sees I'm upset. He begins to ask why, but I stop him and tell him to come here. I hear Grandma saying something to Andy and Tina in a low voice, but I can't make out what she is saying. I get Kelly and we follow Grandma up the stairs to the bedroom that used to be Dad's. We haven't been in there in a long time, and it hurts to see it exactly the way it was when Grandma refused to sell any of his stuff and locked the door so it wouldn't be touched. Matty, Kelly, and I venture in cautiously, almost as if we're doing something we're't supposed to be doing.

"It's okay, he wouldn't mind you being here and I don't either," Grandma says, sensing our hesitation. "I just locked it because they were trying to get me to throw away everything that he was. I don't care where he is, I will never do that. They will never make me forget him or *move on* from him. That is a stupid thing to try to do."

I nod in agreement. That's why I never tell people that my parents and Lauren are deceased. They will never be dead to me, just somewhere else, like on a special trip.

Matty is the first to sit down on what was Dad's favorite chair. He used to sit in it and play acoustic guitar, which was his most favorite thing in the world to do. I sit on my feet on the floor next to Matty. Kelly takes a place next to me, resting his hand on my thigh. I grab it and hold it. I'm like his Mommy now, and I have to do a good job.

Grandma moves to his closet and opens it. The doors squeak, and I wonder if she goes in there a lot or avoids the room entirely because it hurts to think he'll never walk in it again. She pulls out a small DVD case with a DVD in it. It says something on it in black sharpie, but I can't read it from my position on the floor. She turns on the TV and places the DVD in his DVD player after holding it to her chest a few moments. She switches the input and gets it ready to play like a pro. I always thought it was strange that some Grandma's don't even know their way around a remote, when mine is always navigating the newest technology with ease. The only reason the stuff in here is outdated is because she would never change it on Dad.

Grandma takes a seat on Dad's bed and focuses on the TV. I wonder what could be on this DVD. I hope it's something amazing because I really need to feel better, especially with being this close to my birthday. You're never supposed to cry on your birthday, and so far I've stuck to that. I don't want to ruin that now, even though I have every reason to at this point.

The tape starts playing, and we gasp as we see Dad appear on the screen. His face is right up against the camera. It makes my stomach twist. I haven't seen him this young looking before, and I wish it showed a date. He starts adjusting the camera, making the room behind him seem to spin. Finally it stops, and I recognize the room as our living room. The couch is there and the big TV is propped up on the wall. There is even the old record player that never played since I was five and collected dust until it burned away.

Dad moves back from the camera a little and waves at it. "Hey, it's Mackenzie. You probably know that since you're watching it, and that means I'm away on tour and will be home soon. But even if you don't, it's me, and I'm about to have a lot of fun." He smiles brightly and runs his fingers through his jet black hair. I catch sight of his colorful tattoos running all the way up from his wrists to where his t-shirt begins, a little ways above his elbow. I can't believe how much he resembles Andy, everything from the messy black hair, to the bright blue eyes, to the long slender face, and the fun-loving smile. He even has the same sort of tattoos and the same style of clothes. Maybe that's why I love Andy so much. After all, I am my mother's daughter.

"Before I start having fun though, I want to tell you something. Mom, if you're watching this, you're the best mom a guy could have, and I don't think I could have made it to my recent stardom without you. When I see you next, I'll give you a really big hug because I love hugging. If my kids are watching this-Lauren, Matty, Jenna, and any other kids I might have had by the time you're watching this, tell me how much I love you."-he pauses a minute to let us say something. I hear Matty recite what he always said to us in a low whisper. I say it in my mind. "If you said that I love you more than the sun loves to shine on your face, the wind loves to blow through your hair, the stars love to twinkle in your eyes, or the moon loves to smile at you, then you are correct. And I want to protect you longer than gravity keeps the universe in orbit, and I will do that even if I have to give up everything for it. I'm sorry I have to be away on tour or whatever music related thing I might be doing, but I hope you know that and believe that for as long as you live. If my darling is watching this, baby you are the most beautiful, amazing woman in the world, and I was blessed to have you fall in love with me. I don't know how it happened, but it did, and I'm one lucky guy. Call me after you watch this, and I'll tell you a whole bunch of mushy stuff because I'm a hopeless sap when it comes to you." I think I feel my heart skip a beat. I never knew before just how wonderful my own father was. I always knew he was something special, but here I see what an extraordinary soul he was. Not only does my world have a huge gaping hole in it now that he's gone, I think, but the actual Earth must also.

He pauses a moment and has a far-away look, seeming to be thinking hard about something the way Matty often does. "Well, all you need to know is that I will be home soon and can't wait for that. And I hope you smile when you see this." He stops, looking down, and then continues. "I just realized this could be way in the future and I could be dead. Oh wow, you could be watching this in a hovercraft! Sorry I missed that. Whoever you are, whatever year it is, and wherever you are, I hope you enjoy this like I'm about to." He smiles into the camera again and gives two thumbs up. I can't help but smile back; his is so wide it almost seems to be contagious. I look over and see Matty is laughing.

I look back to the screen and see Dad is all the way across the room tinkering with the record player. He places a record on it and moves the needle so it starts to play. I don't recognize the song, but it sounds pretty good. He starts bobbing his head and looks over to the camera. "This is my favorite song!" he yells excitedly. "So I'm going to show you a dance my kids and I made for it. Enjoy!"

He laughs and looks over toward the other side of the room. He beckons to someone I can't see. Matty and I enter, toddling toward him. We look like we're about two years old, and my mouth drops open. This must have been a very long time ago. I have a tiny black ponytail bouncing on the top of my head and am wearing a pretty pink, flowing dress. Matty's shaggy, black bangs hang in his eyes, and he wears little jeans and a striped t-shirt. We smile and wave at the camera as the song starts to play faster and a guy starts singing. The three of us jump around like idiots, Dad making funny faces at us while we laugh hysterically. He then jumps up and down and throws his head around in circles. If his hair was long enough, it would have flown everywhere. Matty and I start running around on our hands and knees and crab walking. It looks as if we're attempting to break dance, but it's just turning out horrible because of our age.

Dad whistles over the music, and a girl who looks about nine runs into the room and begins to strum an air guitar. Her dark hair falls over her shoulders as she wears a cute little green tank top and jean shorts. She starts head banging, and then proceeds to jump to her knees and throw her hands in the air. Dad makes fake fan screams and points to her. She looks up at the camera and smiles, giving rock on signs. I can barely catch my breath as I realize it must be Lauren. It must have been a year or two before she got sick, and she was a gorgeous little girl.

I feel my tears well up and spill out as I think of what a wonderful older sister I would have had. I would have had the best Dad in the world too. It's hard to believe that two people so alive and happy in this video could be cold and motionless in the ground. We hadn't been able to see Dad or Lauren at the viewing because Mom thought it would have upset us too much. The last I saw him was when he tucked me into bed that night, and even then, he didn't look quite like this. Lauren being so sick really took a lot out of his optimistic soul, and he looked tired and hurt. I'd never seen him this bright, vibrant, and truly happy, or at least I don't remember it. I can't think that this guy I'm seeing here could be gone for good, stiff and lifeless.

I start to not be able to breathe correctly as I think of how terrified he must have been in his last moments. He had been helpless to save his first-born and had to watch her die in the car seat next to him after years of suffering. If there's one thing I know about guys, it's that they love to feel in control. They love to feel admired for taking care of their family and keeping them safe. They would be the one who's expected to investigate the noises in the middle of the night, no matter if they're just as scared as the rest of their family. They take pride by making everything alright, and he must have been paralyzed as he realized there was nothing he could do for his little girl. She slipped right through his fingers, and he forgot he was driving on a dark, stormy night. He must have taken his eyes away from Lauren for a split second to see headlights moments before they took his life. Now he could never take care of his family or have his music move the world-the two things he always wanted.

I can barely see the screen through my tears at this point. The music starts to slow down, and I see a little bit younger version of the Mom I knew come out. That makes me cry harder as I try not to think of her limp body being carried out of the house by the fireman. She looks from Dad, to the camera, and says, "He's crazy, but for some reason I love him so entirely anyway." She looks unbelievably happy too, like I've never known her to be. Dad moves toward her and they kiss as the song ends. Matty and I run and hug their legs. Dad puts his hand up in front of the camera, and I spot the ring Matty is now wearing.

"Press the red button Lauren please," I hear Dad say. "Mackenzie, out." Lauren laughs and says, "Lauren, also out." Then the screen goes completely black. We all continue to stare at it, almost as if we're wishing it to keep playing.

"He was always a kid at heart," Grandma comments. "That's what your mother loved most about him. I've never seen two people who cherished each other more." I look over to her and see her eyes are red and puffy. I involuntarily squeeze Kelly's hand and notice that his little body is shaking also.

"I can only hope to find a guy like that," I whisper. After all my crying, I don't have the strength for anything more.

"He reminds me of someone," Matty grins through his tears. I know exactly what he's talking about. He caught that too.

"They say you marry someone like your father."

He nods. "That explains so much."

I feel my chest constrict, like I'm a fish gasping for breath. I hold my head in my hands and clench my teeth to try to fight the pain. I feel weak, and I didn't know it was possible for something to hurt this bad. I know it must be all in my head, but it feels like an elephant is literally sitting on my chest. Maybe this is what heart break is like. Maybe this is real and can get so bad that the heart just gives up. Is that what dying of a broken heart is?

I feel Grandma's arms around me. "Are you okay honey?"

I lift my head to look at her. Matty and Kelly are staring at me with concern too. "I just realized I don't remember him much," I say emotionlessly. "I can't hear that voice in my head anymore like I used to in the first years. I can't picture his face in my mind, except what I just saw there. That's all I've got of such a beautiful soul. I didn't even recognize Lauren there because I don't remember her either. I rack my brain, but I have nothing. Pretty soon I won't remember Mom either, and I don't think I'll be able to take that. Every minute, I lose something precious. I didn't cherish those moments I had because I was so young and thought they would continue forever. I didn't know they were special, so I didn't even care. Now I wish I could go back and live them again so I can remember every little detail. I don't want to regret those times I had with them, but I do. I want a second chance I can never have. It eats me alive that three wonderful, free spirits like that were ripped from this Earth. I can't even remember half my life! How is that fair?!"

I jump up in a fit of frustration and punch the wall. It makes a loud bang, and my hand starts to bleed. I instantly regret that and scream as I attempt to shake the pain out of my hand. Matty grabs me and gets me under control.

"You don't think I feel the same way? Somehow it works out that we remember the things we don't want to all the time, like that fire and Mom and Dad screaming before he left into the storm. We don't remember the little amazing things because our minds can't hold it all. I wish we had that instead of other stupid stuff, but that's not how it works. Some good stuff slips away, but I guess what we learn from it is to live every moment we have like it will be important to remember later."

"You're also lucky that you punch right-handed," he adds. I look down at Mom's ring, still looking perfect on my left hand while the knuckles on my right hand bleed down my arm. I laugh in complete relief. If I would have wrecked the ring, I would never have forgiven myself.

"I guess you're right, but I wish it wasn't like that," I reply to Matty's words about our memories.

"Me neither," Kelly adds, standing up. "Because I never really got to know Lauren or Dad. They were like strangers, and I'm so young that Mom may be soon too."

"I'm so sorry," I cry. I open my arms up and he runs into them. "I wish they didn't have to be gone. I wish they were here with us forever. They were so beautiful inside and out, and it was a big loss to the world when they left."

Grandma joins our embrace. "Their bodies may be still and silent, but their souls will always be here with us. That's how I see it. And I think those souls would want us all to live our lives remembering them, but not grieving them. Should we cheer up with some birthday cake?"

We all say yes and make our way down to the kitchen. I realize three things throughout that celebration of our fake birthdays. We never had a funeral for Mom so we have no idea what happened to her body, I'm really going to miss Grandma when we're living with Andy, and that I appreciate and love everyone in my life that loves me so much that it spills out on the floor. Those three thoughts give me mixed emotions, but I don't know what to do but take Grandma's advice.

46

Matty

I shoot out of bed straight from a laying position to my feet. I haven't done that in a very long time, probably because I haven't been excited like this in a very long time. I am optimistic for once, feeling good about my life to come. I'm going to make this a year of change for the better, where everything is right for a change and I'm not so hard on myself. I am only a kid and need to stop acting like I'm holding the world on my own. Today I turn 14, and this is the beginning of my new beginning.

I look myself in the mirror. I don't look older, and I sure don't feel it, but I am. In reality, I'm getting older every second so each new day I should feel a tiny bit older. It's not like on each birthday you just jump from year to year. It's a steady increase, like a linear graph or a hike up a steep hill. And if you want to get really technical, this is the beginning of my fifteenth year, so I'm really older than everybody thinks.

I stop myself there before I stand here for hours and let my mind race. That is one way Jenna and I are alike-we think way too much. I suddenly want to see her and talk to her about my big plans for my fifteenth year. I think back to last year when I woke up on my birthday. I'd been angry and thought of this day as one more year closer to my death, and one more year that I hadn't been able to conquer time and donate my marrow to Lauren. I'd thought that I didn't deserve to wake up on this day when such a free spirit and good man like my dad would never wake again. I had dreaded the year because I knew it would just make me more depressed, and I would wake up the next year feeling the same as I did then. And to make things worse, Jenna was always happy on her birthday, and it made me mad. I wanted her to feel the same way as me, and I didn't want her to share a birthday with me. It was my day to wallow in my self-pity.

Things are different today though. I am not angry in the least. I don't blame myself for anything anymore. Things happened the way they did, people made decisions that led up to tragic deaths, but it wasn't my fault. It wasn't my job to fix it, even if I could. I still have my life to live, and the best thing I can do for everyone is to live it to the best of my ability while I still can. I do miss Mom more than it's imaginable, and I miss what I still remember of Dad and Lauren. They were amazing people, and they didn't deserve to die so early and the way they did, but everything happens for some reason or another. I just hope that their afterlife is peaceful and happy, and they are proud of what became of Jenna, Kelly, and I.

I also no longer am angry at Jenna for being my twin. I finally understand the way she felt before. She has always wanted to share everything with me and hang out with me like we are best friends, and I have always pushed her away. I wanted to be alone to think and beat myself up all the time. Now I want to go straight to her room and ask her all kinds of questions, like if she felt older, and if she thought this would be a good year, and if she was excited as I was about what Andy and Tina might have planned for us. They had said we were getting something pretty spectacular, and I can't wait to see what that might be. Jenna probably has some pretty good ideas, and between the two of us, we can probably dream up our own wonderland. I love doing that, and I love teasing her about Andy. She really is my best friend that's going to be there for life, and I'm proud to share my birthday with her. I really don't know how some people make it through life without a twin.

I know the first thing I want to do to start this new year, even before seeing Jenna. It is a really big step for me and will take some getting used to after all these years of being set in my ways. I kneel beside my comfy new bed and reach under it. I feel around with my hand until it brushes against the box I am looking for-a small cardboard box. I pull it out and stare at it a moment. I will do this, I tell myself. I open the flaps of the box and pull out a black alarm clock. It has a big shiny front where the numbers will show up and speakers on the top to play the radio. There are buttons next to the speakers and a long black wire coming out of the back. I place it nicely on my nightstand so the numbers will face my bed and can be seen from most of the room. I take a deep breath and plug the wire in the wall. I look up and see the default 12:00 shining in bright red.

"Jeez, this thing is really testing me. Now I have to set it." I can feel my hands shaking a little and realize I'm actually scared. I have survived house fires, deaths, evil hospitals, crazy cops, living in the wild, shoplifting, getting shot at, hiding in a crawlspace, and even jail, but the thing that gets me is...drum roll please...the thing the great Matty is the most afraid of is...setting a clock and looking at the time! Wow, that's pretty pathetic. I've avoided time like the plague for so long that it has officially become one of my fears. But I will get over it, right now.

I look at the different buttons a moment and figure out how to set the time back to 8:39. It blinks and then stays where it is, starting to tell time again. I stare at it until it changes to 8:40. That was one minute of my life, I think. I walk away from it and turn my head quickly, almost as if I'm trying to catch it not doing its job. I feel really stupid and turn away again. The clock actually isn't that bad. It isn't hurting anything, just showing me what people think the time is. Time isn't something that must be measured in a certain way. It's just sort of there, and I still believe that all the time I've ever had in my life is happening right now. And now. I just see different parts of it separately instead of everything at once. Maybe one day I'll be able to sit back and see everything I've ever lived and everything I will live flash in front of me at the same instance, like I dream of doing. Maybe, but for now, I will not obsess over time and defeating it. I will still eat when I'm hungry and sleep when I'm tired instead of fitting a schedule, but I won't fear glancing at my clock every once in a while. I smile, thinking I have found a good balance.

I grab my doorknob and try to twist it, finding that something is stopping me. I let go a moment and the door bursts open. Jenna walks in and says, "Happy Birthday twin! Are you stoked too?!"

I laugh and give her a hug. "Happy Birthday to you too! And yes, like you wouldn't believe."

She lifts her head and looks up at me. For being the same age as me, she still is a good bit shorter than me. Maybe it's me being a boy or that I just had my growth spurt first, because I don't think that three minutes I was in this world first makes that much of a difference. And aren't girls supposed to grow first? Has she stopped? Did I grow a lot this summer and didn't know it? I sure don't remember being this tall before. Maybe I'm catching up to Andy. I shake my head. That probably won't happen. He's like a 6' 3" stick. I wonder how tall Dad was. I heard that each generation of boys is a little taller than the last.

"It's good to see you happy on September 24th for once, even though I can see you're still yourself," Jenna grins, snapping me out of my second wild string of thoughts for the day. "You're over thinking again. I know the face."

"I know. I was thinking about growing, and I'm not exactly sure how I got started thinking about that."

She pulls away and mutters, "I know what that's like." She looks around the room. Her gaze stops on the clock, clearly showing the right time for everyone to see. She stares at it, most likely wondering if it will disappear and she is just imagining it. When she sees that is not the case, she stares at me for an explanation.

"It's a new year," I shrug. "A good one; one for change. I'm not beating myself up anymore, or blaming myself, or obsessing over things that I can't change. I'm going to be happy with myself and my life this year, and that was the first step."

"Wow," she breathes. "That's amazing. I'm so happy today just because of that." I knew she would think that. She hates to see me upset all the time over this. I feel even better now that she is happy along with me.

"I guess my fear will be a little harder to get over, considering our recent experiences," she adds jokingly.

I nod, laughing. "True. Let's just hope they *all* aren't like that."

Her expression suddenly changes to serious. She stares at the wall like she's thinking hard about something extremely important. I open my mouth to ask if something is wrong, but she holds her hand up to stop me.

"I'll be right back. I think I have something I need to do." She runs out of my bedroom, down the stairs, and out the front door, leaving me in a daze. I know she'll probably tell me what she was doing later so instead of trying to follow her, I just head downstairs into the kitchen for some breakfast. Andy is already at the table eating a bowl of cereal and wearing nothing but his boxers. I feel my eyes narrow. He's quite the skinny little thing, and he's really not that great, yet I'm still a tad jealous. I will admit it. He's got enough confidence for me to infer that he's hit on a lot, and more importantly I have a little thing for Tina. As much as I try to tell myself that it's stupid, she'll still be my Krissy in my eyes and he doesn't deserve her. I wish Jenna didn't like him so much either. I appreciate all he's done for us very much, but I wish he wasn't so threatening.

"Hey Matty," he says, looking up from his cereal. "Happy not being a baby teenager anymore."

"Yeah," I smirk. "I forgot about that." I grab my favorite cereal, Honey Bunches of Oats, from the cabinet and pour it into a bowl. I splash some milk on top, grab a spoon, and sit in the seat across from Andy. I try to hide my sudden bitterness.

I glance at Andy's bowl and see there is only cereal. Not a stitch of milk, just dry cereal. I'm not sure I've ever seen him eat it before, so I have to ask, "No milk?"

He looks up and laughs. "No, I don't like it."

I raise one eyebrow. "But it's meant to be or something. That's like eating butter without bread or a jelly sandwich."

"I know. I just have never liked how soggy the cereal gets when there's milk in there since I was a kid. It's a little quirk I have, like I never eat the last bite of a sandwich. While the first bite is always the best, the last is always the worst."

I stare at him, not quite sure I believe what he's saying. I have never heard of someone thinking that before. "You're a weird dude," I finally say.

He laughs even harder this time, making me frown. "You don't know how many times I've heard that along with bizarre, wild, crazy, eccentric, an anomaly, whacked out, off my rocker." He counts off on his fingers as he names them. He shrugs, still smiling. "But, I like it because that's what makes me lovable." That doesn't make me feel good. I look down at my cereal. If that's what it takes to have a girl like Tina love you, then I don't think I'm going to be loved. I wish I had that much confidence in who I am.

"You alright kid?"

He must have noticed me hanging my head. "You would think I'm stupid."

He shakes his head. "Probably not, honestly. But I think you really mean that you're embarrassed to say it."

That's exactly what I mean. I can no more tell him that I want to be him than Jenna can tell him that she wants him. It's just impossible to explain to him that I want his confidence, his luck, his looks, his age, his fiancée, and the fact that he's on his way to achieving all his dreams. It's hard to live with someone who is walking around every day with everything you've ever wanted in life. Jenna would understand what I mean, especially when she sees all the famous author's books getting made into movies and all the musician guys that fill her writing notebook promoting those books. I've heard her crying a lot about that and Andy and Tina's engagement in her room, and the only way she calms down is to do her little act outs where she becomes someone else with different problems. She doesn't think I know about that, but I really wish I could do something like it. Yes, my sister would be able to relate to this. My mom most likely would have too, but right here, he can't.

I feel him staring, waiting to see if I'm going to share, and I just shrug it off. "It's nothing. And I'm not going to let it get me because it's my birthday and I'm going to be happy."

"Okay, well I have something to tell you."

I wait and he continues, "I got the school paperwork done for you, Jenna, and Kelly. I changed the contact information on your little pink cards and got things straightened out. They said they understood that you three had a traumatic summer and are letting you slide on the first three weeks without having to make any of the work up or having all the absent days on your records. You start Monday in 8th grade and Kelly will be in 2nd."

"Thanks. I can't wait."

"I know it's not a great thing to tell you on your birthday, but I thought it was sort of good news, considering the part that you get to start three weeks later than all the other kids without any consequences."

I'm still feeling a little bitter, so I'm not very appreciative. I don't even know my new address, and I don't feel like it is my address at all. It's a little saddening that Mom is no longer who the school calls if I'm at the nurse. Plus, if the teachers know what happened, that means the whole school knows also. They will notice Jenna and I are missing, and the rumors will be flying about what is going to happen to us now that we're "orphans". They are going to come asking questions and trying to be empathetic when all they want is to interrogate us. I really hope that they don't know about our day spent in jail, or else that will be the end of us. We'll not only be the orphans, but the criminal orphans. I'm not sure we can handle all that so soon after this has happened. We just got settled and are starting to try to heal and move on with our lives. I wish we had more time before we get shoved back into something from our old lives. Things are not the same anymore. We aren't the same kids as we were in June. I wonder if we can transfer schools.

I don't want to get into that with him after all the work he's done to make sure we're comfortable. I hadn't thought of it all until right now, and he would probably feel awful that he hadn't either. I look around the house and notice there is a missing member. "Where's Tina?"

"School," he replies, getting up to put his bowl in the sink.

"Oh that's right, it's Thursday." I have to admit I'm a little disappointed. I thought my Krissy would be here for me on my big day.

"Don't worry; she's taking a half day so she'll be home soon." Jeez this guy must read minds. Good thing he does though because I wouldn't have been able to ask that in case I would have been even more disappointed. Now I feel special.

At that moment, Jenna charges through the front door and into the kitchen at full speed. "Matty, Matty, Matty! You have to come here right now!"

"Where have you been?"

"Outside with Kelly. I was talking with him about stuff and all of a sudden he was hearing voices again!"

My eyes grow wide as I understand. "A carving?"

"Yes! You have to come and see it immediately!" She turns to Andy. "I hope you aren't too in love with the wood on the side of your deck."

I feel in between excited and in disbelief that there is another carving. Mom hasn't contacted us in so long, I thought that she moved on or wasn't able to anymore. I thought maybe there wasn't anything important to say, so she'd been spending her time with Dad and Lauren and let us make our own choices. I never would have thought that she would communicate with us again, even if it is our birthday. It is beyond exciting, like a letter from a friend you haven't heard from in months. The only difference is that those months felt like eight years.

Jenna leads me around to the backyard where Kelly is kneeling beside the big, flat side of the deck. Andy is right behind me, not caring in the least that all his neighbors can see him walking around almost naked. I kneel beside Kelly and he smiles at me. "Right there," he says, pointing to where words are carved into the light wood. I read aloud:

Happy Birthday Matty and Jenna dears! I hope you have a wonderful day; fourteen was a good year for me, and I want it to be even better for you. Since I can't be there to celebrate, this is the best I can do. This is the last time I will be able to contact you. I must move on, so I say Happy Birthday to you two for the rest of your birthdays, and to you Kelly for all of yours. I hope you three love your new home and the new additions to your family. Don't worry about school; you may find that things will not be as bad as you imagine. Don't worry about life either, because you three are the most amazing kids that will ever walk this Earth, and you will get everything you ever want and more. I wish I could be there to see it, but that's not the way things worked out. Just know that I am there for you through the rings, and that whenever you feel as if you need to talk to me, you just say it and I can hear. I did the best I could to make sure your lives turned out okay. If Andy is reading this, it may sound strange to him, but he is here not only for himself, but for you three also. Tina and he are your angels. Your Dad knew how things would turn out and found the two best, most wonderful protectors to do our jobs for us. Treat him well, Matty, despite your thoughts, and Jenna, stop crying because you will get what you want in life, including an amazing guy. Kelly, you are the sweetest little boy and the world of music will treat you well. Mother knows best! I am here happy with Lauren and your Dad, and we are all watching over you. Live your lives and remember us, but don't hold back because of what happened. Thank you so much Andy and Tina; take care. Know I love you my three children-my incredible scientist, my famous author, and my moving musician. Lauren and your Dad say the same. Love forever and always, Mom.

Remember kids, embrace yourselves, believe you can do anything, and love life. Matty, nothing is your fault, Jenna, you are the best girl in the world, and Kelly, live my legacy by sharing your beautiful uniqueness that I passed onto you with the world. In fact, all of you do that! Including my young clone, Andrew. Thank you to you and Tina for cooperating with me, even though you had no clue you were. Kids, have your grandmother tell you stories about me so you never forget how amazing I was and will continue to be. I will always be with you and love you more than you will ever know. Happy Birthdays! Love, Dad Mackenzie

I never got to talk to you much or even get to know Kelly, but I still love you. Matty, my death was not your doing. You were too young to donate. Jenna, I always wanted to giggle with a sister about guys, but I never got the chance, so you will have to gawk at Andy's illegal hotness without me. Kelly, you are an amazing little boy, and I wish I could have known you. I am so happy now. I'm not sick, so I guess things worked out anyway. You are the best siblings a girl could have. Love, Lauren

By the time I finish reading, I have tears in my eyes. I'm so happy and sad at the same time. I'm sad that I will never be in these wonderful people's company again, but I'm also happy that they are together and in a good place. I'm also happy that they are watching over us, and that Dad spent all this time making sure we would be alright this summer and for the rest of our young lives. I never knew that any of this could happen, and it actually makes me feel close to all of them. I feel that they actually *will* be with me always, and that I can talk to them when I need to do so. It sounds cliché, but my heavy heart is light now that I know these things.

"Dad and Lauren wrote too," I say through my tears. "I miss them all so much."

Kelly walks over on his knees and puts his arms around me. "They are with us though, all together. That's good."

I smile. "Yeah, it's real good. This family will never be separated. It will keep growing and becoming better."

I look up at Andy, who also has tears in his eyes after reading over my shoulder. I can imagine how he feels, knowing that he and Tina were meant to help us. All of this was supposed to happen, and despite all the bad things that had to happen, all of the good things made everything okay. Believe it or not, life is good. I believe all the things that Mom, Dad, and Lauren said just because they were able to say it, and all the bitterness and fear I had fades away for the moment. I love him just like I love Jenna, Kelly, Mom, Dad, Lauren, Grandma, and Tina.

"Never, ever, *ever* do anything to this deck," Jenna demands.

He shakes his head, still staring at the words. "I don't know how I even could." The great orange Mustang pulls into the driveway, holding more than just Tina. Andy smiles. "It looks like the beginning of your birthday party is arriving."

47

Jenna

The carving leaves us all beyond awestruck. I was discussing the fact that Salamander may be a little more than just a stuffed animal with Kelly when he started hearing voices again. The fact that Mom even contacted us at all after so long is amazing. But Dad and Lauren too? I didn't even know they remembered us, let alone watched us every day and mapped out our entire summer so that we turned out okay. I wonder if they have been watching us all these years, gritting their teeth because they know what we will go through. And were they excited to see Mom again, or dreading it because they know we will lose her like they had? Whatever they were doing, I can't imagine what it would be like to have one chance to say something to people you love so much after almost seven years of leaving them behind. What would I say? Would I be able to fit it on one deck panel? Would I know what they wanted to hear to make them peaceful? I know, being that I am a writer at heart, everything I write is in full detail. I have trouble with the five paragraph limit on essays, and this would be more important than anything else I could ever write. I couldn't do it, I decide. And I give Dad and Lauren props because they gave me everything I need to move on, and I will cherish that until I join them.

Matty leans in and whispers to me, "I'm not jealous," and breaks me out of my wild thought pattern. I hold back a laugh, knowing exactly where he is coming from with that one. The only bad thing about the carving is apparently Mom, Dad, and Lauren know us better than we know ourselves, meaning they know all our secrets. Those secrets we really don't want broadcasted to anyone walking by the deck, especially the owners.

"And I don't cry," I whisper back. We don't need to whisper actually because it is just Kelly, Matty, and I out in the backyard. As soon as the car pulled up, Andy had bolted inside, telling us to stay out here and not look through the windows. He had most likely wanted to get some clothes on before whoever was in the car with Tina saw him. And I if had to guess, they wanted to decorate for our "birthday party" without Matty and I spectating, and Kelly getting in the way. This should be interesting.

"At least not about Andy," I add. "That would just be plain ridiculous."

Matty nods. "Yup. So would being jealous of someone who's twelve years older than you." We are in mutual agreement. We both know the other is lying, and the other knows that we are lying, but we'd rather pretend that we don't know these things.

At that moment, Andy comes running out, looking like he usually does again-worn jeans, striped t-shirt with his colorful arms coming out, and the beautiful Converse shoes that now have many memories on them. "We're ready for the birthday twins!"

"Why are you more excited than us?" I ask, laughing.

"Because you haven't seen what I've seen."

Matty and I exchange looks and start smirking. I have a feeling he's thinking what I'm thinking, and that is this is going to be beyond bizarre, especially if Andy coordinated it.

Andy glares at us. "Stop sharing glances and get in here!"

"Okay, okay," Matty says, throwing his hands up in surrender. We follow him in, and he's almost jumping up and down as he leads us. He's like a toddler who can't keep a secret. I can definitely picture him fidgeting and asking, "Can I tell them?!" continually. I smile, thinking back to when he would chase rabbits through the little forest we were hiding in, or have us hide under his car in the parking lot during a thunderstorm because tires are resistant against lightning. He fits the definitions of "free spirit" and "young at heart", and I can't get enough of it. I hope Dad is right because it's hard to believe my future will turn out. Then again, Dad would know the most out of everyone, considering he and Andy are two of a kind. Maybe there's a third out there somewhere waiting to be mine.

"Did you take your meds this morning?" Matty asks, cracking up. "You seem more fidgety than normal. I might need to start hiding them in your cheese again."

I raise my hand up to say 'good one', and he high fives it, smirking.

"You don't appreciate me enough," Andy sulks. "I do so much, and all you do is bring me down."

"Don't be such a baby," I sneer. He pouts as he opens the front door. He holds his arm out, telling us to enter. Matty goes in first and I hear him gasp. Then I follow him and know exactly why. I have no idea how they did it, but what was once the kitchen, dining room, and family room area just a half hour ago, is now a completely different place. It is an exact representation of where we spent the last few months. Everything down to the trees twisting up through the walls and clumping in the corner of the rooms as brush, to the artificial sand in clumps between the grassy areas and dirt areas, look exactly like our little hideout. As we walk through the trees and push the brush out of our way as we've done so many times before, we find the clearing where a huge inflatable rock looking thing is set up next to a pool. I know it is supposed to represent the lake, and I smile thinking of all our good times there. The landmarks are all there and it is perfect. I can't believe that this has all been set up in just the half hour we were waiting outside. It must have taken a lot of careful planning beforehand, and I suddenly respect Andy so much more for thinking to do this for us. I also understand why he was so excited to show us.

Matty and I finish looking around and stand in the mock clearing with our mouths open and eyes wide. "So do you like it?" Andy asks, still smiling from ear to ear and jumping around with excitement.

We both nod, and Kelly says, "How did you do all this?"

He shrugs. "Well, I thought I'd better make it feel like home, and it wasn't very hard to set up once I had the stuff. I had lots of help."

Tina stands off to the side with a woman I don't recognize. "Well thank you so much," I say to Andy and Tina. I don't know what to think of the other woman.

She comes toward us, holding out her hand. "I'm Andrew's mother. I've heard so much about you three kids." She has a warm smile and her hand feels soft as I shake it, just like Andy's. When I look closer, I can see a resemblance to Andy-not as much as I saw in his crazy father, but still a bit of one. She has shorter, almost white blond hair and those blue eyes I know so well. She is also very tall and thin, so that must have been something he inherited. She shakes Matty and Kelly's hands as well and takes a moment to look at us. "Well I would say you are exactly as I pictured you to be. Adorable and well-mannered, but also wild inside like my children."

That makes us laugh. That's not quite how I would describe myself, so it's interesting to hear how she views me.

"I am very grateful to you three, if you must know. Andrew would have never gotten married no matter how many times I suggested it to him over the phone, and he would have never had any children he loved, especially a girl." She leans in close to me as if that would make it so I was the only one who would hear her. "He was afraid of young girls because he thought they all hated him."

I burst out laughing and look at Andy. He rolls his eyes, and I can see his face growing a shade of red. "Mom, really? You don't know that any of that is true."

She throws her hand in the air as if to swat his remark away with disgust. "Mother knows everything, and you aren't that hard to read anyway."

"Whatever," Andy mutters, looking at a patch of sand he is standing near. Tina puts her arm around him to comfort his embarrassment away, and he smiles at her.

His mom turns back to us. "So you two older ones must be the twins, Matty and Jenna, and the tiny, cute one must be Kelly. I brought you presents because I'm treating you as my three newest grandchildren to spoil."

She pushes aside a few fake trees and pulls out an armful of presents, setting them at our feet. Matty and I say thank you in unison, still getting used to the idea of having another grandparent. She is just about to open her mouth, most likely to urge us to open them, when we spot a car pulling up the driveway. Andy and his mother look at each other, and I can tell they know who is driving it. Andy runs to the front door and throws it open. Matty and I glance at each other and make our way next to him.

A woman who looks a bit older than Andy with long, blond hair, glasses, and a tall, thin frame steps out of the passenger side of the car. A large man with a big shaved head, who looks like he could either be a professional wrestler or a gladiator on the show *American Gladiators*, comes from the driver's side. His muscles look like they are going to explode out of his tight t-shirt in a minute, and I'm pretty sure he could snap the woman in half with no effort. If I were her, I'd be a little frightened, and I feel it as I realize he is coming toward us. Two little boys, one a little bigger than the other, with shaggy, blond hair and matching striped shirts bound up the walk past the other two.

Andy crouches down and throws open his arms. "If it isn't my boys Spencer and Tanner!" They run into his arms, laughing and bumping heads with each other. He picks them up and swings them around so their legs fly around haphazardly. That makes them laugh even harder, and they fall in a heap on the floor when he sets them down. "How are you two?"

"Great!" the larger one whispers loudly. "We were so happy to come down and see you."

The smaller one shakes his head in agreement. "Pretty in here. Trees and sand!" He picks up a handful of sand and lets it fall through his fingers. "Amazing!"

"How did you do this?" the larger one asks, obviously as amazed as his little brother. I wonder why he is whispering, but I don't ask.

"It's magic," Andy smirks, and the little one says, "Uncle Andrew's a magician!!!"

By this point, the woman and man reach the door and take their shoes off as they enter. The woman takes special care to line them up beside the door, and Andy winks at her when she looks over at him. Now that she is up close, I notice she looks just like that picture I saw of him when he had blond hair and glasses. Could this be Stacy? It has to be since the boys she is with said *Uncle* Andrew.

"I see you're doing better," she grins, throwing her arms around Andy. Then she waves at Tina and marvels at her ring. Andy nods at the man who now looks twice as big as he did from faraway. I notice his jeans are ripped, and he is carrying a leather jacket. The way he carries himself shows that he knows he's big and is ready to fight anyone who challenges that fact.

The woman turns from Tina to where Matty, Kelly, and I are standing and laughs. "You must be those kids! Wow, I never thought I'd meet you for real!"

She goes over to Matty first, looking him up and down. "Which one are you?"

"Matty," he replies, wondering just as much as I am what is happening here.

She raises her eyebrows. "Ah, that is a hardcore name. You remind me a lot of my brother, although more sciency than artsy. I like that though."

"Thanks," Matty says hesitantly, almost questioning if that is the right response.

"Oh, you are welcome." She moves on to me next. "Jenna?" she asks.

I nod. "Yeah, that's me. Twin of the hardcore science guy over there."

She chuckles again. "I could really be friends with you! I'm Stacy Thompson, and I guess I could be called your new aunt. I come along with my husband Randy and my sons Spencer and Tanner." She points to them as she says their names, and I cringe as I realize I'll be seeing a lot of Randy the gladiator. Why would Stacy marry him? At least the little boys are cute and don't look like him. Hopefully one day they won't grow that hideous beard and instead look like their uncle. Stacy looks from Andy, back to me, and asks, "Do you like his eyebrow ring? I convinced him to get those pierced when we were teenagers. I think it's pretty hot."

I smile. "Agreed."

She raises her eyebrows. "Wow, I *really* like this one! You can be the little sister I never had, and I'll enjoy you because you remind me of myself. Plus, you have good taste, liking my brother and all. When we were younger, I was beating girls away with sticks. Every time I rode in the car with him, they were trying to throw their numbers in the window, or when we walked on the boardwalk down here, they would buy him pizzas."

"I can imagine," I laugh. I like her, I think to myself. She's funny, and although I can see where she would get a little irritating at times with her ramblings and boldness, she will be an interesting addition to my new growing family. She obviously loves Andy very much and thinks highly of him, and she must have been through a lot with the father they had. Matty seems to be a little intimidated by her personality, but I like her and her mother.

"Well happy birthday to you two," she adds. "Fourteen is a good year; at least it was for me." With that, she kneels down to Kelly's level and looks him in the eye.

"Something you find interesting to look at?" Kelly asks after a few moments.

She grins and points at him. "Spunky little guy. You must be Kelly. I heard you don't talk much, but when you do, it's very important. Andrew was like that when he was your age. Never let his thoughts out and his favorite thing to do was to lie on his back with music in his ears. He would listen to the piano notes in the song a few times and then try them out on our piano. Within hours, he knew the song and it always mesmerized me. Never had that talent; I was more of a sports girl myself, but you strike me as one that would."

Kelly tilts his head to the side like a dog does and looks at her. "I never tried that. Good idea. I guess I could put the notes I see floating around in my head when I listen on an instrument."

Matty and I look at each other. We never knew that about Andy, or Kelly, for that matter. This is completely new for both of us, but Stacy seems to know everything. It makes me feel kind of bad that she knows something about my little brother within minutes of meeting him that I never noticed in almost eight years. I wonder if Matty is thinking the same thing.

"You definitely should," she suggests, rising to her feet again. She looks at Andy and Tina. "These kids are great. You guys got lucky with them."

They both smile. "Yeah, we did," Tina says. For the first time, I see the love in her eyes for us. I guess, in a way, I love her too.

The boys who had been watching us this whole time get up off the floor and go over to Kelly. The older one waves at him. "Hi, I'm Spencer," he whispers. "I have no voice box so I can't speak loud, but if you listen close, it is okay. I'm almost five."

Kelly stares at him for quite a while, almost as if deciding whether he is going to waste his words on this boy or dismiss him. "My mommy died," he finally states, so emotionless that it almost breaks my heart. Spencer must be feeling the same way for his face twists up momentarily as if he is going to cry before it returns to normal.

"That's bad. Do you wanna talk about it?" he asks. His whispers sound raspy like he is a chain smoker. Kelly nods, and Spencer takes his hand and leads him into the living room; they both disappear behind a tree like something straight out of a book. Come to think of it, that would be a great idea for a story. A fantasy land hidden away somewhere with lots of trees and brush where two boys are hand in hand, facing the harsh realities of the world together. Wonder if that one would make the best sellers list? Maybe it's too overused, I think to myself. Unlike my *real* story, which I think is what I'll stick to if I want people to really read what I write. I had to give up the story in my acting to write it because I thought it would be more interesting. Who would have thought that my own life would have more gripping drama for a reader than anything I could come up with in my head? It never used to be like that before this summer. These three months have made me have a completely different life, and it feels like my old one with school and hanging around watching TV, and even my acting hour, is just a dream that I dreamed years ago. I'm not sure if that's okay with me or not.

As I over-think things yet again, Tanner slips away after his brother and his new friend. Matty chats away with Stacy, who I can tell he's taken a quick liking to now that he's past being uncomfortable. He's always liked that spunky attitude. It's not the way he still looks at Tina, but he admires her rather. Kind of like the way I admired and always will admire my dad as the most amazing guy out there, not toppable, and I admire my mom as a strong, caring woman that I should grow up to be like. Andy's mom, who I guess I should refer to as my new surrogate grandmother, is busy doting over the newly engaged couple, asking about their plans and talking a mile a minute as she always seems to do. This makes me the only one to hear the rustle in the trees behind me. As I turn around, I feel a poke on my shoulder. I whip my head at lightning speed, hoping some kind of axe murderer isn't hiding in this fake forest like in a good thriller book.

"Ouch, darling, watch your hair!" I hear and match the voice to my *real* Grandma. I catch sight of her rubbing her face, where I must have hit her with my hair when I turned, with one hand, and pushing a branch from her side with the other.

"Grandma!" I squeal, throwing my arms around her thin body.

"Happy birthday sweetie," she smiles warmly, returning the hug. "You're the most gorgeous birthday girl out there, just like your mother."

I wave my hand in the air as if to swat away that ridiculous comment. "Trust me, you're just biased."

Before she can argue, Matty runs over and almost tackles her. "I can't believe you came!" he exclaims as excitedly as if he got told he's going to be in NASA's space program.

Grandma tousles his shaggy black mane of hair and laughs. "Where else could I possibly be on my grandchildren's birthdays?"

"True," he laughs. He waves his arm around at the landscape. "Do you like it? This is where we have been spending most of our days lately."

Grandma looks around quizzically. "Wow, it's pretty, but I can't believe you survived. I'm having trouble staying here just now, and I'm actually inside." She looks down to see she's standing on sand. "How did that Andrew do all of this?"

Matty and I look at each other and shrug. "*That* will remain a mystery," I laugh. She chuckles along with us as Stacy, Tina, Andy, his mom, and Randy come over to say hello. Stacy and her mom do most of the talking, rambling rather, while Tina just smiles and Randy stands off to the side like a big awkward mess. Andy gets a huge hug from Grandma, and she whispers something in his ear, which I'm sure, is a thank you for putting this all together for us. He grins and nods at her as she pulls away.

I hear another rustle behind me, but this time I'm not as scared as I am surprised. Two strangers stand before me who look to be a couple in their late fifties to early sixties. The man is pretty burly, like he weight-lifted all his life and still goes to the gym periodically. He has white-gray hair and a witty smile, like he's on the verge of making a joke and laughing about it in his head. The woman is much shorter and even thinner than Grandma. She has shoulder length curly hair that is brown on the top and silver underneath. She looks slightly amused as she looks around, like she knows the man so well that she can guess what he's going to say about the scenery. They each hold a perfectly wrapped present with the kind of bow on the top that takes me hours to curl with the scissors. They look absolutely perfect for each other, the kind of older couple happily married for so many years that you see in the movies, constantly bickering in a loving way. I just stare at them, hoping they will introduce themselves. I didn't think Andy had anyone else in his family, unless they are extended, and I certainly don't know them. Why would they attend our party?

"Mom! Dad!" Tina bursts out, ending my wonders. I should have known that they were Tina's parents. The woman looks just like her, and even the man shows some resemblance. I guess I would have expected them to be the sweet and quiet kind, like Tina, rather than the sarcastic, loud kind of person faces I see.

"Hi baby," her mother says to her in a voice like she's talking to someone Kelly's age rather than a grown woman. I have a flashback and realize I do sort of recognize this woman and hope she doesn't recognize me. Our first encounter comes back to me where she and Tina were bickering at her home about Andy and her taking off work. I remember glaring at her as we left, and now I start to think maybe I shouldn't have done that, considering I'm probably going to be seeing a lot of her and don't want her to think I'm a brat. Maybe she never saw it, and I'm just worrying too much as usual.

Tina moves on to give her dad a kiss and her mother looks straight at me. "I could never forget a face like yours." Oh great, I think. The time when I *need* to be worrying too much, I'm not.

I look right through her, hoping I'm convincing her that I'm struggling to remember who she is and why she would remember me. All my troubles are worth nothing though because my idiot brother chimes in the conversation.

"We saw you when Kristina was giving us a ride," he says, having no idea of my internal conflict. I'm forced to pretend that made everything come back to me. I thought twins are supposed to have telepathy or something where they know what is best for each other and always know where each other is. Obviously, Matty missed that one. I shoot him a look that says 'shut your mouth before I kill you later', but he just looks back at me confused. I shake my head in disappointment.

I turn back to Tina's mom and smile my sweetest smile in attempts to counter that glare. "I can't believe I didn't remember that! So much has happened since then; I guess it slipped my mind." I smack myself lightly in the head to play off how much I supposedly think I'm absent-minded. "Thank you so much for coming to our birthday party!"

"Oh, of course honey," she says so nicely that all my worries fade. "I can see why Kristina loves you children so much. We got these for you." She hands one present to me and practically pushes her husband and the present he is holding into Matty.

"I'm not an imbecile you know," he mutters, and she just rolls her eyes. Matty and I time our opening of the presents so we see them at the same time as we always have when opening similar presents. That way one won't ruin it for the other, and we can both be surprised at the exact same time. It takes some talent, but we've had practice, so we pull it off. We both reveal Tanger Outlets Gift Cards at the same time and smile. There are so many opportunities for a great buy in a shopping center like that. Plus, it's getting to be the off season at this point, so the crowds won't make the experience frustrating. I think I'll go on a new clothes shopping spree for our upcoming school year, which is fast approaching, so I hear from Matty.

"Thank you so much," Matty and I say almost in unison. Tina's mother smiles a 'you're welcome' and adds, "We weren't sure just what kind of teenagers you were, so we thought this would cover all the bases."

Tina's father looks around through the trees. "Where is the littlest one?"

"With Spence and Tanner," Andy replies. He looks at Tina's father warily, and I wonder what kind of relationship they have. One corner of his mouth turns up like Matty's does before he's about to entertain himself greatly at my expense.

"I would ask you to go look for them Andrew, but it's a bit windy out. I'm afraid you might just blow away."

Andy's face gets beat red, and Tina glares at her father. "Don't start now please." I get the feeling this is a normal occurrence. Poor skinny, small Andy is in for a life of humiliation.

He chuckles to himself like he thinks that he should have a career in comedy and says, "Sorry, I just couldn't help myself. And he better get used to it if you two are to be wed."

Tina looks over at me. "I felt bad for my boyfriends since I was your age. My type hasn't changed much, and neither has his sense of humor." She rolls her eyes like he is the most embarrassing thing and she's a sixteen year old with her friends.

"Trust me; I know what it's like with this one over here." I point my elbow out to the side in Matty's direction. He throws his hands in the air like he's this innocent little flower and I'm a big liar.

We hear even deeper chuckles and look at Tina's father again, who seems to be struggling to contain himself. He sees us all looking in his direction and bursts out in a loud, obnoxious laugh. "I'm sorry," he says between wheezes, "it's just I was thinking that you guys can't live down here. I mean, without me around, where will you go when there's a water bottle to be opened or ice cream to be scooped? Not to insult you Krissy, but I don't think you have the muscle."

"Oh Dad shut up!" Tina exclaims. Matty obviously thinks that is the funniest thing because he almost falls over laughing and Stacy joins him. I just stand there, wishing I could give Andy a hug and make him feel less small. His mom pats him on the shoulder sympathetically while Tina's mom smacks her husband, who is very proud of his wit at the moment. I see Randy leaning against a tree, his mouth twitching like he is trying to suppress a laugh. He catches me looking at him and composes himself.

At that moment, Kelly saunters in with Stacy's boys trailing after him. Everyone turns to look at them. Tina's parents make their introductions to Kelly and he only nods. It's clear he isn't big on either of them, and he is the best judge of character I know. I'm not sure if I like them that much either. I'll have to see when I get to know them better.

"I think it's time that I give you guys the presents from Tina and me," Andy finally says.

I hadn't even given the concept of Andy giving us birthday gifts a second thought, so when he comes out carrying big, oddly wrapped boxes with tape sticking up in all directions and crinkles and rips in the shiny red paper, I am stunned. He stumbles through the sand as he struggles to carry them to us, and I'm glad he is too busy to see Tina's father's smirks. Finally, he drops them at our feet with a bang, breathing heavily. The largest box of all is marked with Matty's name, and it is nearly as tall him. There is another little box on top of it for him too, and then two boxes for me-one medium sized and one small. I can't guess what any of them could possibly be, especially the enormous box for Matty. I feel a childish pang of jealously for his big box, but then I remember how the best gifts come in small packages.

Our presents obviously aren't similar, so I give Matty the go ahead to open first. He looks more than happy that I did. He attacks the big box like a lion at its prey, throwing the wrapping paper in all directions. Some of it sticks up in the branches of the trees, making it look like Christmas. That was always the thing that I noticed from my brothers-boys rip things apart in a hurry while I take the slow and careful present opening approach.

When the brown box is revealed, Matty looks on all sides to try and read its contents. Finally spotting what he is looking for, his eyes widen, and his mouth spreads into a smile that engulfs his face. "No way!" he screams, gripping the box tightly to make sure it isn't just a hologram.

Andy grins, very happy with Matty's reaction. I look over and see the label that Matty is so excited about. A Hubble telescope, shiny and black, that could provide hours of amazement looking at stars and planets and possibly a comet flying by for my brother. He used to have the exact same one in our old house-Dad had given it to him just before he died-and that was like his baby. He cringed when anyone else even came close to touching it, and I'm pretty sure he tucked it into bed at night. I know it pained him to know that with everything else that burned down and disappeared in that house, his baby was one of them. Now, as he rips through the tape on the box and pushes back the flaps of the lid, it is like he is being reunited with his missing child after years of thinking it was gone forever.

Andy continues to beam as Matty moves on to his other, smaller box. It contains a box of many books about astronomy, theories, and all the things out there that he loves, but my mind can't seem to grasp. There is even one book called "How to be a Young Astrophysicist", and I think Matty's heart almost gives out he's so happy. I can't help but smile at him this way, looking like an excited little kid again. It's been so long since I've seen him so genuinely happy, and it feels good. He's done so much to get us here, just as much as Andy and Grandma and Tina have, and he deserves a reward like this.

When he is finished and proceeds to try to get the pieces of the telescope out of the box, I am encouraged to open mine. I pick the larger box, the one that is long and skinny like a log, and shake it. I hear a 'thump, thump' sound inside like there is something heavy bouncing around. I feel a little guilty, hoping it's not fragile, and start to carefully rip the paper away. It is so shiny, red, and perfect that I make sure I actually rip as little as possible so I can keep some. I see the bottom of a black cardboard box while the top opens up, dropping its contents right out. Before I know it, a pair of clean, new, black and white Converse with blinding white laces fall out in my lap. They look just like Andy's, except smaller and missing all the dirty marks, and I can't help but let my happiness take me over.

"They're so you can make your own memories," Andy smiles, his crystal blue eyes glistening. "And they have brought me luck, so I thought your own pair would for you."

I hug them close to my chest. "Thank you so much!" They are the most symbolic and special present anyone has ever given me, and I know I will wear them everywhere. That way they can collect good and bad memories that I can look back on and smile, and maybe even give me good luck for once on the way.

Andy nods a 'you're welcome' as I use my free hand to get to the smaller present. I don't want to let go of the shoes, nor can I imagine what kind of present could be better than them, following my rule of the presents in small boxes being the best. I try to carefully remove the paper, but it is much harder to do with one hand. I reveal a rectangular black box with rainbow colored words on it reading "you make it you" and a white symbol of lines that reminds me of the white strips on Andy's arms. The cover of the box slides off to reveal a hole holding a long, flat, rectangular electronic device. It is covered in plastic, but I can see through it to a large black screen with a black button at the bottom. Under the button is a shiny, maroon covering, a little darker than the wrapping paper. I carefully pull it out and remove the plastic. It is smooth on the screen part, but a little bit rougher on the red part. There are a few more buttons on the side and a label that says "Zune-hello from Seattle". I turn it over in my hands and see my name engraved on the back, but I'm still lost as to what it is. I look up to Andy for clarification.

He laughs. "It's a special music player. It holds thousands of songs, goes on the internet, plays music videos, holds pictures, and has a place to buy the music, all in a touch screen. It's the most awesome thing I could find for you."

At just the sound of the word music, Kelly comes over to take a closer look. Andy holds down a button on the top. We watch it turn on, a rainbow of color appearing on the screen before it shows a menu. I mess with all the things I can do by just touching it awhile and even let Kelly try.

"There's a wire in there that lets you hook it up to a computer and get your own software to sync and play the music. There are also headphones and an instruction booklet. I got your name on it so if it gets lost, you can prove it's yours."

"Wow, it's amazing, thank you," I whisper, mesmerized by all the vibrant color. I'm so used to the strict red and white of Johnny's music playing that this is like a whole new world. I can tell Kelly is practically drooling, so I add, "I'll share it with you Kells. We can listen together, just like with Johnny."

"Really?" he squeaks, looking up at me wide-eyed to see if I'm joking.

"Of course." He gives me a hug, which makes me think of Mom. I hope she's seeing all this now, how well we're doing and that everything Dad and her did for us, we will be forever grateful.

"I have something for you too Kelly," Andy says, pointing behind him in the direction of the kitchen.

Kelly squeals and disappears through the trees. Spencer and Tanner automatically follow him, and I think that Kelly got himself two little shadows. I take that opportunity to excuse myself so I can let out my happiness. I place my Zune, which I still have yet to name, nicely in its box and make my way up the stairs, my Chucks in hand. I carry them the exact same way I did Andy's when I had them in the waiting room. When I know I'm completely alone, I let out an explosion of squeals. I flop around like a fish on my bed, hugging the shoes and thinking how lucky I am to have such an amazing guy in my life. I'm sure if anyone walked in at that moment, they would have committed me instantly, but it's better than having little explosions in front of anyone. Better to let it all out in the confines of my room and feel better afterwards than when people are watching.

I feel exhilarated after I'm finished, like those moments of my heart beating in overdrive cleansed my body. I bounce down the stairs, holding the Chucks by the laces again so they bump into each other and make a nice thumping sound.

Matty looks relieved when he sees me. "We thought you died up there. It's time for dinner." I ignore the first part and follow them all to the kitchen. Matty leans into my ear so no one else can hear. "So how was that squeal session?"

I just elbow him in the ribs so he shuts up.

48

Andy

At dinner, all I can think about is how well this is going. It took a lot of time and work to plan all of this, so it's very important to me that it's special. It was hard enough just to pick a time when everyone was available. Stacy is always off gallivanting across the country with her lumberjack of a husband who is more than twice my size, and my mom has been sick with worry ever since Dad got moved into the hospital. I'm glad I remembered to take care of asking about this when I called Tina's parents the first time, because I don't think I would have had the courage to go through with talking to her father again. After that, I had to coordinate people coming over at certain times, some to help me set up, and others to be a secondary surprise. I had to order all this crazy stuff from places I won't mention and make sure it looked realistic, rather than like one of those stupid movies where you know it's fake. Plus, I had to think of amazing gifts for the kids to show how much I cared about them and go through the whole 'having the Candy Kitchen worker pull out all the green Swedish fish for me' ordeal. So far, all of it was worth it for how good things turned out, besides my humiliation when Tina's father showed up with his usual hurtful jokes. Even the dinner Tina cooked up, tacos-the kids' favorite-is perfect.

There is one downside, however. I have the two frightening men I've mentioned sitting on either side of me at the table. Randy sits to my right, sticking one enormous elbow on the table in front of me. I look at it and feel quite small and feeble, like that one arm may be able to swallow my entire body. I try not to look at him anymore, but in that attempt, I find myself looking at Jon. He wears that smirk as always as he devours a taco. I have trouble eating; my stomach is twisted up like it seems to be every time I try to eat lately. I think of how I used to feel this way right before my diagnosis, but I shake that from my head real quick. I literally shake my head, and Jon stops eating to look at me as if I grew another head. I shoot him a weak smile, and he just laughs and looks away. I really wish I could get up and walk to shake this fidgety feeling.

Tina sees that I'm feeling this way again-she's used to it by now-and makes subtle air punches, pretending to hit them both. That makes me feel a little better. Jenna catches it and nods in agreement. I laugh and am able to eat a little.

Somewhere near the end of dinner, Jon drops a piece of tomato in his drink, which looks to me as if it is deliberate. He tries to hide a smile as he says, "Oh no, stupid me dropped this." He turns to me and I'm scared of what's coming next. "Andrew, can you reach through this straw and get it for me?" Randy busts out laughing, sounding more like some kind of roar from a bear, and Matty giggles to himself. I still think that kid has a problem with me.

I laugh mockingly at him. "That's so funny. If I were half as funny as you, I'd be a famous comedian."

Jon raises his eyebrows at me. "Sarcastic little sprite, aren't we?"

I feel myself getting red hot angry, the kind of feeling of being ready to explode that I used to have when I would just *look* at my dad sometimes. If only Jones, Tamara as she is being called now, was able to make it. She would have gotten up and punched him in the face for me, and he wouldn't be able to do anything about it because she is a woman. That is the good part about having a tough, police trained girl have a thing for you. At least now that she stopped hating my guts because of it.

"God Dad, just quit for a second! He's beautiful the way he is, and you need to stop trying to intimidate him!!!" Tina is up out of her seat by this point, quite fired up, which I must admit looks good on her. "You're just scared because you think he's taking your only daughter, but that's not what's happening here! I'm being shared, so just chill out and shut your mouth before you really *do* lose me!"

I stand up and grab her wrist to try to calm her down, and she sits down. Jon looks like he actually did get punched in the face and everyone is silent. There goes all that perfect I thought there was down the toilet. I want to melt into my chair, considering I'm responsible for all this. I figure I should speak up and say something, but Jon beats me to it.

"I'm sorry, you're right." He looks down as he says it so he can't see the utter surprise on my face. I'm not sure I actually heard those four words together. But he continues to confirm I did. "I'm being stupid, and I went too far. Kid, I love you for making my daughter so happy. I just have the weirdest way of showing it." He finally looks at me and gives me a genuine smile for once instead of a smirk. "Forgive me?"

I practically laugh out loud in relief. Maybe now he will stop. No, I doubt it, but at least he's not quite as scary anymore. If only I could do this with Randy too. "I guess I have to now."

"Good." He extends his hand so we can shake on it and pretty much breaks all the bones in my hand. I try to shake the pain away when he lets go. "Sorry kid, I forgot who I was shaking hands with."

I just roll my eyes. I guess I can get used to that. A little bit of embarrassment and self-consciousness for a lifetime with Tina is *well* worth it.

"Well, that gets rid of the enormous elephant in the room," Kelly simply states and we all can't help but laugh, filling the room with happiness again. Leave it to little Kelly to save my party. He's one of those people that rarely say anything, but when he does, it's extra special.

W hen Tina gets up to get the cake ready, I follow her into the secluded area of the kitchen.

I help her get the dishes in the sink and pull out the cake. It is a sheet cake-marble with whipped cream icing and has "Happy Birthday Twins!" in orange letters with Matty and Jenna's names in cursive off to the right. I stick a '1' and '4' candle in between the letters and get out the lighter, while Tina gets the correct number of plates and forks. I can't help but think that from now on, this is how life is going to be for us. I sort of like it and can't wait to walk down the aisle in my tux and Chucks carrying her, the kids watching happily. I hear Jean ask how old the kids are turning and Jenna reply 1.4 decades. I grin, thinking of when I introduced that quirk of mine to them. That seems like a lifetime ago, even though it couldn't have been more than two months, if that. I decide to take out the icing pack to write that on the cake.

"Thanks for sticking up for me out there," I say to Tina as I try to squeeze the last drops of the icing out so the words are readable. "I feel like one of those wimpy guys who have to have their girlfriend, excuse me, fiancée fight their battles for them."

"I had to stop him. I can't stand it when you feel like you have to change how you look for him. And I didn't want a repeat of the last time you tried to fight for your own."

"Eh," I sigh, remembering what she is talking about. Long before any of the events of this summer were even planned, Tina and I were in the bar, and some guy almost Randy's size was checking her out. Long story short, my first bar fight landed me in the hospital, and I don't go to bars anymore. "I don't think your dad would have done that to me."

She laughs, picturing it I'm sure. "True, but the situation was better handled with me speaking up."

I shrug. "Thanks anyway."

"Of course." She sets the plates and forks down to move over to me. I run my free hand along her jaw line and kiss her. Forgetting that I'm holding the icing, I involuntarily make a fist with my other hand, sending bright strings everywhere. They fly on the counter, up the wall, and even on the cake, messing up some of the writing I put so much work into. Tina pulls away into a giggle fit while I huff at my stupidity.

"Now look what you made me do."

She throws her hands up. "I didn't do anything! That was all you."

I put down the tube and try to work on fixing the cake. I use a knife to scoop some of the stray icing up and push the letters back into place, but it ends up looking pretty messy. Tina tries to clean the wall, leaving a huge smear of orange against the white. We both can't stop laughing, and she just throws the rag down. We both look from the orange blob on the wall, which has started to look like a fat penguin at this point, to the mangled cake.

"Wow, Andy, wow," Tina says, shaking her head.

"Don't you just love me?"

She looks at me and busts out laughing again. "There's never a dull moment with you, that's for sure."

By the time we get the cake out, everyone is so ready to eat it after waiting so long, that they don't notice how much I messed it up. I light the candles carefully, knowing with how clumsy I am lately, that it would be my luck to light something on fire, and put the lighter far away afterward. Matty sits in front of the '1' candle and Jenna in front of the '4' candle as we sing. I find myself wondering what these poor kids could be wishing for as they blow out the candles in unison. A lot has changed since their last birthday. Maybe last September they were wishing to do well on a test or to get a little extra money to go to the movies with their friends, but now those things seem small and stupid in comparison to what they could be wishing for now. I try my best, but I can't take the place of their Mom, Dad, older sister, house, or the even the life they lost. That makes me feel helpless.

The kids look extremely happy when they open their eyes back up and sit back, and I get the feeling I wouldn't be that strong. I can survive my own pain such as my cancer or being shot, but if my mom or sister died, I would be a mess on the floor. I would even be upset if something happened to my dad, believe it or not.

I cut the pieces of cake so Jenna gets the 1.4 and Matty gets the decades icing. I can tell they love it. I serve the rest of the kids next and then all the adults, except for Jon. He tries to give his piece to me, but with how my stomach is feeling, I'm not sure I want it. Jon insists with a "eat boy, you need to more than me", so I get stuck with it.

When Kelly is finished stuffing his face with cake, he rounds the corner of the table and cups his hand around my ear. "The other cake?" he whispers, then drops his hands and looks at me questioningly. Matty and Jenna have very confused faces as they stare at us. I turn to him and nod, encouraging him to go do what he has to like we planned. He grins and runs full speed out of the room toward the garage.

"What did he say?" Matty asks.

I shrug. "You'll see."

Jenna and he look at me like I'm killing them with that response, but I just choke down more cake that makes my stomach feel worse. Sometimes I think it shrunk from when I was a teenager. Back then I used to eat all day long and never feel this way, but now I think I'm hungry all the time, and as soon as I look at the food, I'm not. It's an evil mind trick, and I think possibly my stomach got tired from eating so much hospital food only to throw it up violently later. It just couldn't take it anymore and shriveled up, but then forgot to tell my brain. I didn't used to be this stick-like with pool stick arms that could snap if I'm not too careful. I wasn't huge, but I would say I was pretty normal sized for a guy my age. But I lost so much weight during my treatment, that I became this way and never recovered. My poor messed up body.

A shrill whistle comes from the garage that literally jolts me out of my head. It takes me a moment to remember the reason I'm hearing it and to get myself together, like I just woke up. "Come with me," I tell the twins, and they are more than happy to be part of this finally. The rest of the guests follow in curiosity, and we all enter the garage. There, on the far corner of the garage floor, where I struggled to put it yesterday, is a small person sized fake cake made out of a cardboard with paper mache and any other art supplies we could think to stick on it. On the top it reads "You made it to 14! Congratulations!" in shaky green sharpie, which Kelly swore was his best hand-writing and that he was just nervous. It looks pretty ghetto, but it's the thought that counts, and it's really important to Kelly.

As the twins move closer, they laugh. "It's beautiful," Jenna jokes. "How long did it take to make?"

"Actually not that long. It was pretty fun." Tina nods in agreement, and I catch Matty beaming that she had something to do with it. I wonder how long it will take for him to stop eyeing her and resenting me for supposedly 'stealing her'.

"Where is Kelly?" he asks when he finally turns away from Tina. Everyone looks around, doesn't see him, and then looks at me like I lost him. I throw my hands up as if to say, 'how should I know? He's his own person.' I make sure I have everyone's shocked attention and make a subtle cough.

"I'm here!!!" Kelly yells, bursting through the top of the fake cake and scaring everyone but Tina and I, who knew what was coming. He laughs like crazy and jumps clear out of the box, brushing pieces of the decorated lid off of his head and shoulders.

Jenna laughs along with him and picks him up from under the arms so his legs swing around. "Did you plan all of this yourself?"

He nods vigorously. "It was my idea. I always wanted to jump out of a cake, and Andy helped me do it." He sounds like he's up on an award show stage thanking me for enabling his dreams, and I can't help but notice what a cute little kid he is. I never paid much attention to a seven year old before, but Kelly seems very unique and much smarter than the average. He's a little weird, but an amazing person to know with an obvious passion for music. A lot like me when I was younger, except about half my size and not blond. I suddenly really want to spend more time with him like I did when we made this cake. Usually the other two kids hog my time and Kelly just sits in the background, but this time the others weren't around and I actually got to talk to him. It made me want to plan more times like that.

Jenna sets him down on the floor, and his black hair spreads out around his head like some kind of river. She tickles his stomach and he squirms around, squinting his eyes and kicking his little legs. "Stop it Jenny!" he squeals.

"You're the best brother in the whole world. Do you know it, Kells? Tell me you know it!"

"I know." He can barely get it out because he is laughing too hard, and tears starts dripping out of his eyes. "I know, I know, I know!"

She lets go of his stomach, gives him a big kiss, and lies down on the floor next to him. I know I should tell them it's dirty down there, but I just let it go. They are having fun, so it doesn't matter that much. I look over to Matty and see he has a twisted expression on his face, almost like he is trying to look happy when something is really bothering him. He stares hard at his siblings, and I think of how Jenna told Kelly he was the best brother in the world. I'm sure she didn't mean better than Matty, she was just teasing, but he must feel like he's not part of this and not good enough. I forgot what it was like to be a fragile teenager where something small that someone else wouldn't notice can eat you for days.

Jenna sits up suddenly and looks straight at Matty. "Why doesn't the best *older* brother join us? It's just not right without him."

Matty's face lights up and he jumps onto the floor next to them. He lays on his stomach, propped up on his elbows, and his legs swinging up behind him. He looks over to Jenna and Kelly who are to his right, both on their backs, looking up. It looks like a perfect scene for a Christmas card picture that they could look at ten years later and remember it completely. I take out my cell phone and snap a picture, just in case that is really a possibility, and they don't even notice. I take pictures of everyone in their positions in the garage and what's left of the cake where Kelly popped out. I snap Jon and Jean leaned up against the wall, smiling warmly at the kids, obviously remembering what it was like to be that young or when Tina was that age. I snap Laura sitting on a little bench, admiring the hard work we put in that cake. I snap Tanner and Spencer bouncing on the floor next to Kelly and laughing hysterically. I snap my mom, who is taking in the whole scene and looks up at me proudly for what I've done for the kids. I snap Stacy with her usual smirk on as she tries to sneak up behind her kids and grab them. I even take Randy, looking like he's about ready to punch someone in the face, crossing his huge arms over his even huger chest and eyeing his wife. It's not very unique because that's how he always seems to look, but I figure it would be rude to leave him out.

Finally, I turn to my most prized possession and the most adorable, beautiful, sexy woman there ever will be, who also happens to be my fiancée, and take the picture that will become my phone wallpaper. She is looking around at everyone, her head full of thoughts, and has a small involuntary smile on her face that reaches her eyes. I stop to admire it a moment and then try to take another one, but she catches me this time and grabs the phone from me. What is it with girls and not liking their pictures being taken? I love my picture taken, especially the nice ones, so everyone can see how good I look. Maybe that's just me being conceited.

"Come on," I tell her, trying to reach for it back. She twists her arm out of my reach and stands back to take a picture of me. I smile sarcastically and give the 'rock on' sign with my left hand. She looks at it, and the small smile she had now takes over her face. She hits the save button and hugs the phone to her chest.

"I love it so much! I'm sending it to me so I can put it as my background."

"Hmmm, we must think alike," I reply, taking the phone back to see that a message has been sent. I quickly change the wallpaper to her picture. She looks over my shoulder.

"No, get rid of that!" She tries to swipe it back, but I'm quicker this time.

I shake my head. "I won't. It's only fair, and plus, it's perfect. Look." I let her see again and she rolls her eyes.

"Fine." Her pocket buzzes and she grabs her phone out. "Oh look, I have a picture message." She opens it, and I laugh at how ridiculous I look. Oh well, it only matters that she likes it.

She sets it as her background and holds her phone up. We click them together and look at our pictures next to each other. "We're such a cute couple," she laughs. She looks over at the kids still on the floor. "With even cuter kids."

"Oh yeah," I agree. I put my arm around her and am glad I took those pictures. Now I can never forget this moment, or this day, when everything was absolutely perfect and we were all together just being ourselves. Who knows when another time like this will come along? Possibly never. I suddenly can't believe how far we've come. What once was just a far off idea of saving the kids from my father, has now been accomplished. In June, I was stuck in a job that I hated, with a girlfriend who could never convince me that we could take it one step further, a nagging mother, a father that I resented, a sister that hated me, and so many dreams that were impossible to chase. Now, merely three months later, I am free of the police force, happily engaged to the woman of my dreams, with a proud mother, a father that I know I will love after he has been helped, a sister who I can actually spend time with, and I am well on my way to achieving my wildest dreams of performing on a stage what is on my mind to millions of fans. Who would have thought that life could change so much in so little time?

As if on cue to make the day even better, my phone rings and the caller I.D. says Ryan. I answer it immediately and he says, "Hey bro, do you want to hear the good news or the great news first?"

I laugh and see Tina is watching me. "Whichever you want man."

"Okay, the good news is that I can make it to be your best man in your big wedding. Now I know you're unbelievably excited because you could never find someone to replace me, but save the celebration and listen to what I have to say next."

"Do you make out with the mirror at night Ryan?"

I hear him giggling on the other end. "I would, but I don't want to risk getting myself too excited. Instead I let lucky women have a taste of this."

"Lucky?"

"Come on now Andy, you know if you were female, you'd have hooked up with me by now."

I shake my head in exasperation, and Tina rolls her eyes, knowing Ryan all too well from living with him for almost three years. "You keep telling yourself that."

"Way ahead of you. Oh wow. I got so caught up in talking about myself that I forgot to relay the great news. This is where you think 'what could be greater than Ryan Young attending my wedding?' Well, I came through and got us a gig. This Saturday, at the Rudder, no less. You know that big sign that we always see when we drive down Route 1 to the beach? Our name is on it advertising us. It says 'Copyright 83' real big for every tourist to see. It's gonna be me on guitar, Ty jamming on bass, Leon our drummer boy, and you as lead with piano and vocals Andyman."

I feel my jaw drop and my eyes widen. I can't help it. I don't know what to feel. I have been working hard lately on editing all the little poems that I've been jotting down over these past months and putting them to music on my piano. I finally got a couple done and brought some of my best music friends over to give them sheet music. We seriously discussed the idea of making our band and our love for music a career. They pretty much said 'it's about time I asked', and we started working on putting our songs together so they sounded halfway decent. We named our band Copyright 83, inspired by the tattoo on my chest, and it fit us because we are all the same age. I was pretty proud of us for just starting out, but I can't even explain how it feels to know that we're going to be performing in the most important bar of the resort area. It is an incredible place to start, but I don't even think the place is what gets me. It's the fact that we actually *are* starting. This is really happening; my dreams since I was even younger than Kelly have a real chance of coming true.

"I can't believe you! This is better than when you signed us up for the musical talent show in senior year of high school and we won! That was kid bands and other kinds of musicians from all over the state of Pennsylvania. I was so angry when you signed us up without asking any of us because I thought we had no chance of even coming close to winning. But we won and didn't make fools out of ourselves. Now you've gone and done something great for us again!"

I think I can hear him beaming through the phone, remembering how he rubbed it in my face how right he was when we held up that shiny, gold 'best band' trophy. "I know how great I am. You don't have to tell me, even though I do enjoy it that you do. We will win again this time. I just know that the trophy this time will be all those fans in a filled up arena screaming for us, and you know I'm always right."

My heart skips just thinking about it. "Yes you are Ryan. I can feel it."

Epilogue

Kelly, Jenna, Matty, and Andy

I lay on the floor of my bedroom, on my back, with my feet bent up onto the top of my bed. I have Jenna's ZuneHD, which she named Brett Bower or Bower for short, laying nicely on the carpet and The Fray blasting in my ears. It's my favorite song, Trust Me, and I smile to myself as I close my eyes and see the notes, beats, and music symbols floating around in perfect symphony. Matty tells me that all he sees is black and some occasional colors when he closes his eyes with music, but I see what you would see on the sheet music. I focus on different parts of the music, starting with the vocal notes and then moving on to the drums, piano, guitar, violin, bass, and so on, and then put it back together again. Then, if I think real hard about a certain song, I can remember all the notes and play them. I know this because I snuck into Andy's music room, taking Stacy's advice. I thought of a song, which happened to be SafetySuit at the time, and played the piano notes I saw pretty well. I went through a lot of different songs, and then decided to try making some of my own. I got pretty caught up and didn't want to stop. I can imagine myself doing that my whole life, and if I'm lucky, sharing it with people and making some good money.

I flip my legs to the floor, grab Bower and Salamander from my bed, and make my way downstairs with the sudden urge to play something. I don't bother tip-toeing because no one notices me anyway. Jenna's always in her room pretending to be someone else or completely focused on her laptop and won't let me see what she's writing. Matty is always outside on the steps or pacing around the yard thinking about some deep science stuff about existence and space. They come in sometimes and hang out with each other, completely forgetting about me. Even when we were hiding, they made the decisions and I was just a tag-along; they didn't really care about what I thought because they figured me a little kid. Sometimes they play with me, and I like that, but it doesn't last long because they get frustrated that I don't talk much. I honestly want to speak only when I have something important to say, or else it won't be as important when I say it. Plus, I'd much rather listen intently to what other people say, how their voices rise and fall to different notes, and the expressions they make to cause what they say to have an effect on people. This is better than listening to the sound of my own squeaky, shrill, little boy voice in my head. I especially like it when people talk in riddles and don't say everything they mean. Then it's like song lyrics or poems where there is an underlying meaning and every word contributes to the reader or listener figuring out what it is. Matty just laughed when I told him this and said I would enjoy talking to girls.

Another thing they laugh at me for is the way I talk sometimes. Some people think I have a speech problem, but that's not the case. I can speak just fine, much better than most kids my age, and always form intelligent sentences. It's just that I don't understand why some people long ago, who created the English language, made some of the words sound the way they do. Some words sound nice to my ears, like they are meant to be that way, but others are just awful. When I hear the bad sounding words, they make me feel dark inside, and I want to hold my ears so I don't hear them anymore. That's why I change some words so they sound nice too. For example, the phrase 'green fishy'. When you say green fishy like it's supposed to be said, it sounds flat and dull. But if you say it my way, geen fissy, it sounds more light and harmonious. Same thing for bracet instead of bracelet, babin suit rather than bathing suit, and canny instead of candy. They all sound more right, and I'm going to say what I think sounds right, no matter what anyone thinks. Sound is my favorite thing in the whole world, so it's important to me. That is all words are after all-a bunch of sounds put together in ways we can understand and remember.

I pass a note in Andy's handwriting addressed to Matty and Jenna on the kitchen table. It says that he went out a little while, and since Tina doesn't get back from school until four, they have to look after me. I chuckle at that. I'm eight years old, and after that long, a lone wolf like me knows how to look after himself. Not that they listened because they are doing their own thing, and I could be dead for all they know. I make my way through the office to Andy's music room, my all-time favorite spot of the house. I run my fingers lightly over all the beautiful instruments and think how great they would sound playing harmoniously. I sit down on the piano bench and tap one key. It rings through my ears and fills my heart. I think of the song I just listened to and follow the piano notes. After a few tries, I have the flow down pretty well and am proud of myself.

I sit back and wonder what Andy would think if he knew I was here. Tina would tell me I was a curious one and talk to me like I'm one of her baby second grade students. But Andy is different. I've liked him since the first time I saw him. I like how he forms what is on his mind, inspired from any life experience to a simple road sign, into well-written poems, and then puts them to music. I'm no good at the writing part; the sound is more my speed. I often think of asking him if he would teach me piano and what the notes were called and all that. Then I could help him bring the sound to his pieces, but I'm scared he'll laugh. He is really nice and relaxed and respects even the wildest ideas, like that cake on Matty and Jenna's last birthday that I jumped out of (it was always a dream I had so I could put on a little performance and have everyone's attention.) However, no one takes an eight year old seriously, even one like me who gets told he's wise beyond his years, and Andy probably wouldn't think I'm good enough for his professional music. I just really want to be as good as him, and I need to learn somehow. I want to make the kind of music that everyone can listen to, relate to, and have it move them. Sort of like where they get done listening and feel like they just watched a movie, read a book, or saw a show they know they will never forget and want to listen again and again. I want to see the day where Kelly Thornton fits the category of Rob Thomas, Jon Bon Jovi, Celine Dion, and Christina Aguilera. Or maybe just Kelly, such as Madonna, Cher, or Sting. Or maybe a band, such as U2, Aerosmith, Queen, Nickelback, or Jimmy Eat World. I can sell out arenas, have fans screaming for me, and a mutual agreement that I made music that changed the world.

I hear Andy's cherry red Mazda Miata MX-5 pulling into the driveway and stand up immediately. I make sure everything is exactly how it was and plop myself in front of the TV in the family room very non-suspiciously. I turn on my favorite channel, Vh1, and clutch Salamander to my chest. The plush, yellow fur on his belly and his red and black back feel nice on my fingers. I place Bower on the ottoman diagonal to me so Jenna will see that I borrowed it and doesn't have a heart attack thinking she lost Andy's gift. She wears those shoes everywhere, cleaning them regularly, and says they are lucky. Matty thinks it's funny that she likes him so much, but I just don't understand it, considering how much older he is than her and about to be married in a month. Maybe it's just the way I admire him, plus other stuff because she's a teenage girl. I'll never know about that thankfully.

I watch a stupid reality show and keep thinking Andy will come in, but he doesn't. I look out the living room window and see him on the front steps with Matty. They look deep in conversation, and since I can't hear it, I return to my spot on the couch. I suddenly feel very lonely and want to at least go sit in Jenna's room, but I hear her voice. That means she's doing her acting and doesn't want to be bothered. I can imagine her yelling that the door was closed for a reason, and that would make me feel worse. I go upstairs, not bothering to turn off the TV, and sit outside her door, hugging my knees. I hear her addressing Mom, Dad, and Lauren. She really has trouble with missing them and telling the pictures she has of them everything she is feeling seems to help. I wish I could go in there and she could talk to *me* about it. I like to be alone and play games with myself sometimes because usually people don't understand me. But, believe it or not, I really don't want to be a loner. It just sort of happens. Now I want to go in there and make her feel better so she doesn't feel the pain of missing them.

As for me, I don't really feel that pain like Matty and Jenna. They either get all choked up or can't stop smiling when they think of Lauren or Daddy, but I feel nothing. I was just about one when they died, and no matter how hard I try, I can't remember a thing about that horrible night. Or anything before or soon after, for that matter. When we watched that video at Grandma's, it was like watching strangers while everyone else cried. The only reason I got upset was because everyone else was, and that kind of thing is contagious for me. Sometimes I feel really guilty about it and wish I remembered too. I'm sure I would have loved them if I knew them, but I didn't, so I can't miss them. I usually am jealous of Matty and Jenna for being older and having more freedoms, while I have to wait around to get old enough for my life to start happening, but in this situation, I'm glad I'm too young. The ache I feel when I think of Mom is enough to make up for it.

Even now, as we reach a year of her being somewhere else, I still think I'll wake up to her making my breakfast. Or asking me the dreaded question of what I want for lunch, full knowing I can never make that decision. Or bringing us down to the beach all day long and then relaxing with us afterwards during a movie, Matty's eyes avoiding the clock at all costs. It really takes my breath away when I realize I will never experience those simple things again. It's all the little things that always make the most impact in life, and most people don't even know it.

For instance, I miss her and how she would dance with me, calling me her little man. Or when she would surprise me with a new album just so she could see my face light up. She once watched me when I listened to music and asked if I saw anything unusual when I closed my eyes.

"Nope, just little pictures floating around," I had replied calmly. I had described them to her, not knowing what they were at the time and that they *were* unusual.

I remember how warmly she smiled, like I had just made all her dreams come true by saying that. "You are my Mackenzie all over again. He'd be so proud." Then she hugged me close for a long time and shook a bit as she tried not to cry uncontrollably. Even then, I knew how special my daddy was and how painful it was for a lot of people to lose him. And I knew I was special too because he passed on his unique mind to me. Now I love him just for that, if nothing else.

Salamander is the only thing I have left of him and that's why I take him everywhere. He's like Matty and Jenna's rings for me, something I can carry with me, pretending I have the actual giver with me. Daddy gave him to me just a few months after I was born because he thought he was as cute as me. My first word was actually Salamander. Matty and Jenna had always called him that, and when he was across the room out of my reach, I pointed and screamed, "Salamander!" The name stuck, and I never wanted to change it. I never wanted to be apart from it either, and Mom used to have to wash it all the time. I don't think I'll ever want to be apart from him. He's my little companion and my guardian angel for when I sleep. I'm pretty sure I'll want him at my wedding. Between him and the gold hoop earrings Mom and Daddy decided to get me when I was born, I can't imagine being separated from them.

I hear Jenna saying Mom's name, and I suddenly wish I'd stayed downstairs. My throat feels like I swallowed too big of a piece of bread with no drink, and my chest is squeezing. I go back to the TV and try to keep my breathing in check so if Andy comes in, he won't question anything and make this worse. I only make it to the doorway of the family room before I catch what is on the TV screen and stop dead in my tracks. I blink a few times to make sure I'm not seeing things and stare wide-eyed. It takes a few moments to get my mouth to work, but as soon as I can form words, I yell, "Jenna, come here right now!" The first time it is just a loud whisper, but on the second try, it echoes through the house.

I grab the TiVo remote, rewind it back a few minutes to the beginning, and hit pause, my hands shaking the entire time. Jenna's door swings open, and she stands over me on the catwalk. "What is it Kells?"

I beckon her down wildly. "Come here. You won't believe what I just saw."

She huffs and joins me in the family room. "What?"

I don't really like the tone she is giving me, but I ignore it and press play. We both watch through it, listening intently and not missing a clip. At the end, Jenna turns to me, almost ghost white with shock and happiness. "You're right. I don't believe it."

I nod smiling. That was pretty amazingly unreal, and we both know it. Almost as if by instinct, we both dash toward the front door at the same time. We throw open the door together and can barely speak as we try to get Matty and Andy to come inside immediately.

Seeing that note on the kitchen table from Andy makes me feel happy. I finally have some time to myself. I nearly have a heart attack when someone comes in when I'm writing, let along doing my acting or talking to my parents. With my writing, it's that I don't want people to see what I'm writing about until it's finished and can show them the final project. I want it to be a complete surprise with no previews. That's a little scary though because it's either the reader likes it from the beginning or hates it, and I would be crushed if I put this much work in and it wasn't any good. I've been working on it since we got to this house, and I'm so close to being done, I can taste it.

As for the acting thing, I just plain don't want anyone to know I do that. I'm pretty sure the people who live in this house know about it, but that's okay because they don't judge me. I think Andy even finds it interesting, and I like that. Anyone who doesn't know me though, I don't want to even have an inkling of this side of me. They would automatically think I'm weird and need a helmet and not want to be around me. Especially boys, because they are vicious about the slightest imperfection, or what they think of as an imperfection. That is exactly why I like older guys at ages between 21 and 35, who have at least some maturity. Sometimes I wish I was older so that I could have a guy like Andy be mine and feel secure in my future, but then I think I'm wishing my life away. I guess I just want to be content and know that the world will love me for the weirdo I am. Matty laughs and says I like old men, but that's not it. He just doesn't understand because he's a boy himself.

Speaking of, I see Matty pacing the front yard out my bedroom window. He is walking back and forth through the grass, looking up at the sky and clouds, and I know he's having profound thoughts like he usually does when he is doing that. I'm safe in the fact that I know he won't be coming in here. Tina is at school getting her classroom together for next year, and Andy is out, where I'm not sure, but he may tell us later. And Kelly is somewhere in the house, but he's a smart kid that knows not to invade my space and would probably like being on his own more anyway. I'm completely free to do whatever I please!

My smile fades as I realize I have no acting ideas. I'm completely dry at the moment, and this is the worst moment for that. Just my luck. I do little half hour sessions periodically throughout most of my days as I get inspiration and an hour one before I go to bed each night. I could be someone else my entire life if that was possible. Between my characters in my writing and the people I switch on and off from in my acting, I would never be the same person a full day.

I think real hard of something I could do, some possible idea, but if I don't flow straight from the beginning, I know it just won't work. I slump angrily in my swivel chair and spin from side to side as I stare at the blank black screen of my laptop. What is wrong with me today? Maybe it's because I didn't sleep at all last night. Andy and Tina's room is diagonally across the hall from mine, and she had another bad headache. Like the sweet, perfect guy he is, he laid next to her, rubbing her head and singing to her until she fell asleep. Usually his beautiful voice would send me straight to dreamland, but this time I ended up crying to the stabbing pain of jealousy again. When I finally got tired enough, I pretty much passed out and dreamed awful things. It was many years in the future and Matty was on the TV for finding a new theory for the fate of the universe, and Kelly was off on his sold-out tour. I tried to contact them, but they disowned me because they didn't want to associate with the panhandler I was that lived in a box on the street. I ended up having to rob a house to get enough money to survive and got sent to rot in prison. No one visited or cared.

I woke up after that one to my whole body aching and scared a hundred times more of the future than I was before. I immediately went to the Internet and looked up how to copyright and publish a novel so I could prevent that dream from coming true. I got about nowhere except with the knowledge that most publishers will deny an author's first book, and I also read a story about how a girl lent her friend the book she wrote to read before it was copyrighted. The friend stole it and got rich off of it. That was far from reassuring, and I was comforted by the fact that I keep my writing to myself.

I rub my head, not really wanting to think about last night ever again, and glance over at the pictures on my desk. They are all from Grandma, and the first frame has two different ones of Dad in them. On the left, it shows him when he was about my age, and he looks like a skinnier version of Matty. He is standing on the jetty of Rehoboth Beach, with one of his friends I never knew, eating water ice. I like it because it is natural. The one on the right is him when he was older, which Mom took. It is located on the steps of our old house where he sits, one knee propped up to support the guitar he is holding. He looks down at his hands, one on the neck holding the chords, the other holding a pick and in the middle of strumming the strings. He looks so into it, and I smile now as I look at it, feeling like I know him a little more just by having this.

The next frame has two of Mom. The one on the left is of her when she was about sixteen and in a cheerleading pose. She has one pink pom-pom to her hip and the other raised above her bright, smiling face. She has on a skirt and a tank top, obviously the uniform, and the tank top reads the name of her school with 'cheer captain' under it. She had told us many times of how that was her favorite thing to do as a girl, and she did it straight through middle school and high school. She had always wanted to be a coach. On the right, there is one of her just a few years before she passed. I remember when we had taken it of her on the boardwalk one night. She holds little Kelly's hand, who has one of those perfect four year old smiles on his face. I miss those days.

Another is of Lauren before her diagnosis. It looks to me like she is about nine, and it is obviously a school picture, for it shows from her shoulders up and her black hair is done nicely. She looks so happy, and it hurts me deep inside to think that she went through so much pain. I wish she were alive so I could have someone to talk to about stuff who would understand. She would be about nineteen now, probably in college working toward her dreams, and I just know she would have been the best sister that I could have.

The last is my parents' wedding picture. It shows Dad when he was a little younger than Andy, which you could have mistaken as Andy at first glance, in his tux. He has added a bright pink bowtie and wears matching Converse on his feet. Grandma laughed when I asked about those and said, "Your father refused to go anywhere where he couldn't express his colorful personality." He holds Mom in her beautiful, flowing, white dress in his arms, and you can see the very tip of his musical tattoos where his jacket sleeves are riding up. They both are beaming, and every time I look at that, I know true love really exists somewhere.

Finally, I look up at my wall and spot the painting Grandma also gave me that she kept of Dad's. Along with music, he also loved art, and he was always designing album covers for musician friends or just doodling on my mom's anniversary cards. Sometimes he would sit down on the beach on a cool day and just paint what was on his mind. I love going through them and being amazed at how realistic, yet original they look. My favorite one is one he painted when he was a teenager. It's a black and white cat lying on its back with its feet and belly in the air. It has the cutest face that almost seems to look at you, and sometimes I wish it would come to life so I can cuddle it. I look back over at the pictures, still not believing that one of these paintings will never be made again, and that my parents had so much talent. Maybe that's where Matty, Kelly, and I get it from, I think.

I suddenly have the urge to talk to the pictures, like I sometimes do when I'm feeling a bit off inside. I know they are just pictures, but I think maybe somewhere they are listening, and it always makes me feel better. "Hey guys, it's Jenna again. You're probably tired of me and my problems by now, but I sort of need you. I'm pretty much the only girl in this house. I love Matty, Kelly, and Andy to death, but sometimes they just don't get it. It's impossible. The only one left is Tina, and I like her enough, but I think her work and the green monster inside me have clouded our relationship. I wish I could come and slip in the bed next to you Mom, and we could talk for all hours of the night again. Or go shopping and I could follow you around the racks because you know how to do it way better than me. Or babble to you about random school stuff when you pick me up each afternoon. Or go to the beach with you, Matty, and Kelly. Every girl needs her Mom."

I gulp and squeeze my eyes shut, for I feel tears coming, and I can't speak correctly when I start crying.

"Every girl needs a sister too. Whether it is a real one, a cousin, or a best friend, she needs someone to get excited and upset with through the days. I don't have a cousin or a best friend that I'm close to like that, Lauren, and I know we would have been inseparable. I wish you could have grown up so I could know who you are. I look at that carving often and trace it, clinging on to that little piece of you that I have. It's not right that you had to be sick. It's just not fair."

I look over to the frame of Dad and think I feel my heart explode. "I know you would be big by now. You would be touching others with what you could create. Sometimes I think it's my fault that you didn't follow your dreams before you died. I'm one of your kids, and between Lauren being sick, and the rest of us being little, you didn't have the time or the budget to continue after the EP. If you didn't have us, you and Mom could be touring everywhere by now. I know Matty thinks it's all on him, but that's not true. Maybe it's not anyone's fault. Maybe the world is just messed up. It seems that the good hearts of the world have horrible things happen to them, like our family or Andy and his cancer, while the bad people come out just fine and hurt others. I can't stand it when amazing guys get hurt. It seems like the world is being robbed because they are hard to find."

I feel a tear escape and run down my cheek. I quickly wipe it away, clench my teeth, and close my eyes. "I want my daddy! I want him to come in and give me a hug and tell me that I'm the most beautiful girl in the world, just like my mother. I want him to tell me that he'll fight off anyone who is mean to me, and that even if I don't find a guy good enough, he will always be here for me. If no one will ever love me and my writing, he will. And that will be alright because he's the most wonderful guy in the universe, near impossible to beat. And more than that, I want him to say that he'll always believe in me, and will never let me live in that dream I had last night." I open my eyes and look up back at his pictures. "I want you to play guitar for me. You shouldn't be dead." It comes out as a whisper because that's all I can manage at the moment.

I need to listen to some music and search all around for Bower. I need to listen to the song "Since You've Been Gone" by Theory of a Deadman. It's perfect for when I feel this way because it seems the words came straight from my heart. It talks about someone breaking your heart by not being there, and you need to hear from them. Bower is nowhere to be found at the moment. Kelly must have him like he always does when I need him most. Luckily, I know all the words to the song and sing it as I sit back down in front of the pictures. At some points, I get choked up and have to stop to breathe a minute before I can finish.

"I'm okay now," I say when I'm finished. "Andy and Tina's wedding is in a month. It's pretty much planned out by now since they've been working at it since last September. It's going to be on the beach like I've always wanted my wedding to be. Ryan, Andy's best friend from the band, is going to be best man, and Tina's best friend Amber is the maid of honor. I get to be one of the bridesmaids and Matty stands on Andy's side, so we get to go to all the rehearsals soon. Tanner and Spencer are little ring bearers, and Tina's niece, who I only met once, is the flower girl. She seems nice enough, so it should be a good time. Tina helped me pick out a pretty dress, and I'm excited to wear that. And she sent invitations to all of her past second grade class right before the year ended, so they will probably be all there, which I think is cute."

"We get to spend the week after with Grandma, so Andy and Tina can go to Hawaii for their honeymoon." I laugh. "I keep telling them that I'm jealous, but Andy says I won't be when I hear he threw up all over the plane during a ten hour flight. I told them to take lots of pictures for me, and Matty said to go to North Shore and ride the waves. Somehow I can't picture Andy riding any waves, especially record tall ones like those. He seems more of a snorkeler to me, but I'm sure that's not what Matty meant. I just know my brother has an image of Tina on a surfboard in her bikini, her hair blowing in the wind, and the Hawaiian sun glistening off the crystal blue water. Teenage boys."

I smile, but then lower my eyes in embarrassment after I glance at the wedding photo. "They really love each other like you guys. I'm positive they will make it. I guess you know that I'm a little jealous of that because I want it. And I know you would tell me it will work out, but that's easy for you to say because you've already got it. Sometimes when I listen to Andy singing Tina to sleep, I just know there can't be a third. It was a miracle he almost matches up to you, Dad. The world just can't be *that* good to contain three perfect guys. I told Kelly that he has to be my boyfriend and never leave me until I find my guy, but he just stared at me like he wasn't even paying attention. So, instead I made up a character that will pay attention. That works for now."

"I don't know how you did it sometimes, Mom," I admit, looking over to the photo of the one with her and Kelly. "You finally had Dad, and then just like that, you lost him. Yet, you were still able to raise us with happiness and love. I don't think I'd be strong enough. I would probably just crumble, and my heart would give out. I'd be one of those people that die of a broken heart. I never really understood what it was like for you until I think about it just now. Here I am thinking *I'm* in pain. I really respect how much of a strong woman you always will be, and I hope I can be like that and make you proud."

"Yes, that's what I'll do. I'll make you all proud. I will not settle until I am everything I can ever dream of becoming." I look over all the photos, through my room, and out of the windows triumphantly. I take all the pictures in my arms and hug them to my chest. "I love you all more than the sun loves to shine on your face, the wind loves to blow your hair, the stars love to twinkle in your eyes, and the moon loves to smile at you. I want to protect you longer than gravity will keep the universe in orbit, and I will even if I have to give everything for it."

I hear footsteps thumping downstairs and the faint sounds of the television. They seem to soothe me as I stand there, hugging pictures and spinning in my swivel chair with my eyes shut tight.

"Jenna, come here right now!" Kelly's voice echoes through the house, and it sounds frantic. I don't really want to go down there at this moment, but it is my responsibility to help him if he needs it. I place the pictures nicely back where they were on my desk and swing open my door with force. I walk out to the catwalk to see Kelly standing in the family room, holding the TiVo remote and looking like he just saw a ghost. The TiVo is paused, but the glare makes me not be able to see what's on it from this angle. It's probably some new album he wants and is excited to show me about it. But something about his face seems to tell me this is something more.

"What is it Kells?" I ask, hoping something isn't seriously wrong.

He beckons me down wildly with his free hand. "Come here. You won't believe what I just saw."

I can't help but let out a little sigh at having to leave what I was doing. This seems important to him, and I'm curious as to what he thinks I won't believe, so I join him in the family room. "What?" I look at him expectantly. He looks like he's going burst with anticipation in a moment. I smile to myself at how interesting he is as he hits the play button.

302

The TV clip starts to play and I completely understand all the emotions I saw in him. I feel my eyes widen as I stare in disbelief at what I'm watching. I watch through it, not daring to miss a second, and when it's over, I want to watch it again. It was beautiful and just perfect in all ways. I love it. "You're right. I don't believe it."

He nods, smiling, and I can tell he feels the same way about it. Matty and Andy have to see this. I remember involuntarily hearing his car pull up, but he never came inside, so they must be both outside. Kelly must have been thinking the same thing, because we both dash for the front door at the exact same moment. We both pry open the door together, and Matty and Andy look up at us quizzically.

"You guys have to come in and see this. Kelly, go rewind it again so it's at the beginning." They both look completely confused but get up as Kelly rushes back to the family room. We hear the nice purr of a muffler and look up to see Tina's orange Mustang GT pull in the driveway. Perfect timing. She should be included for this too.

"Matty, go get Tina and bring her in here too," I order, and he's more than happy to oblige. "We'll be inside waiting."

He nods and runs down the sidewalk at full speed, meeting her just as she gets out of her car.

I pace the length of the front yard that's parallel to the sidewalk and twists around the front of the house to the garage, back and forth, over and over. The grass feels soft on the bottoms of my bare feet, and the cool June wind feels refreshing as it rushes through my hair, across my face, and makes the front of my clothes stick to me. I look up at the sky and squint as the sun fills my sensitive blue eyes. A stray, white, puffy cloud slides over in front of it and makes it comfortable to look up. I smile. "Thanks for that," I tell it and feel ever more thankful that it seems fairly large and is moving slowly. That way I have some time.

I tilt my head as far back as it is comfortable, and gravity causes my hair to slide off my forehead and ears and hang from the back of my head in a cone shape. My jaw falls open a little, which I also blame gravity for doing. I shove my hands in my pockets and take a seat on the top step, keeping my head in the same position. This is my favorite thing to do. Something about sitting outside on a nice day, just watching the bright blue sky and harmless white cumulus clouds, is the most peaceful thing I will ever experience. I could stare at it for days and never get tired of it, just like in that barn. So, while Jenna is inside writing and Kelly is lying down listening to his music, I'm out here watching the sky and pondering life.

A lone bird glides in front of the cloud and flies in a circle. I wonder what it's like to be a bird, flying up there alone and looking down on the rest of the world. I like to look down from an aeroplane and see all the little squares of farmland and the cars traveling down the highway that look like dots. I think being a bird would be just like that, except more free because you are suspended in mid air, not strapped to a seat that's been thrown up on multiple times. I can't help thinking that that bird is lucky to be able to feel that.

I watch the sky a bit longer and see some more clouds slowly moving in toward the sun. They seem so close that I could reach out and touch them, yet they are miles and miles away, and if I touched them, my fingers would most likely freeze and fall off of my hand. For me, the sky is like looking up at another world or alternate universe full of wonder that we all know someday we may reach. My mind always races at even the thought of it.

I have always loved science, everything about it and every subject, but astronomy will always hold my heart. I guess I like it so much because there is so much we don't know and so much to learn. And best of all, some things we will never know for sure, so there's room left to make guesses. It seems crazy to me that this world, which we think of as so vast compared to us, is so miniscule compared to the rest of space. How small does that make us? Do we even have a purpose? Space and even our universe was doing just fine before any kind of life came along, so why did we?

They say everything has to start from nothing to become something, but my mind can't grasp that word nothing. There must have been some kind of small atom that started off everything and blew up in the Big Bang Theory and kept expanding until we had space and all the stuff in it. But does that mean that there is an infinite supply of nothing for space to expand into and fill up? What is nothing anyway? Even air and space have *something* in them.

I shake all those thoughts out of my head before I give myself a major headache. I focus on the sun, a small circle beneath the clouds. The only thing that gives us light and heat and keeps our world from floating off into space in all directions forever and ever. It's hard to believe that I'm made out of the same stuff as the sun. I hold up my hand and look real close, but all I see is my tan skin with some blue veins visible underneath. It looks pretty solid, but all it is is a bunch of cells packed together in intricate ways to make everything in my body. And all those cells are made of atoms from stardust, just like every other living thing on this planet.

I start to get the feeling that the glue holding all my pieces together could stop holding any minute, and I could crumble into a million invisible atoms, never to be found again. I cringe at that thought and say to myself, "Okay *that* won't happen. I hope." I shake my arms around wildly to make sure nothing will fall off and am happy to see that everything stays intact and no big chunks fall away. I imagine little pieces that I can't see falling off silently until one by one, I'm chipped away to nothing. I pull my arms close to me and lower my head to ground level.

I look out over the horizon and suddenly feel very alone. I imagine Mom, Dad, and Lauren sitting just at the point where the blue sky reaches the land. I could keep running after them forever but never reach them, because the world is round, and the horizon will always be the same distance away. I miss them very much and hope if they are that there, somewhere I can't see, that they are together watching me and feeling very proud. I hope they know I do love them and wish they were here, but I will live my life to the fullest without them. I will let the ghosts of their memories fill me with happiness that they *were* there instead of sadness that they aren't anymore. I didn't want to have to go on without them, but I certainly can. It's my duty.

"You did well by me. I love you more," I say to that horizon where I imagine they are, one corner of my mouth turning up in a genuine smile. "Well, you know the rest."

I hear a car and look over to see Andy returning from his mysterious endeavor. He waves to me as he gets out and walks up the sidewalk toward me. I wave back, and he comes up and stands off to the side next to me.

"What are you doing out here?"

I shrug. "Just watching the sky and thinking."

"Mind?" I shake my head, so he takes a seat beside me on the steps. His long legs have to reach down two steps so his knees don't touch his chest.

"Where'd you disappear to?" I ask, noticing that he looks just as bothered as me.

"Saw my dad," he replies, refusing to look at me. I analyze him, and it occurs to me that we aren't much different. Just because he's older, doesn't mean he can't think, worry, and get excited about the same things. I never thought about that before.

"Yeah? How did that go?"

He looks up at the sky, involuntarily tracing the strips of color on his arms. "I don't know. I guess he's better, but I'm not used to him like that. Nice and all. I still feel really bad for putting him there, even though it was to help him, and I would rather get yelled at for it than have him tell me he understands my reasons. It sounds completely ridiculous, but the yelling would make me feel better."

I laugh. "Yeah, it sort of does. But I get it."

He smiles too, his eyes growing narrower. "Stacy was there too. She dropped by just as I was about to leave. I'm still getting used to her being nice to me too. When we were little, we used to be best friends. We went everywhere together, and one of us wouldn't want to get candy in the supermarket unless the other was getting some too. Then she got to be sixteen, got a car, and thought she was too cool for a twelve year old. She never really came home much; she was always at parties or out doing God knows what with her friends and guys. When she did come home, she didn't say two words to me unless she needed money or to mess with my fragile mind, and before long, I hated her. Not like I want to kill you hate, but I don't want you around until you grow up kind. Especially when she would scream and fight with everyone about her life choices and how she was a mature adult who could make decisions. I was always more mature than her, and that is saying something."

He looks over to me and I can't help but laugh. Andy is definitely not the most mature person you will ever meet, and I'm sure it wasn't any better when he was a kid. Stacy must have been really bad. He laughs too and continues, "When I got cancer, she came around to visit some, but it always seemed like she was uncomfortable and had other things she'd rather be doing. I really missed the time with her at first, but it faded by the time Tina came around, so I told her, 'If it is a chore to come see me, then don't do the chore.' She didn't come back."

"Her brother had cancer and she thought it was a chore to visit? What's her problem? You could have died."

He nods. "Yeah. But something was always messed up with her that she didn't care that much. Maybe it was denial that she honestly didn't believe I was fighting for my life, and she had nothing to worry about. I'll never know. Anyway, when I recovered, she decided the best thing to do was to pick up smoking and flaunt it in my face every time she saw me. She thought that was showing me that it was just bad luck that gave you lung cancer, and that she wasn't scared."

I honestly can't believe that. I don't know much about lung cancer, but I heard it's very painful, and it's unlikely that you recover. More than leukemia. Stacy's little brother could have died, and she wouldn't have cared. I wouldn't leave Kelly or Jenna's side if it happened to them. I start to feel bad that I ever didn't like this guy. He did so much for us and he is a great guy. My admiration for him turned to jealousy before I knew it. My stupid jealousy, for no good reason, and some need for dominance got in the way of me seeing that. I suddenly feel really ignorant, and I'm embarrassed of that. That admiration is coming back.

"Now that has all changed," he continues. "Just like everything else. Most of it is good and I guess this should be too. But she hasn't been a part of my life for so long, and now she's trying to push into it. It's not that easy. She's different than when we used to be best friends, and it's like trying to get to know a stranger. Does that sound awful?"

"No," I reply, shaking my head. "It makes perfect sense. I never knew she was ever that mean to you. I'm glad Jenna isn't older than me. Not that she would do that to me, but I don't want to take the risk. I would call us close twins, and I don't want to lose that."

He smiles warmly. "I don't think you will." He looks me over, like he's analyzing me, and his expression changes. "What have you been thinking about out here?"

I take a deep breath. "Way too much to talk about."

"I know you don't really like talking to me or like me at all. I get that, but I don't want something bothering you."

"No, it's not that. I actually do like talking to you. I may not like you like Jenna does, that would be creepy, but you're pretty awesome, and I'm grateful to you. Without you, we'd be rotting in jail or dead maybe. Sometimes I even want to *be* you. It's just that what I was thinking about was deep. It was all about the universe, how small the world is, how my atoms could stop sticking together, and that I could run forever and not reach the horizon. And birds are lucky to fly in the alternate universe of the sky, and that maybe my parents and Lauren are somewhere watching me."

As soon as I say it, I know it sounds crazy. I can tell by Andy's face he does too. "I told you it was way too much to talk about," I add in a mutter.

"I'm just surprised. You've got quite the scientific mind. I never thought about any of that. I thought about nothingness and how people see the world differently, but never stuff that deep."

I like to hear that. "I want to be an astrophysicist, so maybe I can answer some of these millions of questions that go unanswered in my mind. Can I ask you one of them?"

"I'm positive I won't know the answer, but sure."

I look out back over the horizon. "Do you think there are other people out there? Not on Earth I mean. Not even in this galaxy. There are so many objects in space-planets, comets, asteroids, stars, meteors, and some things we may not know about. Do you think, somewhere too far away to ever travel in a lifetime, there are other living things? Things that can love, hate, cry, laugh, talk, think, write, play music, dance, and do math problems? Do you think they are busy studying their own world and their own universe and wonder the same things about how it all began? Most importantly, do you think there's one of them right now wondering if we're out here thinking about them?"

He laughs to himself a little and looks over at me, his eyes glistening. "I never even thought about that. That would be so cool. Maybe there are other people really far away that look really weird and have their own society, completely oblivious to ours. Maybe they are looking for us while we're looking for them, and one day we'll find each other. Then they'll think we look weird because they think three eyes and fifty arms is the norm."

"Imagine what it would be like if there was breeding between us and them."

His eyes widen. "Oh, now *that* would be an alien!"

"Our worst fears in horror movies would come true."

"Yeah," he agrees. "I'm glad I'll be dead by the time we find them."

"Maybe it's best we don't. Maybe we should just stay here and feel a connection with them because we know they are there, and they can do the same."

We laugh hysterically together thinking of some three-eyed, fifty-armed creature sitting on the steps of its home, looking out over the horizon of its world and wondering if we're out here doing the same. In that moment, I feel really glad that things turned out the way they did. My life just wouldn't be the same without Andy and his strange mind in it or Tina and that strange feeling she gives me. Or their families and how weird those gatherings can get. We never had those before, so we didn't know what they were like. I'd much rather be here at this house with them and the great things that lay ahead of me than anywhere else, especially with the creatures we talked about. In some twisted sort of way, things turned out for the best with what we had left.

When we stop laughing, Andy stares at me and smirks. Before I can ask what he's thinking now, he asks, "You ever heard that song "Time" by Hootie and the Blowfish?"

I think a bit before it comes to me. "Yeah, I think Dad had that album."

"It reminds me of you."

I think of how it's all about how time is the enemy and how the one line says 'I don't believe in time.' I don't feel that way as much as I used to, but there still is some truth in it. "That's understandable. Any weird song reminds me of you."

I look to see his reaction, and I'm glad to see he gets the joke. People who get all mad and uptight about that kind of thing don't mix well with me. "Great. So you think I'm off my rocker?" There's a hint of sarcasm in his voice.

"No," I correct. "I think you never *found* your rocker."

He laughs and his laugh makes me laugh. It's all squeaky and dramatic. "That's a new one. I'll never find it though. I'll stay here with my dry cereal, three-fourths eaten sandwiches, and crazy thoughts, hoping people love me."

"That's *why* people love you."

"Well then good. I'll do well in life." He leans in real close like what he's about to say is a big secret. "Just so you know, I don't think you ever found yours either. Especially with all those deep thoughts you were just having."

"And I wouldn't change a thing."

The front door bursts open with great force at that moment, and we turn around to see Jenna and Kelly standing in the doorway. The matching expressions on their faces make me wonder what in the world they have been doing. You would have thought those creatures had come to get them while we were out here making jokes about it all. We wait to see if they are going to tell us to come save them.

"You guys have to come in and see this. Kelly, go rewind it again so it's at the beginning." Jenna sounds very serious, and it makes me really confused. I glance over at Andy, and he is obviously feeling the same way. Kelly runs inside as he is told. We stand up to go inside and see what's going on, when that gorgeous Mustang appears in the driveway. Tina is home from school.

"Matty, go get Tina and bring her in here too," Jenna orders, and I feel like going to see her. "We'll be inside waiting."

308

I nod and run down the sidewalk as Andy and Jenna go inside to where Kelly is. I meet Tina just as she is getting out of the car and closing the door. She is carrying a lot of things, and I take some for her so she doesn't drop it.

"Kelly and Jenna just came out and said they saw something really amazing. We have to go inside immediately and see it. I have no clue what it could be."

"Well then, we better go find out," she replies, walking with me toward the house. I feel so happy now that Andy and I are friends, and I'm being gentlemanly by helping Tina. I know that whatever is waiting inside will make me only feel happier.

I've always been afraid of hospitals. Not that I just don't like them-I'm truly afraid. I always think that all the air is just swirling with germs ready to silently creep inside me and attack my body. If I hurt myself when I was younger and had to go to the hospital, I would shake and cling to myself, hoping maybe I could shrink inside myself and not be touched by the air. Then Stacy would push me, and I would fall on the waiting room chair, screaming and feeling contaminated with flesh-eating bacteria. Stupid fear? Yes, but it never went away. All that time I spent locked away in a hospital room during my cancer treatment certainly didn't help. It was a bit better because I was already pretty much dying and didn't think any of those germs could make that much worse. But still, every time I had to go to a hospital after that, it was like telling me that after nearly a year of hell, now that I was out, I shouldn't be afraid of being sucked in and burned again. It doesn't really work that way.

Stupid fears are my thing though. I used to think that if I walked across an open field, I would fall into one of those hidden traps that people hide with sticks and leaves to make it look like the regular ground, and even the strongest person can't claw their way out of and save themselves. I'm clearly not the strongest person, so I would die a slow death down there of starvation or something of the sort, alone. I never told anyone that. I just made up a really good excuse why we should walk somewhere else.

Of all my fears, and trust me there are a lot, the worst is my father. Sometimes I would get so angry with him, I would do what I knew he would hate deliberately. But when the adrenaline wore off, I would just get scared of what he'd do to me for it. I feared he would get fed up and kill me. I knew he was crazy enough for it and smart enough that no one would be able to prove it. That fear is what drove my entire life into shambles. Funny to think those kids were my saviors.

Now here I am, sitting in my car, staring at the large building ahead of me, all my worst fears welling up inside. A mental institution is the worst kind of hospital, and my father is inside it. Not only that, I put him there, and there is no telling how he'll react. I'm pretty sure the doctors won't let him hurt me, but I can't help my mind going to the worst case scenario. He has already attempted to murder me once.

So many times I have done this. I've spent hours convincing myself that I'm strong enough to just march in there, and I've sat here in this same position every time. Then I start not to be able to breathe and turn the car around toward home like a coward. This time will be different. I have to do it this time instead of just thinking about it constantly.

It takes everything I have inside me to step out of the car and make it within reach of the door of the building. "I'm so weak," I curse myself and my fears. "I'm about to be married and I'm still a little baby boy." I'm disgusted with myself for this feeling of sheer terror at something stupid. Other people can just come in easily. Hell, people *work* here just fine, and here I am, a grown man about to burst into tears. Sometimes I wish I can have some time away from myself, but I'm not that lucky. I wonder if anyone else feels that way.

"It can't be that bad," I convince myself, thrusting open the door and charging in with determination. "I'm strong, smart, and amazing."

I make it to the desk, and an elderly woman looks up at me. "Hello, are you here on a scheduled visit?" She asks, smiling.

I nod. "Yeah, I'm here for my dad, Andrew Thompson Sr."

Her smile fades. "Are you sure? You've cancelled very often."

That is the last thing she should have asked because I am not sure at all. I hear a shrill scream echo through the building, making everything worse. I feel my whole body tense up, quickly losing all that nerve I'd taken so long to build up.

The woman senses my fear and touches my hand to comfort me. I nearly jump out of my skin, making her jump as well. She quickly recovers herself and says, "That's just Maria. She thinks the meds are given to her to poison her. Every day she screams when they try to give them to her. You don't have to worry."

I imagine a skinny, sweaty woman in ragged clothes trying to hurt the doctors that are trying to give her her pills, completely out of her mind. I shake it away and reply, "Yeah, okay."

"Really," she assures me. "You can stop shaking." I look down and see my hands are shaking uncontrollably. I clench them into fists to stop it.

"Can I go now?" I want to get this over with more than anything. I know I will feel so much better then.

She nods. "I would just tell you what room, but I'll be nice and escort you."

I give her a weak smile and follow her down a long hallway past many closed doors. There are windows on each of them, but I don't dare look in them. Instead, I focus on my new tattoos. I got one on each bicep just a few months ago on March 3rd as my birthday treat to myself. My left arm has a large, beautiful G clef. The kids, especially Jenna, encouraged me to get it because their dad had one just like it. Plus it fit me. On my right arm, there are two eighth notes connected by a beam, with a tiny heart underneath. Obviously it means I love music, and the beamed eighth note has always been my favorite symbol. I smile, feeling very proud of them and how good they look next to the colorful bands winding around my triceps and the tiny palm tree on my left hand.

The woman stops at a door, and looking down at my arms, I bump right into the back of her. I snap my head up and apologize.

"This is your father's room," she says, obviously getting a little fed up with me.

I stare at the door. It looks exactly like the other ones, except there's a plaque next to it reading "A. Thompson". I gulp, thinking it said the same thing next to *my* hospital room. The woman still stands there, so I open the door just a crack. I hold it there a minute, fighting the urge to close it and run, and give myself a chance to calm down. She encourages me to keep going, so I swing the door open all the way, step inside, and close it. I watch her walk back down the hall through the window. I've come this far, I think. There is no way I'm turning back now.

I whirl around and see my father sitting on his bed. There is a nightstand with a picture of Mom on it next to him, a chair across the room, and a bare-looking table. I look back to my father, and he just stares at me. No ragged clothes or dirty hair. No bony, sickly figure from refusing to eat. No beady eyes nervously searching the room in paranoia. Just my father, looking as he always has, sitting on a bed and looking at me.

"Hello Andrew," he says calmly. I try to read his expression, but his face is showing no signs.

"Hey Dad," I shuffle my feet, trying to think of something to say. I come up with, "How are you?" How original.

He smiles, and it isn't a sinister smirk either. It's a genuine smile that lights his eyes. "I'm much better, and I have you to thank." He walks over to the chair and slides it my way. I sit reluctantly, still not sure if this niceness is an act. "You look good kid. What's been going on? I thought you'd visit me sooner. You're the only one who hasn't."

I look down, suddenly unable to meet his gaze and feeling a bit silly. "I've been busy," I say, only half lying. "That sounds awful. I'm sorry. Not just for not visiting, but for putting you in here. I know what it's like to stare at four bland walls so long with nurses tiptoeing around you."

He chuckles. "Yes, I'm about to break down the walls and run away." I let my mouth twitch a bit in a small laugh, still looking at my memory filled Chucks. "Andrew, look at me."

I lift my eyes to meet his. "It's really alright," he assures me, and I can tell it's genuine. I feel a rush of relief flood over me, making every fear I had of coming here spill out on the floor. They really helped him.

He continues, "The only thing you should be sorry about is not bringing me here sooner. I know I wasn't very willing, but it hurts me to think of all those wasted years. All that time in blind, crazy rage and all I put you, your mother, and Stacy through. I'm so deeply sorry for ruining your life. I completely understand why you wouldn't want to visit me."

"My life isn't ruined," I argue. "You were ill. It's not your fault that things happened. I only didn't come because I was a bit scared you'd lash out at me."

He throws his hands in the air, disgusted with himself. "This is what I've done. I've made my own son afraid of me. I was always hardest on you because I had this vision of my son being a clone of me. When I saw you weren't headed in that direction, I got so angry and used that fear you had to force you into what I wanted. I would have done anything." He sucks in air. "I can't believe I went so far. I was so wrong. To think that you could be dead by my hands makes me sick."

I watch his expression become hard, and one small drop of water escapes his eyes and falls on his cheek. He wipes it away with his thumb. This is a first for my eyes to see. I've seen him fuming, throwing things, screaming, and acting like an animal some days, but never crying.

"Dad, I'm fine." I have absolutely no hard feelings towards him. Yes, he did more than you can ever imagine over the years and mentally abused me and my family, but that man is not sitting in front of me. He was sick and things have turned out for me anyway. I've had time to let myself forgive him. "I have a bullet-hole scar on my chest, but it makes me look tough. Goes well with my chemo scars."

That smile returns, making me feel better. "On a lighter note, how have things been with you? I want to know who my Andrew truly is."

I beam, eager to share. "The kids have been living with me since you got in here and are doing well. I love them so much, and I think you would too once you patched things up. I can't imagine what they would be going through if I hadn't come along. And," I pause for effect and continue casually, "I'm engaged."

His eyes widen. "How long?" How come your mom or sister didn't tell me?"

"They thought you'd want to hear it from me," I shrug. "I proposed, in song no less, back in September, and my big day will be at the beach next month."

His face falls when he hears that. "I wish you the best the luck."

"I was thinking, if you're up to it, I could get you out of here to attend."

"Up to it? I wouldn't miss it." He winks at me. "What do you think of a second Mrs. Thompson?"

"Hmm. Mrs. Thompson to her next class. Kristina Lynne Thompson. I love it." I truly do. It sounds so right, so meant to be.

He laughs at my answer. "I say it's about time. And you have those kids around the house already so you can focus on other things. I'm looking forward to making amends with them and your bride."

I nod. What he said about focusing on other things jolts my memory. "I made this for you." I pull a wrapped CD from my breast pocket and hand it to him. "I'm sort of in a band now, so I thought I'd let you hear a bit of our music. I'm lead, so I wrote most of it."

He holds it and leans back, as if trying to look at it from another angle. "God. You're talent and potential were always what I hated, but now I'm just thinking of how I'll be flying in your private jet to Fiji when you get rich and famous."

I laugh in relief. That's his way of saying he supports and believes in me. I'm not sure how to take it. That's something I've wanted my whole life and gave up on long ago. Now I have it and feel so light and happy. I know he will love my music no matter what. That's all that counts.

The door creaks open, and I turn around to see Stacy standing in the doorway. She is surprised to see me. "Andy? Wow, never thought I'd see you here."

"Just visiting as you are Stacy."

"I just came to give Dad this," she says, holding a book. She turns to him. "It's from Mom. She couldn't make it." He laughs when he sees the cover and thanks her.

"Sure. I'm going to visit later in the week. Right now I've got Spencer and Tanner in the car. We're going to Funland."

"Ooh!" I cheer, showing fake enthusiasm. "Randy too?"

She laughs out loud. "Of course not! He's off with friends."

I get an image of Randy in Funland, the loud, crowded, chaotic amusement park of the Rehoboth boardwalk, and know it was a stupid question. "Shouldn't you be wedding planning with your fiancée?" she asks, putting emphasis on the last word. "Or spending time with your kids? I'm sure Jenna misses you. That girl *loves* you!" Dad raises his eyebrows, and I tell him not to listen to her.

"Making amends with Dad was most important, and I'm so glad I did." I look to him, and he nods in agreement. "Plus, Jenna has a harmless crush. That's all."

She rolls her eyes, smirking. "Sure, sure. I just never thought I'd be fighting off young girls too when you're older. I should have known though because every girl has always hit on you. My sexy little brother, who looks just like me."

She kneels next to me and puts her arm around my shoulders. "You wish," I joke.

She gasps, acting like that hurt her tremendously. "We're more similar than you know. Both were never into the school scene. I was out shopping and partying while you were busy having jam sessions. Now we're both chasing our dreams-me with my fashion and you with your music. We're going to be very rich siblings."

I nod. "Oh yeah. Even if we both took the long route to success."

"Funny how life works. I hope we can be best buds again."

We could at least try. "For now I think you better get back to your kids."

Her eyes widen as she remembers her boys. She jumps up. What a fabulous mother she is. "I'll be back soon. Before I depart, you must notice Andy's newest ink additions." She points to my tattoos. Dad was never really big on them, and I know she's just instigating.

"Very fitting," he comments, admiring them. I shoot Stacy a 'haha you didn't cause a fight' look, and she sulks.

"I think I better follow you out," I tell her. "I left the kids home alone."

I get up and Dad follows. "It was really nice to see you." I nod in agreement, and he pulls me into a pretty awkward hug. He pats me on the back, making it a bit difficult to breathe. "I love you Andrew, even if I don't show it sometimes."

"Love you too Dad." I pull away.

"If you're not too busy, I'm hoping to see you again before the wedding."

It seems like a question, so I reply, "I'm sure I can make time for you." Now that I know what it's like in here, I have no reason to be afraid to come. I take one last look at my father and follow Stacy down the hall confidently. Even the woman at the desk notices and smiles at me as I leave, heading back to my Miata. Next time I see her, things will go way more smoothly.

I take the way home slowly, enjoying my car. She's my beauty, no matter how much Ryan wants to make jokes. He says she's so small that if I ever got in an accident, I would snap like a twig. I just have to be careful and try to fight my unwilling attraction to fatal situations.

I start to become nervous. I grip the wheel and eye every car like it's going to come careening through my windshield. A bird flies by, and if anyone were around, they would have thought a three year old girl watching a horror movie was driving.

I want to fall out of the car and dramatically kiss the ground by the time I make it to the driveway. I refrain from that though because Matty is outside on the steps, and he already thinks I'm weird enough. I casually stroll up the walk and ask him if I can join him. He doesn't suspect my recent panic attack, so I feel safe to talk.

Out of the three kids, Matty is the one who confuses me most. It's clear where Jenna stands with me-she thinks I hold the world on my shoulders and can do no wrong. I don't dare tell her that's far from the truth and risk crushing an amazing young girl. Kelly seems to look up to me too, even though he is afraid to show it most of the time. I see so much talent and potential in that kid, and I'm committed to letting him know that I love and support him. But Matty is different. He likes Tina a lot, but has some problem with me. He didn't trust me from the first time he saw me, and something tells me he's threatened. Whether he thinks I'm trying to replace his dad or challenging his leadership, I don't know. He has grown up too fast, way more than the other two, and has taken the position as protector of his family. I think the only reason he let me help is because of those incredible carvings, and now he's just putting up with me. All I want to do is take care of things for him so he can be a kid. My childhood was rocky, and I didn't have it *nearly* as bad.

When I came into this, I was afraid the girl and the little kid would be the problem. What an interesting turn of events. I just want him to love me like I love him and his siblings. I may be no good with kids, get all nervous trying to talk to them, and rely on Tina for stuff like packing lunches and signing midterms, but I'm giving everything I have to be there for them and give them semi-normal lives, and I always will. Plus, even if they have no clue, they give me so much in return.

I jump at the chance to talk one on one with Matty, maybe have him open up a little and clear things up. I awkwardly sit on the steps beside him, my stick legs reaching down two steps. And talk we do. He asks about my morning's endeavors, and I tell him about visiting my father. I leave out the fear I had, but pretty much spill otherwise. I tell him about how things were with Dad and Stacy when I was younger, how Stacy and I used to be very close but she changed and forgot about me, and how that felt. I've never said much to the kids about Stacy, mainly because I was bitter, but now I say everything. How she treated me during my cancer, picked on me afterwards, and just recently is trying to be friendly. I tell him how both her and my father are trying to be nice and make up for lost time, but it's not that easy for me. To me, they are strangers pushing their way into my life after I'd patched up the hole they left long before.

Matty seems like he genuinely cares and feels comfortable to share what he's been doing all morning. I can't hide my surprise when he tells of his deeps thoughts of the universe and life. I know he is a wise and mature science kid, but this kind of stuff takes a certain kind of extraordinary person. I feel like I could learn so much from searching his brain and feel stupid that I thought of falling in traps and jumping into crowds of fans when I was his age. Even now I'm not that insightful. I think of some deep things, especially with my different eyes theory, but they don't seem that deep compared to his thoughts.

He makes my mind go crazy places with his questions of other life forms in space. We describe aliens from far away galaxies and horror movies coming true and end up laughing hysterically. I'm sure that I've made progress with him today, and as I make jokes with him, I realize how similar we are. I can't help but wish things were this easy all the time, but something tells me that I don't have to worry.

Jenna and Kelly burst through the door behind us frantically. We turn around to see what's going on, and by the look on their faces, you would have thought a zombie was chasing them through the house with a chainsaw. Or those aliens from far away galaxies.

"You guys have to come in and see this. Kelly, go rewind it again so it's at the beginning." Jenna talks like she's going to burst soon. Kelly runs inside eagerly and Matty looks over at me, just as lost as I. We rise and are about to follow her in, when Tina rolls up the drive. I smile. Nothing better than a hot girl in a hot car.

"Matty, go get Tina and bring her in here too," Jenna orders, and he is more than happy to do so. "We'll be inside waiting."

Matty runs toward Tina, and I pretty much get drug inside by Jenna. "Are you two okay?"

Jenna nods vigorously. "More than okay." Kelly's knuckles are white from clutching the TiVo remote so tight. Whatever they want to show us is on TV, and I start to get the feeling I know what it is. I just didn't know the moment would come so soon. I act dumb though and just arch my eyebrows at them. Matty and Tina walk in, both carrying files and school things. They place them on the kitchen counter and stand next to us, waiting for Jenna and Kelly to reveal what the big deal is about. I try my best to hold in the grin that is trying to spread across my face.

"Watch this," Kelly says, pressing the play button. "Although one of us already knows exactly what is going on and decided to be sneaky." Jenna and he glare at me, and Matty and Tina eye me suspiciously. I can't hold that grin in any longer. I point to the TV, and they all turn back to watch.

What we all see next is a sort of commercial, but not quite. It is advertising the newest Vh1 You Oughta Know Artist, or rising musician that Vh1 decides to outline-a little band called Copyright 83 that I seem to know a little about, starring me, Ryan, Ty, and Leon. We talk about how it's always been our dream to write music that could be shared with the world and people would want to listen to over and over again. Ryan talks first, flipping his shoulder length curly blond hair as always, and telling the kind of music in which we specialize. His green eyes shine and it's obvious he loves the attention. Then comes Ty, Italian with his black Mohawk that makes mine look amateur, chocolate eyes, and darker skin, who talks about his dreams of the big stage. He has that brooding attitude and soulful look in his eyes that most girls seem to like. Next is Leon, long, light brown hair pulled into a ponytail, and his beard, stretching from sideburn to sideburn, curves up into a mustache. He always seems like a mountain man to me, like he belongs bundled up and hiking snow-covered mountains. Here he talks about going into his own world when he plays drums, and now he has the chance to do that for a living. Finally, I come up and tell my story about the inspiration for following my dreams of music. I then explain the song, Pictures of Life, and the meaning behind the video. Everyone turns to look at me, following the mention of their names, and have no clue what pictures I could be talking about.

I feel very proud of myself when the video begins. This is my little moment of fame, a time to shine in front of everyone and show them what they mean to me. It shows us all performing on the beach right near the forest I know so well, myself right in the middle on piano, Ryan jamming on his favorite guitar, Ty on bass on my other side, and Leon in the back going crazy on drums and making strange facial expressions like he always does. I sing, Ryan providing backing vocals, and the scene keeps switching back and forth from that to all those pictures I took during the twins' 14th birthday party. The pictures show everyone from Stacy, to Laura, to the kids on the garage floor, to Tina, which is my phone wallpaper. Everyone laughs when the picture of Randy shows up. I even added a few pictures of the forest, the lake with the big rock, Laura's house, Jenna and my shoes, Salamander, a green fishy, Matty's telescope, the carving in the deck, the kids' rooms, my music room, Tamara's barn, and our cars. I included every single significant thing about our journey this past year and how life could take so many twists and turns. These are the pictures of my life, and the song pretty much backs that up. I worked really hard to put this together, and I can see on the faces of those around me, they appreciate that.

The video ends with a picture I took recently of Tina and the kids in the kitchen. She is showing them how to use the end on the icing tube to make professional looking flowers. I thought it fitting because I learned it's important to know how to properly apply icing and to stay focused or else the cake may be ruined. Plus, it is a perfect natural picture, the kind they put in frames with a wise quote underneath and sell. The picture pretty much wraps up how far we've come since last June, and it fades out into the sun setting over the ocean, with the aid of my final piano notes.

Our band is advertised next, and the self titled album we plan to get out in about a month. We're pretty much finished recording the rest of the songs, bit by bit, since we've already been signed. Then we have to put it all together into an album that we can be proud of, me providing the art I drew. It seems crazy to me how this is all coming together. I never thought that one day I'd walk into the music section of a store and see my album on the shelf, let alone advertised on TV. I just stare at the screen minutes after it's done and thrust my phone out of my pocket. I dial Ryan's number and he mutters a "yes?" like I just woke him up.

"Did you know our sexy selves are on the television?" I ask.

He starts laughing like crazy. "Oh yes Andyman. I saw that the other day. I can't believe you just noticed. We're gonna make it big now. How can people not love us? They are sweating us *hard*."

"I know, especially with your hair flips, mountain man Leon's sob story there, and Ty's act of dark and mysterious."

"And don't forget those cute kids and your girl. And I guess you too, if nothing else."

"Oh come on now, you know you wanted me after you saw that."

"Yeah, why don't you come over and we can make out in the basement?"

My laughs come out in wheezes and Tina rolls her eyes at me. That makes the kids laugh too. "Yo bro, did you know we're wanted for a photo shoot next week?" Ryan asks when I calm down.

"What? No."

"I'll call you back later with more details. I just know they want most of you, Andrew the poster boy. Right now I just stumbled into bed from a long night, so leave me alone. Unless you want to take me up on that offer and join me."

"As much as I'd love to, I think I'll pass."

"'K then. Suit yourself." He hangs up on me, and I put my phone away. "I'm wanted for a photo shoot obviously." I tell them.

Tina's eyes widen. "First the video and now a photo shoot? I'm marrying a rock star!"

That makes me grin even more. I pull her in and the kids jump in and hug me too, telling me I'm great. As much that has changed since last year, I still am not a hugger unless I initiate it. I break it up by asking, "Who wants to dance?"

Everyone is in agreement that it sounds like a good idea at the moment. Kelly runs upstairs and comes back with one of his millions of albums. I stick it in my DVD player, which also plays CDs, and the music fills the room.

Andy a rock star? It sounds crazy, but it is coming true. Soon we'll see him up on the big stage performing for a bunch of fans. Then we can tell people that we know him and see gaping mouths. Maybe then I can get an in, and it won't be quite as hard for me to pursue a career of my own when I'm older. As a matter of fact, I won't sit around and wait for life to happen. I'll work toward my goals now, not caring if I'm only eight. I can still do something. I'll ask Andy for piano lessons and learn from him about music as a business so I'm better prepared for later. Maybe he'll even be nice enough to let me give him some tips on the sound for some of his songs. That sounds perfect. And I won't be afraid of my voice. I deserve to be heard. I'll make my parents and Lauren proud of me and feel peaceful because I turned out okay, even though they had to leave. I *will not* settle for less, and that thought makes me smile wider than I have in a long time.

I clutch Salamander as Andy cranks up one of my favorite albums, and the beautiful sound fills the entire house. I close my eyes a moment and soak it all in, seeing the symbols in my mind, and then I open them to start dancing with the others. As I dance, I think about how much I love my ears and what a beautiful invention music is. I also love that my particular mind is able to appreciate it so much. I guess I am a lucky kid after all.

I look around to all these people I love in this great home. Life may have horrible things in store at times but guess what? It goes on, and sometimes things work out like this-just fine.

K̲elly is so adorable, filling his entire body with the music, Salamander in hand. I love that little kid more than I ever thought I could. In fact, the same is true for everyone that I'm dancing with now. Matty, even when he's annoying, I thank the heavens every day I had a twin. It's an experience only a few lucky people get to have. Tina, how sweet and caring she always is and how perfect she fits in with us. Andy, how much he did to save our lives and how cute he looks right now dancing happily. I can't wait until he is up there on the stage pouring his heart out, and then jumping off of it, completely trusting his fans to hold him up. He deserves that and so much more for how absolutely perfect he is to us.

All that I was feeling earlier fades away. I feel Mom, Dad, and Lauren with me, and they always will be, watching over and making sure things are okay for me. And Tina and Andy are perfect for each other. I will have a guy of my own one day, but for now, I just like them both around, and I wouldn't change a thing.

Matty looks over at me when we start dancing and whispers, "Familiar?" in my ear. I look over at Andy and see a flash of that video Grandma showed us of Dad and us dancing around to music. How perfectly coincidental. I wink to let him know that I understand what he's talking about, and he just laughs and turns away.

So here I am, blessed with all this-this home, these siblings, these angels sent from Mom and Dad to look after me. And I know in this moment that when I get our story out there in book form, it will be a best seller. After all, who wouldn't just adore us and our journey?

I̲ was right. Seeing that video of Andy and all the pictures of our journey the past year made me even happier. I no longer feel bitter toward Andy. He's just a good guy that's trying to help us not be messed up out there on our own. And he's great for my Krissy. I'll just settle for being her little man. One day, I'll be listening to his music, thinking about this moment when the future lies ahead of us with so many possibilities. What looked so glum in the aftermath of that fire, turned into this. Jenna and I will be in high school in just a few short months, Kelly will be moving on to third grade, even though he could probably pass fifth already, Andy is on his way to being a rock star that everyone will be jealous we know, and Tina is about to have her big wedding day and change her name plaque outside her classroom door.

I look around at everyone dancing and wonder again if in another galaxy there could be creatures just like us that lead these wild lives. If not, that is okay, because in this moment, I feel so far from alone that it doesn't matter. Andy reminds me of Dad dancing around with us in the living room in that tape Grandma had. In fact, this is like an accidental reenactment, and I have to see if Jenna realizes that.

I get her attention, and then slide in close so that I can whisper "Familiar?" in her ear. She looks up for a minute to process what I said, and then winks at me. I just turn away, laughing. This is what I love about having a twin. We get each other, and that's pretty useful in most situations. All that time I pick on her is just for fun. I totally understand why she feels the way she does now, and there's nothing to show you love someone more than to tease them to the point of humiliation. That's just how we roll in this home.

Like I said, one day I'll look back on this and think "man how did I get so lucky?" I don't think I'll ever know the answer to that question, but I'll take the luck. I don't mind it.

Who would have thought twelve short months, about 365 days, can take you on this roller coaster ride? A normal year for me would have included suffering case work with my father and Detective Jones' hatred for me, fighting with Stacy as she dropped off her kids, listening to my mother beg me to propose as Tina's pleading eyes say she wants me to, but her mouth tells me she loves me enough that it's okay, and overall being moderately miserable. Nothing important happening, nothing special affecting me forever. Just dull moments filling non-memorable days that mixed into one messed up life I had. There was no way out.

Then there came a case that teamed up with my wild, imaginative mind, and before long, I was on the ride of my life. This year I will never forget. Each day was important, each moment making up this happiness that I feel. I am going to achieve my dreams in the future, and I can't wait. I will be a big music star who's married to the best girl in the world, living in a resort area. My dad is well again, Stacy and I are on our way to be being better, and best of all, I have these kids. I'm free, and I owe them everything I will ever have.

To Matty, who taught me how strong a young boy can be when trying to protect his family. One day I'll be so proud when I see him making new discoveries important to our kind.

To Jenna, who taught me how amazing a young girl can be and just how much of a hold she can have on your heart. One day I'll be so proud to see her books out there on the shelves with all those awards on the covers.

To Kelly, who taught me that it doesn't matter how young you are, you can still make a great impact on the world. One day he'll replace me up on the stage and probably be a million times greater. For now, I'll pass on what I know.

Tina and these kids are everything that I've grown to love. They are my family in some messed up way that only we can have. Ah, what a weird bunch we are.

About the Author

Nikki Dumigan is a sophomore in high school, living just outside of the beach town of Rehoboth, Delaware. Writing of any kind is something she has never been able to live without since elementary school, when she wrote her first short story, and also something she never expects to grow out of. The things that happen to her at the beach are inspiration enough to keep all of her stories set somewhere near there. Balancing hours of writing with school work and spending time with family and friends, she hopes to put out as many books as she has ideas floating around in her head.

CPSIA information can be obtained
at www.ICGtesting.com
Printed in the USA
BVHW041409160519
548500BV00012B/255/P